Blue Bird

Trish Finnegan

Burning Chair Limited, Trading as Burning Chair Publishing
61 Bridge Street, Kington HR5 3DJ

www.burningchairpublishing.com

By Trish Finnegan
Edited by Simon Finnie and Peter Oxley
Book cover design by Burning Chair Publishing

First published by Burning Chair Publishing, 2020
Copyright © Trish Finnegan, 2020
All rights reserved.

ISBN: 978-1-912946-13-6

To everyone on the thin blue line

Trish Finnegan

Prologue

Nobody heard the scream, cut off by a rough hand crushed against the girl's mouth. Nobody saw the sack thrown over her head or the men throwing her into the back of the van. Nobody would be able to provide a description of the men, not even the girl.

She had seen the van come down the lane. No company name, no side windows. It looked bottle green, but it was hard to tell for certain: the street lights were widely spaced on this road. Twice the van had slowed down as it passed her, but she had not been able to see the occupants in the dark interior.

She felt uneasy, regretting her decision to take the short cut home from the youth club disco, regretting going down the lane that took her past the dark playground, and regretting rejecting the boy who had asked to walk her home. She would feel safer when she was by the houses and could knock on a door for help, if necessary. If she walked quickly, she would be home in five minutes and next time she would stay on a well-lit road.

She spun around as she heard a shuffle behind her, but nobody was there. She laughed to herself; it was probably a hedgehog or a fox in the hedge that bounded the playground. An owl hooted in the distance, adding an eerie atmosphere to the lonely, unsettling location. Humming a song so she didn't feel so alone, she continued her journey home. She could see the lights of the first houses ahead of her; three or four minutes and she would be in her own road, then safely home.

The van came from a side track and drove directly for her, blocking her route to the houses. She turned and ran back up the dark lane but the van accelerated and mounted the pavement in front of her. A man disguised by a scarf tied around his lower face, leapt out and grabbed at her, missing by a hair's-breadth. The girl shrieked and turned away, racing towards the welcoming light of the houses. The man cursed and ran after her, while the van turned awkwardly in the narrow road.

The girl suddenly veered off and threw herself into a gap in the hedge, dragged herself through to the other side, and ran for the dark trees near the houses. If she could reach them she could hide, she could scream for help.

The van drew up beside the panting man and he climbed in. The driver stamped on the accelerator and sped along the hedge towards the houses. They waited but the girl did not emerge. The man climbed out and crept along the hedge, listening for movement; but the girl was silent.

'She's gone,' he called.

The van drove away.

After a few moments, the girl stood up and peered over the hedge. Everything was quiet, the van was gone, and the houses were almost in reach. She crept to the gate from the playground but, just as she reached it, the man leapt from his hiding place, threw a sack over her head and crushed a hand over her mouth, silencing her scream.

The van emerged from the dark and pulled up beside them. The driver got out and opened the back doors. The girl kicked and bit at the hessian-covered fingers that covered her mouth. The driver grabbed her legs and the men threw her into the van. They banged the doors shut and hurried to the front, and in less than ten seconds were gone.

Chapter One

'It's Monday, 24th May 1976 and this is the Radio Peninsula News at One. The search continues for missing schoolgirl, Julie Wynne—'

Mum leapt up from the table and stabbed the radio off button.

'Leave it,' I said. 'I might be drafted into the search and it'll be useful to hear about it before my shift.'

Mum sat down but the radio remained off. She looked tense. Stress had etched lines across her forehead and had given her crow's feet that reached her temples and made her look older than her years.

'They should excuse you from things like that.'

I rolled my eyes. 'It doesn't work like that. I'm operational now and stuff like this will be my job. Try not to worry.' As I spoke, I knew I might as well have asked the Earth to stop spinning.

Mum erupted. 'Try not to worry! You've chosen to put yourself in danger every day and I'm expected not to worry? I don't want to have to identify your body.'

I sighed. 'Mum, we've spent hours talking about this. You're going to give yourself a heart attack if you carry on.'

'Why couldn't you have become a nurse or a teacher? Police get killed all the time.'

'No, they don't,' I argued.

'There were two shot just last year.'

'You've told me that almost every week since I applied. You also told me you were proud of me.'

Mum stared at me for a moment. 'I am proud, but…'

'I can use my experience to help others.' I shovelled the last of my beans on toast into my mouth. 'I'd better get ready, my shift starts at three.'

I went upstairs with another little bundle to put on my guilt pile. Maybe I should have gone to university like Dad wanted, but I knew in my heart it wouldn't have stopped Mum worrying. She felt responsible for me, I got that, but it was stifling.

I quickly showered and put on my uniform. Black tights, plain skirt, and a jacket with silver buttons down the front and on the epaulettes. It had grown comfortable during training. Week by gruelling week, the stiffness had eased. Even the ridiculous hostess-style hat had moulded itself to the shape of my head. I attached the chain of my whistle to my waistband and dropped it into the skirt pocket. A pointless accoutrement; if I needed to call for help, I'd use the radio like every other modern copper. I pushed my fringe to one side and put on my hat. In this uniform I looked smart, strong and capable. Who was I kidding?

Mum watched as I backed my old Triumph Herald onto the street. I waved, then set off to my new posting at Wyre Hall Police Station, my new home-station.

*

It was just after 2.30pm when I drew up in the station car park. Wyre Hall was a grey, two-storey 1960s building named after the long-demolished old mansion that had once stood on the site. It had the architectural charm of a shoebox. Laden down with bags of kit, I took a deep breath to control my racing heart and pushed my way into the enquiry office.

'Hi, I'm Samantha Barrie. I start with B Block today.'

The bobby behind the desk grinned at me. 'Well, you're going to come as a surprise.' He opened the side door and gestured for me to go through. 'Be with you in a moment,' he said to a member of the public who had come in after me.

'I don't know where to go,' I said.

'Parade room. Follow the corridor and it's the end door facing you.' He looked at my bags. 'Leave them here. You can collect them after parade when you have a locker.'

I gratefully dumped my bags in the office and followed his directions to the parade room. On my left were windows looking out onto the yard. Liveried police cars were arriving, presumably the morning shift coming in to hand over to the late shift. On my right were offices and a glass-surrounded control room.

At the end of the corridor, just as I had been told, was the parade room. I took a steadying breath and pushed open the stained, mustard-coloured door.

I gazed around in dismay at a poster-lined, putty-coloured dump of a room that reeked of feet, fags and farts. A table, twice as long as it was wide, was at one end with three chairs behind it. Facing that was a larger wood table, with three short rows of chairs lined up behind that. High windows ran along two walls, letting in light but preventing anyone from seeing in, or out.

The eyes of a dozen policemen turned my way and nailed me to the spot. My face grew hot and I began to hyperventilate. I hated being the centre of attention. I gave what I hoped was a friendly smile, but my lips felt so numb with nerves I couldn't be sure it didn't look like I was snarling.

'I'm starting with B Block today.' I gulped.

'Bloody hell, it's a bird.'

I couldn't see who had spoken, but his powers of observation left me underwhelmed. I waved in the general direction of the voice. 'Surprise!'

'What's your name, love?' a burly constable sitting at the table asked.

'Watch it, Phil; you're a married man,' said a fair-haired, younger officer sitting on the first row of seats behind the table.

'I'm Samantha Barrie. Sam.'

'Shurrup, Steve.' Phil said. 'You'd better sit down then, Samantha Barrie Sam. It's almost three and parade starts shortly.' He gestured over his shoulder to the rows of chairs.

There was a definite hierarchy there, despite us having been told at the training school that all constables are equal. The drivers, identified by their flat caps, sat at the table; the foot patrols, all younger men with traditional helmets, sat on the seats behind them. Then it struck me that I really was a stranger in a strange land; I was the only female in the room. My breathing ratcheted up a notch, but I forced myself to take long, slow breaths. I was going to pass out if I didn't get my breathing under control. I was in a police station; these were my work colleagues and I was safe.

'Sit here, darling.' Steve, the fair-haired lad, a similar age to me, patted the chair next to him.

'Oh, hello. Steve's right in there,' said one of the other foot patrols.

'Wazzer,' Steve replied.

I sidled along the row and sat down. Steve had a slim build. Fair hair curled over the edge of his helmet. He'd be getting pulled up on that before long. His number was close to mine so he hadn't had much more service than me: five or six months I estimated

The door opened; everyone put on their headwear and stood to attention. I followed suit a couple of seconds later as an older sergeant entered the room carrying a heavy, hard-bound book almost as long as his arm. Grizzled. Not a word I normally used, but he was grizzled with short, salt and pepper hair, large jowls and wire-rimmed glasses.

An inspector followed him, carrying a couple of folders. When I had been given my posting, I had been told Inspector Gary Tyrrell headed B Block. He looked younger than some of the constables and was half a head over six feet. I had always been drawn to very tall men; not that I had ever done anything about it, but I liked to look. I mentally chastised myself, this was my boss and I had no business ogling him. I was at work and it was time to be professional.

'As you were.' Inspector Tyrrell pulled out his chair and sat down.

We sat and the officers at the table arranged their handcuffs and truncheons in front of them, next to their pocket notebooks. Producing their appointments: another anachronism. None of us at the back did that; it was too crowded, and whilst I had handcuffs and a pocket book, I didn't have a staff. In neighbouring forces, the girls were given a handbag-sized baton, which the lads at the training school had dubbed dildoes, but here on the Peninsula we had nothing to defend ourselves, except our soft leather handbags and devastating charm.

'Over to you, Sergeant Bowman,' said the inspector, turning to the grizzled sergeant.

'Thanks, Sir.' Sergeant Bowman looked around the room. 'We're a bit short-staffed today because of the search over in Tynvoller division for Julie Wynne. Try to pick up the slack.'

When I saw police searches on the television, I used to wonder where all the police came from. Now I knew; they were drafted from other stations, maybe to the detriment of that area, but some things had to take precedence over everything.

'She's dead,' said Steve just under his breath, but Sergeant Bowman heard him and lanced him with a look.

'We cannot assume that, Steve.'

Steve didn't back down under Sergeant Bowman's scrutiny, which I thought impressive from a probationer. 'She's from a decent family and not coming home is out of character, Sarge. Also, her sixteenth birthday is just a few days away. What kid would miss a party? Also, she's been gone over a week, the media are all over it and still we have no leads. Everyone knows that hope fades with each day she's gone, Sarge. I think the team will find a body.'

I couldn't argue with his logic. Sergeant Bowman pursed his lips in a way that told me that he also agreed with Steve's reasoning; however, he said, 'Until a body is found, she's still missing. There is hope, and the search goes on.'

But they all secretly believed it was hopeless. My stomach

knotted.

A few seconds' silence filled the room before the sergeant spoke again.

'Has the recruit arrived?'

I put my hand up. 'Here, sergeant.'

'Stand up, let's have a look at you.'

'She is standing, she's only little,' said Steve, breaking the sombre atmosphere.

'Thank you, Steve but I doubt she would have passed the medical if that were true,' said the inspector over the laughter.

I stood up and sneaked a look at Steve. It was difficult to judge with him sitting down, but I got the impression he was quite tall. Not as tall as the inspector, but tall just the same. I turned my attention back to Sergeant Bowman, adopted the "at ease" stance, and fixed my eyes on the middle distance. In my peripheral vision I could see the inspector watching me, and my cheeks burned.

'It's customary for recruits to report to the sergeants' office before parade starts,' said Sergeant Bowman.

Great! My first parade and I'd dropped a clanger already. 'I'm sorry, Sergeant, nobody told me.' The burn in my cheeks spread to my ears.

'Do you have a locker yet?'

'No, Sergeant. I left my bags with the front office staff. If they're in the way, I'll leave my stuff in the ladies' toilet until I'm allocated a locker.' Not ideal, but it seemed like the best solution to me.

He grunted. 'Best not. You get some dodgy people in police stations.'

'And that's not counting the public,' Steve whispered. I stifled a smile. I wanted to make a good impression, so I needed to maintain a professional demeanour to make up for not going to see the Sergeant.

'I'll fix you up with a locker later,' Sergeant Bowman signalled for me to sit down.

'There'll be a woman in the locker room; bear that in mind if you are changing, and try to keep the dirty talk down,' he announced to the room. 'Phil, you can puppy-walk the sprog.'

'Yes, Sarge.' Phil shifted in his seat at the table and his shoulders slumped. Just what I needed; a tutor-constable that didn't want me.

Sergeant Bowman gave out duties, beats, and refreshment periods to everyone, and I followed their lead and jotted mine into my pocket book. Next, he gave out a lot of information about ex-prisoners returning to the area, suspect activity, and a lot of other stuff that went over my head. Finally, he doled out paperwork, making odd comments on some.

He tossed an accident booklet to Steve who caught it with ease. 'The admin department appreciated your diagram of the accident scene, Steve, but they say you didn't need to include the dog that happened to be sitting on the pavement.'

'Just trying to be thorough, Sarge,' Steve replied.

I gaped at his audacity. We'd never have got away with that at training school. Things were very different in division.

Sergeant Bowman turned to the inspector. 'Over to you, sir. '

'Thanks. The good news is that we will be getting our new sergeant, next night shift.' He turned to Sergeant Bowman. 'That'll lighten the load a bit, eh?'

'Not before time,' Sergeant Bowman replied. 'I began to think I wouldn't be able to retire next year.'

The inspector scanned his folders. 'Svetlana Jones has gone off again,' he said. 'Phil, will you make the usual enquiries, including St Agnes' High School?'

The groans and headshaking around the room were a diametric contrast from the reaction to Julie Wynne's continued disappearance.

'Do you want me to take the sprog with me?' Phil asked.

'Why not? It's a straightforward enough job, so it'll be an easy introduction for her,' Inspector Tyrrell said.

I put my hand up. 'Is there a description please, sir?'

'Oh, right. I forgot you won't know her. She's a regular. Five foot four inches tall, brown eyes, proportionate build, long dark hair usually worn in a ponytail, and last seen wearing jeans and a blue tank top.' He smiled. 'She looks a bit like you, except she's fifteen.'

Fifteen! I looked up from my pocketbook in shock.

'Shouldn't...?' I stopped speaking as all eyes turned to me again.

'Go on,' the inspector said.

I gulped and tried to ignore the heat in my cheeks. 'I mean, sir, the search for Julie Wynne was on the lunchtime news today. I know that she's not from this division, but are we going to do something similar for Svetlana?'

The others chuckled. I glanced around, confused at their uncaring response.

'You think we should use the same resources on them both?' The inspector shook his head. 'No. Svetlana has only been missing a few hours. We don't have the manpower to launch straight into another major search, so we must prioritise. Julie hasn't absconded before as far as we know, and she's been gone a while. As I said, Svetlana is a regular and has been for about a year, just like her sister before her. She'll be back.'

I could see what he was saying but I still felt uncomfortable. It seemed to me that, although she had been labelled a persistent absconder, there was a chance that Svetlana might not return home and precious time might be lost before a search began. I knew how important lost time could be to the outcome of a case like this.

'Is that all?' the inspector asked.

I wanted to say more but I couldn't articulate my muddled thoughts. Everyone was watching me, so I just said, 'Yes, sir.'

'Right. It's tranquil out there, let's keep it that way.' The inspector gathered his folders and stood up. Everyone else stood as he and the sergeant left. As soon as they left the room, everyone crowded out after them. It was worse than mealtimes at the training school. I hung back a few seconds; I wasn't claustrophobic exactly, but I was very uncomfortable in a huddle of people.

When I got onto the corridor, Phil was waiting by the open door of the sergeants' office.

'Here she is,' he said to someone in the office.

'You go on to St Agnes', Phil. The boss wants a word with her. I'll call you back when she's ready,' Sergeant Bowman said from inside the office.

I watched Phil's retreating back for a few seconds. I would have to work hard to impress him; he would do weekly reports on me and would decide if I was ready to go solo in a month.

'Steve's right, you're not very tall; you must have just scraped through the medical,' said Sergeant Bowman when I peeped around the door.

That was true; I was only half an inch over the minimum height requirement. I remained silent as Sergeant Bowman looked me over.

'How old are you?' he asked.

'Twenty-one, Sergeant Bowman.'

'You look younger.'

Yep, the bane of my life. I was always getting questioned in pubs, and sometimes they refused to serve me. I'd probably love it when I was forty.

'You're going to ride with Phil Torrens. He knows the town well and doesn't have too many bad habits. He's got a couple of little girls, so he's used to dealing with incessant questions.'

I was a little offended at Sergeant Bowman's assumption that I would prattle like a child, but I smiled just to be polite.

'He's an experienced constable, so listen to him and learn,' he continued. 'The public won't care that you don't know your arse from your elbow; they'll just see the uniform and expect you to solve their problem.'

'Yes, Sergeant.'

'You can call me Alan.'

'Thank you, Alan.' It felt wrong to be calling a man older than my father by his first name.

He took a key from a grey key cabinet and handed it to me. 'Your locker key: number 39. Don't lose it. Come on, the boss is waiting.'

I put the key in my pocket then followed Alan upstairs to the Inspector's office.

Chapter Two

Inspector Tyrrell was on the phone when we arrived at his office. He waved us in and pointed at the chair opposite. I sat down, back straight, ankles crossed, hands neatly folded on my lap like we did in our class photo at training school. Alan shut the door and leant against the wall with his arms crossed.

I let my eyes wander across the muddle of notices pinned to the board. Front and centre was a poster of missing person, Julie Wynne: *"misper"* in police jargon; there was a lot of that I had to get to grips with. Julie, dressed in her green St Agnes' uniform, smiled from the poster. Not a perfect smile, one front tooth crossed over the other, but attractive all the same. It wasn't so unusual that Svetlana and Julie attended the same school. St Agnes' High School was a huge, all girls, Roman Catholic secondary school and pupils came from all over the Peninsula.

The inspector finished his call and, for a moment, he looked as if he had the heaviest weight on his shoulders. I wanted to put my arm around him.

'Problem, Gary?' Alan asked.

I noted the use of the boss's first name. Perhaps that was a privilege of Alan's age or length of service, or maybe they were friends outside of work.

'That was Tynvoller division. Ports Police found a body washed up in Lyseby. They think it's the Wynne girl. No official ID yet but the clothing's the same and they're calling off the search,' the inspector said. 'She's been in the water a while, so they're using dental records.'

Her poor parents wouldn't even be able to see her one last time. A dentist would confirm if the body was his patient. Her parents might get a piece of jewellery or an item of clothing to identify as hers. My hands clenched involuntarily.

Inspector Tyrrell studied me for a few seconds. 'You can't repeat what you've just heard to anyone outside the station. An announcement will be made when she has been formally identified.'

'I understand, sir,' I said.

'What do your family think of your joining the police?' he asked.

I thought about Mum's conviction that I was going to be killed, but I said, 'Dad was a bit disappointed when I didn't go to university. He's supportive though. He and Mum were really proud when I passed out at training school.' Which was true.

'What have you done since school?'

'After A levels, I went to Canada and worked in my uncle's restaurant. I stayed there for a couple of years before I applied for the police.'

The inspector's gaze shifted slightly to my left. I turned and saw Alan Bowman thin his lips and slowly shake his head. The inspector smiled slightly and turned his attention back to me.

He leant his elbows onto the desk. 'So, it's safe to say you have limited life experience?'

I nodded. I knew I had led a sheltered, even restricted, life. Working for my uncle had been the first step in my self-prescribed rehabilitation. It was far enough away for me to push bad memories aside, but I was still close to family. It had been a good move that had enabled me to rebuild my confidence, although I did have the occasional wobble.

I heard Alan shift position behind me, and Inspector Tyrrell's eyes flicked to him then back to me.

'You will probably find life in the Peninsula Police very different, not least because there are so few females apart from the typists and cleaners. You'll spend your first month here in company with Phil.'

I smiled and nodded. I was beginning to feel like a donkey, all teeth and nodding.

'When you do go solo, you will still be on probation…'

My mind drifted as I watched Inspector Tyrrell's mouth move. His lips had a natural upward curve that gave him a friendly, approachable appearance.

'…and Alan was my tutor-constable back in Odinsby. I think he did a decent job.'

I zoned back in and hoped I hadn't missed anything important. Even worse, a family was about to be shattered while I daydreamed. Something else to put on my guilt pile. The inspector leant forward, and I thought I'd been caught out. I was making lousy first impressions.

'I know about Hogarth Acre,' he said, his voice low and serious.

I shivered and pressed my hands between my knees to control the shaking. I didn't want to think about that place.

'Nobody on B Block, apart from Alan and I, knows you were involved yet. Do you want it to remain that way?'

I needed to fit in. I decided it would be easier if I didn't have to worry about gossip behind my back or, even worse, questions to my face. I couldn't face that yet.

'Yes.' My voice was almost a whisper.

'Very well,' Inspector Tyrrell said. 'But you know I can't guarantee that one of the lads hasn't been talking to someone from Odinsby division, and you know how gossip spreads.'

'I understand.'

'Go down and introduce yourself to Derek and Ray in the control room.'

'Yes, sir.' I left and was walking towards the stairs when I heard Alan's voice through the open door.

'They're taking the mickey, Gary. Minimum height and no life experience. How's a girl like that supposed to cope with life on the spike? Do you think a little thing like her will be any good when The Capstan pub kicks off? It's only been a few days since we had the last fight there. They should have kept the policewomen's department and left the rough stuff for the lads.'

'You're a dinosaur, Alan. Same pay for the same job now.'

'What about a fatal RTA, Gary? Or a cot death?'

'We all find those hard, Alan. If she can't hack it, she'll have to find alternative employment just like the lads would have to.'

My legs shook as I made my way downstairs. How would I cope with a cot death or a fight at The Capstan, a well-known pub and roughhouse? I knew when I joined that I might be called to disturbing incidents, but it hadn't felt real, even during role play exercises. Now it hit me: I really might have to go to a fight, deal with a dead baby, or speak to a family like the Wynnes. I inhaled deeply and beat my palm against the bannister, as was my habit. The rhythm grounded me when my thoughts started to run away. I had worked hard to get here, and I would cope; I would.

I went into the tiny control room, which had no natural light. As I had seen previously, it was surrounded by half-glazed walls so some light could creep in from areas that enjoyed an outside view. Additional light was provided by a long fluorescent light covered by a milky-grey fly graveyard. On one side, the control room staff had a clear view through to the enquiry office and on to the door to the sergeants' office the other side of the enquiry office. The other side offered a clear view to the corridor.

A tall, slim man in his late forties sat in front of the radio studying one of the maps of the town that lined the remaining glass wall in front of him. The town was divided into four areas; west, town, north and south marked as Mike One, Mike Two, Mike Three and Mike Four respectively. One of the country's arterial rivers ran along the east side. Each area was further divided into the smaller foot beats.

The man stubbed out his cigarette in a well-filled metal ashtray and spun around in his seat. 'You must be our recruit.'

'I'm Samantha Barrie.' I shook his extended hand, which was the size of a dinner plate.

'I'm Ray Fairbrother, this is Derek Kidd. He usually takes the calls and I allocate them.'

I shook hands with Derek. His wide-spaced eyes and large abdomen brought to mind Toad of Toad Hall.

'Have you been in a control room before?' Ray asked.

'I spent a day in the control room in Egilsby. This is smaller.' Much smaller. Egilsby was our divisional headquarters—the "DHQ"—and so had more phone lines and more control room staff. All divisions had a DHQ and a secondary station. Some had satellite stations too, often little more than a portacabin.

Back in Wyre Hall, behind the control room was a smaller room, little more than a beige painted, windowless cupboard, in fact, it might well have once been an actual cupboard. Inside were the telex, a bookshelf packed with folders, and a lockable filing cabinet. An aged electric kettle, half a dozen brown-stained mugs and a crusty bag of sugar sat on a rickety table shoved into a corner. There was no way in or out other than through the control room.

'Aye, they do fancy themselves in Egilsby,' said Ray puffing smoke from his nose. 'We're not grand here but we get the job done. We don't have Talkthrough like Egilsby. There, everyone can hear everyone else on air and patrols can talk to each other. Here, everything comes through me and you'll only hear me, or Derek on the air. Our superintendent thinks it's less confusing. Also, you'll have to take your turn covering here from time to time when we take leave.'

'Or when you're gadding off in your cricket whites,' Derek added.

'Do you play cricket?' I asked Ray. I didn't follow cricket, but I was glad to have something to talk about.

'He's on the force team. Goes off all over the country and gets given the time for it,' Derek said.

I was impressed. Being on a divisional sports team was good, but being chosen for the force team, be it cricket, football, rugby, or anything else, was remarkable.

Alan came into the office. 'Sam, go and get your bags and stow them in your locker,' Alan said. 'Then go to the collator's office and say hello to Irene Ward. I'll send someone to get you when Phil's back.'

'Yes, Sergeant Bowen,' I said.

I turned to get my bags from the front office and crashed into Inspector Tyrrell, who was just entering the crowded room. I bounced backwards, and he grabbed my shoulders to steady me.

I looked up into blue eyes surrounded by long lashes and my cheeks flushed. 'I'm so sorry, I didn't see you there.' I ducked my head and scurried off to retrieve my bags.

*

The locker room was about the same size as the parade room. The rows of green lockers arranged in bays made it look small and crowded, and the high long windows above them offered little light through the layers of cobwebs on the inside and bird poo that coated the outside. I found my locker at the far end of the furthermost bay, removed the card bearing the service number of the previous occupant and wrote my own number, 4912, on the other side. I then reinserted it into the slot, marking my own little place in this alien world. I stowed my things and went to the collator's office.

Unlike most offices in the building, the door to the collator's office was closed. I looked through the glass panel into a room only slightly larger than the control room. It was lined along two walls with head-high filing cabinets and the remaining visible wall was covered with the ubiquitous maps and notices. Afternoon daylight struggled in through ever-present, high strips of windows. I wondered if anyone ever cleaned them. A sharp-elbowed woman with dark, cropped hair sat at a table, typing on an ancient machine. She looked up and smiled when I tapped on the glass and waved me in.

'Are you Irene?' I asked.

'Yes, and you must be the sprog. Shut the door so we can have a chat.'

I closed the door behind me and approached the table. 'I'm Sam Barrie.'

'Hi, Sam.' Irene shook my hand. 'Excuse the mess, it's always like this. Take a seat.' I sat down and put my hat on the edge of the table.

'First things first.' She pointed to a metal basket filled with what appeared to be waste paper on top of a filing cabinet. 'Don't ever remove that or take out bits of paper. The lads scribble any information, whispers, or rumours they come across—any scrap sheet will do—and then put it in the basket for when I'm on duty. I transfer all this information into the system then shred the paper.' She waved a hand over her shoulder at the filing cabinets. 'Also, I do a bulletin of the latest news and info every day; you probably heard it during parade.'

I didn't remember hearing a bulletin, but then I had been a bit overwhelmed by the mass of information passed out.

'How will I know what to pass on? I wouldn't know what's important.'

'I wouldn't expect you to at your stage of service, so you put any snippet you hear into the basket. It might mean little to you, but it could be the last piece of evidence needed to complete an investigation.' Irene glanced at the clock then fished her epaulettes from her bag and attached them to her blouse. 'The superintendent usually pops in for an update around four and he likes me to have the eps on.'

I noted the chevrons on the eps. 'I didn't realise you were a sergeant,'

Irene grimaced. 'I'm not sure many do. When the policewomen's department was disbanded, they couldn't demote any peewees with rank and they couldn't move the men on to make room for us, so we were slotted into various low-key positions. I landed on my feet here though.'

Peewees, police slang for policewoman: more jargon for me to learn.

'It'll be different for me, we've joined under the same conditions as the lads,' I said.

'You'd think so, wouldn't you.' Irene laughed. 'Congratulations, you've won the right to attend fights and to mop up after fatal RTAs.' She made a *"peace"* gesture at me. 'Right on, sister.'

I liked Irene and, despite the ten year or so age difference and the jaded attitude, I felt I would be able to count her as a friend.

'Can I ask you something?'

Irene waved her arms over an imaginary crystal ball. 'I am the collator: all seeing, all knowing. Ask me anything.'

I laughed. 'On parade, the boss said a girl called Svetlana Jones had gone missing.'

Irene's eyes rolled. 'Again!'

I snapped my fingers. 'That was the reaction on parade. But she's only fifteen so why isn't there more of a fuss? Especially as Julie Wynne has been found dead.' The collator was sure to be aware of them finding Julie's body, so I was pretty certain I wasn't going against the inspector's instruction to not say anything about this.

'That's not confirmed yet.'

I knew she would know about it. 'But it is her, isn't it?' I persisted.

'Probably,' Irene agreed. 'Now, Svetlana is a different kettle of fish. Glynis was never the most devoted mother so Svetlana and her older sister, Consuela, have never had boundaries. We have to prioritise resources, so we circulate Svetlana's description to patrols and surrounding divisions, and Julie Wynne gets the search. Svetlana will be back tomorrow.'

'Unless she isn't. It doesn't seem right,' I said.

Irene shrugged. 'We do our best with what we have. It isn't ideal.'

We lapsed into silence. It seemed I wasn't the only one to feel uncomfortable, but I had yet to come to terms with things the way Irene had.

'Svetlana and Consuela?' I said. 'Unusual names for around

here.'

'They're known as Lana and Connie, which sound more conventional. Glynis always says she wanted something exotic because the name Jones is so common. The standing joke is that they were named for the nationalities of their fathers, but I don't think Glynis knows who their fathers were because she goes on so many ships.' Irene laughed. 'Don't look so shocked. You'll get used to dealing with prostitutes. Most are okay.' She yawned. 'Sorry. It's been a long day.'

The door opened and Derek came in. 'You two discussing shoes and men?'

'No, Derek. We were discussing you,' Irene snapped.

'Ooh, catty.' He turned his attention to me. 'Phil is on his way in to collect you.'

'You'd better go then.' Irene said. 'Pop in when you have a minute; it's nice to have someone to chat to.'

I pulled my hat on and followed Derek into the control room to wait for Phil to take me on my first proper operational patrol.

Chapter Three

'Are we going to St Agnes' school?' I asked, eager to begin.
Phil got comfortable in his seat before he turned to me and said, 'I did that while you were with the boss.'

'Oh.' I was disappointed. 'Will we do follow-up enquiries?'

'The other addresses are not on my patch,' Phil said. 'Someone else will do that and report back.'

'Oh.'

'Let's get a few things straight before we go out,' Phil said. 'First, set your watch by the control room clock before you go out; that way, when you make up your pocket notebook, the times will tally with the job sheet. Secondly, you don't get out of the car unless I tell you to. Thirdly, if I tell you to be quiet, you be quiet. If we are dealing with someone, you stay quiet unless I instruct you otherwise. Fourth, if you hear anyone shout "Scramble" on the radio, you fasten your seatbelt and hold tight. A scramble is a shout for assistance; it takes precedence over everything, so it isn't shouted lightly. Got it?'

'Got it.' All the excitement drained from me. Phil considered me to be a liability and he was probably right. I had a head full of theory but, as Alan had said, I didn't know my arse from my elbow. Fine, I would keep quiet and try not to annoy Phil.

After five minutes, I couldn't stand the silence. I was about to say something when Ray's voice came over the radio.

'Mike Two.'

Phil nodded his head towards the radio. 'Answer it.'

I picked up the handset, pressed the transmit button and replied, 'Mike Two; go ahead. Over.'

'Domestic dispute; Gilmour Street.'

'Tell them "Roger",' Phil said.

'They haven't told us what number.'

'No need, it's a regular,' Phil replied.

'Roger. Over and out.' I replaced the handset.

Phil flicked a couple of switches. At once the two-tone siren sounded and reflected blue light pulsed across the bonnet. I felt a little thrill as the traffic opened up and Phil accelerated through.

'You know, saying "over and out" and so on identifies you as a sprog.' Phil wove through some traffic lights, raising his hand to thank the other drivers.

'That's what we were taught at training school,' I said. 'You say, "Over" after a transmission and, "Over and out" when the conversation is ended.'

'We're not so formal in division. Listen to Ray and me on the radio, you'll get the hang of it.' Phil turned into a dismal, terraced street. The tiny, beige-painted houses opened straight onto the pavement. Soot-stained red brick peeked through the patches where the paint had peeled off the walls. It was a shame the council had painted over it in the first place.

Phil pulled up and, without saying a word to me, got out of the car and strode up to the house. So what was I supposed to do: stay put because he hadn't told me to get out, or ignore him? I needed to attend incidents to learn so I hurried after him, hopscotching past dog dirt and chip papers, pretending I didn't notice the neighbours peering from behind their curtains or unashamedly staring from their open doors.

Phil hammered on the door but there was no reply. The smash of breaking china made me jump. Phil immediately drew his staff, marched to the entry at the end of the terrace, and cut around to the rear of the property. I ran after him into a stinking, cluttered back yard. Instead of knocking, he simply walked into the house.

I had to swallow bile down when I stepped into the kitchen. Green scum surrounded the dish-piled sink, used milk bottles lay on the filthy worktop, congealed food stuck to a frying pan, and a rotten tea towel lay beside the grease laden cooker.

I kicked away a piece of newspaper that had stuck to my shoe and followed Phil into the living room, which was little cleaner than the kitchen.

A middle-aged man and woman screamed at each other across shards of broken china. It wasn't the obscene language that shocked me so much as the female's attire: a tight corset and bra bit cruelly into blue-veined, blancmange flesh that undulated with each shove she gave the bald man.

Phil slammed his staff onto the scratched Formica table and sat on one of the plastic-and-metal chairs. 'Rose, put something on.'

Rose, whose name didn't suit her, stamped to the kitchen, pausing briefly to inspect me. She pulled a nylon overall from a hook on the door and continued to watch me as she buttoned it up.

'What's it about this time?' Phil sounded bored. How often had he been here?

'Him!' Rose jabbed a finger towards the man, who smirked, displaying rotted stumps of teeth. 'He's been at Nita's house again.'

Phil turned to the man. 'Arthur?'

'If a man can't get what he wants at home, he'll go elsewhere.'

Arthur folded his pasty arms across breasts that were bigger than mine and tapped his brown-stained fingers against his elbows. I suppressed a shudder. It was bad enough to think about older people having sex at all, but these two... I swallowed hard.

'And what about what I want, eh? You can't keep it up for more than thirty seconds for me,' Rose screamed. 'But maybe Nita's happy with the shrivelled bit of gristle you pass off as a dick.'

Now there was a picture I really didn't want in my head.

Phil put his hand on Arthur's shoulder and guided him past Rose and me, into the kitchen, talking quietly to him.

I stood in the living room trying not to brush against anything while Rose stared at me. I didn't know what to do, but this was my first proper incident and I felt I ought to take some part instead of letting Phil do everything.

I smiled at Rose. 'Have you tried speaking to this Nita?'

Rose made a show of looking me up and down. 'Have you ever been married, or even engaged?'

'No,' I admitted.

'Piss off then. Coming here thinking you know best. Smug cow.'

I didn't think I knew best. I'd never met anyone like these two and I didn't have a clue how to handle this incident.

Rose stalked to the kitchen door. 'Hey, Phil. Why are you bringing kids to the house?'

Phil put his head around the kitchen door. 'She's new, Rose.'

Arthur joined Phil at the door and stared as if he'd only just seen me.

'By heck, look at her. She's about the same age you were when I first met you, Rosie.'

Rose looked back at me and her expression softened. 'Aye, she is.'

Arthur turned his attention to Rose. 'I didn't think I was in with much of a chance when I asked you to dance.'

'You were a good-looking lad then. I didn't think you'd notice me,' Rose said.

'I couldn't believe my luck when you let me walk you home.' Arthur held out his hand and Rose gently took it. 'I think I'll lay off the beer for a while, then I'll be able to keep my rosebud happy.'

I closed my mouth, which had fallen open, and turned to Phil, who indicated that it was time to go by jerking his head towards the back door.

'Okay, Arthur,' he said. 'Good idea about the beer; brewer's droop is no fun. Stay away from Nita. Make an appointment with the Marriage Guidance Council and get yourselves sorted out. I can't keep attending like this, there are serious incidents that need our attention.' Phil toed a fragment of china on the floor. 'One of you is going to get hurt.'

'Yeah, you're right, Phil. Have they found that girl, Julie, yet?' Rose asked.

I glanced at Phil, who answered without missing a beat. 'She's still logged as missing.'

His quick thinking and diplomacy impressed me. He had maintained confidentiality, and he hadn't lied because, until she was formally identified, Julie would remain on the outstanding misper list. I had to remember how to do that when I was patrolling solo.

'She's the same age as our Lana, my niece's girl.'

My ears pricked up, there couldn't be too many girls with that name in this area.

'Have you seen your Lana recently, Rose?' Phil asked.

'Yeah, this morning in Nelson Square. She said she was going to her friend's flat.'

'What time was this?' Phil got his pocketbook out ready to log the details.

'About eleven,' Rose replied. 'Did the soft bitch bunk off school again?' Without pausing for an answer, she addressed Arthur. 'I said it was odd, didn't I. She told me that she had a free period and didn't have to be back until after lunch, lying cow. I'll tell our Glynis.'

'Do you know her friend's name and where she lives?' Phil asked.

'Mel, Milly. Something like that. Dunno her address.'

'Thanks Rose. Come on, Sam.'

I followed Phil to the door but, before I could leave, Rose tapped me on the shoulder.

'He's a good lad. Stick with him and he'll show you what's what.'

'Sam.' Phil called from the yard.

'Hang on.' Rose pulled a knife from the pile of dishes in the scummy sink and prised the lid from a stained biscuit tin. She held out a digestive biscuit to me. 'Sorry I called you a cow. Here, have this with your tea back at the station.'

I would starve to death before I ate that biscuit, but I took it, smiled my thanks, and went after Phil, who did a double take as I walked towards the Panda car with the biscuit held out in front of me.

'Rose must like you; she's never given me a biscuit.'

'Want it?' I held it towards him. Phil snatched the digestive and tossed it to a passing dog that didn't care where it had come from and crunched it up in a second.

'Was she talking about Svetlana Jones?' I asked as we got into the Panda.

'Yes. I didn't know she's Rose's great-niece.' Phil started the engine.

'You hid that well.'

'It doesn't do any harm to let people think you know more than you do. They're more likely to open up then.' Phil pulled out and drove slowly down the road. 'What did you make of Rose and Arthur?'

'I've never heard my parents scream at each other like that. I couldn't believe how soppy they got in the end. I think they love each other really.'

'Culture shock is a big part of your first year. I'm glad you saw that last bit, it reminds us that these are not just jobs we have to sort out, they are real people with feelings.'

'I couldn't believe the state of the place. Is it always like that there?'

'It's not normally that bad,' Phil said. 'You will go to worse places. Wash your hair with Derbac or something like that occasionally.'

I was aghast. 'The nit shampoo! You mean I could actually catch lice or something?' My scalp began to tickle and I scratched it quickly, which made Phil laugh.

'You wouldn't be the first if you did.'

Phil picked up the handset and radioed in the information that Rose had told him about Lana.

'We'll go to Nelson Square and mooch around in case we see Lana,' Phil said. He pointed at the glove compartment. 'Pass the bottle from in there.'

I flipped open the door and found a miniature spirits bottle filled with white liquid, next to a bag of liquorice allsorts. I passed the bottle to Phil.

'What is it?'

'Dilute disinfectant. Hold your hand out.' Phil spilled a few drops of the fluid into my cupped palm. 'Rub that into your hands. Then pass me the bag of sweets.'

I quickly rubbed the disinfectant into my hands. I made a mental note that I should bring in my own bottle, and some hand cream to counteract the inevitable dryness. Then I passed him the liquorice allsorts. Phil took a pink coconut wheel and passed the bag back to me.

'Have one, but not a coconut one. They're my favourites.'

I preferred the stripy ones anyway. I popped a sweet into my mouth and Phil pulled away.

'Brewer's droop,' I mumbled through masticated liquorice. 'I haven't heard that expression before. Does it mean what I think it means?'

Phil made a small choking noise and swallowed his sweet. 'Hellfire. Ask your mother.'

'So I'm right. If a man has too much beer it interferes with his performance, and that's what Arthur has.'

Phil wiggled a finger to demonstrate and I fell into a fit of giggles. I laughed until we reached Nelson Square, a small park facing the town hall, surrounded by Georgian houses that had long been converted into restaurants, clubs, and offices.

Phil parked up opposite the town hall that gave us an unobstructed view of the crowds. A young woman walked around the corner into Nelson Square and did a swift about-turn when she saw us.

'That was Connie.' Phil accelerated after her.

'Oh, hello Mr Torrens,' she said as the Panda car drew up beside her.

'Hello, Connie. Heard anything from your Lana?' Phil asked through the open window.

'I'd ring in if I had.' She glanced over to the recently built apartment block, Belvedere House.

I looked across too. Unlike the dated tenements in the area that were being demolished, and the replacement maisonettes being thrown up a short distance away, Belvedere House was an exclusive address that overlooked the river. It was the first step of a great plan to rejuvenate the area and attract a different demographic. The hoarding outside trumpeted this block as "Desirable Urban Living for Professional People", and referred to the flats as apartments. When I looked for my own place, I would not be looking here, not on a police wage. Why would it interest Connie?

'Why do you keep looking at Belvedere House?' I asked, breaking one of Phil's rules.

'Someone is moving by a window and it distracted me.'

Sounded reasonable.

Phil cleared his throat. 'Going back to your Lana, your mum's Auntie Rose told us she met her this morning and Lana told her she was going to visit a friend who lives around here. Do you know who that friend might be?'

Another glance at Belvedere House. 'No, Mr Torrens. Look, I do have to get on.'

I looked over and saw a man standing in the car park looking across at us. He hadn't been there a minute ago. He turned away and walked out of sight.

'Who's he?' I asked.

'How should I know?' Connie snapped.

'Okay, Connie. Let us know if you hear from Lana.' Phil revved the engine.

Connie checked out the flats again then continued away from us, in the opposite direction she had been going when we first saw her. Even I, with my lack of experience, could see something wasn't right.

'She's not being straight with us, and she was going the other way before,' I said to Phil. 'I wonder if Lana's friend lives there.'

Phil nodded. 'Let's go back and look in the collator's system for Belvedere House.'

Chapter Four

At the station, Inspector Tyrrell was in the sergeants' office with Sergeant Bowman, who called us over.

'What are you doing back?' Sergeant Bowman asked.

'We saw Connie Jones near Nelson Square, and she was most interested in Belvedere House,' Phil replied. 'I wanted to check it out with Irene. We'll do our reports on the domestic after scoff if that's okay. By the way, did you know Rose is Glynis Jones's aunt?'

Sergeant Bowman cocked his head. 'That's interesting. It gives us another address to check when Lana next does one.'

'I don't know how long we'll be with Irene so, if it's okay, we'll go for scoff straight from there, Alan,' Phil said.

Police never seemed to say "meal time" or "break time"; they preferred the earthier "scoff", which could refer to the meal break period or the food itself. This was interchangeable with "ref", from the word refreshments. At this rate, I would be speaking fluent copper in no time.

'No problem.' Alan said. He turned to me. 'So, you met our Rose and Arthur.'

'She gave me a biscuit, but Phil threw it to a dog and gave me one of his sweets,' I replied.

Inspector Tyrrell came to the door, laughing. 'Phil gave you one of his precious allsorts?'

'Not the coconut ones; they're his favourites. I thought he was dead grumpy at first but he's not so bad. He was really nice to Rose and Arthur, apart from banging his staff on the table.' I realised I sounded like an overexcited toddler, so quickly added a 'sir' then shut up. Maybe Alan's assessment of me, and choice of tutor-constable, wasn't so far off the mark.

Inspector Tyrrell grinned. 'Go with Phil.'

'Yes, sir.' I hurried after my tutor-constable.

'How was it?' Irene asked me when we got to her office.

'We went to a domestic at Gilmour Street,' I said.

'Rose and Arthur? Those two were fighting when I first joined. Was she complaining about him seeing another woman again?'

'Yes, someone called Nita. I can't imagine anyone wanting to be intimate with either of them.' This time I didn't suppress my shudder. 'Did you know that Rose is Svetlana Jones's great-aunt?'

'Put that in the basket and I'll add it to the system.' Irene glanced over to Phil who was scanning the indexed drawers. 'What are you after?'

'Anything on Belvedere House. We saw Connie Jones hanging around by there a little while ago.'

'House hunting?'

'Probably making sure there was enough garage space for her Bentley.' Phil laughed, Irene and I joined in. Were we being unkind? Perhaps; not that we could afford an apartment in Belvedere House or a Bentley either.

Irene pulled open a couple of drawers and fruitlessly flicked through the cards, while I found a scrap of paper and wrote out my little bit of information. I popped it in the basket and felt an absurd rush of pride that I had provided my first bit of information to the system. I joined in the search of the drawers and found cards on Glynis Jones, Consuela Jones, and Svetlana Jones. Lana's card logged her frequent AWOLs, Connie's showed she had followed Glynis into prostitution. Both had convictions for CPL: Common Prostitute Loitering. Lana was living with two active prostitutes. Not one: two!

'Why haven't social services taken Lana into care?' I asked.

'She isn't beaten or hungry, she goes to school most of the time and is adequately dressed, so she probably hasn't come to their notice,' Phil said.

'She's in moral danger.' Was I the only one to be concerned?

'It's 1976 not 1876. As far as we know, Lana is not out selling herself, so the social services won't be interested,' Irene said. 'It's a matter of prioritising resources. It's not ideal.'

No, it wasn't. So much was very far from ideal, but I had no idea how to change things.

*

After refs, Phil showed me to another dingy, putty-coloured room, dominated by a wood table surrounded by grey plastic chairs. He pointed to a large, grey filing cabinet. 'You'll find all the forms you need in there. You should put the most used ones—like the crime and Road Traffic Accident booklets—in your bag. When you've completed your form, you put it in the large drawer by the sergeants' office.'

'Control to Phil. Return to the control room please.'

Before I could comment on the informality of the call, he left. I looked in the cabinet but had a brain-freeze moment. I stared at the piles of paper, but my brain felt like a rusted cog, grating as it struggled to move. It was no good, I would have to ask someone which form to use. I went to the door as Derek, the control room operator that resembled Toad, came around the corner.

'Derek, can you help me please?'

'Anytime.' Derek bounded over, grabbed me by the wrist, and pulled me close.

In a fraction of a second, my heart rate trebled and I had to bite back a scream. I shoved him hard and he crashed against the wall. *If he came at me again, I wanted something behind me, so I could give him a hefty kick.* I caught his look of shock and I realised that I was hyperventilating and had adopted a defence stance, ready to repel the next attack. I took a calming breath and lowered my hands.

This wasn't the same as that time.

I deliberately kept my voice level. 'Do not do that again. I just want to know which form to use for a domestic dispute.'

'General report.'

'Thank you.' I turned my back on Derek and fished the form from the cabinet, aware that he remained watching me for a few seconds before going on his way. Nice one, Sam; how to get a reputation as the block weirdo in one easy step.

*

I was just putting the completed form into the drawer next to the sergeants' office when Sergeant Bowman came out.

'What's that?'

'The report from that domestic, Sarge,' I replied.

Alan held out his hand. I passed the form over and watched him read it. His deepening frown didn't fill me with confidence. He handed the form back to me.

'Sam: first, this reads like something from *Jackanory*. You must be more succinct. Second, you don't do a general report form for a domestic; it has its own form that's specifically laid out so you know what information is required, and that does not include Arthur's affliction.' Sergeant Bowman tapped the report where I had described the exchange between Rose and Arthur. 'Phil's supposed to be helping you with this. Where is he?'

'He was called away and Derek told me to do a general report.'

Alan ripped up the report. 'It was probably a joke. I'll have a word with him. Get the correct form done and I'll send Phil to help you.'

I trailed back to the report writing room, seething with Derek. But I couldn't put all the blame on him; we had practised these forms in training and I had forgotten.

*

34

I was still livid with Derek when Phil and I went out, after I had completed the correct form.

'Why would Derek tell me to do a general report form?' I complained. 'Sergeant Bowman thinks I'm useless. I bet it was revenge.'

Phil looked sideways at me. 'Revenge for what?'

'Derek grabbed me, so I pushed him and he fell against the wall.'

Phil shrugged. 'Fair enough. It would just have been a joke. The sprog always gets teased. The same thing happened to Steve Patton then Ken.'

'I remember sitting next to Steve on parade. Which one is Ken?' I asked.

'Ken Ashcroft. He was sitting on your other side. He was the sprog before you. Nice lad.' Phil flipped down the visor against the late, low sun and drove out of the yard.

'Mike Two.'

'Mike Two; go ahead.' I was getting the hang of the radio.

'Make Collinwood Place, report of a drunken man; disorderly and shouting in the street,' said Ray.

Phil took the handset from me before I could answer. 'I've got the sprog, remember.'

'It's Stan,' Ray said.

Phil's face relaxed. 'Right. Roger that then.'

'Why did you say that?' I asked as I replaced the radio.

'I didn't want to take you to a kick-off on your first day here,' Phil replied. 'But Stan's harmless. A nuisance, but harmless.'

I considered his comment for a minute, then said, 'Phil, you won't hesitate about going to jobs just because I'm with you, will you? I need to gain experience before going solo even if it means wading into a fight.'

Phil swung the car around the corner. 'Yes, I am going to think twice.'

That wasn't the answer I wanted, although I appreciated Phil's chivalry. 'Same pay, same job, Phil,' I said, paraphrasing the inspector's words.

'Hrmph.' Phil pulled into a narrow street and a short, scruffy, extremely drunk man staggered off the kerb into the road in front of us.

Phil wound down his window. 'You've started early tonight, Stan.'

Stan turned and raised two fingers at us. '…koff!'

'Now then, Stan, you can't be using language like that tonight. I have a young lady with me,' Phil said.

Stan fell against the car and peered into the window. 'I'm terribly sorry, madam. I didn't see you there,' he slurred whilst trying to sound refined. 'You see I've had a bit to drink.'

Phil jabbed a thumb over his shoulder. 'You know the drill. Get in the back and, if you behave yourself, young Samantha and I will see you to the hostel.'

Stan tottered to one side then sat heavily on the road. Phil sighed, and we got out of the car. I didn't wait to be told.

'Come on, Stan. If you can't get up the hostel won't take you.'

'Don't care. I wouldn't mind a nice warm bed in your bridewell, especially if she's there too.'

'Don't be cheeky,' Phil said. 'It's a police station, not a doss house.'

Stan grinned. 'Okay then.' He threw his head back and bellowed, 'All coppers are bastards, except Samantha. All coppers—'

'Stop that, Stan, or Samantha will arrest you,' Phil snapped.

'Me?' I wasn't ready, I couldn't remember the caution or anything else.

'You need experience.' Phil took hold of Stan's arm and tried to stand him up, but Stan sat in the road and sang *Goodbye Sam, Hello Samantha,* loudly and off key. Phil heaved Stan up and I supported his other side. He draped an arm across my shoulders, which I would actively discourage usually but, before I could move away, he tripped on nothing and brought us both down onto the road. I felt my tights give at the knee. Luckily, I had a spare pair of tights into my locker, but if I was going to be dealing with people like Stan in future, I'd better bring several pairs in.

I wiped away the gravel on my legs and stood up. Phil pointed at the now prone Stan. 'D and D. Off you go.'

'I'm arresting you for being drunk and disorderly. You are not obliged to say anything unless you wish to do so, but anything you do say will be taken down in writing and may be given in evidence.' I had remembered the caution!

'Thank you.' Stan belched.

Phil and I took an arm each, manoeuvred Stan over to the Panda, and poured him into the back. I slid in beside him, Phil got into the driver seat and, after informing control that we had one in custody, he drove us back to the station.

As we passed Belvedere House, Stan stirred and waved a limp hand towards the apartments.

'That's where you should be. Lock up the bent bastards and perverts that live in there.'

Phil glanced over. 'Just because they're rich, it doesn't mean they're bent or perverted.'

'There's some bad 'uns in there. They talk about them in the hostels. Gangsters. Drugs, girls and orgies...' Stan's voice trailed off and his eyes closed.

'There's bad 'uns everywhere, mate.' Phil caught my eyes in the mirror.

'Orgies?' I whispered.

'Some people resent rich people.' Phil swung the Panda off Nelson Square and Stan slumped against me. I pushed him back.

Phil was right; some people would resent the residents of Belvedere House simply because they were well off, but that didn't mean their prejudice was without basis. Perhaps the apartment block wasn't as nice as I thought. I would put a note in for Irene.

In the receiving yard we tried to get Stan out of the car but he remained a dead weight, sprawled across the back seat, humming. I was getting sick of that song.

The bridewell officer came out. 'What's the delay?'

'Give us a hand,' Phil said.

The two men took an arm each and hauled Stan to a sitting position. Stan belched then vomited in the car. They let go and leapt backwards, while Stan flopped backwards and lay in the puke. I covered my mouth and swallowed hard to keep the contents of my stomach in place.

Phil leant his forehead against the Panda. 'Hellfire, couldn't you have waited until you got outside?'

'What's going on out here?' The bridewell sergeant came out and took stock of the situation. 'Whose prisoner?'

'Young Sam here. Her first,' Phil replied.

The bridewell sergeant eyed me for a few moments then said, 'Phil, you clean the car. Help me get the prisoner out first. The lass can wipe him down and book him in.'

'Hellfire,' Phil muttered.

Between them, the three men pulled Stan from the car and propped him against the mesh fence while I gingerly eased the sick-soaked jacket from him and then used it to wipe the worst of the puke from his face and shirt. I should have listened to Dad and gone to university.

'What do you want me to do with this, Sarge?' I held out the jacket.

'Chuck it in that bucket over there,' he replied, nodding towards a large metal pail in the corner of the receiving yard.

'But how can I book it into property if it's out here?'

'It's not coming inside stinking like that. Leave it there and I'll put a note on the charge sheet.'

I obeyed the sergeant and threw the jacket in the bucket, but I would make sure he did put that note on the charge sheet. It might only be a sicky jacket, but it was Stan's sicky jacket and, if he lost it, it would be me that would have to explain things.

While we walked Stan into the bridewell, Phil went to the caretaker's cupboard, got a mop and bucket and a very large bottle of disinfectant, then trudged back to the Panda, muttering all the way.

With the sergeant's help, I booked in and fingerprinted Stan, installed him in his cell for the night, dealt with the property, and wrote my statement. I had just completed the file when Phil came in.

'The car's clean but it stinks.' Phil stowed the mop and bucket and put the empty bottle of disinfectant in the bin.

'I have some cologne in my locker. Do you want me to get it and we can sprinkle some in the car?' It would also give me the chance to get a new pair of tights; my knees were hanging out of my current pair.

'Why not?' Phil said. 'The car can't smell worse than it does now. I'll do my statement while you're gone.'

I hurried to the locker room, congratulating myself for bringing in cheap cologne. Actually, I hadn't thought of it; it was a tip from training school.

The sun had set and it was getting dark; the locker room was cast in shadow. I got the bottle and tights from my locker and was just locking it again when I heard voices from the doorway.

'Someone's in here.' I recognised Steve's voice. A second later he peered into my bay. 'It's the sprog.' He rushed in and wrapped me in a bear hug. My heart rate increased but I didn't want to overreact. The logical part of my mind knew he was just messing around, but I struggled to get away.

Steve squeezed me tighter. 'Do you want to try a spot of bondage? I've got my handcuffs.'

Another policeman from parade, whose name I didn't know, came into the bay. 'I've got mine here too.'

If they handcuffed me, I would surely lose my mind. I couldn't be restrained like that again and remain sane. I kicked at Steve's shins and threw my head backwards towards his nose, but still he held me. My racing heart almost burst from my chest and I began to feel light-headed.

'Get the 'cuffs,' he called.

Everything I had fought so hard to suppress flooded back. My throat closed until I felt I was suffocating, and I couldn't have screamed even if I tried. I could feel the burn of the duct tape around my wrists and ankles. *I kicked the side of the van until my shoes fell off and I hurt my feet.* I kicked against the locker in the hope someone would come to investigate the noise.

Alan stepped into the bay. 'What's going on?'

Steve immediately let go and I sagged against the locker. I felt tears welling up, but I pressed my tongue hard against the roof of my mouth to stop myself crying; a trick an instructor at training school gave us for when we dealt with upsetting incidents. It worked.

'Just horseplay, Sarge,' Steve said.

'Get out, both of you,' Alan growled.

They left at once. Alan took a step towards me and I instinctively flinched.

'Sam, what just happened?'

I felt my lip tremble. Steve and his pal would probably be puzzled over my reaction to what they considered to be a bit of fun. I didn't believe I had been in any danger, but I couldn't have coped with being restrained like that.

'They were going to handcuff me. Like Steve said, it was just horseplay, Sarge.'

'Sam…' Alan reached out a hand as if to pat my shoulder, then thought better of it. 'Do you want to crime this?'

'Crime it?'

'Report it officially so it is recorded as a crime,' he explained. Another bit of jargon for me.

I shook my head. 'I don't believe they intended any harm. It's just me…'

'Maybe you should let people know what happened,' Alan said.

It was a thought. I wanted to keep it quiet, but if I continued panicking then someone would do a bit of digging and it would all come out anyway.

'I'll think about it,' I said. 'They were just messing around, no harm done.' I gripped the bottle of cologne to stop my hands shaking. 'A prisoner was sick in the car. This is to help it smell better. I must get back to complete the file. Phil's doing his statement.' I could hear myself babbling but I didn't want to stop speaking in case Alan asked me any more questions. I retrieved the dropped packet of tights from the floor and moved towards the door.

Alan stepped back to let me pass and followed me onto the corridor. I could feel him watch me as I walked back to the bridewell.

I knocked at the door and Phil let me in. 'You took your time.'

I held out the bottle of cologne. I didn't have the energy to argue; the adrenaline was leaving my system and I felt a headache starting.

Phil took the bottle from me. 'I'll go and do this while you submit the file. My statement's done.'

I got the file from the office and trailed off to the submissions drawer, stopping off at the ladies' toilet to change my tights.

I had just put the file in the drawer when the door to the sergeants' office opened and Steve came out into the enquiry office, his cheeks burning red.

'Where's Phil?' he asked.

'Bridewell,' I replied.

Steve walked to the bridewell and, after a few seconds, I followed; close enough for him to know that I was headed to the same place, but far enough to know I was not speaking to him. I felt a glow of satisfaction that Alan had given him a dressing-down.

In the bridewell, Phil came in from the now-dark receiving yard and handed me the half-empty cologne bottle.

'It smells like a tart's boudoir but that's better than eau de vomit.'

Steve groaned. 'I've got to sit in that! Alan says he wants Sam to spend the last hour in the office, so I've got to come out with you. He's done this on purpose.'

I normally would have objected to Alan so obviously taking on a paternal role, but I felt a bit shaky, and I didn't want to sit in a smelly Panda car, so I waved a cheery goodbye and left Steve to his misery.

*

I went off duty with a sense of disquiet that Lana still had not returned home. Enquiries into her absence would continue into the night, despite Rose's sighting of her earlier on. Lana's description had been passed to the other forces and to the ports. Soon, they would have to decide whether to up the ante and bring in the media. I hoped she would return before then.

Chapter Five

Next day, I arrived at the station about half two, ready to start my shift at three. I went into the locker room, pausing at the door to listen for voices. There were several, but I couldn't expect the room to be empty all the time. I made sure I made a noise as I entered.

A couple of faces peered out of other bays and nodded a greeting to me.

'Afternoon,' one said.

'Afternoon, gents,' I replied and went to my locker to get my hat and put on my jacket.

I heard people leave the room and relaxed, until Steve looked into my bay. I wasn't going to make a scene but I watched his movements. If he came too close with handcuffs, he was going to get a shoe in the balls.

He hovered at the top of the bay for a moment, exchanged a few words with someone as they left the room, and then turned back to me. The locker room was silent. I remained still and waited for him to say something.

He scuffed his feet along the ground. 'About yesterday. It was just a bit of fun, you know.'

'Your idea of fun is to assault me?' I asked.

'I didn't assault you,' he argued.

'Look up the definition sometime before you finish your

probation. I think you'll find you fulfilled all the elements,' I said.

'Look, when you come to a new block you have to expect a bit of teasing,' he said. 'Regard it as an initiation. I had it and so did Ken.'

'Lads roughing up lads as a joke is one thing, two men grabbing a female and threatening to handcuff her is something else entirely. I could crime it, you know.'

Steve blanched. 'You make it sound sinister, but it was just meant as fun. The most we would have done is handcuff you to the locker. We get closer and rougher than that when we have to arrest people sometimes.'

'You were not arresting me.' I kept my voice low, even though I wanted to beat him to death with his own truncheon. 'You threatened to handcuff me.'

Steve remained silent for a moment. 'We really upset you, didn't we.' He didn't wait for me to reply. 'I'm sorry; it really was just a joke.'

'Emptying the contents of the hole puncher into my hat is a joke, this… This was…' I shook my head.

Steve stared at the floor. 'I'm sorry.'

I watched him for a moment. 'All right. I accept your apology. Just be aware that if you—or anyone else on this block—touch me again, I will crime it. You can spread the word.'

'Friends?' he asked.

'I suppose.' I knew he had meant no harm, but I was going to make him work hard to make up for scaring me like that.

*

'All right,' said Ken Ashcroft as I sat down between him and Steve. 'How was it yesterday?'

'Not bad,' I replied. 'A domestic and a D and D. I got my first arrest over and done with. There were a couple of pranks, but it was okay.'

'I overheard Alan giving Steve a right rollicking in his office.'

He smiled, showing off straight white teeth, which were offset nicely by his dark brown hair.

It seemed nothing was secret in this place.

'I'm glad you're here,' Ken continued. 'You'll take the heat off me.'

'You can join in the fun now,' I muttered.

Ken shook his head. 'Not my style. Steve was the sprog before me and, as soon as he was off the hook, he became the biggest pest of them all. My girlfriend, Gaynor, is a cadet; she's going to the training school in November. I don't like to think of her being bullied, so I won't do it to others.'

'You think this is bullying? I thought it was just my initiation.'

'It is your initiation. It's also bullying.' Ken stopped speaking as the door opened. Everyone stood as the inspector and sergeants entered, and parade began.

'Lana Jones is still missing,' Sergeant Bowman said after he had given out the duties. 'It's been longer than usual so step up the enquiries, would you, Phil?'

'Yes, Sarge,' Phil jotted in his book. 'She was seen by Rose yesterday,' he added.

'Yes, but she wasn't home and hasn't been cancelled.' Alan Bowman shuffled his papers.

'Does this mean we'll have to start a search like Tynvoller division did?' I whispered to Ken.

'Not yet,' he replied. 'They'll widen the enquiries first, then consider a press release. Nothing for us to worry about until we're directed to become involved.'

I turned my attention back to parade. Inspector Tyrrell was giving out observations and warning us to stay away from a particular road in case we disturbed a CID operation. If I were to stray into the area, it would be because Phil had taken me there.

'That will be all.' Inspector Tyrrell brought the parade to an end and, as yesterday, I held back while everyone swarmed out.

*

As we walked out to the yard, Phil stopped me. 'What's that?' He tilted my hat forward and a snowfall of paper bits tickled past my nose. 'Someone's emptied the contents of a hole puncher into the rim of your hat.'

Steve was the prime suspect, probably pinching the idea I gave him in the locker room. This was the type of lark I could appreciate. I took my hat off and shook out the paper.

The inspector came across the yard. 'You go on, Phil. I want to talk to Sam for a minute.'

Phil went to the car. I replaced my hat and stood "at ease" in front of the inspector with my eyes cast downwards, wracking my brains for any transgressions that would earn me a rollicking.

'I understand you were subjected to a prank,' Inspector Tyrrell said.

He evidently knew everything, but I didn't want him to think I was weak.

'It was nothing, sir.' I tried to meet Inspector Tyrrell's nice eyes, but I finished up gazing at the silver buttons on his breast pockets. He was going to think that beetroot was my natural colouring, seeing as I had blushed every time I had been near him.

'There will always be an element of teasing for the sprogs, but there is a limit. If you have any concerns, or if someone oversteps the mark, you must speak to Alan or me.'

'Thank you, sir.'

He dismissed me, and I hurried over to Phil and got into the car.

'What did the boss want?' Phil asked.

'Just asking how I was finding it,' I replied.

Phil pointed to the glove compartment. 'Pass me an allsort.'

I got the bag of sweets out, took one myself, and held out the bag.

'Did I offer you one?' I knew by his expression that Phil was joking.

'Sorry, do you want it back?' I made to spit out the chewed

liquorice.

'Don't you dare. It was bad enough cleaning up after Stan last night,' Phil said.

I shook the bag and, just as Phil selected a coconut wheel, Ray's voice crackled over the radio.

'Mike Two.'

'Mike Two; go ahead,' I responded.

'43 Sandringham Boulevard. A sudden death.'

Phil took the handset from me. 'Do we have any further details?'

'That's a bad cold, Sam; your voice has gone husky.' Ray joked.

'You can tuck me up in bed later, Ray,' Phil said.

'I look forward to it.' Ray's voice became business-like. 'It seems straightforward. The deceased is seventy-four years old: Henry Albiston, who lived with his sister. He went up for a post-lunch siesta and passed in his sleep. Doctor has been informed.'

'Roger.' Phil turned the car towards the outskirts of town, and I felt butterflies in my stomach. This would be my first dead body.

'It's important to remain professional at sudden deaths,' Phil said. 'Often there are weeping relatives and it can be hard to remain composed, but the families have enough to deal with without coppers blubbering all over the place. If you can't keep a lid on it, take yourself back to the car until you can.'

I had that tongue pressing trick but, if that failed, I would follow Phil's advice and get out.

Phil pulled up at a red traffic light. He hummed tunelessly as we waited for them to change.

'Why don't you put on the lights and siren on?' I asked. 'You would get through the traffic faster.'

Phil slipped into gear as the lights changed and pulled away. 'What for?'

'He's dead.'

'Then he's not going to get any worse, so a small delay won't make a difference. Blues and twos are kept for urgent situations. This isn't logged as a suspicious death so, whilst it's distressing for the family, it's not an emergency. Dodging around traffic at high speed can be dangerous because it isn't law for other drivers to let us through, although most do. If anything goes wrong, it's on our head.' Phil turned into a road lined with neat, post-war semis and drew up outside number forty-three.

I saw the curtains twitch at the adjoining house, number forty-one. 'We have an audience.'

'Nothing new there.' Phil opened the gate and I followed him up number forty-three's path, which was lined with azaleas. Before we could reach the front door, a woman came out of the next door house.

'Hello, hello. Coo-ee.' She scuttled over to the fence. 'Is everything all right?'

Phil paused briefly. 'We just need to see your neighbour.' He continued to the front door and knocked.

'Henry has been proper poorly recently. His sister won't appreciate being disturbed,' the woman said.

'Shouldn't be a problem with the death certificate if he's been ill,' Phil murmured.

The door opened a crack and a slim, elderly lady peered around. When she saw us, she threw the door wide open. 'Thank you for coming. Please come in.'

I gaped as I entered the hall. I had never seen so many religious artefacts in one place outside of a church. From the Sacred Heart picture on the wall to a small, china plate with the image of Jesus painted on it, beside the telephone; the place was stuffed with religious knick-knacks and pictures.

'Are you Henry Albiston's sister?' Phil asked.

'Miss Maud Albiston. You may call me Maud.'

'Thank you. I'm Phil and this is Sam. Where is Mr Albiston?'

'Upstairs in the rear bedroom. He went up for a lie-down and, when I checked on him, he was gone.'

'May I?' Phil pointed up the stairs.

'Of course.' Miss Albiston and I followed him upstairs. 'Henry had rheumatic fever as a young man and his heart was never strong afterwards. He needed someone to look after him after his wife died, so he came to live with me.'

'It must be a dreadful shock to you,' I said.

Maud turned and smiled. 'When you get to our age, you know that it won't be too long before the Lord calls you home.'

'Is there anyone we can call for you?' Talking to Maud made me forget my nerves and made me feel I was doing something productive.

'You are kind but there's only Henry's son in Australia. I'll let him know myself. He'll be terribly upset. Last year, after his mother's funeral, he invited Henry and me to Australia, but Henry was too frail to travel that far. I couldn't leave him here alone, so I stayed too.'

The doorbell rang and Maud went downstairs to answer it.

Phil and I entered a dull room, cluttered with more religious items and heavy, dark wood furniture. Henry Albiston lay on a chintz coverlet that matched the curtains. He wasn't scary at all. His passing had been peaceful.

'He looks asleep.'

'Aye. When it's my time, I hope I just slip away in my bed,' Phil said. 'His sister seems to be coping well.'

I looked at the wooden cross fixed to the wall above the bed. I didn't doubt that, if I went into Maud's bedroom, I would find a similar cross over her bed. I wasn't sure if I still believed, but if people found comfort in such things, good luck to them.

'It must be wonderful to have such faith that death is almost seen as a reason to rejoice,' I said.

'Rejoice is perhaps a little strong, but death is not a cause for sorrow.' Maud came into the bedroom followed by the doctor, a man of about forty-five with floppy, dark hair just starting to fleck through with silver.

'Hello, Dr Owen,' Phil said.

'Hello again, Constable Torrens. Who is your companion?'

'This is Sam Barrie, she's new,' Phil said.

'Hello, Constable Barrie. I expect we'll meet from time to time in the future. Phil and I are old friends now,'

'Please, call me Sam,' I said.

'Thank you. Away from incidents I will, and you must call me Tom.' He turned to Maud. 'And how are you, my dear. I know this isn't entirely unexpected but it must have been a shock. Do I need to prescribe something for you?'

Maud shook her head. 'Allow the Lord into your heart and he will sustain you. I will miss Henry but he's in Paradise now and God will support me, Dr Owen. As you said, he's been ill for a long time and I knew this day would come.'

Would Julie Wynne's parents feel the same? I wondered. Maybe they wouldn't ask God to give them strength but would demand to know why their child had died. I would. If there was a Great Plan, I would want to know which part of it demanded a child's death.

'Would you all like some tea?' Maud interrupted my thoughts.

'Yes please,' we chorused.

Maud went downstairs while the doctor carried out an examination of Henry and officially pronounced life extinct.

'We could have told them that much,' I whispered to Phil.

'We're not medically qualified so, even when it's evident, it has to be confirmed by a doctor. Radio in and let Ray know what's happening,' Phil said to me.

'What is happening?' I asked.

Dr Owen grinned. 'Your first one?' I nodded. 'You have a bit of a problem. I can't issue a death certificate because I haven't actually seen him for a few weeks, so you'll have to inform the coroner so an inquest can be arranged. However, I know Henry well and I don't anticipate any problems because his ticker has always been a bit iffy. By the way, Henry wanted the Cooperative to deal with him.'

I relayed all the information to Ray back at control, just as Maud came back carrying a tray with four bone china cups filled with tea and a plate of assorted biscuits. She placed it on the dressing table and handed each of us a cup, passed around the biscuits, then took the remaining cup herself.

'How long has Henry been unwell for this time, Maud?' the

doctor asked

'About three weeks, but you know we don't like to bother you with every little thing. Should I have called you?' Maud nervously nibbled on a Rich Tea biscuit.

'I don't think it would have made any difference to the outcome, but as I have just been telling the officers, I can't issue a death certificate because I haven't seen him for a while. There will need to be a post-mortem to confirm the cause of death.'

'Oh dear; he won't like that. I wish I had called you.'

Dr Owen put a hand on Maud's shoulder. 'Don't you worry, Maud, it's just what the rules say. The undertaker will come shortly to take Henry to the mortuary.' He finished his tea. 'Right, I need to get to my next call. Now, Maud, if you do find that you can't sleep or you feel otherwise overwhelmed or unwell, you must ring me.'

'I will, Dr Owen. Thank you,' Maud said.

He bade us all goodbye and left.

Phil drained his own cup and put it back on the tray. 'We'll go to the mortuary and see Henry is safely booked in, and we'll make sure the report goes off today. It shouldn't be too long before you can make arrangements.'

Maud smiled at Phil. 'You're very kind.'

We went downstairs when the undertakers arrived, to give them more room to manoeuvre Henry from the room.

'Is there anyone here we can call?' I asked Maud. 'I don't like to leave you alone like this.'

'I'll be fine.' She studied my face. 'Were you a St Agnes' girl?'

'I went to the Grammar,' I replied.

'Oh, I thought I didn't recognise you. I'm normally quite good at spotting our old girls. I was head of maths at St Agnes' until I retired.' Maud opened the door to let us out. 'A St Agnes' girl lives next door. Janice Alderman. She's growing up so quickly. When she's out of uniform you would hardly believe she's only just turned fifteen. You met her mother, Pamela, on the way in.'

Immediately Pamela from next door appeared at the fence.

'Maud, what's happening? Is there anything I can do?'

Maud half smiled at me. 'The Lord told us to love our neighbour, didn't He?'

'He did.' I might be agnostic, but I still remembered scripture lessons from school.

Maud sighed. 'Henry has passed away, Pamela. The officers need to go to the hospital now. Would you mind sitting with me for a while?'

Pamela stared as the undertaker wheeled Henry's bagged body out to a plain grey van. As they slammed the van door shut, she seemed to shake herself.

'Of course, I'll come over at once. Poor Henry. I'll bring some biscuits.' Pamela scurried inside her house.

'You go, I'll be fine,' Maud said to me.

'Someone will be in touch soon, Maud,' Phil called.

'Thank you for being so kind. I'll mention you both in my prayers tonight.'

Phil and I got back into the car as Pamela bustled from her house into Maud's, carrying a biscuit tin. She waved briefly before disappearing inside.

Chapter Six

The hospital was an ex-workhouse built of ornate brick interspersed with engraved tablets proclaiming that *"Work Leads to Salvation"*. I was sure the previous occupants had appreciated that reminder as they endured their wretched existences.

Phil pulled up next to the undertaker's grey van outside the mortuary.

'As sudden deaths go, this hasn't been too bad,' Phil said. 'We should book in the property and get this boxed off in no time.'

We went through the quarry-tiled vestibule into a corridor and turned into a door on the right. Henry was lying on a trolley opposite the bank of fridge doors where bodies lay until a relative came to view them, or an undertaker collected them to prepare them for the funeral.

The mortuary attendant came in and greeted us. 'You're new,' he said to me.

'Yes I am.'

'Have you seen the fridge?' He went over and opened one of the doors. Curious, I peered in and was surprised that interior was an open space with long trays arranged on a large rack. The little doors allowed convenient access to each tray without disturbing the others. There were a couple of sheet-wrapped bodies inside, and soon Henry would join them.

'I didn't expect it to be all open like that,' I said. 'It's all a bit brutal, as if a person is just a piece of meat.'

'Once someone dies, that is all they are,' the attendant said.

I imagined Julie Wynne lying on a tray awaiting identification. I shivered and tried to shake off the images in my mind.

The attendant must have thought I was cold because he said, 'Bodies have to be refrigerated because they go off very quickly.' He shut the door. 'You have very pretty eyes.'

He was chatting me up in front of a fridge of dead people! I moved swiftly over to Phil.

'Sam, can you nip out to the car and get me a form from my folder please. We may as well make a start on it while we're here,' Phil said.

I went out to the car and was rummaging through Phil's leather folder when Ray's voice came over the radio.

'Mike Two.'

I hesitated in case Phil answered via his personal radio.

'Mike Two,' the call came again.

Phil didn't respond, so I picked up the handset and answered, 'Mike Two; go ahead.'

'Will you be free for another job shortly?' Ray asked.

'We're still at the mortuary, over,' I replied. Damn, Phil had said that made me sound like a sprog; but then, I was the sprog and everyone knew it. No reason to fret then.

'Not to worry. Shout up when you're free.'

'Wilco control. Over and out.' Okay, maybe I was revelling in my sprog-ness a bit too much. I replaced the handset and went back inside, where Phil was folding an item of clothing ready to go into the property bag.

'Ray called. I think jobs must be piling up.'

'We'll be another fifteen or twenty minutes here.' Phil put the folded clothing into the property bag.

The attendant went over to the desk and picked up a black marker pen and wrote, *"Albiston. H,"* along Henry's calf. At the same time, I realised that Henry was now naked. I'm not sure what my face did as I tried to process the scene, but Phil immediately grabbed a towel from the rail by the sink and threw it across Henry's hips. I turned and fled back to the Panda.

*

I had brought my breathing under control, but my cheeks were still burning when Phil came back to the car, carrying the property bag and jewellery envelope.

'That was a fast exit.' Phil threw the bag onto the back seat.

'I thought I should leave.' I nodded towards the bags. 'Do they go into the safe at the station?'

'The jewellery does, the rest go into the property store until the coroner releases the body.' Phil climbed into the car and picked up the handset.

'Mike Two to control.'

'Go ahead,' Ray answered.

'Finished at the mortuary. We just need to bring some property in and submit the file. Do you have a job for us?'

'We had an alarm earlier and everyone was committed but the boss has gone to it. See you back at the station.'

Phil replaced the handset and started the car. 'He's a good 'un our boss. I can't think of many inspectors who would turn out to a job like that.'

I was forming a very favourable impression of our inspector.

'To tell the truth, I think he likes it,' Phil went on as he drove out of the hospital. 'He wants promotion, but he doesn't like the way he's had to move away from operational policing. Anyway, you coped with this job much better than I thought you would.'

I was pleased at the praise. 'It was okay. Sad, but somehow right, like the end of a cycle.'

'How come you broke the land speed record out of there?' Phil asked.

I wriggled in my seat. 'I think he'd have been embarrassed to know I was there while he was naked.'

'We have to undress them, Sam. We need to take possession

of jewellery and suchlike for the family. Also, what appears to be a straightforward death sometimes turns out to be murder. We need to preserve a crime scene quickly, so gathering the property gives us a chance to do a brief inspection before the more detailed medical examination. Not that I thought there would be anything off about Henry's death.'

'We can't pronounce death because we're not doctors, but we can strip people to see if a death is suspicious. That seems wrong.'

'I did say we only did a brief inspection.'

I wasn't placated. 'Writing on the leg? I thought they used toe-tags like on the telly.'

'Labels get lost, legs don't,' Phil replied.

'Would Julie Wynne have been stripped off and left naked in front of strangers and had her name written on her decomposing leg? Would I have...?' I became aware of my rising volume and stopped speaking. My heartbeat throbbed in my ears and I stopped before I let slip something I didn't want to say.

'Hellfire! Calm down. Would you have what?' Phil braked, hard.

'Never mind.' I turned my head and stared out of the window.

Phil drove on in silence for a minute. 'I think there's more to this. Have you seen a naked man before?'

I felt heat rise across my cheeks. 'I know what a man looks like, Phil.' Yes, I knew what a man looked like but that was as far as it went. I lost more than my liberty and peace of mind that night; those bastards also stole my chances of a normal relationship. Working in my uncle's restaurant had been great for learning how to talk with people my own age again, but I had refused all requests for a date because dating led to kissing and kissing led to sex. I wanted a boyfriend. God, how I wanted a boyfriend; but if a man so much as put an arm around me, I had a panic attack. I would probably die a reluctant virgin.

'Did you know Julie Wynne then?' Phil asked.

'No, I just thought of her when I saw Henry lying there. I hadn't realised it was all so undignified. I don't want to be left exposed like

Henry was and have a creepy attendant write on my leg.'

Phil rolled his shoulders. 'Nobody said it was ideal, Sam, but we have procedure to follow to ensure everything goes smoothly and the right property goes to the right family. You'd better get used to it because sudden deaths are one of the bread and butter jobs. We get at least one a week.'

'It's just not like I imagined.'

'What did you imagine?' Phil asked.

'I don't know; something nicer.'

'A nice, sudden death?' Phil gave a wry grin. 'Sorry, but we only get sad ones or nasty ones.'

'I know, but I don't have to like it.' I would never like it.

'None of us like it,' Phil said.

We got back to the station at the same time as Inspector Tyrrell and all walked in together. Phil carried the jewellery and I had the bag of clothing.

'How did Sam's first sudden death go?' the inspector asked.

'Fine, until she ran out of the mortuary,' Phil replied. 'I think it was because we undressed him.'

I could have killed Phil. 'I'll go and do those property cards,' I said and scuttled into the station.

I literally ran into the ladies' toilet and splashed my face with cold water to take down the beetroot shade. Bobbies loved a good gossip and I had no doubt that my swift exit would be the subject of discussion at scoff.

*

By 10pm all paperwork had been completed, so Phil and I went out on patrol for the last hour of the shift. We cut around Nelson Square on our way out because, Phil said, the restaurants and clubs would be busy now it was dark, and the staff there liked to see a police presence as it deterred bad behaviour. Nelson Square was filled with people. Some gave us a cheery wave or a thumbs-up, which I returned.

'That's Lana!' Phil exclaimed.

I looked over to where Phil was pointing. Off Nelson Square, in a narrow alley that ran beside Belvedere House, a lone figure walked towards the main road. She did look a little like me.

Phil zoomed over to her and pulled up just in front of her. 'Hop in, Lana. We've been looking for you.'

Lana threw down her cigarette and climbed in.

'So, where have you been?' Phil asked.

'I went to a friend's,' Lana replied.

'Which friend?'

'Molly, if it's any of your business.'

Did she have any idea of the work that went into dealing with girls like her? Phil didn't respond to her jibe, so I remained quiet.

'Let control know we've located Lana and we'll take her home,' Phil said to me.

While Phil drove off while continuing to talk to Lana, I radioed Ray as instructed, then Ray relayed our information to the patrols and cancelled observations. Derek would be telexing the other forces to cancel her.

Phil pulled up outside a neglected, terraced house in a warren of run-down, narrow streets near to the docks. Each street had a nautical name: schooner, clipper, yacht and so on. Lana and her family lived in Schooner Street. I let Lana out of the back and she shot to the closest front door.

'Thanks for the lift. See you.'

'Not so fast. We need to speak to Glynis,' Phil said.

'She probably won't be in.' Lana slipped into the house and tried to shut the door.

Phil casually leant against the door, keeping it open. 'Then we'll wait.'

'You'd better come in then.' Lana reluctantly allowed us entry and we stepped directly into a small living room filled with a threadbare suite and the largest television I had seen outside of *Radio Rentals*. How the hell did someone living in this street afford something like that? Rhetorical question; I could guess how.

'Did Molly give you that money, Lana?' A bony, bottle-blonde woman came from the kitchen and jumped when she saw us.

'Hello, Glynis.' Phil folded his arms and awaited her response.

'Mr Torrens, what are you doing here?'

'Returning your daughter, the one you reported missing,' Phil replied, his tone judgemental.

'Where've you been, I've been so worried.' Glynis tried to hug Lana who stepped backwards out of her reach.

'What money?' Phil asked.

'What?'

'When we came in, you said, *"Did Molly give you that money?"*' Phil spoke slowly. 'This makes me think that you were expecting Lana, which means she wasn't really missing, and that you were expecting a pay-out. Also, who is Molly?'

'Thank you for finding her, you can go and close the case now.' Glynis pushed past us and held the door open.

'We want to establish who this Molly is in case Lana skips off again,' Phil insisted.

'She's just a friend,' Glynis said.

'From school,' Lana added.

'Right. And why would she give you money?' Phil asked.

'I lent her some dinner money,' Lana said.

That sounded reasonable, we certainly had no grounds to challenge it, but I was sure there was something they were not telling us.

'Okay then, Lana. Try to keep your mum informed of your whereabouts so she doesn't worry.'

Lana rolled her eyes and snorted. 'Yeah, we wouldn't want that. She only reports me because the school or the social services will come down on her if she doesn't.'

I followed Phil to the Panda. I was beginning to see why the block was exasperated with her; I had only just begun my dealings with her and I was already frustrated.

Chapter Seven

I hated earlies, really hated them. I had always been more owl than lark, and getting up at five thirty for a seven o'clock start almost killed me. I'd only done a couple of early shifts, but I already knew I preferred the late shift. I would reserve judgement on nights until I had completed a shift.

I yawned as I walked towards the parade room.

'Are we keeping you awake?' Alan called from his office as I walked past. He was always first in and always the last to leave.

I looked in. 'Morning, Sarge. I don't think I'll ever get used to earlies.'

'I bet you like the early finish,' Alan said.

'I'm too exhausted to do anything with it,' I complained.

'Be glad you're not in Odinsby; they start at six.'

I grimaced. I couldn't imagine getting up at four thirty. The night sergeant came in to start the handover with Alan, so I let them get on and continued down to the parade room.

A notice taped to the door declared, *"Room out of use. AM parade in the report writing room."*

I opened the door and peered in. There was nothing to indicate why the room should be out of use, but there was nobody around, so I went to the report writing room, where I waited and waited…

*

It was 6:55 before it finally dawned on me that I'd been caught out again. I grabbed my stuff and scarpered back to the parade room, but not before Alan and the inspector had arrived.

'Sam, where have you been?' Alan asked.

'I'm really sorry but there was a note on the door saying the room was out of use and to go to the report writing room. I've been waiting there.'

'Didn't you notice there was nobody else there?' Inspector Tyrrell asked with an amused glance at the assembled men.

'Eventually,' I muttered. I took my seat and tried not to glare at everyone.

'As I was saying,' Inspector Tyrrell said. 'The coroner has ruled that Julie Wynne died accidentally of drowning.'

'Sad news, sir,' Alan said.

Everyone nodded or murmured agreement. I wasn't sure if it was the early hour or whether it was the sad news, but there was not the same banter I had become used to.

*

Phil and I had been on patrol for a couple of hours when Ray called us on the radio.

'Can you make St Agnes' School? A pupil has failed to attend, and when they checked with the parents it seems she didn't return home last night. The parents are at the school.'

'Roger,' I replied and replaced the handset. 'Why are they all going from Aggie's, Phil? Don't the other schools have the same problem?'

'I suppose it goes in cycles. We had a problem with the secondary last year but that's settled down now,' he replied.

A couple of minutes later, we arrived at the school. Phil parked outside the main door and we went to the school office. The secretary ushered us into the head teacher's comfortable office, where we found Pamela Alderman, Maud's neighbour from

Sandringham Boulevard, and her husband, already waiting.

A stout, wiry-haired woman stood up from her chair and shook our hands. 'Thank you for coming so quickly. I'm Miss Ashton, headmistress of St Agnes. These are Janice's parents, Mr and Mrs Alderman.'

We nodded our greetings.

'I'm Constable Torrens and this is Constable Barrie. We met Mrs Alderman a few days ago,' Phil said.

'My neighbour, Henry, died,' Pamela explained. 'I sat with his sister, Maud, for a while.'

'Would that be Maud Albiston? I believe that she lives in Sandringham Boulevard?' Miss Ashton asked.

Pamela nodded. 'Number forty-three.'

'Oh dear. I must arrange for some flowers to be sent. Maud used to teach here.' Miss Ashton pulled forward a couple more chairs. 'Please sit down. Would you like some tea?'

Mr and Mrs Alderman each had a cup of tea, so Phil and I accepted the offer.

Miss Ashton opened the door to the school office and spoke to the secretary. 'Would you please arrange tea for the officers? Also, could you organise some flowers to be sent to one of our retired teachers, Maud Albiston, forty-three Sandringham Boulevard. I've just learnt that her brother passed away. Thank you, dear.' She returned to her desk. 'Maud taught me when I was a pupil here. A lovely woman. Very astute and a natural teacher.'

A few minutes later, the school secretary came in and placed two cups of tea in front of us.

'Thank you, dear. Could you make sure we're not disturbed for a while?'

'Of course, Miss Ashton.' The secretary left and shut the door behind her.

'Right, let's get started. I need to ask a few questions and get a description,' Phil said. 'Your daughter is Janice Alderman?'

Pamela nodded and sniffed back a tear. 'She's just fifteen.'

'When did you last see Janice?'

Pamela took a gulp of tea then placed her cup on the desk. 'Yesterday afternoon after school. She told us she was going out with her friend and would stay the night then go to school from there. This morning, the school told me that she had not turned up. I rang my husband at work and he came home at once.'

'Who is her friend?' Phil asked.

'Lana Jones. I don't know where she lives or I would have gone there to check on them,' Mrs Alderman replied.

'Lana hasn't turned up at school either,' Miss Ashton said.

'Lana hasn't been reported missing yet,' I said.

'Maybe her parents don't know. You need to tell them.' Pamela bobbed in her seat as if she was about to rush off. Mr Alderman patted her hand to calm her.

'Janice said they were going to meet someone called Molly,' Mr Alderman volunteered. 'We don't know her; she must be a friend of Lana's.'

'Does either girl knock around with a Molly at school?' Phil asked.

Miss Ashton shook her head. 'There's nobody named Molly in their year. I've had all the other registers checked and we only have two girls of that name in the school, both first formers and both present today.'

'Okay, I need a description,' said Phil.

'She's not tall, five foot three inches, average build, long fair hair, blue eyes. She was wearing her pink dress and brown boots. She had her school uniform with her in a bag.' Pamela dabbed her eyes.

Phil quickly completed the misper form and finished his tea. 'We'll be in touch as soon as we hear anything. Please ring us if she makes contact, and if you could get a photograph for us to attach to the file, it would be really useful.' Phil stood up and shook hands with Janice's parents.

'What are you going to do now?' Mr Alderman asked.

'We'll go to Lana's house and make some enquiries. We'll keep in touch so try not to worry.'

'I'll ask our secretary to find her address for you.' Miss Ashton reached over for her intercom.

'No need.'

'The police know where she lives! I said that girl was a bad influence on our Jan,' Pamela said to Mr Alderman as we left.

Miss Ashton came onto the corridor with us. 'Lana isn't such a bad girl, despite her family. I remember Consuela, her sister, and before that their mother, Glynis…' She left the sentence hanging, which told me more than words could.

'Svetlana is quieter, more thoughtful. If she had more support at home, she could make a better life for herself,' she continued.

A skinny girl, perhaps thirteen years old with lank, mouse coloured hair pulled back into a tight ponytail, passed us and gave me a shy smile. I smiled back.

'Bernadette, why aren't you in class?' Miss Ashton asked the girl.

'I have to go and see Miss Hughes,' Bernadette replied.

'In that case, would you please ask Miss Hughes to come to my office when she is able?'

'Yes, miss,' the girl, Bernadette, replied and hurried off.

'Another good girl from a dubious family. I pray daily that these children are guided away from trouble.'

'Are the girls aware of Julie Wynne's death yet?' Phil asked.

Miss Ashton nodded. 'It was in the paper a couple of days ago. The news shot around the school as if it had wings.'

'How have the girls coped?' Phil asked.

'They're still a little unsettled; so are the staff to be honest. Julie had been a bit of a handful in her last days here. Some teachers regret that their last interaction with her was to send her to detention. We had a special assembly yesterday and offered prayers for her family, which seemed to help. A few teachers and I will attend the funeral. I might take the head girl with me to represent the pupils.'

'Her family will appreciate that,' I said.

I saw Bernadette hurrying back. 'Miss Ashton, Miss Hughes

says would it be all right if she dealt with me first. She'll be about ten minutes.'

'Thank you, Bernadette. Tell her that will be fine.'

Bernadette glanced at Phil and me, smiled again, and went back to Miss Hughes.

'Bernadette has her fourteenth birthday during the summer holidays so she's eligible for a place on the camping trip run by the church for the children of our poorer families. It costs them nothing for the week, but we do need parental permission and her mother has not responded. Miss Hughes is head of pastoral care and has taken it upon herself to chase it up. I think she cares more about the girls than some of their parents do.'

'I went to a church camp as a teenager. It was good preparation for national service.' Phil quirked his mouth. 'Come on, Sam, let's get those enquiries done.'

I trotted after him. 'Did you really go on a church camp?' I asked when we were out of Miss Ashton's hearing.

'Yeah. I was only two when Dad was killed. His ship was torpedoed during the war. Mum was left alone with me and twin babies. Things were a bit tight growing up, so we qualified for camp. It piddled down every day, the site was a quagmire, and I got the runs. I've never been camping since.'

I chuckled despite the tragic circumstances. Phil wasn't the only child to have lost his father during the war.

We arrived at Schooner Street and parked up near the Jones's house. A yellow Lotus Elite looked out of place on the grim street.

Phil nudged me. 'That's worth a note to Irene.'

I jotted down the registration. It would be nice to be able to provide her with something that might prove useful.

We could see movement through the bare, streaked window as we got out of the Panda.

'There's Lana in the blue top,' Phil said. 'There's someone else with her. I bet it's Janice.'

Before we could knock, Connie Jones opened the door. I was mesmerised by the bruise that surrounded her left eye and flowed onto her cheek. That hadn't been there when we'd seen her previously.

'Is Janice Alderman here?' I asked. I glanced at Phil; I wasn't sure I should be taking an active part yet, but he said nothing.

'You'd better come in,' Connie stepped back.

Phil and I went into the living room. A muscular, well-groomed man in his late thirties sat on an armchair. Lana sat on the threadbare sofa next to another girl of a similar age, who folded her arms and glowered at us as we entered.

Lana groaned theatrically. 'I can't believe your mum called the fuzz.'

'Show respect,' snapped the man. I could imagine him on the door of a club; he'd have no trouble with rowdy crowds.

Lana's shoulders sagged. 'Sorry.'

The man got up from the armchair and sat astride a hard-backed chair by the kitchen door. 'Please, sit down.'

I sat on the vacated seat and Phil sat on the sofa, closest to Lana. The man stroked his fashionable Mexican moustache and watched us silently.

Despite his outward charm, I felt uncomfortable around the man. From his expensive clothes to his manicured nails, he was as out of place in the shabby room as the yellow Lotus Elite was in the street. It was reasonable to assume he was the car's owner. I kept an eye on him as Phil began questioning the girls.

'Hello, Lana. This must be Janice.'

'Duh!' Janice rolled her eyes.

'I said show respect.' The man's voice rolled like thunder.

Janice pursed her lips and turned to the man. 'To them?'

'Apologise, Jan,' Connie said. I caught an urgent tone to her voice.

Lana nudged Janice who immediately lost the attitude. 'Sorry.'

'People have been worried about you.' Phil directed this at Janice, who glanced towards the man. The girls seemed edgy, but not about our presence.

'Are you a relative?' I asked the man.

Phil picked up on my interest. 'What's your name?' He asked the man.

Lana twisted around to face Connie. Our questions had elicited a mild panic. A brief communication of eye movements and shoulder twitches followed between the two that wasn't too hard to follow. I cocked my head as I waited for an answer.

'Robert,' the man replied, his tone careful.

'Robert what?'

'My boyfriend,' Connie cut in. She moved behind him and put her arms around his shoulders, but her brow was furrowed. 'Come on into the kitchen, Robert, and I'll make you a cup of tea while the police talk to Lana and Jan.'

Robert followed Connie into the tiny kitchen. I would visit Irene when we got back and see what I could unearth about the mysterious Robert and the yellow Lotus. I would send a card to DVLA and find out if Robert was the registered keeper. It would take about five days, but might answer a few questions. Meantime we had a problem; we needed an adult with us to interview two juveniles. Would Robert-in-the-kitchen count?

The front door opened and Glynis came in.

'Hello again, Glynis,' Phil said. 'We were just about to talk to your Lana and her friend. Janice's parents have reported her missing and we'll have to take her back. Lana didn't go to school today either. Did you know?'

I watched Glynis's reaction. She peered into the kitchen and edged towards the door as she shouted at Lana.

'Scowing again? You told me you'd go in today. You'll have the education board on me.'

Lana shrugged but her mother was already giving all her attention to Robert's presence.

Glynis finally addressed us. 'Have you finished?'

'Not quite,' Phil said. He turned to Janice. 'So, where were you?'

Janice twiddled with her skirt. 'Staying with a friend.'

'Which friend? Phil was not letting go.

'Molly.' Lana jutted her chin.

Ignoring the posturing, Phil turned to Glynis. 'Molly again. Molly does have a wide social circle.' He turned back to Janice. 'How do you know Molly?'

'School,' Janice replied but her eyes never left Lana.

'We spoke to Miss Ashton earlier and she told us that there is no Molly in your year. Just a couple in the first form.' I said. 'Are you meeting a first former?'

There were more twitches and eye communication between Lana and Janice.

'Molly doesn't go to our school,' Janice finally answered.

'That's interesting because Lana told us that she knew her from school, and she had borrowed dinner money.'

'I meant that we meet sometimes before school,' Lana said.

Good come back, but I still didn't believe them. 'She must be local then,' I said.

'Where does Molly live? We'll need to speak to her,' Phil said.

'Glynis!' Robert's summons to the kitchen was not a request.

'Who is he?' I pointed to the kitchen.

'He's… He's… Glynis's fingers twisted around each other as she stuttered over her reply.

'I told you he's my boyfriend,' Connie cut in from the kitchen.

'Yes. Our Connie's boyfriend.' Glynis suddenly sounded confident. 'Enough questions. They've told you they were with a friend. No harm done. Take Jan back to her parents. Connie, see them out.'

Connie came and opened the door, and Glynis went into the kitchen.

Phil walked towards the door. 'See you soon, Glynis.'

I stood up. 'Come on, Janice.'

Janice scowled, but followed Phil out to the Panda car without argument.

Outside, I turned to say goodbye and over Connie's shoulder I saw Robert hand a very full envelope to Glynis. He looked up and saw me watching. The charming veneer dropped and his whole demeanour became defensive. He turned fully towards me and lifted his chin in a tacit dare. I never responded well to dares.

'What was that?' I demanded. 'What was in that envelope?'

'None of your business,' Glynis said. 'Connie, shut that door.' It seemed that Robert's demand for respect to the police did not extend to her.

Phil called me from the street.

'You'd better go,' Connie said and shut the door.

I really wanted to march into the kitchen and demand to see what was in the well-filled envelope but, in the absence of a crime, I couldn't do that. For a second, I considered if I would have grounds if I said Glynis had been hiding Janice, but Lana had just been hanging around with Lana, so that would be a step too far. I would just have to content myself with passing notes to Irene.

I spun around and walked to the Panda, sitting beside Janice in the back. I didn't expect any trouble from her, but it was protocol.

'What were you doing?' Phil asked.

'As I was leaving, I saw Robert hand an envelope to Glynis and I wanted to know what was going on. He got very defensive and Glynis told me to mind my own business. Do you think there might be money in it? Can you think of a way we go back and demand to see it? Maybe if we said they were hiding Janice they'd have to let us see.'

Janice caught her breath.

'Do you know anything about this?' I demanded.

She shook her head so hard, her dangling earrings jangled.

'Who is Robert?'

'Connie's boyfriend,' Janice answered.

'Tell me the truth or I'll charge you with lying to a police officer and you'll have to go to court. You'll go to prison.'

Phil coughed gently and raised one eyebrow at me in the rear-view mirror.

I took the hint and backed off.

'Did you see the size of the telly in that tiny room? Where did Glynis get money for that?' I said to emphasise my argument.

'I don't doubt what you saw, Sam, but it could have been anything. We don't have the right to demand to see private mail unless it's relevant to an investigation.' Phil turned on the engine and headed back to the station.

*

The Aldermans had beaten us to the station and rushed us as we entered the enquiry office. Pamela grabbed Janice's shoulders and alternately shook her and hugged her.

'Where have you been? Why didn't you call us? How could you do this to us?'

Janice shrugged off her mother. 'I went to a party with Lana and we stayed over, that's all.'

'Why didn't you ask us? Are we so terrible that you couldn't ask us?' Pamela shouted.

'I didn't think you'd let me go to a party on a school night,' Janice replied.

'Don't ever do this again, do you hear?' Pamela wiped the tears that had started to flow down her cheeks.

'Sheesh. You're such an embarrassment.'

'Don't talk to your mother like that,' Mr Alderman admonished. 'It'll be a long time before we trust you again.'

Janice rolled her eyes. However suspicious I thought Robert was, he was a damned sight better at commanding Janice's respect than her parents.

'So the party was at Molly's house?' Phil asked.

'It's not a house, it's an apartment.'

'Can you remember where the block is?' Phil asked.

'Dunno. We were driven there.'

'Was it in town, by the river, somewhere else?'

'Not sure. Towards town I think, but I could see the river through the window.'

'Who drove you?' Phil asked.

Janice glanced around, a hunted look in her eye. 'Connie's

boyfriend.'

Robert. I definitely needed to speak to Irene and to persuade Phil that we needed to speak to the classy Robert, who dated prostitutes from dilapidated streets and even felt safe to leave a very expensive car in the road.

'Just to straighten things out, Molly doesn't go to your school?' Phil asked.

'No,' Janice replied.

'Probably goes to the secondary,' Pamela said. 'I can't imagine anyone from the Grammar having parties on a school night.'

'You get off now, Janice. Don't worry your parents like that again.' Phil turned to me. 'Let's get the job signed off.' I followed him to the door. 'And I want a word with you,' he whispered.

He'd been quiet during the drive back to the station, but I had pushed my apprehension away. Now I knew he was unhappy with me. The first rule of sprogging: do not piss off your tutor-constable.

We updated Ray in the control room then went to the report writing room. Phil held open the door and I went in and sat at the table.

'That Robert was out of place and I think we should think of a way to bring him in for interview.' I always gabbled when I was nervous.

'He was a bit out of place, but it might be nothing. However, it doesn't give you the right to lie to the customers or try to concoct ways to exceed your authority. I'm rather disappointed, Sam.'

I hung my head.

'If you go down that road, Sam, where does it end? That's the type of thing that can come back to bite you in the bum and you'll find yourself on a fizzer. Be truthful or be silent; do it properly or don't do it at all, then you can never be criticised. Some will disagree with me, but in my book the ends do not justify the means. If you cannot adhere to that, you should find another tutor.'

That was me put firmly into my box. 'I'm sorry.'

Phil nodded. 'All right. It's wasn't so terrible, and no harm's been done this time, but it's a slippery slope, Sam. Don't ever go there.'

Phil's censure was worse than any disciplinary hearing. He had made it clear I had breached his principles and he had effectively pulled me back on track. I wouldn't let him down again.

'Anyway,' Phil continued, his voice brighter. 'Most people are nervous when police are in the house. If Connie has found herself a sugar daddy, good luck to her.' He scratched his head. 'We would need evidence or at least reasonable suspicion, not supposition, before we waded in.'

I bowed to Phil's experience, but I was frustrated I couldn't just act.

Chapter Eight

At refs, Phil disappeared upstairs to play snooker while I went to get my sandwiches from my locker. As I walked past the control room, Alan called me in.

'Sam, after scoff, will you cover the control room while Derek goes for his refs. Then will you cover the enquiry office for the rest of the shift? Anything you're not sure of, ask me or Ray.'

'Yes, Sarge.'

The inspector came into the control room. It was crowded with all of us there including Ray and Derek. I would have left but Alan was blocking the door to the enquiry office and Inspector Tyrrell was blocking the door to the corridor. I couldn't even dodge into the cupboard-sized telex room as Steve was there making tea, and there was only one way in and out anyway. I was hemmed in and felt my breathing rate increase.

The inspector looked at me. 'You all right, Sam?'

'Fine, thank you. Just a bit hot, sir.' I fanned my face to emphasise the point. Better he thought I was overheating rather than considering shoving him to one side and running away.

'It is hot in here. All yours, Derek.' Ray stood up and Derek moved from the phones to Ray's seat to cover the radio. Steve dished out mugs of tea, then slid into Derek's vacated seat to man the phones. 'Time to dine; come on, Sam.'

I sidled around Inspector Tyrrell and went with Ray to the refs room.

*

After scoff, Ray and I returned to the control room. Ray took over the radio and I took over from Steve.

'Were you shown how to log incidents in Egilsby?' Ray lit a cigarette from the stub of his last smoke.

'Yes.' I stifled a cough as the smoke tickled the back of my throat.

'I'm going for my run, Ray. You know where to contact me.'

I looked up and saw Inspector Tyrrell in the doorway wearing a white t-shirt and blue shorts. I didn't mean to stare but those shorts revealed toned thighs and a nicely rounded bottom.

'Righto, sir,' Ray said.

The inspector headed out to the yard and I leant far back to gain the best view of his retreating behind. I turned back and, from the corner of my eye, saw Ray watching me. I had two choices: admit I had been ogling the boss, again, or pretend it never happened. I opted for the latter. He might know it had happened but, unless I confessed, he wouldn't be able to prove it. Or, in police slang, *"No cough, no job"*.

'Where does the inspector run?' I impressed myself with my fake nonchalance.

'The spare garage across the yard. Someone moved in a treadmill and some weights. He runs there during his break most days.' Ray grinned. 'Looks good in shorts, doesn't he? Don't worry, I won't tell him you sneaked a peek.'

Busted! I gasped and buried my scarlet face in my arms on the desk as Ray creased up with laughing.

*

When Derek and Steve came back, I went into the telex room to make a cup of tea for everyone before going into the enquiry office.

Inspector Tyrrell came in from the yard. His t-shirt stuck to his body and his damp blond hair flopped as he walked. He put his head around the door of the control room.

'Give me ten minutes for a shower, Ray, then I'll be available. Sam, I'd love a cuppa when I get back. Milk, no sugar. Ta.' He gave me a wink and jogged upstairs.

In my peripheral vision, I could see Ray grinning at me. I grinned back and finished serving tea for everyone. There was no harm in a spot of window shopping.

*

The following days were peaceful and I was not subject to any tricks, which probably should have made me cautious.

On the last day of earlies, after parade, I went into the control room to collect my radio and do my test call, as I did at the start of every shift.

'Message for you, Sam.' He handed me a sheet.

'Please ring Mr C Lyon about his incident,' I read aloud. 'Who's he?'

Ray shrugged. I went to the report writing room to make the call. After a few rings, a man answered it.

'Hello.'

'Hello, is that Mr Lyon?' I asked.

'Are you having a laugh?' the man said after a moment's pause.

I was confused. 'I'm Constable Barrie of the Peninsula Police. I received a message to ring Mr C Lyon. Is he there please?

The man began to chuckle. 'Are you new?' I admitted I was, which made him laugh harder. 'This is the private staff number of the zoo. You've been had, pet. Think about it. C Lyon.'

It took a few seconds for the penny to drop, then I had to laugh too. 'Of course. I'm sorry to have disturbed you.'

'Don't worry, pet. You're not the first one who's fallen for that.'

I returned to see Ray and Derek in the control room.

'Good one. You got me,' I said to the chortling pair.

'That one never fails. Phil's in the yard waiting for you,' Derek said between laughs.

I tried to do my test call, but it was hard between giggles. Eventually I managed to get a coherent call out and went to meet Phil.

'Did they get you?' Phil asked when I got into the car.

'Hook, line, and sinker.'

'Everyone's had that one. C Lyon or G Raffe.' Phil drove out of the yard and we joined the morning traffic.

'As pranks go, that was quite funny,' I said. 'The rest gets a bit tiresome. Has anyone ever said, *"I'm getting fed up now and I want it to stop"*?'

'It wouldn't make any difference if they did; in fact, it might make it worse. You just have to tough it out: they'll get bored eventually.'

'That's what I thought.'

'Mike Two.' Ray's voice came through the radio.

I picked up the handset. 'Mike Two, go ahead.'

'Report of an RTA corner of Civic Avenue and Village Road. Two vehicles; persons reported. Tango Alpha Four One also making. Ambo and fire en route.'

'Roger, making from Town Way.' I replaced the handset, pleased I had mastered another bit of jargon. Police don't always "go to", or "come from"; they "make". Probably derived from "making our way", but I might be wrong on that.

'Sounds nasty.' Phil flicked the switch activating the siren and lights.

'Persons reported what?' I asked.

'Persons reported trapped. That's why the fire brigade is attending; they might have to cut them out,' Phil replied. 'This is a bad junction at the best of times, so we'll probably have to close roads in each direction.' Phil eased the Panda through the narrow gap created as drivers moved over to let us through.

As we approached the junction a couple of minutes later, I saw two damaged cars skewed across the junction and a lamppost leaning at an angle. From my view, it seemed that a brown BMW had come from the side road and had knocked a white car into the lamppost. Traffic was backed up for some distance in all four directions and pedestrians gathered near the scene. The sound of horns added to the confused atmosphere.

Was anyone in immediate danger? Nothing apparent. Casualties? Uncertain. I could see someone moving by the BMW, but there was no movement by the white car. Upgrade that: casualties likely. Other issues? People milling around might be in danger if the lamppost fell.

'Hellfire, we're first here. What a mess. We don't have the equipment to deal with this properly.' Phil pulled over and silenced the siren but left the lights flashing.

'What do you want me to do?' I asked.

'We need to assess the injuries and report back, then I hope traffic will be here because we need to block these roads but make sure ambo and fire can get through. Then we need to get witness details. We also need to contact the council to get someone out to make that lamppost safe.'

'I'll take the white car,' I said.

'Okay but keep an eye on that lamppost.' Phil picked up the handset. 'Mike Two to control.'

'Go ahead,' Ray said.

'At scene. Two vehicles; probably multiple casualties but that's unconfirmed. Please update the ambo; also inform the council there's a damaged lamppost leaning over. They need to get here and assess it for safety ASAP.'

'Roger. Tango Alpha Four One says the heavy traffic is delaying them, probably tailbacks from the RTA. Mike Three and Mike One are making to help with the road closures.'

'Thanks.' Phil put back the handset and swore. 'We're it for a while.'

Butterflies jived around my stomach, but I needed to project calm confidence and authority. We got out of the Panda and I took a deep breath then went to the white car, shouting to bystanders to move away in case the lamppost came down. To my surprise, most of the public moved a few feet away.

I braced myself and looked into the car. It wasn't too horrible. A young, blood-covered woman slumped against the steering wheel. Her legs were trapped by metal pushed in from the impact with the lamppost, but at least there didn't seem to be any bleeding from there. I pressed a hand against her neck and was relieved to feel a pulse and movement as she breathed. She had a gash on her head, probably caused by the steering wheel. I used my handkerchief to stem the blood. When it healed, she would have a similar scar to mine. I took a quick glance into the back of the car in case a passenger had slid to the floor, but it was clear. The dashboard hung down, obscuring my view of the passenger-side footwell, but nobody would fit there. Where was that ambulance?

Across the junction, I saw Phil talking to a balding, middle-aged man in a suit beside the brown BMW. A girl in a St Agnes' uniform wept beside him. Janice Alderman! What was she doing here? We were nowhere near Sandringham Boulevard and this wasn't a route from her home to Aggie's.

I looked around the gathered crowd. Did they think we were here just for their entertainment? Ghouls. I rebuked myself. Maybe I was misjudging them, they could be witnesses waiting to speak to us.

'Did anyone see the accident happen?' I called to the crowd.

Most avoided eye contact but a couple shouted out that they had seen what had happened.

'It wasn't her fault. The BMW just came out and hit her,' one woman called.

'I'll need to speak to you later, so please don't leave.' My initial assessment had been correct. I would tell Phil when I got to talk to him again.

'Can I help?' a male spectator asked.

I thought for a moment. 'You can help by stopping the traffic.' I directed him to one side of Village Road. 'Make sure you let emergency vehicles through though.'

'Right. I'll make sure nobody else gets past.' He hurried off to take his post.

I caught the eye of another young man. 'You can stop the traffic from the other side.'

He went off and I directed another couple of people to cover Civic Avenue. I needn't have worried about coping; I could see what needed to be done and I could send people to do it. Alan was right, people didn't notice or care that I had about five minute's service in. I was in uniform and I was in charge.

'What can I do?' asked the woman witness.

'It would be really helpful if you were to collect the names and addresses of any other witnesses then give them to me. I'll need to speak to everyone who saw this.'

The woman scrabbled in her bag for a sheet of paper and began to work her way through the crowd.

'If you did not witness this accident and if you do not have a job allocated to you, would you please leave the area,' I shouted.

A couple of people shuffled off, but I was sure that the majority that stayed hadn't witnessed a thing. Never mind, that was all bases covered as far as I could see. Now, if only the ambulance would get here to help this driver. The woman stirred and groaned so I stroked her cheek and made reassuring noises. There was little else I could do.

Phil sat the other driver in the Panda then came over, pushing a set of keys into his top pocket. 'What have you got here?'

'Unconscious woman with trapped legs. A lady is gathering witness details for me and I've sent some bystanders to stop the traffic.'

Phil made a small 'hmm' noise.

'Have I done something wrong?' I asked.

'If anything goes wrong and someone gets hurt, you will be writing for a very long time. You might even find yourself up before the Chief, or worse.'

Just when I thought I was doing all right. 'I thought it would help until another patrol arrived. I can't leave this woman.'

'I suppose it'll be all right. Sometimes we do have to improvise.'

Right. I improvised and I would do it again. I wouldn't feel bad about my actions because I could justify them in my report.

'Is that Janice?' I asked, nodding towards the BMW. 'Because this is a strange way to Aggie's from her house.'

'Yes. Her uncle was taking her to school,' Phil replied. 'God only knows how much he drank last night. He swears he didn't drink anything this morning, but when I breathalysed him, the crystals turned grass green.'

'Aren't you worried he'll run off?' I peered over to the Panda where the driver sat in the back seat.

Phil shook his head. 'I've 'cuffed him to the arm rest.'

'Inventive. What's his name?' I asked.

'Gerald Mount. A bank manager, would you believe. Janice is refusing to seek medical treatment and wants to go to school, but I think the ambo will take her to casualty anyway. I've asked Ray to send someone to her address and to contact the school.' He paused. 'Can you smell that?' Phil touched his fingers to the ground and sniffed them. 'Petrol!'

'Move back and no smoking, there's petrol on the ground,' I called to the onlookers, while Phil radioed in with the new information. Ray and Derek would disseminate it around the fire and ambo control rooms.

Phil and I circled the car, looking underneath for the leak. Then I spotted it. Fuel dripped at a gentle rate from a small crack in the petrol tank.

'It's not so bad,' I called to Phil. 'Just a drip.'

'The fire will need to neutralise it before they begin work just the same.' Phil looked up as a vehicle approached. 'Here's the ambulance. Four One is still caught up in the gridlock.'

'I didn't hear that on the radio,' I said.

'Where is your radio?' Phil gestured to my harness.

I put my hand to the empty harness. 'It must have fallen out when I leant into the car. I'll get it back when the woman's out.'

Phil went back to the brown car with one ambulance man,

while the other came over to me and checked the woman as best he could.

'Vital signs stable. Her legs are trapped but the injuries appear non-life threatening. We need the metal to be cut.'

'Be careful, there's petrol about,' I fretted.

'Don't worry.' He placed a neck brace around the woman.

Phil came over and handed me a waxy, yellow block.

'Mark up the position of the wheels. We'll have to get our measurements later.'

'Won't it get washed away?' I asked.

'Not this stuff; it'll stay until it's cleaned off. By the way, other patrols have taken over the road closures up Village Road and Civic Ave.'

While I was drawing lines around the wheels, the fire appliance arrived closely followed by a second ambulance and, finally, Tango Alpha Four One—the traffic department car—arrived. Phil pointedly looked at his watch.

'All right, Phil. Sorry about the delay, the whole town is gridlocked because of this. What have we got?'

'We've got one injured female in the white car. The passenger in the BMW has slight injuries but is refusing medical treatment. However, she's a schoolgirl so the ambo will be taking her anyway. Ray's contacting her parents. Young Sam here has organised the collection of witness details and we're just waiting for fire to spread neutraliser and cut this car up, then the driver can go to hospital. The council have been informed about the lamppost. I've got the driver of the BMW in the Panda. Positive breathalyser.'

'Sounds like you've got it covered. I'll let you take the job as you know the circs. I'll just do the follow-up at the hospital,' said the traffic officer.

'I need to get my prisoner back, so you'll have to get your hands dirty this time,' Phil grumbled.

The traffic officer grinned. 'I suppose it is a bit more complicated than your usual RTA. Best leave it to the professionals.'

'Wazzer.'

It wasn't personal. I had learnt on my attachments after training school that all the departments worked hard in their role, but each one thought they worked hardest and mocked other departments.

The firemen quickly spread foam around. Then, like a plague of locusts, they got out the big cutters and set to work on the car. In less than thirty seconds, the roof was separated from the body, then they gently cut away some of the metal by the woman's legs, which allowed the ambulance crew to gently pull the woman free. I could see why they referred to the cutter as "the jaws of life".

The woman was whisked off to an ambulance and I leant into what was left of the car and felt under the seat for my radio. As I pulled it out, a baby's bottle rolled forward and fell into the ruined foot well. It felt warm when I picked it up. It was another hot day, but I would not have expected the milk to be that temperature. The back of my neck tingled; something was not right.

'Phil!'

He turned from his conversation with a fireman. 'What is it?'

'A baby's bottle.' I opened the top and sniffed. 'It's still fresh.'

Phil and the fireman came over.

'There's no baby here,' Phil said.

'Then why would she carry a freshly-made bottle of milk?' I peered into the car, trying to see if a child could have got underneath a seat. Behind the fallen dashboard? No, a baby would be in a carrycot and that would be too large. Wouldn't it? I felt a little ball of tension in my stomach. I had looked underneath the car for the leak and I hadn't seen anything, neither had the firemen as they had cut the metal. Surely, she wouldn't have travelled with a baby loose in the car. Had it been thrown?

'Maybe she dropped the baby off somewhere and forgot the bottle,' Phil said.

'We can't be sure.' I reached in and tried to move the dashboard, but it was wedged.

Phil gingerly knelt in the foam and peered underneath. 'How the hell did that get there?'

'Can you see a baby?' the fireman asked.

'No but I can see what's left of one of those new carry seat thingies. It must have shot forward and slid into the engine space.'

The fireman knelt beside Phil and looked under the car. They straightened up and exchanged a look. I knew what that look meant.

'Sam, would you go back to the Panda and get an RTA booklet please?' Phil said in a desperately calm voice. 'Remind Mr Mount that he's still under arrest and I'll be with him in a little while.'

No. I was not going to leave until I knew for sure that the baby had not survived. I elbowed my way between them and looked under the front of the car. The remains of a backward-facing baby car seat poked up through twisted metal.

'We'll have to cut the front off the car to get it out,' the fireman said.

'No. If you do that the rest of it will fall and completely flatten it,' I cried.

'Any child in there couldn't have survived.' Phil gently laid a hand on my shoulder. 'Go and get that booklet while we get the baby out.'

My breath shuddered and a large teardrop ran down my cheek. I crushed my tongue against the roof of my mouth. I had to stay professional here. Phil radioed in that it was now apparently a fatal accident; the inspector would have to attend.

He stood up and pulled on my arm. 'Come on, Sam. Let the firemen do their job.'

I shrugged away as I heard a small whimper. 'Hush!'

'Sam, it's dead.' Phil was losing patience.

'No, I heard something too,' The traffic officer said.

Another faint wail came from the engine area.

'We need to get under,' the fireman said.

'I won't fit under there,' Phil said.

'Nor me,' said the traffic officer.

The fireman just patted his stomach.

I lay flat and wriggled under the car, knocking my hat off, soaking my uniform with petrol and foam, and wrecking another pair of tights. I peered back. 'I fit.'

'Wait! We need to put in supports underneath.' The fireman waved towards the fire appliance. 'Blocks. Now!'

'I can touch the seat,' I called back.

A couple of firemen ran over and wedged blocks under the chassis. I wriggled further under the car and almost whooped with joy when a tiny arm moved. I forced myself to remain calm; it might be alive, but who knew what injuries the child might have.

'There's a live baby here, just a few weeks old by the look of it,' I shouted. 'Somehow, it's landed in the tiniest space by the engine. A couple of inches either side and it would have been crushed.'

I couldn't leave the child there; injured or not, I was going to have to bring it out. The seat was wedged, I was going to have to release the baby. I no longer heard the hubbub at the accident scene; it was just the baby and me. I stroked the child's head, clicked the buckle and moved my hands underneath its body. The baby jolted, then wailed.

'Hush. Come to Auntie Sam.'

I managed to slide the baby into my arms and draw it towards me, taking care to keep it away from the road surface. When it was close enough, I tucked it into my jacket. A little boy. Tears flowed down my cheeks and dripped onto the child, who wailed his objection.

'Come on, little man. Let's get you out of here.' I wiped my cheeks, then I realised I didn't have room to hold the baby and lever myself out.

I shook my leg and shouted, 'Pull me out!'

Someone grabbed my foot and gently pulled me from under the car. A couple of firemen helped me sit up.

'Are you all right, Sam?' Phil knelt beside me.

I felt nauseous, but I swallowed hard and nodded. I opened my jacket to reveal the tiny boy. I caught one of the firemen crouched beside me staring at my legs. Cheeky bugger, we were in the middle of a serious incident. But then I looked down and saw the state of my legs: my tights were more hole than material, and my knees were bleeding from where I had scraped along the road surface. Stones had embedded themselves under my skin and blood trickled along my legs. Strange, I hadn't felt a thing. Was I going to spend the rest of my service walking around with scabby knees like a schoolboy? I pulled my skirt down over my ruined tights and tried to regain my dignity by replacing my hat.

The inspector had arrived when I was under the car. He came over and knelt beside me.

'My God, this looks like a nativity.'

I looked around and giggled. Instead of angels, kings, and shepherds; police, fire, and ambulance surrounded the child. I handed the baby over to the ambulance crew.

'It looks like just a few scratches, but we'll take him to the General to make sure. That's where his mother's going isn't it?' said the ambulance driver.

'Yeah, but we don't have a name yet,' Phil said.

'We'll soon sort that out. I'll follow them to the hospital,' the traffic officer said.

'I've got one in the Panda, Boss. He blew positive.' Phil pointed to the car.

'Go back now in that case; we'll need to get bloods or urine from him,' the inspector said. 'Take Ken with you.'

Phil returned to his Panda and the baby was rushed away. A couple of the firemen pulled me to my feet. The one who I had caught looking at my legs kept hold of my arm longer than necessary. He smiled at me when I looked at him.

'That was really brave,' he said.

'Anyone would have done it; I was just the one small enough to fit.' My legs felt weak and I leant against the wrecked car.

'You're shaking.' He put an arm around my shoulder. Surprisingly, I didn't mind; in fact, it felt nice. Maybe I was too sick to bother.

Inspector Tyrrell gave him a stern look. 'I'll take over from here.'

Even my dad wouldn't have so blatantly chased off a man showing interest in me. The fireman let go. I didn't have time to ponder on the boss's behaviour because I was overtaken by another wave of nausea. The inspector put his arm around me and guided me to the ground as I retched. The fireman moved towards me but Inspector Tyrrell waved him away.

'I said I've got her. You go and help clear this mess up.'

I leant back against the car. The inspector took my hand and stared into my face as he ran his thumb across my knuckles. 'Adrenaline and petrol are never a good mix. Do you feel better?'

I nodded but he didn't move away. I stared down at our hands. Was I misreading the signals? The woman I had asked to get witness details came over and held out a sheet of paper. The inspector cleared his throat and released his grip on me.

'I got some names. Some people here didn't see anything, they're just gawping,' she said.

Inspector Tyrrell took the paper from her. 'You get that a lot at incidents like this. Thanks for doing this. Someone will be in touch in the next day or so to make arrangements to get a statement from you.'

'Yes, thanks,' I echoed.

'No trouble. My name is at the top of the page. I hope everyone's all right. You're quite the heroine.' She turned to the inspector. 'I think you should give her a reward.'

'Chocolates please,' I said.

Inspector Tyrrell smiled. 'We'll have to think of something; but meantime, perhaps you would like to write to the chief superintendent at Egilsby to tell him about Sam.'

'I certainly will.' She jotted my number on the back of her hand and withdrew back into the crowd.

'We should formally thank her for her help,' I said. 'And the others I sent to close the road. I think they're still here.'

'I'll put in a report and request the chief superintendent writes to them,' the inspector replied.

'The recovery vehicle is here for the cars, boss,' the traffic officer said.

'Can you manage? I'm going to get the ambo to take Sam to

the hospital.'

'I don't need to go to hospital,' I protested. 'I just need to go back and put some clean clothes on. I'll be fine in a little while.'

Inspector Tyrrell and the traffic officer looked doubtfully at me.

'Very well,' Inspector Tyrrell said. 'I'll take you home to change, but if you feel unwell, you must tell me.'

I readily agreed, and we left the others to mop up.

Chapter Nine

Mum's car was on the path when Inspector Tyrrell pulled up outside our house. I had forgotten it was her day off.

'I'll wait here for you,' Inspector Tyrrell said.

'Mum's home and she'll be offended if she knows you're waiting out here.'

Inspector Tyrrell got out and followed me up the path. I opened the door and called out, 'Only me, Mum.' I turned to the boss. 'Come in, sir.'

Mum came out of the kitchen. 'What are you doing home now?' She paused when she saw the inspector behind me. 'Oh, hello.' Her attention immediately returned to me. 'What on Earth have you been doing?'

'I got mucky at an incident. Mum, this is Inspector Tyrrell; he's in charge of our block. Sir, this is my mum.'

'Pleased to meet you Mrs Barrie,' Inspector Tyrrell extended his hand.

Mum shook his hand. 'Call me Liz. I'm pleased to meet you too, inspector. Come through and I'll make you a cup of tea, or would you prefer coffee?'

'Tea is fine, thank you, Liz. Milk, no sugar.'

'I'll go and get changed. Won't be a tick.' I ran upstairs as Mum and the boss went into the living room.

*

All clean and presentable once more and with dressings on my knees and a couple of packets of tights in my pocket, I went downstairs. Mum and the inspector were getting on well, judging by the laughter coming from the living room.

'…and this was Sam when she was bridesmaid at her cousin's wedding. She looked lovely.'

'Yes, she did,' Inspector Tyrrell agreed.

I felt a little warm glow until the significance of the conversation struck me.

'We were so proud of her. After what happened we weren't sure she'd be well enough on the day, but she was a little trooper. The headdress hides…'

I marched into the room. 'Mum?'

'Hello, Sam. I was just showing Gary some photographs.'

She was calling my boss by his first name and showing him the family album! 'Muuum!'

Inspector Tyrrell handed the album back. 'Thank you for the tea, Liz. We have to get back now.'

'It's been lovely meeting you. Feel free to pop in for a cuppa if you're passing'. Mum stood up and walked the inspector to the hall. 'He's nice,' Mum whispered as Inspector Tyrrell went back to the Panda car. 'Nice looking too.'

'Why did you show him the photos? He's my boss; he won't be interested in them.'

'He seemed to be. He liked the one where you were a bridesmaid. I was just telling him about the headdress hiding your scar.' Mum stroked her hand down my arm. 'Anyway, Gary told me all about this incident. He's going to recommend you for a commendation. I'm very proud of you.' Mum bit her lip. 'Maybe that was supposed to be a secret. Pretend I didn't tell you.'

Blooming heck, a commendation before I was solo! It would look good on my record if Mum was right. I glanced over to the Panda car. Inspector Tyrrell was talking into the handset of the radio. 'I'd better go.'

As I reached the Panda, I saw the girl from the house opposite. She stopped momentarily, then deliberately turned her back to me before going into her house. I had known her almost all my life. We had walked to school together and had giggled over Cathy and Claire's problem page in *Jackie*. We even wrote to each other when I was in Canada, but now we didn't speak. Her choice. Her mother had been locked up for shoplifting shortly after we had left school and she probably thought, erroneously, that I was laughing at her now I was a police officer. When I had first noticed this change, I had told myself that if someone was going to stop speaking to me because of my job, they weren't worth having as a friend, but it still hurt.

'Ray says the mother has woken up and they say her injuries are not life threatening. The child is being kept in overnight for observation and, all being well, he can go home with his father tomorrow.' The inspector beamed at me.

Hurt feelings forgotten, I beamed back. 'That's good news.'

As we drove off, I said, 'I'm sorry about the photos, sir. I didn't imagine she'd bring out the album.'

'Your mum is very proud of you. You look like her, you know.'

'I know.'

'Is that your father in the picture over the hearth?' Inspector Tyrrell asked.

'Yes. He's away working on the North Sea rigs. Mum wanted a picture of all three of us together, so, last Christmas, Dad arranged it as a present for her.'

'It's a good picture. What was your mother saying about your headdress hiding something?'

I squirmed. 'A scar that runs along my hairline. From Hogarth Acre. It's why I have a fringe.'

'Oh.'

That was a conversation killer.

We drove past Belvedere House and I caught a glimpse of a yellow Lotus in the parking area.

'Hold on, sir. Can we go back and have a look at the new apartments please?'

'Thinking of getting your own place?'

'I quite fancy the penthouse,' I joked. 'Seriously, I think I saw a Lotus Elite in the car park. There was a yellow Lotus outside the Jones's house when Phil and I went to get Janice Alderman back. I sent off an enquiry card to Swansea and the registered keeper is Robert Molyneux with an address in the city. Janice said that they had been to a party at a flat and that Robert had driven them there, but she didn't know exactly where it was.'

Inspector Tyrrell swung the car around and drove slowly past the flats. Sure enough, in the parking area was a yellow Lotus Elite. I had never seen another Lotus in the town so, a pound to a pinch of dust, it was the same one we had seen in Schooner Street. I jotted the number down. I would check back in my pocketbook to see if it was the same registration as the one I had seen in Schooner Street.

'Robert Molyneux might have lied to Swansea about his address. Can I do a voter's check to see if he lives in Belvedere House or would that be overstepping my authority?' After what Phil said. I didn't want to go rushing in.

'No, that would be reasonable,' Inspector Tyrell said. 'But he might just be visiting someone. We'll be back at the station in two minutes so why not do it then.' He drove quickly back to the station and I went into the telex room behind the control room to check on the electoral roll for Robert Molyneux's address.

'Making us a brew, Sam?' Ray called from the control room.

I pointed at the large book. 'I have to check this, but I'll make you a drink when I've finished.'

I switched on the kettle and put teabags into five mugs. One each for Ray and Derek and me, one for Alan, and one in case the boss came in. As I waited for the water to boil, I scanned through the residents list and found two Roberts, neither of whom were Molyneux. One on the top floor and one lower down. I also searched just for the surname Molyneux, but I couldn't see it.

The kettle boiled and clicked off, and I made the teas. I passed them to Ray and Derek, and left the boss's tea for him in the telex room. After having a quick slurp from my own mug, I carried the remaining mug to the sergeants' office for Alan. As I approached the door, I heard the inspector's raised voice.

'No smoke without fire and you can tell him I said that.'

He paused, then said, 'Fine, but I'll be watching him. One foot out of place and I'll hit him so hard with a fizzer, it'll knock him into next week.'

I hesitated outside. I wasn't eavesdropping, honest, I just didn't want to interrupt his phone call.

'All right, Sam?' Derek called over.

'Yes, the boss is in there. I'll get his tea too.' I went back to the telex room, collected the inspector's mug, then went back to the sergeants' office just as Alan opened the door.

'Nice timing,' he said.

I carried the mugs in and placed one on the desk and one beside the inspector.

'Thanks.' He smiled but it didn't reach his eyes, and the red tinge across his cheeks showed he was still angry.

I smiled back, glad that it wasn't me that had upset him, and left the office. I was pleased with my efforts to trace Robert but less pleased, though unsurprised, that I found no trace of the mysterious Molly when I had checked. The baby and mother were all right and I was being put forward for a commendation. Overall, it had been a good day for me, if not for the boss.

At knocking-off time, I put my hat and jacket into my locker, picked up my bag and walked towards my car. Ken was already in the yard and fell into step beside me.

'Ray said you were looking for a Robert Molyneux,' he said.

'Yeah, I keep seeing his car around. A yellow Lotus, very swish,' I said.

'I was chatting to the door staff at The Basement Club in town,' Ken said. 'They told me they're employed by Capri Securities in the city, which is run by a Robert Molyneux, and they're sent to clubs all over the place. He likes the finer things in life so that car would fit.'

'If it's the same bloke,' I said. 'But that's helpful, thanks Ken.'

*

The rest of the earlies shifts were fairly quiet and warm. The sun came out and the rain stayed off. I liked warm weather and I intended to make the most of it, because sunny weather never lasted long in England. I was pleased when the inspector gave us permission to leave off our jackets; it seemed to get warmer each day and it would have been unbearable to try to work in full uniform.

I dealt with shoplifters, nuisance youths, and domestics. Even after my short time at the station, I was starting to see a pattern in the type of incidents we dealt with. There was always some overlap, but in general each shift had an emphasis on a particular type of incident. Apart from RTAs, sudden deaths, stolen vehicles, and people missing from home, which could happen at any time, earlies—the 7am to 3pm shift—meant more burglaries were reported. Usually discovered when shopkeepers opened up or residents got up. Shoplifters. Every day, especially Saturdays, several people were caught helping themselves to stock from the shop. Some were professionals who regarded arrest as an occupational hazard, others took stuff to sell to fund their drug habit. Then there were those I pitied: old people or desperate mothers with a tin of ham or a box of baby milk. Once I saw Phil surreptitiously take coins from his own pocket and hand them to the manager. The lady in question was given a talking-to by Phil, banned from the store by the manager, and sent on her way with the goods and an unblemished character.

Lates—the 3pm to 11pm shift—meant drunks and domestic incidents, often both together, particularly on Friday and Saturday nights, and Sunday afternoon after the pubs shut. Complaints about youths causing a nuisance, especially at the weekend, and neighbour disputes, usually long-standing and petty.

I was keen to find out what a week of nights would bring. Between 11pm and 7am, I expected fights and rowdiness when the pubs and clubs kicked out, but I didn't know what else to expect. Phil told me that it was busy before refs, but after refs it was mostly patrol and property checking. Responding to alarms and looking out for suspicious people mooching about. I was more concerned about staying awake. I had had my share of late nights, but I had never stayed up all night before.

Chapter Ten

At exactly 11pm, everyone stood to attention as Inspector Tyrrell, Alan, and an unfamiliar sergeant came into parade. Average height, average looks, dark, short hair; nothing remarkable about this newcomer apart from his deep-set eyes that darted everywhere, taking in everything around him.

'As you were,' Inspector Tyrrell said. 'We've had authorisation to remain on shirt sleeve order because it's so hot.'

'Shirt sleeves on nights; it's not right,' Alan said. He went over to the fan on the wall and flicked it to maximum as he couldn't open a window. 'I suppose we should make the most of it; it's been a few days now, so it'll probably piss down tomorrow.' He abruptly stopped speaking and glanced my way.

The inspector held his hand out towards the newcomer. 'This is Brian Lewington, he's come to us from Odinsby. Some of you might already know him.'

'All right,' Brian said.

He got a few muted 'all rights' back. I might have thought the block were being unfriendly, but my own introduction hadn't gone much better. Meanwhile, I had another concern. Odinsby was the division that covered Hogarth Acre. I hoped he wouldn't have done any digging on his future workmates before he came here, but I guessed he had because, if I'd been able, I would have. I felt his darting eyes rest on me. I looked up and knew he knew; it was only a matter of time before he told the others. I had to decide quickly: tell the block before I was ready, or ask him not to reveal what he knew.

I tried not to make eye contact with him throughout parade. Instead, I concentrated on my notebook, frantically scribbling down my duties and instructions. The volume of information was making sense to me now and I could pick out the bits relevant to me.

After parade, I made my way to the control room to collect my radio with Phil.

'A message for you, Phil.' Derek passed him a memo sheet.

Phil scanned the note. 'Interesting.' He held the note towards me. 'It's from traffic, about that RTA. Janice Alderman's parents say she doesn't have an Uncle Gerald.'

'Maybe he goes under another name. Gerry, Ged, or something like that,' I suggested. 'Or maybe he's an honorary uncle. I call my dad's best friend, Uncle Peter.'

'No, listen,' Phil said. 'She had been allowed out to stay at a friend's house on the understanding that she went straight to school.'

'Who was the friend?' I asked.

'It doesn't say,' Phil replied.

'I wonder if it's the mysterious Molly. Maybe Mount is her father,' I said.

'I wouldn't waste too much time on that, he was only driving Janice to school,' Brian said from directly behind us. I hadn't heard him approach, neither had Phil judging by the way he jumped.

'Over the limit,' I said. 'And he caused a bad accident.'

'Well, you won't be able to do much in the way of follow-up on nights,' Brian said.

'No, the traffic department will do that. They only told me out of courtesy because I was the arresting officer for Gerald Mount,' Phil pushed the note into his pocket.

'If she was staying with Molly, why wasn't she in the car too?' I wondered aloud. 'But she goes to a different school doesn't she?

Maybe that's why they were going such a strange way to Aggie's.'

Phil stared at me for a moment, opened his mouth as if to speak but then his eyes moved to Brian and he closed his mouth without saying anything.

Brian turned to me. 'This is your first night, isn't it, Sammy?'

I hated being called Sammy, but I held my tongue. 'Yes, it is, Sarge.'

'Will you be all right after what happened?'

'It's not an issue,' I mumbled, wishing an asteroid would land on his head. I wasn't ready to share my past.

'Brian, got a minute?' Inspector Tyrrell called from the corridor. His expression said that Brian had better find that minute.

Brian stood up and went off with the boss.

'What was that about?' Ray asked.

'Nothing. It was nothing,' I replied.

'Strange thing to say, though,' Ray said.

'Why are you all hanging around here? Get out,' Alan shouted from his office.

Everyone filed out to the Pandas or to their beats. I mouthed a "Thank you" to Alan. He gestured for me to come over.

'It's only a matter of time before they all know, Sam,' he said. 'Why not tell people; what's the worst that can happen?'

I didn't know what the worst thing was. I just wanted to be treated like a normal person and to find my place at Wyre Hall without all that.

'I'll think about it,' I said. I heard Phil call my name. 'I'd better go, Sarge, I think we've got a job.' I hurried into the yard after Phil.

*

'Gerald Mount is divorced with no children,' Phil said as soon as I got into the car.

'So why would Janice stay with him? Why would she lie about him being her uncle? Why would she lie to her parents?'

'Why indeed.' Phil rubbed his chin.

'Phil, do you think he might be her boyfriend?' It sounded ridiculous, I mean, he was at least twenty-five years her senior.

Phil half smiled. 'Not her boyfriend, but I do think we need to have a closer look at Mr Mount. I'll put a note in for Irene and let traffic know so they can speak with her parents again. I think I'll have a chat with the boss.' Phil started the Panda and we left the yard.

'Was it deliberate that you didn't say anything in front of Brian?'

Phil grunted. 'It seemed wisest to keep quiet at that point.'

'You don't trust him. Do you know him from another station?' I asked.

'Not personally, but I heard some whispers about him taking bribes. Nothing could be proved.'

'It might all be rumour,' I said.

'Yeah, it's probably nothing.'

But those alarm bells rang loud and clear all the same. Phil left the yard and we began patrol.

I liked working nights. It was a bit hectic at first when the pubs kicked out, but then the streets cleared and sound carried for miles. Shakespeare called it "fairy time", a time when dreams and reality merged, and that exactly described the atmosphere. The almost tropical heat added to that. We had all the windows open as we drove, which kept it comfortable in the car but, when we stopped, heat wrapped around you like a moist blanket. Still, there had been almost a week of sun so the weather was bound to break soon. Phil concentrated the patrol around the back roads, ever on the lookout for suspicious movement.

'Can we have a mooch around Belvedere House?' I asked.

'What are you looking for?' Phil turned the Panda towards the apartments.

'I'd like to see if that Lotus is there again. The boss reminded me that he might just be visiting but, if we see it, it's likely that Robert lives there.'

'The car alone won't prove anything, you know,' Phil said. 'You're better off sending a card to Swansea to get driver's details.'

'I already did that, but it gave a different address. Ken told me a Robert Molyneux ran Capri Securities in the city, so he might have used that address. I wish there was a computer where we could get stuff like that, same day. I heard something like that is being trialled in London.'

'Typical. The Met always get first dibs. Check Yellow Pages for that address.' Phil pulled in beside the apartment block. The Lotus was there. Phil walked into the car park, but the view of the river distracted me. It was a working river, wide and busy. During the day, the occupants of the apartments would look out over a major port with cranes, ferries, and tugs, but at night the countless lights that lined the riverbank threw glistening jewels across the black water. It was spectacular.

'It's beautiful isn't it, Phil?'

Someone grabbed me from behind and pinned my arms to my side. I could tell my assailant was shorter than Phil and not as stocky, and I instantly reverted to survival mode. I kicked backwards as hard as I could. I would not be taken and terrorised again. I felt breath tickle against my ear as my assailant said, 'Kick away, Sammy. I love it when girlies put up a fight.'

I screamed; it was instinct.

'Sam!'

I heard Phil run towards me from the car park. Abruptly my captor released me, and I crumpled to the ground, gasping for breath. I twisted around and saw Brian Lewington leering down at me.

'What's going on?' Phil demanded.

'I've just given your sprog a bit of a scare.' Brian held out a hand towards me. 'Sorry. I wouldn't want to resurrect bad memories.'

I ignored Brian's hand as I stood up and skittered away towards Phil. I tried to catch my breath, but my heart was still pounding.

'Where did you come from?' Phil looked around. 'Where's your car?'

'I decided to reacquaint myself with the area on foot. The river is lovely at night.'

Something felt off. I couldn't put my finger on it, but I was sure Phil felt it too because he stared at Brian for several seconds before saying, 'Come on, Sam. Let's get on.'

It was hard for me to maintain a professional veneer when I was all but running away. Phil put a reassuring hand on my shoulder until we reached the Panda. I slammed the door after me and locked it. I stared at Brian as Phil pulled away. The bastard was laughing.

Phil drove for a few minutes then stopped in a side street. 'I think you should tell me what's happening, Sam. Brian evidently knows something about you and it would make life easier if I knew too.'

Alan was right; with Brian around, I was going to find it tough to keep my past secret. It was time for me to tell my secret.

'When I was fifteen, two men snatched me off the street as I walked home from the youth club one evening and threw me into the back of a van. I heard them talking and they were taking me to Hogarth Acre. I was scared because it's really deserted there and nobody would hear me shouting for help.'

Phil nodded. 'I know Hogarth Acre. You get the odd dog walker but that's it.'

'Another man was waiting there, they called him Lou,' I continued.

'Hogarth Acre. Hellfire, of course: Barrie. I hadn't made the connection.' Phil exclaimed.

'One of them tried to assault me in the van but the driver stopped him because this Lou paid to go first.' I gulped before continuing. 'I managed to break free before we got to Hogarth Acre and I jumped out of the moving vehicle to escape but I was knocked out. Before I regained consciousness and told people about them, they kidnapped another girl, Tina Smiley. Her body was found in a copse on Hogarth Acre.'

'That explains a few things. So why the secrecy? It's not like you did anything wrong, you're the survivor,' Phil said.

'I don't want to be "the survivor"; I want people to look at me and see plain old Samantha Barrie.'

'They were caught after killing Tina. One's now dead and the other is still in prison,' Phil said.

'Tina died because I escaped,' I said. I wiped a tear from my cheek.

Phil rubbed his chin. 'Tina died because two perverts abducted and killed her. You shouldn't feel guilty. Does the boss know?'

'Of course, and Alan.'

'Right, okay. You know, Brian's going to tell people, don't you?' Phil started the car and began patrolling again.

'Yeah, I know. I would prefer people to hear it from me than him,' I said. 'I'll do it at parade tomorrow.'

'Why not when we knock off at seven?' Phil asked. 'Everyone will be there.'

I thought for a moment. 'Yeah, why not.'

'Pass me an allsort.' Phil held out his hand.

I opened the glove compartment, popped a sweet into my mouth and handed a coconut wheel to Phil, and with that everything felt normal again.

*

At refs, I went into the kitchen for hot water to make up my instant soup. I couldn't see through to the dining area, which was accessed through an arch from the kitchen, but could hear the lads chatting and the clack of snooker balls. A radio played in the background. I was surprised to hear Derek in the dining area; it was normally Ray that had the same scoff as me. They appeared to be discussing the roles of women. No prize for guessing who had triggered that. I remained still and quiet beside the hot water geyser; I might as well practice eavesdropping skills.

'They only join to find husbands you know,' Derek said. 'Once Margaret got her claws into me, she resigned; and once that sprog has hooked one of the lads, she'll do the same, mark my words. If you want a fish, you go where the fish swim, and this is a very well-stocked pond.'

'You're talking bollocks,' Ken said. 'In the old days, women had little choice but to leave work to look after their husbands and babies. Now they have more choice and finding a husband is not a priority. My Gaynor is going to have a career if that's what she wants.'

'Wind it in, Derek. I've seen nothing to suggest that's her motivation,' Alan said. 'You need to stop being so bitter that Margaret divorced you.'

I saw a shadow approach the archway and I moved swiftly over to the hot water geyser.

'Hello, Sam,' Ken said. 'I didn't see you come in.'

The conversation in the dining area stopped at once.

'I just came in for some hot water.' I filled my mug with hot water and went and sat at the table where Derek and Alan were now chatting about football. I wouldn't let on I'd heard anything but, day by day, I was building a picture of my block mates: and some of them were not looking good.

'Soup? That's not a meal. You can't beat a good old cheese and Branston pickle butty,' Derek said.

'Or spam and piccalilli,' Alan added, waving his doorstep of a sandwich at me.

'It's 2am; I'm not really hungry,' I said.

'If you don't eat now, you'll wake up hungry about eleven and it's a bugger to get back to sleep. Then you'll feel like death tomorrow night.' Alan bit into his sandwich.

A useful tip, but nobody had taught me how to retrain my body clock to cope with the rapidly changing shifts. I couldn't cope with a sandwich yet, but a mug of soup was fine. I would have some toast before going to bed and hope that would be sufficient.

As I drank the last of the soup, Steve put his head around the door of the refs room.

'Sam, before you go out, can you go to the bridewell? There's a female prisoner that needs searching.' He disappeared again.

'Will do,' I called after him.

'It'll probably be a D and D from the clubs,' Ken said.

'Yeah, there's been a few drunk and disorderlies in tonight,' Derek said. 'I was talking to the city control room earlier and there's a woman in the city station saying she's been sexually assaulted.' Derek took a huge bite of his sandwich then said, through a mouthful of cheese, 'What do women expect gadding about late at night, dressed like tarts?' He shook his head.

'We don't know the circumstances,' Alan said.

I agreed with Alan. 'You think that if a girl is raped, she has brought it on herself because of the way she's dressed, Derek? What about those who don't go to clubs? Girls who are attacked in the street as they walk home, minding their own business? "No" means "no", whether you're drunk or not.'

'Did she say "no" though? We've all heard cases where the girl has made allegations to hide a one-night stand.' Derek looked around the table seeking but failing to win support. 'What's a bloke supposed to do when he's led on?'

'He should show some restraint,' I said.

'Women shouldn't attract attention to themselves if they want men to leave them alone. A bloke would be less inclined to go after an ugly bird.'

I was actually immobilised by anger.

'Rape isn't about attraction, it's about power and control,' Ken said.

I was awe-struck. Ken was brilliant! Where did he learn this stuff? Wherever it was, every bobby should go there as part of their training.

'A woman should be able to have a night out, wearing whatever she likes, without having to worry about being attacked, and without having to cope with judgmental coppers if she is, you misogynistic tosser.' I pushed my chair back and stalked off, unable to remain in Derek's company a minute longer.

I could hear him laughing as I went into the ladies' toilet to splash my face. I knew there were more men than Derek who felt that way, but it didn't make it right. I wiped my face and took some deep breaths to slow my racing heart, then went to the bridewell to deal with the prisoner. It was early, but I didn't want to go back to the refreshment room; Ken would wash my dirty mug for me.

Chapter Eleven

Steve let me in to the bridewell. I put my radio on the charge desk and followed him to the female cell area; a radio hanging around my neck would get in the way during a search.

'She hid behind the door when I took her a drink,' Steve said. 'I'll wait here in case there's trouble.'

I went into the cell ready to fend off an attack, but there was nobody there. I turned to see if she was crouched behind the door, but all I saw was Steve pulling the heavy door shut. I lunged forward but it was too late, the door was locked fast. I shouted and banged on the door but, unsurprisingly, Steve did not come to release me. I pressed the alarm several times but still nobody came. My radio was on the desk in the charge office so I couldn't even radio control to let them know where I was. I backed up to the bunk and sank onto the plastic mattress. I could feel panic welling up. I closed my eyes and hit my palms against the edge of the bunk to keep myself calm, but my memories overwhelmed me. I could smell the dust and plastic inside the van, feel the rag in my mouth. My throat felt tight. I kept banging my hands against the bunk.

'That was then, I'm safe now. That was then, I'm safe now. Safe, safe, safe…' I banged my hands and chanted until I lost track of time.

*

Even through the hessian, I could smell rank body odour. I was dumped, kicking and scratching, onto a hard surface and knew I was inside that lurking van. Someone tied my hands behind me and bound my legs. I made as much noise as I could, but unless someone was on the playground, nobody would hear me. One man with stinking breath pulled the sack from my head and pushed a rag into my mouth. I baulked and tried to dislodge it, but it was there to stay.

When the van moved off, I made myself calm down and took stock of my surroundings. Once, at school, we had had a talk from a police officer. During the session he mentioned how helpful careful observation had been in gathering enough information to solve a case. I needed to gather information.

There were two men, one of whom stunk of old sweat. Moonlight shone through the small rear windows and reflected on tools and plastic dust sheets strewn around. It was a workman's van. Judging the tools, the owner worked in construction: a joiner maybe. The van itself was open in the back with a thin, metal wall behind the passenger and driver's seats, and a narrow opening between them to allow direct access to the back. All useful to pass on to the police when I escaped. If I escaped. No! I couldn't afford to think like that. I was going to get away and I would make sure these men went to prison.

The streetlights were close together, so we were still in a built-up area. Despite the late hour we might pass someone, so I kicked the side of the van until my shoes fell off and I hurt my feet, and screamed as hard as the gag would allow, to no avail. The streetlights became further apart; we were going into the countryside and my chances of escape were diminishing by the second.

Stinker left the passenger seat and climbed into the back. I cringed away from the wicked look in his unblinking eyes. It wasn't hard to read his intentions. I struggled uselessly against my restraints. He knelt beside me and grabbed my breasts. I wriggled away but he yanked me back. He undid his trousers and the smell of stale pee and sweat attacked my nostrils. I turned away in disgust as he let loose his penis. Stinker yanked the gag from my mouth, almost taking my front teeth with it, and pushed his pelvis towards me.

I strained away from him, but he grabbed my hair and forced my head towards him.

Think! If I threatened to bite him, he'd kill me, but they weren't trying to hide their faces, so they probably planned to kill me anyway. Decision made, I bared my dry teeth and snapped towards him like a rabid dog. He jerked backwards.

'Bitch!' He backhanded me across the face, splitting my lip. Blood ran onto my chin. He rolled me onto my stomach and yanked my knickers down, ripping them.

I screamed, bucked, and squirmed but he pinned me down. I braced for the pain of penetration.

'Lay off! Lou goes first, and he expects unblemished skin for the camera. We'll get our turn when he's finished,' the driver shouted.

Stinker let go and I caterpillared away and propped myself against the side of the van. If he came at me again, I wanted something behind me so I could give him a hefty kick in his rancid balls. If I was going to die, I would die fighting.

'Why should that shithead go first?' Stinker whined.

'Because he paid good money,' the driver snapped. 'Sit down; we'll be at Hogarth Acre soon.'

Hogarth Acre was an area of deserted scrubby land with a small copse, up a single-track lane off a rarely used road. It was extremely quiet even during the day, and it was unlikely we would encounter another car at night. If I remained here, I was doomed.

Stinker grabbed my hair and, for a horrible moment, I thought he was ignoring the driver. My heart drummed in my chest, but I managed to draw my feet up and smash them into his ribs. He fell backwards but recovered quickly, grabbed a Stanley knife from a toolbox and held it against my face. I whimpered and twisted away as far as I could.

'You'll pay for that. I'll enjoy giving you some special attention. I might carve my initials on to you.'

'Great, leave clues,' I croaked with more bravado than I felt.

'Initials! You can barely hold a crayon, you thicko,' the driver

scoffed.

'*Shut up! It's not my fault,*' *Stinker shouted. He moved back to his seat, grumbling loudly about the driver mocking his illiteracy, leaving me bound, with my tights shredded and the remains of my knickers around my knees. I'd worry about my dignity later. The Stanley knife lay on the floor just a couple of feet away from me. I wriggled around until I could get hold of it and contorted back to use it on my ankle ties.*

Stinker turned around and looked at me. I froze. Then he turned back, apparently satisfied that I was still secure. '*If you ask me, Lou will have his hands full with this one.*'

The driver chuckled. '*He enjoys a challenge…*' *He stopped speaking as lights moved behind us.* '*Lou said the road to Hogarth Acre was quiet.*'

Stinker glanced back. '*Slow down, perhaps it'll overtake.*'

I had to make my escape right now. No time to free my hands. I frantically kicked my legs, feeling the remaining threads of duct tape bite into the skin before breaking, then I rolled across to the door, knelt up and fumbled the door handle with my limited hand movement, praying it was unlocked.

'*She's free!*' *the driver shouted.* '*Stop her!*'

Stinker squeezed between the seats and lurched towards me, but the door flew open and I launched myself towards the lights. The car behind braked and swerved to avoid me. My head cracked against the road and skin ripped off me as I rolled to a stop. The last thing I saw before oblivion descended was the van lights go off and Stinker standing at the doorway as they raced away.

*

I heard movement outside the cell but I couldn't raise the will to shout; part of me was still in the back of that van. I could see and hear everything, but I felt wrapped in plastic.

The door opened. Steve and Alan came into the cell.

'Sam, I'm sorry.' Steve looked worried.

I stood up and walked out of the cell without speaking, or even looking anybody in the eye. I couldn't even enjoy it when Alan slapped Steve across the head.

Inspector Tyrrell flew out of the charge office, gripped Steve's lapel, and shook him like a rat. 'The cell alarm panel was disconnected! You don't ever disconnect the alarm panel.'

'I'm… I'm sorry, sir,' Steve stammered. 'It was a joke.'

Inspector Tyrrell propelled Steve towards the door. 'My office, NOW!'

Steve ran from the bridewell. I was unable to make the smallest decision, so I stood in the corridor, staring at a poster on the wall.

'Sam?'

I turned my head towards the inspector but found it difficult to focus on him.

'Sam, speak to me.'

I could still feel that gag and the duct tape. I allowed my head to drop and I stared at his shiny shoes while my mind took itself off for a wander. I had never got the hang of bulling shoes. I could never achieve that high mirror gloss. In training school, where bulled shoes were mandatory, I had reached an arrangement with another student: I'd pressed his uniform and he'd bulled my shoes for me. You could see the unblemished results in the class photo. That thought triggered another memory.

'He said Lou wanted unblemished skin for the pictures,' I whispered.

'I think we should get the police surgeon to look at her,' the bridewell sergeant said. 'He's down in the male cells checking someone who says they're diabetic. He won't be long.'

I jerked from my trance. I looked at the clock and was surprised to see I had been incarcerated for only half an hour. 'I just remembered that one of the men mentioned that a man named Lou wanted unblemished skin for the pictures.' I gulped. 'If they were going to film me, they probably filmed Tina.'

Nobody except Inspector Tyrrell had a clue what I was talking about.

'You did a statement at the time,' he said.

'Yes, but I don't know if I remembered that then. I remembered it in the cell. If I'm right, somewhere out there are the last pictures of Tina Smiley, and maybe her attackers.'

'One offender is in prison and the other committed suicide, so I wouldn't worry too much about not remembering,' Inspector Tyrrell said.

Yes, the driver had hung himself with ripped sheets and Stinker would be incarcerated for decades yet, but Lou was still out there.

'There was another man waiting at Hogarth Acre, who has never been traced,' I insisted.

Inspector Tyrrell stared at me for several seconds, and I could almost hear the cogs turning in his head. 'I'll check back with Odinsby CID on that, but I think they will already be aware. I can't imagine the offenders they caught would have wanted to shoulder all the blame.'

'Go and get a cup of tea then come to my office,' Alan said. 'I'll tell Phil to go out without you.'

'I'm going to rip Steve a new arse.' Inspector Tyrrell put a protective arm around my shoulder and walked me to the refs room. He was a decent bloke and he was just being caring, so I ignored the urge to punch his gut and run.

'Sam, I think it's time to let the block know what happened. Everyone knows there is something not quite right, and I think trying to keep this a secret is adding to your stress.'

'I spoke to Phil earlier and I'm going to do it at the end of shift if that's okay,' I replied.

'Good.' Inspector Tyrrell gently kneaded his fingers into my shoulder as we walked, and my urge to punch and run was replaced by the urge to rest my head against him and wrap my arm around his waist.

At the top of the stairs, I saw Steve waiting outside the inspector's office.

'Sam…' he began.

I held up my hand and turned away.

Inspector Tyrrell released my shoulders and jabbed a finger at his office. 'Get in.' He turned to me. 'Let me see your hands.'

I held out my hands for inspection. I hadn't realised I had bruised them, but a blue tinge crept from my wrists towards my palms. I couldn't say if they came from banging on the cell door, or my attempts to calm myself by hitting the edge of the bunk.

'Right,' Inspector Tyrrell said. 'No rush, Sam. Enjoy your tea.'

I went into the kitchen and made a brew while Inspector Tyrrell went into his office and slammed the door. We could never normally hear conversations in the inspector's office unless the door was open, but I heard this one. He clearly spelled out the implications should Steve interfere with bridewell equipment again. Then he started summarising the ordeal he had put me through, which sounded awful even in cold policing terms. I hadn't considered that what had just happened was False Imprisonment, but that's the charge Inspector Tyrrell threatened to lay on Steve. He'd be sacked for sure, and possibly end up in prison.

Alan came into the refs room, followed by the police doctor.

'Dr Owen?' Apart from incidents outside, he often came to the station to deal with unwell prisoners and take blood from drunk drivers, but I had never seen him on the upper floor.

'Hello young lady. Your sergeant has asked me to examine you. Do you want to stay here?' Dr Owen asked.

I raised an eyebrow at Alan.

'I hope you don't mind, Sam, but I thought it would be best. He was here anyway,' Alan said.

I sighed. Maybe this would convince everyone that I wasn't a weirdo.

'Will I have to get undressed?' I asked. My choice of location depended on the answer.

'Only if you want to,' Dr Owen quipped.

'Then let's stay here,' I said.

Alan left the room and I sat at the table where the doctor took my blood pressure and pulse, shone a light into my eyes, waved a finger in front of me, and looked at my bruises.

'Everything appears normal and the bruises are not severe,' the doctor said. He put his equipment back into his bag. 'Your sergeant told me about what happened to you in the past. It was a terrible thing. I remember it clearly.'

I blinked in surprise. 'Were you at the hospital when I was taken in?'

Dr Owen shook his head. 'No, I was in general practice. Tina Smiley was one of my patients.'

I drew a deep breath that turned into a sob at the mention of her name. The doctor put his hand on mine.

'What is it that still bothers you from that time?' he asked. When I shrugged, he prompted, 'Come on, tell Uncle Tom what's wrong. Is it that you survived?'

I felt tears spill over onto my cheeks. I didn't want to cry but they ambushed me. Even the tongue pressing trick failed.

'It wasn't your fault, Sam.'

I pulled my hand back and put my hands over my face. 'Every time I look at the scar on my head, I think of Tina. I never knew her, but I'm forever connected to her. If I'd been a bit stronger and remained conscious for a little longer, I could have told the other driver about the van at once and the police could have stopped them before they murdered her. They'll have been angry that I got away and that will have made it worse for her.' I bowed my head and wept.

Dr Owen patted my shoulder. 'I'm probably breaching patient confidentiality here, but I don't suppose she would mind. I can tell you that Tina died quickly of a fractured skull. One single blow did it.'

I wiped my eyes with the back of my hand. 'One blow?'

'One catastrophic blow that fractured her skull and killed her outright. She wasn't tortured, if that is what you were thinking.' The doctor looked over my shoulder. I turned and saw the inspector standing at the archway to the kitchen. Steve and Ken stood behind him. Steve's eyes were red rimmed and his cheeks looked pale. Had the inspector really made him cry?

'How long have you been standing there?'

'Long enough,' Steve croaked. 'I thought it would be a good joke. I was locked in too when I first came here. I thought it was funny. I never intended to harm you or upset you.'

'The boss asked me to come and sit with you,' Ken said. 'But if you want me to get lost, just say so.

'And I came to speak to the doctor,' Inspector Tyrrell said. 'I'm glad I heard you; I'm not sure you would have been so open with me.'

Dr Owen stood up. 'You have friends here, Samantha. That does more good than any tablet I can give you. Be honest with them. It won't eradicate the memories, but their support will help you cope.'

'We have a good doctor. Wyre Hall is lucky,' I said.

Dr Owen patted my arm and left with the inspector, while Ken and Steve sat at the table with me.

'It would have been better to tell people as soon as you arrived,' Ken said.

'Maybe,' I admitted.

'Can you forgive me?' Steve's plaintive expression was hard to resist despite the distress he'd caused me. Thanks to his antics, I had remembered the comment about the camera. Also, the doctor told me Tina had not died a prolonged, agonised death. I had had repeated nightmares about that for six years. Impulsively, I pecked Steve's cheek. He slapped a hand onto his face, his mouth and eyes round.

'Don't get excited. I was just saying thank you. Because of you, I might start sleeping better.'

Steve exhaled. 'Thank God.' His eyes grew round. 'I didn't mean it to sound like that, I mean you're really pretty and if I wanted a girlfriend, I would definitely consider you... No, that didn't sound right either...' Steve blushed. 'When in a hole, stop digging,' he muttered.

'Jeez, Steve, you're such a berk sometimes,' Ken said.

I understood that Steve hadn't meant to harm me when he

played his tricks; he was being mischievous rather than malicious.

I nudged him. 'Let's just be friends.'

'Cool.'

I thought for a moment. 'I need to apologise to Derek.'

'What for? The prat deserved everything you said to him,' Ken said.

I laughed. 'Yeah, but in the interest of block harmony, I should apologise.'

We trooped downstairs and I went in to see Alan, who sat me on the chair by the key cabinet. Inspector Tyrrell came in shortly afterwards, closed both doors to the office, and perched on the desk. He did a lot of perching; he seemed to prefer it to sitting in a chair at a desk.

'I thought you'd at least put Steve on a fizzer,' Alan said.

'I thought about it, but I don't think there's much to be gained from tainting his record with a charge this early in his service. I put the fear of God into him by threatening to lock him up for False Imprisonment.' The inspector focused on me. 'Are you settling in here?'

'I'm still finding my feet,' I replied.

'That's a polite way of saying "no".'

It was time to speak out, about everything. 'I'm on guard all the time, it's exhausting. Even when someone is nice to me, I'm waiting for the punch line. I can't relax: and I still get caught out.'

'Do you want me to step in?' Inspector Tyrrell said.

'Please don't. I'm sure it's not malicious; I have to find my own place here.' Did I even *have* a place here?

'Are you claustrophobic?' Alan asked.

'I wouldn't have been able to get under that car for the baby if I was claustrophobic.'

'You *chose* to go under the car,' Alan pointed out.

True. I was in more danger, but I wasn't trapped. Maybe he was on to something. Perhaps it wasn't just the guilt over Tina's death that affected me.

'I'm fine. Just cross and embarrassed.' I forced a smile.

Inspector Tyrrell stood up. 'Right. I have a mountain of paperwork I need to get finished. Alan, can you pop up before we knock off?'

'Will do.'

Alan and I also stood as he left. I wondered if they wanted to talk about me and what the doctor and Inspector Tyrrell had talked about.

When the inspector had gone, Alan signalled for me to sit down again.

'You gave Derek a right scolding in the refs room.'

I shifted in my seat. 'I don't know what came over me. I didn't mean to come across as rude.'

'You came across as angry.' Alan held his hand up as I opened my mouth to lie about how I wasn't angry. 'Don't worry about it; I'm quite impressed that someone of your short service would confront someone with as many years as Derek has.' He paused. 'In this job, we see so much of the underside of life; we tend to become cynical, which isn't an altogether bad thing. You will come across women who make false accusations.'

'They make it more difficult for genuine cases to be believed,' I said.

'They do indeed,' Alan agreed. 'And it's good for us to be reminded that not all allegations are false; but do you understand why we have to treat allegations with some scepticism? It's not for the men to prove their innocence, we have to prove guilt.'

I sort of understood. In general, I thought the premise of *"innocent until proven guilty"* was right, but to treat a victim as if they were the offender was wrong.

'When we take a complaint of theft or burglary, we might have reservations about what happened but we take the report and investigate it without interrogating the complainant as if they were the offender,' I said.

'The women who make allegations of rape get a harder time in court than we give them,' Alan said.

'Because this is a man's world. It shouldn't matter whether a woman wears a short skirt or lipstick or whether she has had pre-marital sex.'

'It shouldn't, but it does.' Alan nodded, signalling the end of the conversation. 'Okay, it's not worth your going out now, so just finish some paperwork.'

I went into the control room and Derek narrowed his eyes.

'I'm sorry I shouted at you,' I said.

Ray spun around and leant forward. 'What have I missed?'

'Did Alan tell you to apologise?' Derek snapped.

'No, he said it did us good to be reminded that there are some genuine people around. The apology was my idea. I shouldn't have shouted.'

'But you don't regret saying what you said?'

'I stand by my sentiments, Derek, but I shouldn't have called you a misogynistic tosser.'

'Misogynistic tosser! Love it.' Ray held his sides as he laughed.

Derek glared at him as he spoke to me. 'No, you shouldn't have. But it's what you think, isn't it?'

'I shouldn't have shouted it at you,' I said.

'Stop being churlish and forgive the girl,' Ray said.

'I forgive you,' Derek said grudgingly.

'Thank you.'

Ray turned back to the radio. 'I'll wheedle it all out of Derek later. Failing that, I'll wait for the gossip at knocking-off time.'

I smiled. 'Actually, I was going to do this later, but I'll tell you two what's going on now.'

Ray spun back, and Derek cocked his head.

'Do you remember the Hogarth Acre incident?' I asked.

They nodded and then Ray gasped. He had figured it out, but Derek needed a bit more.

'I was one of the girls that were taken. It's left me with a few issues that I am trying to address. I wanted to keep it quiet, but so many people know now, it's daft to keep that up. I don't want it to affect how people treat me and as far as I'm concerned, it's business as usual.'

Derek pursed his lips. 'A bad do that was. No wonder you got angry.'

'I take it Phil knows,' Ray said.

'He does, so does the supervision. Ken and Steve overheard me talking about it to the doctor, and now you know. I'll let everyone else know later.'

'Right then. Put the kettle on while you're doing nothing,' Derek said.

I gladly went into the telex room and put teabags into the mugs. I should have done this before. Inspector Tyrrell had been right; it wasn't so terrible. I could continue doing my job; in fact, while I was here, I could check the Yellow Pages for the address of Capri Securities.

Chapter Twelve

I woke up just after 4pm feeling well rested. In fact, I hadn't slept so well in ages. I'd been foolish to try to hide my past. What happened, happened; it didn't define who I was now.

I showered, belting out *Convoy* into the showerhead, put on my cool cheesecloth shirt with the drawstring neckline and a pair of linen trousers, then went downstairs. Mum was still at work. I drank a mug of tea and tried to read the paper, but my attention kept wandering to the yellow Lotus and the mysterious Robert. The address DVLA had was indeed that of Capri Securities, so Belvedere House could well be Robert's home address. Brian Lewington crept into my mind too, but I pushed him aside. On impulse, I grabbed my bag and drove down to Belvedere House. I had no plan, but I wanted to see if the yellow Lotus was there, and maybe I would also see Robert. That would firmly link him to the flats.

I parked up on the main road and walked past the apartment block towards the river. The yellow Lotus was there again. I walked down to the water's edge and sat on a wall, ostensibly to watch the passing ships, but I angled myself so that I could see any movement in the car park.

Very little happened. After fifteen minutes, I was about to leave when I saw a girl in St Agnes' uniform walking across the car park. It wasn't Lana or Janice, but maybe she was visiting Molly.

I watched her go into the flats. I jumped down from the wall and sauntered over to the apartments. The door was locked. I examined the panel of door buzzers to the side, but no names were attached to the numbers, so I was no better off.

I dodged around the corner as an MG convertible swept into the car park. A woman, with her hair pulled back in a gypsy headscarf, got out. As she was furtling in her bag for a key, I strolled back around the corner and followed her. She held the door for me.

'Thanks,' I said.

She smiled. Her clothing, although similar in style to mine, was of much better quality. She would not be found rummaging around the market on a Saturday afternoon. We got into the lift together.

'Top floor please,' I said, desperately hoping she would get out before that.

'Thank goodness. I did wonder if you were one of those girls.' She pressed the buttons for the top and third floor.

I relaxed against the rear wall as the lift purred to the first stop. 'What girls?'

'The ones that come here looking like strumpets. You must have heard the noise. Parties and screeching late at night. I suppose you are protected from it up there.'

Ignoring that she had just told me I looked like a strumpet, I said, 'Have you contacted the police about it?' I tightened the drawstring on my blouse.

'I don't want to cause trouble. I mean, I'd still have to live here after they left.' The doors opened, and she snorted. 'There's one of them now.'

The St Agnes girl was knocking on the door opposite. She had taken her blazer off and had unpinned her hair.

The woman stepped out of the lift. 'See you.' She turned sharp right and out of sight.

'Bye,' I called after her. I stepped forward to see the girl better, but the doors slid shut again.

I rode the lift to the top floor, then held the sliding door and looked around. There were four apartments on the floor. Nothing else to see, so I pressed the third floor button again.

That floor was laid out just like the top floor. The door to the apartment where I had seen the girl was number 11. Apartment 1, the caretaker's flat, was on the ground floor and there were 4 apartments per floor, so now I could work out which floor any number apartment was on. Another snippet for Irene; you never knew when such information would be useful. I let the doors slide shut and travelled to the ground floor.

When I stepped out of the lift, I saw Glynis and Lana coming towards the outer door. I ducked into the stairwell and peered through the glass panel. Had Lana been alone I would have assumed that she was visiting Molly, but Glynis's presence threw me. She hadn't struck me as the most concerned parent, so would she escort Lana to visit Molly?

I waited until they were safely in the lift then I watched the display change as it ascended then stopped on the third floor. Right then: the third floor was significant. Could number 11 be Molly's address? I needed to speak to Phil or Irene.

I trusted that there was sufficient distance from apartment 11 that nobody would recognise me out of uniform, but I kept my head down as I hurried back to my car.

My stomach rumbled. I checked my watch and was surprised that I had been at Belvedere House for over an hour. I could get something to eat in one of the restaurants or takeaways in Nelson Square. There was a chance I might see something interesting happening by Belvedere House if I stayed nearby, so I left my car and walked the short distance to the Square.

Hari Kapoor, the handsome son of the owner of the Golden Temple restaurant, was clearing one of the tables they had set up on the outside. He was a similar age to me, and we had met a few days previously when he had called us to move on some rowdy customers.

He waved when he saw me. 'Hello Constable Sam.'

I went over. 'Hi, Hari. How's business?'

'Lunchtime was busy. We have several bookings for tonight.' Hari smiled, flashing his white teeth and obsidian eyes. He was far too popular with the girls for his strict father's taste. 'It is not busy now and I see you are not in your uniform. Why don't you stay and have something to eat?'

'I don't really like spicy food, Hari.' I hoped he wouldn't take offence. My only exposure to curry had been from a packet of Vesta, which was horrible, and from my local chippy, which had been so hot it had almost blown my head off.

'There is lots of food that isn't spicy, Constable Sam. Sit down and I'll bring you something you will enjoy.'

'How could I refuse an offer like that?' I allowed Hari to seat me at a table and pour me a glass of water.

'I will be back soon with delicious surprises.'

It felt quite continental to sit outside in the sun and look at people passing by. When I was in uniform, people got a bit paranoid if I watched them, but nobody took any notice of me dressed like this and with my hair loose.

Hari returned. 'Samosas,' he announced and placed a plate in front of me.

I picked up my knife and fork and attacked the pastry triangles. Meat and rice fell out and delectable savoury smells wafted up. I tested a small piece and it was scrumptious. I cleared the plate in no time.

Next, Hari brought me red chicken with a yellow rice and salad. 'Tandoori Chicken with pilau rice.'

I poked it with my fork, then took a small bite. It was just as tasty as the samosas. As my dad would say, it didn't touch the sides on its way down.

'Did you enjoy that?' Hari asked.

'I certainly did.'

Hari cleared my plates and brought me a small metal bowl. 'For dessert, we have something most exotic.'

I laughed as he placed a bowl of vanilla ice cream in front of me. I crunched up the wafer then started on the ice cream.

'You look like you're enjoying that.' I instantly lost my appetite and put my spoon down at the sound of Brian's voice. He came over and sat uninvited at my table. 'Don't stop on my account, I like watching girlies lick cream.'

'Inappropriate.' I picked up my bag, ready to pay the bill and leave.

Brian leant forward and sniffed. 'That's lovely perfume you're wearing. You're an attractive girl. Do you want to go for a drink?'

'No thanks, Brian. I have a boyfriend,' I lied.

'You don't wear much make-up, even off duty,' Brian said. 'That's nice; I prefer the natural look.' He leant to the side and scrutinised my torso. 'And you've got curves.'

'Are you calling me fat?' Two insults in one afternoon was almost too much.

He laughed. 'Far from it. Those skinny models are all very well, but most men like something to hold on to. If you're interested in a bit of moonlighting, I know someone who would like to meet you.'

'I earn enough for my needs, thank you.'

'Everyone could do with a little extra. I could be useful to you.'

I'd had enough of Brian and his weirdness. 'Can I have the bill please, Hari?'

Hari looked shocked. 'No bill. You helped us, now this is our thank you gift to you.'

'Hari, this wasn't a cup of tea and a biscuit, I've just eaten a three course meal. I can't accept that, it's too much.'

'My father and I will be most offended if you refuse.' Hari's mouth turned down.

'In that case, thank you.' I wasn't sure of the protocol, but I was sure I would have to declare it to someone back at the station. Phil would know.

'You can declare your meal to me,' Brian said.

It seemed he did have his uses.

Hari nodded in satisfaction. 'You should come here with your boyfriend. Tell Constable Phil too.'

'I will.' I would tell Phil, but I doubted I would go back that often. I had enjoyed the food but I suspected that, if I went back, it would prove to be a very cheap night out and I didn't want to take advantage.

'Is your father in the back, Hari?' Brian asked.

'Yes, he's in the kitchen, Sergeant Brian. He's expecting you.'

Brian disappeared into the back. I was curious about what business he would have with Mr Kapoor, but I didn't want to hang around anymore. Mum would be home by now and wondering where I was.

*

'You did what?!' Phil exclaimed when I told him about my afternoon's adventures. 'Hellfire, Sam! You went into the flats without telling anyone: off duty, alone, and without means of calling for backup if you got into trouble? What were you thinking? How do you know that the CID or Vice or Drugs or anyone hasn't already set something up, maybe on that very flat? You might have compromised a surveillance operation. I thought I'd taught you better than that.'

'If they wanted us to stay away, they would have said so on parade,' I said.

Phil shook his head. 'Sam, Sam, we get told when it isn't too important. There are operations that are secret, even from us. There's stuff happening right now that we have no idea about. If we have information that makes us want to snoop about unnoticed, we tell Irene or the boss, then it will either tie in with an ongoing operation or be the start of a new enquiry. Either way, it gets passed from uniform to the jacks: the detectives. We're the visible presence, the deterrent. The jacks are the investigators.'

'I thought you'd be pleased,' I whined.

'Pleased that you put yourself in danger? Hellfire!'

'Sam, can you come to the office, please.' Sergeant Bowman gestured from the doorway.

I peered into the office and saw the inspector perched on the desk.

'Come in and shut the door,' Alan said.

'I'll cut straight to the chase,' the boss said. 'Phil has completed his assessment and we've decided that you're ready to go solo.'

'OH YEAH!' I did a little hopping dance of celebration, which made the boss laugh. I beamed and Inspector Tyrrell returned my smile with something more. I hesitated because I couldn't be certain what that look meant, but I was sure I had seen something, and so had Alan judging by the way his narrowed eyes ping-ponged between us.

'You still have a lot to learn, so don't get cocky. If you come across anything you're not sure of, ask for help,' Alan added.

'I will,' I promised.

'Off you go. Enjoy your remaining time in company because, on lates, you're on your own.'

I skipped out of the office and found Phil in the report writing room.

'I'm going solo on lates,' I said.

'I know, I signed you off. Although I might have thought twice if I'd thought you were going to go off half-cocked like you did this afternoon.'

'All right, point made. I promise I won't do that again,' I said.

'Good. Right, you might as well let Irene know what happened and then we'll get out. I'll meet you in the yard.'

I quickly jotted everything I had seen and learnt at Belvedere House onto to a piece of A4. Then I added the snippet about a Robert Molyneux owning Capri Securities. I folded it and popped it into Irene's basket. I hoped my information would be useful; it would be a shame to have annoyed Phil for nothing.

'Not out yet, Sammy?' Brian leant against the doorway.

'I was just putting some information in for Irene.'

He glanced at the basket. 'Right, off you go then.'

I edged past Brian, who made no attempt to move aside, and hurried into the yard. That man just made my flesh crawl.

Chapter Thirteen

It was almost midnight when Ray announced that Janice had been reported missing, again. We drove over to Sandringham Boulevard and were let in by Janice's father. Her mother, Pamela, hovered by the window, peering out every two minutes.

'When did you last see her?' I asked. Phil was letting me take the lead in preparation for going solo.

'This morning at breakfast. We argued because she wouldn't eat anything, then she left for school as normal.' Pamela flitted back to the window.

'I thought that she'd have learnt her lesson last time. I made it plain then we would not tolerate this behaviour,' Mr Alderman said.

'Do you mind if we check her room?' I asked.

Mr Alderman just waved a hand in the general direction of the stairs.

Phil and I went to the bedroom, a typical teenager's room with make-up strewn across a dressing table and posters on the wall.

Phil got straight to business and began to rummage under the bed. I checked in the wardrobe and pulled open the chest of drawers in the hope of finding something useful to our enquiry. In the knickers drawer, I found a small packet of pills.

'Look here.' I shook the box.

'Contraceptive pills?' Phil took the box from me and opened it.

Three pills were missing from one of the strips, corresponding with the last three days. 'Where did she get them from? I didn't think doctors could prescribe them to under-sixteens.'

'Welcome to the twentieth century, Grandpa. I've heard of girls going on the pill early, but I thought the doctor had to inform the parents if they were underage.'

'Inform the parents of what?' Pamela came into the bedroom.

'Does Janice have a boyfriend, Mrs Alderman?' I asked.

Pamela shook her head vigorously. 'We wouldn't allow that yet.'

Phil handed the pills to her. She read the label and sank onto the bed.

'This can't be. Birth control is a sin.'

I wondered how the Aldermans had only one child with such a belief, but perhaps there was a medical problem. I didn't want to pry.

Mrs Alderman sprang from the bed and began to pull out the bedside cabinet until she found a diary. She flicked through it and threw it onto the bed.

'She's still mixing with that Lana.'

'Did another officer come to speak to you about the crash?' Phil asked. It sounded casual.

'Yes. He said she was with someone called Gerald. She told the officer he was her uncle. Neither my husband nor I have any relatives named Gerald.'

'So, you have no idea who this person might be?'

Tears welled in Pamela's eyes. 'We tried to speak to her about it… Well, you know what teenagers are like. I wonder if this Gerald is related to Lana somehow, and our Jan calls him uncle because Lana does.'

Phil grunted. 'Okay. If she comes home, please ring at once, and we'll contact you if we find her.'

Pamela showed us out and I spotted Maud next door peeping from her bedroom window. I gave a little wave and she waved back. I wondered if she was lonely without Henry.

'We could do with speaking to the traffic department,' I said when we got back into the Panda.

'They're already following up that side of things,' Phil said. 'We should follow up what we have so far, but a note to Irene would be in order.'

'Mike Two.'

I picked up the handset. 'Go ahead.'

'Ken has been to Schooner Street and spoke to Connie. Lana is absent but had not been reported. He's taken a misper report on her.'

Phil reached over and took the handset from me. 'Thanks, Ray. I think we can assume the two girls are together. I'll call around to Gilmour Street and make some enquiries.'

'Can we go to Belvedere House?' I asked Phil.

'Let's go down the usual routes first.'

'I think we should at least knock. If I was solo, I'd go there.'

'Don't get cocky.' Phil cautioned. 'We'll go to see Rose and Arthur before we do anything else.'

'Oh joy.'

*

Our arrival at Gilmour Street was a lot more tranquil than our previous visit there. Phil knocked at the door and Rose answered it. I was relieved to see she was clothed, albeit in a tight, pink nylon nightie topped with a gaping, quilted dressing gown. A pink, nylon scarf held a hedgehog of rollers across her head.

'All right. I was just making Arthur a cup of tea before we went to bed. Want one?' She ushered us inside where Arthur was ensconced on an armchair. He nodded a greeting.

To my relief, Phil said, 'No thanks, Rose. We've not long had one. Sorry to disturb you this late but Lana has done one again with another girl, Janice Alderman. Have you seen them?'

'I saw our Lana yesterday.' A kettle whistled, and she went into the kitchen, which surprisingly looked a lot cleaner than the last time I had seen it. It still smelled though.

'Last time we were here, you mentioned that she visited a girl, Milly or something. Has she mentioned her since?' Phil asked.

Rose came out of the kitchen carrying a cup of tea. 'No, but I remember her name. It was Molly not Milly.'

'Now can we go to Belvedere House?' I whispered.

'Okay,' Phil agreed. 'Thanks, Rose. Would you let us know if she turns up here?'

'Okay.'

We returned to the Panda and Phil radioed in for Ray to update the job sheet that we were headed to Belvedere House.

'Okay, Mrs Almost-Solo, what's the plan?' Phil asked.

'Well, I suppose we could go to apartment 11 and ask for Molly.' It felt strange to be making the decisions.

'If Lana and Janice are there, ringing the bell will give them a couple of minutes to hide.'

'I could ring the caretaker's bell,' I said. 'It's late, but isn't letting us in part of his job?'

'Not necessarily, but it's not a bad idea.'

*

As we approached the apartments, I could see a Panda already in the car park.

'That's Mike Sierra Two, the patrol sergeant's car.' Phil pulled in beside it.

Brian came out of the block, holding Lana by the arm and with Janice tottering on sky-high heels behind him. Phil and I got out of the Panda. Lana glared but allowed herself to be guided to the car.

'Hellfire, they don't look fifteen,' Phil murmured.

'All right you two. I was nearby so I thought I'd cover this.' Brian opened the door of his car and Lana climbed in.

'You should have let control know; it would have saved us a job,' Phil said.

'Sorry, mate, I didn't think.' Brian couldn't have sounded less sorry if he tried.

Phil nodded. 'Jan can come with us since we're dealing with the file.'

Brian hesitated then turned to Janice and murmured something. Lip reading would be a useful skill in this job. Maybe there were classes; I should make enquiries about that. Janice hung her head and teetered over to us. I opened the door and she climbed in. A flurry of hand gestures passed between Janice and Lana, none of which I understood.

Brian radioed in to tell Ray that he would take Lana home and that we were returning Janice. While Brian was occupied on the radio, I whispered to Phil, 'I don't remember you mentioning which apartment we were going to?'

'How did you know to where to go?' Phil asked when Brian had finished on the radio.

'I spoke to the caretaker. A couple of the residents had complained to him about the noise from apartment 11.'

'That's what we were going to do,' I said. I didn't want Phil to let slip that I had been snooping around.

'Great minds...' Brian chuckled. He got into his car. 'Anyway, I'll get this one back.' He left the car park, leaving us alone. I looked up at the apartments and saw faces at some windows. By my calculation, none of them was apartment 11.

'How did he even know to come to Belvedere House?' I said. 'Other patrols can't hear our transmissions unless we're on Talkthrough, and I know Ray didn't mention it on air.'

'Maybe he was in the office and heard us,' Phil said.

'Do you believe that?' I asked.

Phil didn't answer. We got into the car and set off to Janice's home.

'So, Janice. Is this where Molly lives?' I asked.

'Fuck off.' Janice folded her arms and slouched down in the seat.

'Apartment 11. We'll know where to come to get you next time.'

'You can't. You mustn't...' Gone was the sullen child. Janice appeared genuinely scared.

'Tell us about Uncle Gerald,' Phil said.

Janice's eyes bulged. 'I can't...'

'We know he isn't your uncle. Who is he?' I asked.

'You can't make me talk. I want a lawyer.'

'Why do you need a lawyer?' Phil asked. 'We're not accusing you of a crime; we just need to know why you keep worrying your poor mother half to death. You know she was crying when we were there.'

For a second, Janice looked contrite, but only for a second. 'I'm a child and you can't question me without an adult.'

'I'm an adult of the same gender,' I said, although I thought the rules intended that it should be a non-police adult. 'Besides, like Constable Torrens said, we're not questioning you about a crime. You're not under caution so the rules are a bit different.'

I thought Janice's eyes were going to pop.

'Uncle Gerald?' I encouraged.

'He's not my uncle; he's a friend of Molly's.'

'Molly has a lot of friends.'

'Yes.'

'She wasn't in the car with you and Gerald when it crashed?' I asked.

I saw a flicker of uncertainty in Janice's eyes. 'She...' One side of her mouth tugged in a half smile. 'She was but we dropped her off first.'

I had the distinct feeling I was missing something.

Phil interrupted my thought process by asking, 'Do you have a boyfriend, Janice? Only, we found some contraceptive pills in your drawer.'

'Shit! You didn't tell Mum, did you?'

'She's seen them,' I said.

'Shit! Shit! Shit! She'll kill me. She'll drag me to confession tomorrow. I'll spend the rest of the week saying "Hail Marys".'

'Why do you need to take the pill if you don't have a boyfriend?' I asked.

Janice turned her head and refused to say another word.

*

At Sandringham Boulevard, we hadn't even got out of the car before Pamela raced down the path and hauled Janice onto the pavement.

'Look at you!' she screeched. 'You look like a tart.'

Mr Alderman hurried out. 'Hush Pam, the neighbours...' He took her arm and led her inside. We followed with Janice.

'Where have you been?' demanded Mr Alderman.

'A party at a friend's house,' Janice answered.

'Another party? You're turning into a harlot and no man wants soiled goods. Your mother has shown me those pills. I've thrown them out.'

Janice blanched. 'You had no bloody right—'

Slap!

Janice howled and held her cheek. Mr Alderman raised his arm again but Phil stepped forward and held his arm. Mr Alderman bit his lip and nodded. Phil let go but stayed near.

'Tomorrow we'll go to speak to Father Thomas, Pam. We need guidance on this. Perhaps he knows somewhere we can send Janice.'

'You're going to send me away? No! Dad, please don't send me away,' Janice cried. 'Mum, tell him not to...' Janice clutched at her mother.

Pamela was crying but pushed her daughter away. 'Dad is right; you need help. You're on the devil's path. You won't listen to us.'

Janice rubbed her red cheek. 'I hate you! I hate you both and I hate your precious, bloody church. First chance I get, I'm going to London. I can be a hostess or a model and work in films.' Janice fled upstairs.

'I'm going to go to the school tomorrow and tell them that our Jan isn't to mix with that Lana. All this started when she began to hang around.' Pamela rubbed her eyes.

'We'll leave you to it,' Phil said. He lowered his voice. 'Seek the advice you need but if you want my opinion as a father, kids need to know that their parents love them unconditionally. That's probably the best way to bring her back.'

'We'll see what the father says tomorrow, but I'll bear that in mind.' Mr Alderman saw us out and quietly closed the door behind us.

'Hello?'

I turned and saw Maud Albiston leaning out of her bedroom window. 'Hello again, Maud. How are you? I hope we didn't wake you.'

'Not at all, dear. I'm often awake in the night. I'm quite well, thank you. I'm going to Australia to visit my nephew. It's very exciting.'

'Sounds fantastic,' I said.

'It will be wonderful, but I'll be there for some time. My poor garden will suffer in this heat. I thought we'd have had some rain by now. I save washing-up water for my azaleas now we can't use hoses; but I can't ask neighbours to do that, they have their own gardens to tend. I heard they are going to put standpipes in the street if this heatwave continues.'

'It can't last much longer, so it probably won't come to that,' I said.

Maud nodded towards the Aldermans' house. 'I saw Janice this afternoon. A man dropped her off after her mother had gone out, and she ran inside and came back a few minutes later with a bag.'

'Did you recognise the man?' I asked.

'No. He had a super car though. It was yellow and very sporty looking.'

'What make?' I asked.

'Oh, my dear, it's pointless asking me things like that, I haven't a clue.' Maud laughed.

'Never mind. Thanks, Maud, and enjoy Australia.' I turned to leave.

'Do you think I could help with next door, a little prayer perhaps?' Maud asked.

I turned back. 'It wouldn't hurt.'

'Goodnight then.' Maud closed her bedroom window.

'Come on, Sam.' Phil called

I got into the Panda, and Phil set off back to the station.

'Do you think the sporty, yellow car Maud mentioned could be the Lotus?' I asked Phil.

'Could be. But there might be other sporty, yellow cars around.'

'In this town?' I laughed. I didn't need to say any more.

*

The following night, at refs, Ken handed me an invitation to his and Gaynor's engagement party. I squealed and hugged him.

'Congratulations! But I thought you were going to wait until she completed her initial training?'

'We were going to wait, but it's what we both want so what's the point? We won't tie the knot until she finishes her probation. By the way, we're limited in numbers so I'm being selective about whom I invite. Be discreet please.'

'Who's coming,' Steve asked.

'Phil, Alan, Inspector Tyrrell, Ray, and their plus-ones, and you two.'

'I'm looking forward to this.' I put the invitation into my bag and sat next to Steve. I felt a little thrill to be among the chosen ones.

'Ray doesn't normally attend parties, does he?' Steve said.

'I hope he does come, he's a good bloke,' Ken said.

'I wonder who his plus-one will be, I've never heard him talking about a wife or girlfriend,' I said.

'Perhaps he's widowed,' Ken said.

'Have you got a plus-one for Ken's do?' Steve asked. I shook my head. 'Me neither. Why don't we go together? You can pick me up unless you want to come on the back of my motorbike.'

'I'm not riding on the back of that thing. I'll collect you at eight.'

'It's a date.' Steve winked.

'A date? You two are seeing each other?' One of the lads called over from the snooker table. I groaned.

'You must have a silver tongue, Steve, for her to forgive you for pulling that cell stunt,' Phil said.

'Sam knows I meant no harm,' Steve replied. 'Now it'll be all over Wyre Hall,' he whispered to me. 'Oh, I'll warn you: my brother, Richard, will be home on leave. He'll probably try to garner you for his harem. Just tell him to get lost unless you like being one of many.'

'Thanks for the warning. He's a marine, isn't he?' I said.

'Just like Dad,' Steve said.

'You were a military child? Didn't you want to join up too?'

'Dad wanted me to join up, follow the family tradition, but it didn't appeal. He was happy when I joined the police. Richard thinks I sold out.'

'Policing is not selling out,' I said.

'Try telling Richard that.' Steve crammed the last of the sandwich into his mouth.

*

'I spoke to the boss about Molyneux, Mount, Janice and Lana. He wants us to pass it to the CID,' Phil said just before we knocked off.

I pouted. I wanted to be the one to make the kill so to speak.

'Don't look like that; you know we and the jacks have different roles,' Phil said.

'I know, I know.' But I didn't have to like it.

'It's not about who cracks the case, because we're all on the same side. It's about the case getting cracked and a conviction being won.'

'So why can't we be the ones?' I grumbled.

'We're too busy mopping up drunks, alarms, and domestics.' Phil yawned. 'My bed's calling. I'm off.'

'Yeah, see you.' So, that was that. I knew I was bottom of the heap, but did they have to rub my nose in it? I hefted my handbag onto my shoulder and stalked out to the yard.

Chapter Fourteen

I had liked working nights, but I was glad to be back on the three-to-eleven late shift. I was going solo. I was excited and scared. Also, being around in the afternoon gave me the chance to speak to Irene, the collator.

After parade, I hurried to her office and closed the door behind me. 'Irene, something strange happened while I was on nights.'

Irene laughed. 'That comes with the job.'

'No, I mean really strange. Brian asked if I was interested in moonlighting. He kept ogling me and saying he could be useful to me.'

Irene thought for a moment. 'Did he ask you out?'

'He did, but I told him I have a boyfriend.'

'I heard you were seeing Steve,' Irene said.

I rolled my eyes. 'That got around fast. For the record, I'm not seeing Steve. I don't have a boyfriend really, I said I did to put Brian off. I wanted to ask what you know about Brian. Is he as dodgy as he seems?'

Irene glanced at the door and sighed. 'This is mostly gossip, so don't repeat it.'

'I won't,' I promised. A bit of dirt on Brian Lewington would make me very happy.

'He's been moved around a bit because he sails close to the wind. Most recently he's been suspected of taking bribes, protection money even, from businesses, but nobody can prove anything. He has a lifestyle that would be hard to maintain on a copper's pay, so he must be getting a little extra from somewhere.'

'Maybe he moonlights, and he really was just trying to be helpful to me,' I suggested. Several bobbies supplemented their earnings by using skills from prior employment. For instance, Phil was a qualified electrician and did jobs for colleagues.

'Maybe he does, but Gary's just waiting for him to put a foot wrong. He never wanted him here.'

Irene went over, pulled a card from the drawer, and held it out to me. 'Going off the subject, I have a little information for you and Phil. Gerald Mount moved here from another area where he came to police notice for his liking for young girls. The investigation of that RTA in Civic Avenue unearthed a previous address in Manchester for Mr Mount. Traffic passed it to me because of the suspicious circumstances of Janice Alderman's presence. I rang the collator in that area and he kindly shared what he had.'

I took the card from Irene. 'Was he convicted of anything?'

'Sadly, no. He always managed to keep just this side of the law, but he was suspicious enough for a card in the system. He liked to walk his dog past the youth club and sometimes engaged the youngsters, usually girls, in conversation.'

I shuddered as unwanted memories tried to surface.

'The kids didn't think anything of it, but the staff were concerned enough to mention it to the neighbourhood officer. The police were unable to act against him, because it isn't an offence to walk your dog, or chat to kids who want to pet your dog, but he changed his route when a Panda parked up by the club for a few nights. Then he came to notice again because a couple of girls at the bank he was working at complained to management that he had touched them and made lewd suggestions.'

'Was he arrested then?' I asked.

'The manager brought the police in because he had had to send one girl home in tears and he thought what she described amounted to indecent assault, but the girls wouldn't make a statement so, without their evidence, it was no cough, no job. Mount said it was just a bit of fun and they had misinterpreted his remarks.'

I scanned the card. 'It says a couple of mispers there were found half naked at his address.' I handed the card back. 'How did he get out of that one?'

'He said one of them was the daughter of a friend. He spotted her with the other misper and persuaded them to go back to his house and contact their families. However, someone else saw them go off with him and contacted the police, and the police arrived before they had a chance to phone.'

'Oh, come on!' I said.

'He said they were dishevelled and he had allowed them to use his bathroom to clean up.' Irene held up a hand. 'Yeah, I know, the bobby wasn't convinced either, but the girls corroborated "Uncle" Gerald's story. He moved away soon after and ended up here.'

'Are CID aware?' I asked.

'Are CID aware of what?' The delicious Irish brogue of DC Eamon Kildea slid into my ears and down my spine like warm honey. The dimple-cheeked detective came into the office.

Irene sighed. 'I swear; one day, Eamon, I'm going to find a way to bottle your voice and bathe in it.' She fluttered her eyelashes.

Eamon sat on the edge of the desk and leant towards Irene. 'I've got a mental image of you in the bath now, m'darlin'.' His voice was low and deep, and sexy as hell.

'Behave yourself, DC Kildea, I'm sure you didn't come down here to think of me in the bath.'

'No, but it's a lovely distraction, Sergeant Ward,' Eamon grinned. 'I've actually been sent down to speak to you about the information you got on Gerald Mount.'

Irene handed him the card with Mount's information on it. 'That's what we were talking about.

'Was that other information I sent helpful?' I asked.

'What information?' Eamon said.

'The information about Belvedere House. I saw a St Agnes girl at apartment 11, and then I saw Glynis and Lana Jones.'

'I know nothing about this,' Irene said.

'Me neither.' Eamon rubbed his chin.

'But I put a sheet in the basket when I was on nights.'

Irene looked a little troubled but said, 'Never mind. Tell us now what the information was.'

I recounted all the information I had been able to glean including the significance of apartment 11. I also told them about Capri Securities. Irene and Eamon listened carefully.

'What type of security, Sam?' Irene asked.

'From what I can gather, he specialises in bouncers, door staff,' I replied. 'It's a real company, it's in Yellow Pages.'

'Such people often have legitimate businesses to launder money from illegal operations,' Irene said.

'All that fits in with some intel I have,' Eamon said. 'Sam, m'darlin', when you met this Robert, what happened?'

'Phil and I went to Schooner Street to get Janice when she was reported MFH for the first time. Robert was there with Lana and Janice. Connie was there too, then Glynis came in and she went into the kitchen with him and I saw him hand over an envelope.'

'What was in the envelope?'

'I don't know but it was well filled. Phil said we didn't have the power to demand to see private correspondence that wasn't connected to the incident.'

Eamon sighed. 'Shame. When did you see him again?'

'Well I haven't exactly seen him again, but there was a yellow Lotus Elite outside the Jones's house that day, which belongs to a Robert Molyneux. And I keep seeing that same car in the car park at Belvedere House but, when I sent off a card to Swansea, it came back to an address in the city.'

'Right, that's very helpful, m'darlin', because the Vice Squad have been working on a pornography case centred on a warehouse in the city. One of the names that cropped up on the periphery is Robert Molyneux. We need to speak to him.'

I knew Eamon wasn't including me with that, but it was nice to know that my bit of information was going to help. Where had that sheet gone? I decided to leave Eamon and Irene to their flirting and left to start my first solo patrol.

I passed the control room on my way out and saw Brian regaling Derek with some story. They looked very matey. Irene had said that Brian gathered a clique. Was Brian buttering Derek up? Ray caught my eye and grimaced. Brian did spend a lot of time indoors for a patrol sergeant. I grinned my sympathy and went out.

The town was tranquil, so I decided to cut through the industrial estate and walk to the river and then maybe go back and sneak a look around Belvedere House. It was still light, and the heat wave showed no sign of abating. I loved it and hoped we would have a few more days before the rain returned.

I passed people, usually men in varying stages of sobriety, as I walked but none were causing a problem. A couple of blokes stared at me and turned to follow my progress.

'Bet she's going to see about the prozzies.' I heard one say to the other.

'Can I help you?' I asked.

'You're not going to The Capstan, are you?' the other one asked.

'Do I need to?' I replied.

'No, but if you do go, take a mate with you, 'cos you're dead little and it's dead rough in there.'

How sweet, they were concerned for my safety.

'Don't you get many foot patrols down here?' I asked.

'Cars go past sometimes but we don't often see bizzies on foot,' said one.

'And we never see diddy girl bizzies like you,' his mate added. 'A bird in blue.'

'Blue bird,' said the first man. The pair chortled at their joke.

'If you're looking to see what the cows are up to, try Municipal Road by the docks,' the second man said.

I surmised that, as I was unlikely to run into a bovine herd by the docks, it was local slang for the prostitutes the men had been talking about when we met.

'Okay, thanks for telling me.' I considered turning back but, curiosity piqued, I continued down the road until I came to The Capstan. It was a typical dockland corner pub with alternate clear and opaque windows displaying the brewery logo. I walked past, pretending not to see the faces pressed against every window watching each step I took, and went on to the docks.

I saw a girl come through the gate to the quays area a short distance ahead. My first thought was that it was Lana Jones but she was older, nineteen or twenty perhaps. She was half running and glancing behind her.

'Are you all right,' I called.

The girl paused and turned to me. I approached, noting the rapidly forming bruise on her cheek.

'What happened? Is someone chasing you? I can help you.'

The girl shook her head. 'I'm fine, just in a hurry to get home.'

'You don't look fine; you look scared and hurt.' I looked over into the dock area but there was nobody else around.

'I said I'm fine. Thank you.' The girl couldn't wait to get away.

'What's your name?' I asked.

'Why?' she countered. Belligerent.

I smiled. Phil had taught me that a smile in the face of aggression often disarmed people and made them more inclined to speak to me. Of course, there were other times where it made no difference whatsoever. The girl's expression softened. Good, it was working.

She folded her arms and smiled back. 'I'm Ruth. What's your name?'

'Sam,' I replied.

'What are you doing here by yourself, Sam?'

'Patrolling.' Hang on, when did our roles reverse? 'I'm concerned for you, Ruth.'

Ruth patted my arm. 'Well don't you worry about me, I'm fine.'

'What about that bruise?'

Ruth touched her cheek. 'I walked into a door.'

'You know I don't believe you.'

'You know I don't care.'

'Don't be like that,' I wheedled. 'If you tell me who assaulted you, I will arrest them.'

Ruth stepped away from me. 'There's no need for you to become involved. I really must get back now.'

If she wasn't willing to talk to me, or complain about an assault, there was little I could do. A job without a complaint was no job at all. Frustrating. Ruth resumed her journey at a more sedate pace. I considered walking over to the quays and nosing around, but I didn't want to tread on the Ports Police's toes, so I turned back to the streets and trudged back towards The Capstan. I would leave a note for Irene when I got back.

A couple of women teetering across the cobbles in platform shoes stopped as I walked past.

'Aw God, look at the size of her,' said one with inch-long dark roots to her blonde, feathered mane and, as my dad would say, legs up to her armpits. 'Here, love. Coo-ee, hang on a minute.'

I stopped and watched the women approach.

They drew level and smiled down at me. I really wished I had my platform shoes on, so I didn't have to look up at everyone I met.

'What are you doing down here, love?' Roots asked.

'I'm patrolling.'

'All by yourself?' She looked around as if expecting to see a Panda car hidden around the corner. Did I really look so lost and vulnerable that even the local prostitutes were concerned for my safety?

'You want to be careful being seen chatting to a copper. It'll get back,' Root's companion said.

Roots snorted. 'I work for myself, so I decide who I talk to. She's all right, look at her face; like a little angel's.' Roots gently pinched my cheek. 'What's your name, love?'

There was something infectious about Root's friendliness. She had been drinking but wasn't disorderly.

'Samantha Barrie,' I replied.

Roots squealed. 'I'm Samantha too; Karen Samantha Fitzroy. Ooh, we're like twins. That's my house there.' Karen pointed to a grey-painted, pebble-dashed terrace a few yards down the road. 'Want to come in for a cup of tea? Don't mind, do you?' She asked her friend. 'I know we said we'd go back to yours, but we can do that tomorrow.'

'Just what we need: you to befriend another copper.' Her friend folded her arms. 'Be careful, Karen.'

'Don't worry. See you tomorrow.'

Her friend sighed and walked on.

Karen turned back to me and said, 'Do you want that cuppa, Samantha?'

I could almost hear my mother shouting *Don't you dare!*, but Karen would be a useful person to know.

'I'd like that,' I said. 'Perhaps you can tell me about a girl named Ruth on the way. I met her earlier and she had a right shiner but refused to tell me anything.'

'Ruthie? A customer getting a bit too frisky probably. It happens.'

'Does she have …' I wondered how to word it. '…someone to look after her?'

'A pimp?' Karen wasn't so coy. 'She's one of Molly's girls. Molly doesn't like them to attract police attention. Ruthie probably wouldn't speak to you in case it annoyed Molly.' Karen paused awkwardly, and I guessed that, however police-friendly she was, she'd revealed more that she'd intended.

Molly the Madam: that was going to Irene. My subconscious gave me a nudge, so I listened. Molly was not such a common name in the town. Lana and Janice kept going off with Molly. Janice had contraceptives in her room despite being fifteen and a Roman Catholic. Lana's mother and sister were prostitutes. Janice and Lana were prostitutes. Oh no no no: Lana and Janice must be prostitutes.

'Let's get that tea. I've got bourbons too.' Karen pulled on my arm but, before I could take a step, a Panda car turned the corner and slowly came towards us.

I recognised the figure in the driver's seat. 'It's Inspector Tyrrell, my boss.'

'Gary!' Karen seemed equally excited to see him.

'You know Inspector Tyrrell?' I squeaked.

'I remember when he was a sprog in Odinsby. He patrolled the patch where I grew up and locked me mam up for CPL more than once. He was always polite, not like some of them.'

Well, she was fluent in police jargon, and so blasé about CPL: Common Prostitute Loitering. I would have died of shame had it been my mother. It also went some way to explain why Karen ended up working the docks.

Inspector Tyrrell pulled in to the kerb and wound down his window. 'Hiya Karen, how's business?'

Karen crouched down and rested one arm on against the car door. 'Busy. I've been on my back all afternoon.' She gave a filthy, Sid James laugh, and I couldn't help but join in.

'You are being careful, aren't you?' Inspector Tyrrell asked.

'One beating was quite enough thank you. I might be a common prostitute, but I don't loiter anymore. I only bonk the officers now. They prefer a bit of class.'

I giggled.

Karen winked at me. 'Isn't Samantha lovely?'

Inspector Tyrrell looked over to me and drew in a deep breath. I waited to hear his verdict, but he exhaled without answering.

'I just invited her in for a cup of tea, do you want one too? I've got Bourbons.'

'Sorry Karen, I came to find Sam; I need her somewhere else.'

I went to the passenger side. 'Another time, Karen.'

'Hey, Gary.' She jerked her head in my direction. 'It's been a while and you could do worse.'

I gasped and pressed my hands against my cheeks.

'Got to go, Karen. See you around.' Inspector Tyrrell drove towards the park and pulled over and picked up the car radio.

'I've found Constable Barrie on Municipal Road. All in order.'

'Roger, sir.' Derek replied. Ray must be away from the radio.

'You found me?' I was confused.

'You didn't answer your radio.'

'What!' I checked it was switched on although I had just heard Derek's voice come through it. 'I haven't heard anything, sir. I would never ignore my radio.'

'Sergeant Lewington was in the control room, Sam. He confirmed that Derek called you. Karen can be a bit full-on,' he replied. 'But you must still listen out for calls even when you are talking to people.'

'But there was nothing. Honestly, sir.'

'Maybe you were in a blank spot.'

Blank spots were the bane of police officers' lives. Sometimes, because of buildings or trees, or sometimes for no reason at all, radios refused to work. At least the boss seemed to accept that I hadn't received the transmission.

'What's the incident you need me for?' I asked.

'There isn't one. I just came looking for you when you weren't answering the radio. I didn't want to say so in front of anyone,' Inspector Tyrrell said.

'Was Karen beaten badly?' I asked.

He nodded. 'She was just eighteen. She almost died. I was the jack dealing with it and tried to encourage her to get out of the business, but it's all she's ever known. She grew up in that environment so it would have been really hard for her to think of anything beyond that, not that she got any encouragement from anyone.'

'Karen told me you locked her mother up. It's a bit like Lana Jones now: her mother and sister are prostitutes, and everyone expects that she'll follow suit.' I sighed.

The inspector was silent for a moment before speaking again. 'Phil told me what you did on nights.'

I examined my nails as I considered my answer. Phil did once say he would tell the boss if something was criminal or safety was compromised, and I suppose I had jeopardised my safety. I trusted Phil enough to know it wouldn't have been malicious, but I wished he had kept his mouth shut.

'I did it on impulse, I didn't mean any harm and I hope I didn't disrupt any operation. I did get some useful information for Irene.'

'Phil told me that too. In future, don't do something like that without letting someone know.'

'Phil explained it to me. I won't go off like that again.' I paused. 'Tonight, I saw a girl called Ruth, Karen told me she was one of Molly's girls. Janice and Lana keep going off with someone called Molly and up to now we've believed that she was a school friend, or at least someone a similar age to the girls. Last time Phil and I were at Janice's house, we found contraceptives despite her being only fifteen and Roman Catholic. Is it reasonable to suspect that Molly is an adult and Janice and probably Lana are working for Molly as prostitutes?'

Inspector Tyrrell nodded. 'That would be a reasonable assumption. Are you going to pass that on?'

I chuckled. 'Of course, although last time I put something in, it went missing. I promise I won't be rushing off into dockland to uncover a brothel.'

Inspector Tyrrell laughed. 'Glad to hear it. Just bear in mind that things happen in the background that you don't know about.'

'Can we let social services know?' I asked.

'That side of things will be dealt with, don't you worry.'

Back off, Sam. I got the message.

'I'll let you out here.' He leant over and opened my door. For a second our cheeks were an inch apart. I could have just leant forward and let my lips brush against his skin, but instead I climbed out and resumed my beat. The inspector drove off towards the station.

Chapter Fifteen

I knew it was going to be one of those days when I was sitting in parade and Alan slung a Form 52—crime booklet—across to me. It slithered onto my lap and fell to the floor before I could grab it.

'Sort that out,' was all he said.

I retrieved the booklet and flicked through it. It was one I had submitted a few days previously, only there was no crime number written in the box. When it came back from Divisional HQ, it should have been allocated a crime number. Also, the centre pages had been removed so only half the report was there.

'I submitted this once and it was intact, Sergeant Bowman.' I caught Brian's eye. 'You saw me submit it, Sarge.

'I never saw you submit a crime booklet,' Sergeant Lewington said without letting my gaze go.

Alan and Brian Lewington went back to dishing out the duties and I gazed uncomprehendingly at the booklet. Brian had been there, right next to me in fact, but he just now had looked me in the eyes and denied seeing anything.

Other pieces of work had gone missing apart from the information I had put in Irene's basket. Strange, all very strange.

Ken leaned towards me. 'You're due your quarterly review with the big boss soon, and he's red hot on paperwork.'

'You think I don't know that?' I snapped, which I instantly

regretted. 'Sorry, Ken.'

'I have something that might stop you getting stressed out,' he said. 'St John's Wort. I'll give it to you after parade.'

'What are you two whispering about?' Brian called across. 'Making arrangements for a secret tryst? Looks like you've been binned, Steve.'

'Sorry, Sarge. We were just discussing this 52,' I replied. I put my head down.

'Sam!' Sergeant Bowman sounded exasperated.

My head shot up. 'Yes, Sarge?'

'Concentrate, girl. You're covering for Ray in the control room from four o'clock.'

'Yes, Sarge.'

I caught Inspector Tyrrell watching me, his eyebrows were drawn together but not in an angry way. He looked as puzzled as I felt.

'Steve, you can cover from seven to let Sam go for her scoff, then stay on until eleven,' Alan said.

'Yes, Sarge. Is Ray off cricketing?' Steve asked.

'Merchant Navy reunion,' Alan replied.

'Do you think he took part in the Atlantic convoys?' I whispered to Ken.

'He's not quite old enough,' Ken whispered back. 'He's got some fantastic stories though. Get him chatting about it sometime.'

*

As soon as parade was over, I met Ken by his locker. He pulled down a box and rooted through it, until he settled on a small glass bottle with a dropper lid.

'Here you are. Just a couple of drops every few hours and you'll feel less stressed.'

I took the bottle from him, opened it, and sniffed the dark liquid inside.

'This is legal?'

'Do you think I'd have it in my locker if it wasn't? It's just a herbal remedy; it won't harm you,' he assured me.

I took a couple of drops, then slipped the bottle into my handbag. 'Thanks.'

Ken's eyes moved to the left, just as the force of a hard slap to my bottom pushed me forward. I spun around holding my stinging behind.

'Brian! What the hell! That hurt,' I shouted.

'I said you were planning a tryst.'

'This isn't a tryst; he's letting me have some St John's Wort.' I pulled the bottle from my bag and shoved it under his nose. He was lucky I didn't shove it *up* his nose. 'See.'

Brian scrutinised the bottle. 'I heard you're into weird, witchy stuff, Ken.'

'It's herbal, not witchy,' Ken retorted.

'Whatever.' Brian handed the bottle back. 'You need to get outside instead of getting cosy in here. You're slipping, Sammy, and people are starting to notice.'

I felt tears prickle, but I would not let Brian see; it would give him power over me and I didn't want that toe-rag to have any power over me.

'That's uncalled for, Sarge,' Ken said, bless him. 'She had no problems when she was with Phil.'

'Everyone does okay in company; the testing time is when you go solo.' Brian jerked his head towards the door. 'Out, both of you.'

Ken and I trooped past Brian and, as I passed him, he squeezed my bottom.

I spun around. 'Keep your paws to yourself.'

'Lighten up, Sammy.'

'Touch me again and I'll crime it.'

Something flared in his eyes but he laughed. 'Don't make threats you can't follow through. Now, get out.'

Inspector Tyrrell had once told me to speak to him if I had any concerns. I did have concerns, but what could I say? If I mentioned this latest incident, the inspector would be obliged to act, but it would be my word against Brian's and, if I really was failing my probation, it might be construed as me lashing out. But there had a few odd occurrences apart from the latest, and I was fairly sure he had deliberately lied on parade. I decided I should start keeping a diary.

*

At 1600 hours, Derek took over the radio from Ray while I made us both a hot drink. The boss came back from his run and, as usual, called into the control room.

'Good run, sir?'

'Not bad thanks, Derek. Care to join me tomorrow?'

Derek lolled back, patted his generous abdomen, and sighed in contentment. 'I prefer a leisurely game of snooker, thank you sir.'

'Let me know if you change your mind.' Inspector Tyrrell turned to me.

'Milk no sugar,' I said.

He winked. 'Good girl.'

He jogged upstairs while I popped a teabag into a mug, ready to add hot water when he was showered and changed.

'What are these lights doing here, Derek?' I kicked at the lanterns that were usually found at the side of roads hanging on skips and suchlike, but now cluttered the telex room.

Derek twisted around in his chair. 'They need to go to the equipment room. Will you take them up when you've done the tea?'

'I thought they went outside in that end garage.'

'Cones and stuff go there; those lights go into the equipment room upstairs because they're electric and the damp gets to them. It's next door to the gents' toilet.' Derek waved a hand in the general direction of the stairs. 'Take them now while it's not so busy.'

I knew where the gents' loo was, but I had never been into

the room next door. I picked up three of the lanterns and went upstairs; I would have to come back for the rest.

I counted along the doors and stopped at the one after the gents' toilet. There was no handle on the door, so I turned my back and pushed against it. I was surprised to encounter a second door and for a moment I wondered if I had entered the men's toilet by mistake. I pushed backwards through the second door and turned around.

A towel hung on one of the pegs that ran along a wall and the air was thick with pine scent.

Men's showers! I turned to get out pronto, just as Inspector Tyrrell emerged, dripping wet and unselfconsciously naked. He stopped so quickly he skidded, and I whirled around to face the opposite wall only to find I was facing a long mirror that gave me an unrestricted view of the inspector's gloriously unclothed body.

'What the hell are you doing?' Inspector Tyrrell shouted as he grabbed the towel and held it in front of him.

'I'm so sorry,' I cried and spun back to face him and scrunched my eyes shut. 'Derek told me this was an equipment room.' I sidled towards the door.

'Does this look like a bloody equipment room? Get out!'

I juggled the lights to free a hand, so I could open the door. 'Derek said it was. This isn't my fault.' I ran out.

As I exited, a loud cheer went up. Derek and half the station stood outside. I glared at Derek, who held his sides as he laughed.

'Derek, you absolute sod…' Hang on, we both were upstairs. 'Who's got the radio?' I shouted. I dropped the lights, pushed past him and ran downstairs.

'Mike Two to control,' Phil called as I burst into the empty control room.

How long had he been calling? I snatched up the handset. 'Go ahead Mike Two.'

'Just to let you know that the water board say the works in Village Road will go on for a few days. Can you update the sheet?'

'Will do.' I moved across to my seat and marked the sheet of the incident Phil had been sent to, relieved that it had been a routine call.

Derek came in, still chortling and carrying the lamps I had dropped. Brian came in with him.

'I said it would work, didn't I?' Brian whispered to Derek, just loud enough for me to hear.

'Phil was calling on the radio and nobody was here! What if it had been a scramble?' I was breathless with embarrassment and anger.

'I was here,' Brian said.

'No, you weren't; the office was empty when I got here!'

'What's going on?' Alan came in.

'Young Sam here has just disturbed the boss in the shower.' Derek dumped the lights on the floor and started to laugh again.

'You told me it was an equipment room,' I wailed.

'The equipment room is that end garage outside,' Alan said.

'I know, but he said the lights would be affected by the damp because they're electric and they had to go upstairs.'

'How much damp do you think they're exposed to at the side of a road? They're designed for that,' Alan explained, slowly.

'I didn't think of that.' Why hadn't I thought of that? It was so bloody obvious.

'You have to know where to draw the line, Derek,' Alan said.

'It was just a laugh, Alan.' Derek wafted his hand around dismissing Alan's concerns.

'You left the radio—' I stopped speaking and turned away as Inspector Tyrrell, now back in uniform, came in, but he must have heard me.

'Derek, a word.'

Derek shot me a dirty look. 'Yes, boss.'

Inspector Tyrrell looked past Derek to Alan. 'Would you cover the radio for a few minutes?'

'Yes, Gary.'

Inspector Tyrrell looked down his nose at Brian. 'You're not needed here. Go out and do some patrolling.'

Alan sat at the radio, and Inspector Tyrrell gestured for Derek to follow him.

'You need to be careful of making allegations, Sammy,' Brian said from the doorway. 'Derek would never be so irresponsible as to leave the radio. He asked me to cover while he went upstairs.'

'But you weren't here, you came in with Derek,' I argued.

'But I was.' He turned to Alan. 'Wasn't I here when you came in?'

Alan regarded him for a moment. 'Put those lights into the equipment store on your way out.'

Brian picked up the lights and left. I sat down and put my head in my hands.

*

Derek came back about fifteen minutes later with a face like thunder. Alan gave up his seat and returned to his office with Inspector Tyrrell, no doubt to discuss what had just been said.

Derek stuck a finger almost under my nose. 'In this job, we stick together. We don't go ratting to the boss.'

I slammed my hands onto the desk and stood up. 'Don't you dare blame me because you're in trouble, Derek Kidd. Take it up with your new best friend. This is your own fault for toadying up to Brian. You embarrassed the boss as well as me and you did leave the radio unattended. Brian was not here.'

'Sam,' Alan called across the enquiry office. 'A minute, please.'

I briefly looked back at Derek, but he was responding to a call. I went into Alan's office.

Alan sat at the desk and Inspector Tyrrell was on his usual perch. I felt my cheeks take on their usual red when in his presence and stared at the floor.

'Sam, what happened, happened. There's no point getting all awkward about it. We have to work together so we need to move on.'

'Yes, sir.'

'Look at me, Sam.' Inspector Tyrrell said. I raised my eyes and chewed my lip.

The inspector cocked his head. 'See: it's not so bad. If I can get over it, so can you.'

'Yes, sir.' I immediately lowered my eyes.

'I just need to ask you about the radio. I know Derek was upstairs because I heard you shout at him. What happened after that?'

'I got to the office and heard Phil shouting up, so I answered. Derek came in after me and Brian came in with him. Then Alan came in.'

Alan nodded in agreement.

'Are you sure the office was empty when you got there? Could Brian have been in the telex room or the enquiry office?' Inspector Tyrrell asked.

'The office was empty,' I said. 'Brian wasn't in the enquiry office; he came in from the other side with Derek.'

'Okay, thanks. I'll speak to Brian later. Dismissed.'

'Thank you, sir.'

I returned to the control room and Derek glowered at me but I ignored him. I had other things on my mind, like how was I ever going to stop myself blushing around the inspector, especially now I knew what he kept in his shorts.

Chapter Sixteen

After refs I went out on patrol. I was getting used to walking out by myself and even found it liberating. I had my beat and I could go in whatever direction I chose in that area. It was up to me how I dealt with incidents and, so far, I hadn't encountered anything that I hadn't been able to handle. I decided that, despite Brian's comments, my next review would be all right and I would be able to continue with my probation.

Instead of drifting over towards Belvedere House as had become my habit, I walked to the new maisonettes. It was still sunny and hot so I wasn't surprised to see that several flats had washing hanging from racks attached to their window sills. One or two had tea towels hanging from their letterboxes. It seemed a strange way to air washing but who was I to judge.

As I approached, the towels were whipped back through the letterboxes by unseen hands. I was pondering on this when Ray's voice came over the radio.

'4912 from control. Location for Mike Sierra Two, please.'

Oh great, why was Brian looking for me? It better had not be about the Derek incident. I was not going to lie for him; that control room had been deserted. '4912, I'm on High Lake Road, near the post box.'

'Remain there. Mike Sierra Two will RV with you.'

'Roger.' I would have to ask someone about the tea towel thing later.

I probably alarmed the residents as I paced up and down a twenty-foot length of road, awaiting Brian's arrival and rehearsing scenarios that might come from the day's events.

'Hop in, Sammy,' Brian called through the open window as he drew up.

I climbed in and waited for him to speak first.

'We've got to help ambo pick up a loony. The doctor and social services are there to section him, but he isn't cooperating, so they need us there.'

This was one type of incident I had never dealt with, and I inwardly boiled at Brian's callous attitude.

We drove to a house near to where Karen Fitzroy lived, and pulled up behind an ambulance. A male aged about forty was rampaging around the pavement, naked except for a blanket wrapped around his shoulders. His screams and shouts had brought neighbours to their doors.

'It's little Samantha. Coo-ee, Sam, it's me!' I turned around and saw Karen waving.

'Friend of yours?' Brian asked.

'Not exactly,' I replied. I waved to Karen. 'Can't stop, work to do.'

Karen scuttled over to me. 'Poor John's not been well for a while you know. In fact, he's not been right since he left the army. It's been hard on his mum.' She pointed to an older, distraught woman sitting on the doorstep.

'We're here to take him to hospital,' I said. 'You said his name's John?'

'When you've quite finished yattering...' Brian shouted from the ambulance.

'Misery arse.' Karen scowled towards Sergeant Lewington.

'That's our new sergeant, Brian Lewington.'

Karen stepped—no, stumbled—back one pace. 'Brian Lewington?'

'You know him?'

'I know *of* him. I thought Lew was in Odinsby.'

'Lew ?' I gulped as I did whenever I heard that name. I shouldn't let it affect me still. People played with names all the time, and it was almost to be expected that someone named Lewington would be called Lou, or maybe given how the name was spelt: Lew.

'Sam, move your arse,' Brian shouted.

'Better go. I'll be in touch.'

Karen nodded but her eyes never left Brian.

When I got to the ambulance, Brian was talking to the doctor, a short Indian man I hadn't encountered before. John's mother was still sitting on the front step, weeping. My heart went out to her; I couldn't imagine the pain of watching her son suffer in this way.

'Sam, you keep the doors open while I help the ambo get him into the van,' Brian said.

Three men strode towards the screaming man and grabbed hold of him.

He immediately lashed out in every direction, connecting soundly with Brian's nose. Brian staggered back, cursing loudly as blood ran onto his lip. John's mother stood up and wailed for him to stop. John grabbed the ears of one of the ambulancemen and his cries joined in with the cacophony of sound. Unable to stand John's distress any longer, I ran over to him and slapped his bare arm.

'John, stop that at once!'

He paused and focused on me. I braced myself for an attack, but his eyes widened and he released the ambulanceman.

'Mary!' John fell to his knees in front of me. 'I prayed you would come to me. Hail Mary, full of grace, the Lord is with thee...' John's voice became unintelligible as he bent forward and buried his head in his hands.

Uh-oh. I pulled his arms. 'Get up.'

John remained crouched before me, muttering Hail Marys. I saw Karen slip past the crowd and put her arms around John's mother. She really was a caring person; I liked her. She and John's mother looked at me expectantly. The crowd had become silent and even Brian looked on, slack-jawed.

'What do I do?' I mouthed at Brian.

'Get him in the ambulance,' he mouthed back.

I leant forward and tapped John on the shoulder. 'John.' He looked up but didn't make eye contact. 'John, stand up.'

John slowly raised himself up and stood before me with his head bowed, hands folded in front offering a modicum of modesty, thank goodness.

'Look at me, John.'

John slowly moved his eyes to meet mine, although his head remained bowed.

'John, I want you to get into the ambulance. These men will take you to hospital.'

He looked anxiously around.

'It's all right; they're here to help you.' I took his arm and guided him gently to the ambulance and he meekly climbed in and sat on the bench. I heard the crowd murmuring.

'Well done, Sam,' said Brian.

'I don't like pretending to be the Virgin Mary,' I said.

'Oh, I don't know; it seems apt to me.' Brian winked.

'Tosser.'

'Mary, Mary, don't leave me,' John shouted as I stepped back onto the road. He leapt up as the ambulancemen tried to close the door.

I climbed the step into the ambulance and pointed at the bench. 'Sit down and be quiet, John.'

He immediately did as I requested. His rapturous gaze was unnerving.

'You've got the magic touch,' the doctor said.

'Why does he think I'm Mary?' I asked.

The doctor pointed to my hat. 'The sun keeps glinting off your cap badge. He's probably seeing that as a halo.'

I snatched my hat off, but John's expression didn't change. The damage, if you could call it that, had been done.

'I don't suppose you could spare your lady policeman for a

couple of hours, could you?' the doctor said to Brian. 'She calms him. I think it would be a good idea for her to come to the hospital with him.'

I shook my head. I didn't want to remain with a naked man who thought I was the Holy Mother, but Brian agreed.

'That's all right isn't it?' the doctor said to the ambulance driver.

'Sure. It'll make a nice change to have a pretty face on board.' The driver winked at me.

I politely laughed, then resentfully sat opposite John, who promptly fell to his knees again. At least that was better than him sitting opposite me displaying his family jewels.

'Get up, John. My name's Samantha, not Mary.'

John showed no sign of understanding me, but he sat back on the bench, whispering prayers. The ambulance man threw the blanket across John's lap and closed the doors, and so began the second most uncomfortable journey of my life.

*

John was still praying when we arrived at the hospital forty minutes later. I had repeatedly told him I was not Mary but, in the end, I had given up. He shrank back when the doors opened and a couple of men in white coats boarded the ambulance.

'John, relax. They just want to make you better,' I said. John did relax.

'He seems to listen to you; will you come to the ward with him?' asked one of the men.

'Do I have time?' I asked the ambulance crew.

'Sure. We'll go and get a brew. Meet us in the canteen when you're finished.'

I stood up and indicated to John he should follow me. He stumbled from the ambulance and obediently walked to the ward flanked by the men in white, while I brought up the rear.

The ward wasn't as I expected. Instead of the terrible, bleak asylums of fiction, it was a bright place with several rooms offering different activities from TV to arts and crafts. The only difference was, instead of the open desk of a regular ward, the nurses were in a locked, glass-fronted office positioned in a corner to see everything that was happening.

'Leave him to us now,' said a male nurse who had left the office as we arrived. I did a double take—male nurses were rare—but it seemed that mental health had men in greater numbers. It occurred to me that he and I were in the same position; we were both minorities in our professions.

'What's your name?' I asked.

'Peter,' he replied.

How apt. I touched John on the arm and he bowed his head. 'This is Peter. I want you to go with him. He'll look after you.'

John looked uncertainly at Peter. 'Don't leave me, Blessed Mary. I love you.'

'I have to go, John. Do what Peter tells you to do. He'll keep you safe.'

Peter took John's arm and gently led him away. Although compliant, John stared at me over his shoulder until he disappeared into another room.

I exhaled in relief. I had no paperwork to deal with, as Brian was doing that back in Wyre Hall, but I needed to update my pocket book. I found my way to the canteen and joined the ambulance men.

'Brew?' the driver asked.

'Yes please. Are there any biscuits?' I figured I might as well take advantage of the situation. He pushed a minipack of shortbreads towards me. I took a biscuit and dipped it in my tea. It was a good time to write up my pocket book, which reminded me about the tea towel in the letterbox.

'I saw something strange today,' I said.

'Apart from John?'

I smiled. 'Before that, I saw a tea towel hanging out of the letterbox at a couple of houses. It seemed odd.'

'It means they're selling,' the ambulance driver said.

'Selling what?' I asked.

He leant towards me and lowered his voice. 'Drugs: they're indicating they're available for sale.'

My jaw dropped. 'Why don't they teach us this stuff at training school?'

'They probably think everyone knows already.' He finished his tea.

'Well I've never heard of it.' I felt a bit foolish.

'That's because you're a nice girl and your parents have probably protected you from the nasty side of life,' he said. 'Ready to get back?' They stood up.

I grabbed the last biscuit before following them out of the hospital for the ride back to Wyre Hall.

*

Brian dropped to one knee and genuflected when I walked into the office.

'Don't,' I said. 'It was bad enough having John think I was Mary.'

'The Virgin has spoken.' Brian stood up and brushed the dust from his trousers.

'Stop teasing her, Brian,' Alan said. 'Have you finished that file?'

'I just need Sammy's statement and report from the hospital, and then it can go off.'

'Do the statement then get back out for the last hour,' Alan said to me.

I went to the report writing room and scribbled my version of events. I wanted to go back to speak to Karen before I finished duty, so I was in a hurry to get outside.

I took the finished report to the sergeants' office and handed it to Brian.

'I'll give you a lift out, Sammy,' Brian said.

I didn't want a lift out with Brian; I didn't want to be near him and I didn't want him to know where I was going, but I couldn't say that. Instead, I mumbled a, 'Yes, Sarge,' and trailed after him. The sun had set but it was still sweltering. Surely this weather couldn't hold for much longer.

'You were mistaken about the office. I was there,' he said without preamble.

'Stop lying.' I was past being polite with him.

'Your word against mine and Derek's.' He grinned.

I didn't grin. 'I'm telling the truth. You are lying, and I think Alan and the boss know that.'

He looked sideways at me. 'Be careful, Sammy.'

'Or?' I really didn't have enough service in to be goading a sergeant—he could cause me to fail my probation—but I was irritated and let it show.

He didn't answer. We got into the Panda car and he said, 'Did you give any thought to our conversation the other day?'

'No, because I don't want to moonlight; it's frowned upon, as you should know, and I don't want to go out with you.' I didn't even try to be polite.

'Shame.' Brian drove across Nelson Square and then on, into the docks. This was Ports Police territory; we had no need to patrol there.

'Where are we going?' I asked trying to hide my alarm.

'I like looking at the river. It's peaceful and beautiful and hides so much.'

My heart thumped and my breathing quickened. There were plenty of places to view the river without going into the docks.

'I think I should go back to my beat.'

'You're with me so you won't get into trouble if the boss sees you.'

'Even so, I would like you to take me back.'

Brian continued past a block of shipping containers and turned down to the waterside. I couldn't hide my agitation any longer; as soon as he stopped, I jumped from the car.

'Where are you going?' Brian called.

'Back to the station. I shouldn't be here.'

'You shouldn't be back at the station either.'

True, but I felt very unsafe where I was. I could radio in for assistance, but what would I say? My sergeant had taken me off my beat to look at the river? It was weird but not criminal.

My legs shook as I struck out towards Belvedere House. I had no plan, but I guessed that Brian would try to divert me. I wasn't wrong.

'Come on, Sammy, stop messing and get in. I'll take you to the main road if that's what you want.'

'I'll walk, thank you,' I called back.

Brian started the engine and spun the car around and pulled up beside me. I stood with my thumb hovering over the transmit button: part warning, part reassurance.

'Give me your pocketbook.'

I handed my notebook to him and hoped he didn't notice my hands shaking.

'Now get in the car so I can drive you back or I'll write in here that I reprimanded you for being off your beat. You have a review coming up, haven't you?'

Police notebooks are classed as official documents and a remark like that would be seen by the inspector and the superintendent. I couldn't risk a comment like that in my note book. I reluctantly got into the car.

'That was blackmail.'

'Yes, Sammy. It was, and it worked.' He handed my notebook back.

'Bastard.'

'It's been said,' Brian laughed.

He drove to the main road and dropped me off. 'I'll see you at knocking-off time.'

I didn't look back as I walked off, back straight, head high, tongue pressed hard against my palate. As soon as he was gone, I slipped into an alleyway, took a deep breath and let the tears flow.

Chapter Seventeen

It was the following afternoon before I could call at Karen's house. She ushered me in and bustled about with the kettle.

'Is John settled in?' she asked.

'I think so. He was compliant enough when I left him.'

'I hope they keep him in for a while,' Karen said. 'Give his mum a rest.'

'Doesn't he have medication?' I asked.

'Yes, but as soon as he starts to feel better he stops taking it and ends up ill again. His poor mum is at her wit's end.' Karen disappeared into the kitchen.

'I wanted to ask you about Brian Lewington,' I called through. 'You seemed rattled when you saw him.'

She came to the door drying a mug on a tea towel. 'I've never seen him before, but I've heard the name several times. There's a lot of rumours about him being involved with some bad people. He looks after them and they look after him.'

Everything connected to Brian was rumour and gossip. Surely some of it had to be true. I nibbled my thumbnail, then stopped because it was something the inspector did, and I was starting to copy him.

'What do you mean?' I asked.

'I don't know the details, but I heard he's involved with a gang who specialise in prostitution and pornography. Lew's not above deflecting police attention from them and, in exchange, they let him use the girls they control. Story is Lew once caught the clap, so he only goes for the young ones now. Molly's cornered that market around here, so Molly and Lew have a mutually beneficial partnership going. But there are others beside Molly.'

Molly. There was that name again.

'Brian "keeps them clean",' I said, air-drawing the inverted commas. 'How did you hear about this?'

'People talk to me, tell me things,' Karen replied.

Yes, I could see people talking to Karen, she had experience on the streets and on the ships. She had maintained her sympathetic and caring nature and was possibly the only source of compassion and empathy they had. She was the ideal person for people around here to talk to.

'This sounds like a gangster movie. We don't have proper gangsters here.'

Karen put the mug down and poured out the tea. 'We have real live gangsters right here. And kids who like to think they're gangsters. They know they have nothing to fear around here, nobody is going to report anything.'

'Are they scared?' I asked.

'Of course they're scared.' Karen said.

'That's why your friend told you to be careful about being friendly to police when we met,' I commented.

'I'm an independent, they don't control me; not that they haven't tried to recruit me.'

I accepted a mug of tea, which tasted awful but I drank it anyway. 'Isn't it dangerous to refuse to cooperate?'

Karen sat down with her drink. 'As long as I keep out of their way, they leave me alone.'

'I always imagined those types were in London.'

Karen giggled. 'Kids around here grow up knowing who not to cross.'

'Who?' I asked.

Karen paused before answering. 'Molly and Ted Bulwer.'

'Who's Ted Bulwer?'

'He runs an operation in the city. Molly does some recruiting for him.'

'And Brian is in with these people.'

'It's only rumour.' She cocked her head. 'No, more than that. Let's call it… unconfirmed intelligence. And if anyone asks, you didn't hear it from me; Molly can be a bit rough with people who attract police attention.'

I should report what she's told me, but I didn't want to put her in danger. It also explained why Janice was so cagey and anxious we didn't track down Molly. I needed to speak to Irene, or Eamon, or the boss. Even Phil.

My radio crackled disrupting my thoughts. '4912 from control.'

'Go ahead,' I responded.

'Can you make Schooner Street? Janice Alderman has been reported missing again and it's believed she is with Lana Jones.'

I rolled my eyes. That girl was a pest. 'Roger. Has Lana been reported, too?'

'Negative,' Ray replied.

I swigged the last of my tea. 'Got to go, Karen. Thanks for the tea and the info.'

'Go carefully, Sam.'

That wasn't just someone saying goodbye. There was something about her look that told me it was a genuine warning. I felt a chill run down my back, but I smiled and waved as I left.

*

It only took me five minutes to get to Schooner Street from Karen's house. As I turned into the street, I saw the yellow Lotus Elite parked in the street. I nipped into an alleyway behind the houses and peeped out at the car. After about five minutes, I saw the well-dressed Robert come out of the Jones's house with Janice. They stopped on the pavement and he handed Janice an envelope much like the one I had seen in Glynis's kitchen, but not as obviously filled. They exchanged a few words, then he drove off and Janice returned to the house. What an interesting little exchange. Was Robert one of those people Karen had been talking about, I wondered? He evidently wasn't worried about being seen with Janice. And what was in that envelope? I radioed in to ask for a car to meet me in a nearby street. Maybe I was being over-cautious, but I didn't want Janice to see me and make off before I could stop her.

Phil pulled up a couple of minutes later. I quickly explained the situation to him and together we knocked at the Jones's door.

'For fuck's sake,' Connie said when she opened the door. 'Jan, you've got to stop bringing coppers to our door, Molly's going to hit the roof.'

So it seemed that Karen was right. Even Connie was concerned at the frequency of our visits to Schooner Street, and Molly's reaction.

We stepped inside. Janice was sitting on the sofa, counting money from the envelope Robert had given her.

'That's a lot of cash,' I commented. 'Where did you get it?'

She stuffed it back into the envelope and scowled at me. 'Nothing to do with you.'

'I think it is. I saw Robert give it to you. We need to speak to him.'

Janice blanched. 'You can't.'

'I warned you about drawing attention to us, Jan,' Connie said.

I got a little subconscious kick again. Did Robert work for Molly, maybe as an enforcer or something?

'Come on, let's get you home.' Phil went outside. Janice scowled at me, then followed him, and I brought up the rear.

*

In Sandringham Boulevard, Pamela alternately screamed at then hugged Janice, while Mr Alderman paced the hearth rug. When they were spent, and I could get a word in, I said to Mrs Alderman,

'Does Janice have a bank or a savings account?'

'What? Yes. A post office account.'

'Can I see the book please?'

Janice's head spun around. 'That's mine.'

'Don't worry, I just want to look at it.'

Pamela disappeared for a minute or two and returned white-faced with the book in her hand. 'Janice, how did you get so much?'

Janice snatched the book, but Mr Alderman took the book from her and looked inside.

'Seven hundred pounds!'

'How much is in the envelope, Janice?' I asked.

'What envelope?' Janice feigned innocence.

'The envelope in your bag.'

Pamela seized Janice's bag and tipped it onto the carpet. Mr Alderman grabbed the envelope that fell amongst the makeup and tissues and pulled out the money.

'There's...' he flicked through the notes. 'Seventy-five pounds here.'

'It's mine. I earned it,' Janice wailed.

'How?' Pamela asked.

'I have a job.' Janice jutted her chin.

'No Saturday girl I know of earns that,' Phil said.

'What do you do that pays so much?' Mr Alderman shouted.

'I'm a model. A photographic model,' Janice shouted back.

Mr Alderman threw the money at her. 'Jezebel!'

Janice scrabbled on the floor for the notes.

'We need to speak to the photographer,' Phil said to Mr Alderman. 'They probably have no idea she's only fifteen. Do you know who it is?'

Phil didn't know what I knew. I didn't think that the photographer would give two hoots about her age, and I doubted that she was modelling this season's fashions.

'Janice, who is the photographer?' I asked.

'I don't know his name. He's in a studio in the city, near the river.'

'How did you get involved in something like this?' Pam Alderman asked. Her voice quiet, defeated.

'A girl at school does it.' Janice hung her head.

'Which girl?' Mr Alderman snapped. 'Lana?' Janice nodded. He turned to us. 'I want you to arrest that girl.'

'We'll speak to Lana,' I said. 'However, I think both girls are being exploited by someone else.' I addressed Janice. 'Please get out of this situation. Just stay away from Molly.'

'It isn't that easy,' she said.

'Of course it is. You're forbidden to go to Lana's, you don't go to the city, and you don't speak to Molly again,' Mr Alderman said.

Janice shook her head. 'You wouldn't understand. Lana and I are buddies.'

I was beginning to get a glimmer of understanding. It was easy, even fun to start with, but then it was hard to break away from Molly.

'Let's leave these people in peace, Sam,' Phil said.

We went back to the Panda.

'Can you give me a lift into the station?' I asked. I wanted to complete the file and pass the latest little snippet on to Irene and, if he was around, speak to Eamon.

'Sure, hop in. I was going back there for refs anyway.'

I looked at my watch. 'I hadn't realised it was that time. Perfect.'

*

Neither Irene nor Eamon were there when I got back. I didn't want to leave a note in the basket after the last piece of information I left went missing, so I went to the CID office intending to leave a message directly on Eamon's desk. However, as I approached, I could see Brian was already there, rummaging around the DS's desk. Nobody else was around. I was not going in there, and now I knew to be careful what I left in the CID office too.

Without drawing attention to myself, I went for refs.

Chapter Eighteen

Ray knocked on the glass partition as I walked past the control room on my way out. He held his thumb and pinkie to his face, indicating that I had a phone call.

'It's a woman who insisted on talking to you. She wouldn't tell us what she wanted,' Ray said when I went in.

I picked up the telephone handset. 'Hello, Constable Barrie speaking.'

'Is that you, Sam? It's Karen. You've got to get to Quay Five right away. Welsh Elsie has gone on board a container ship. I didn't want to tell the bloke I just spoke to; they wouldn't take it seriously, but I knew you would.'

The docks were divided into several quays that were known simply by their numbers. Quay Five was the deepest and used by the largest ships, which were popular with the prostitutes. I had never met Welsh Elsie but her tough reputation was known throughout the town. It was rumoured that she was strong enough to take on any man in a fist fight—and win. That she went onto the ship was not unusual.

'What's your concern, Karen?' I asked.

'She's got her daughter with her. Bernadette is only thirteen or fourteen. It's not right, but Elsie said it was time to introduce her to the job.' Karen's voice had that slight high pitch that told me this was a genuine call. 'You need to get here before it's too late.'

'Okay, calm down, Karen. I'll round up some help and come over.'

I heard Karen's sigh of relief. 'I knew I could trust you. I don't like grassing on one of the girls, but this is wrong.'

'It certainly is. It might be an idea for you to lie low, I've heard Welsh Elsie can be rough and she won't appreciate that you made the call.'

'It's nice of you to think of me, but I'm not by myself here.'

I heard others clucking in the background, confirming what Karen had told me.

'Okay, leave it with me, Karen.' But this was more than I could deal with alone.

'Trouble?' Ray asked as I replaced the receiver.

'I think there's a child in danger. I need to speak to the boss.'

Ray pointed to the sergeants' office. 'I saw him go in there.'

I went to the sergeants' office and peered in through the open door. Alan was sitting at the desk and Inspector Tyrrell was perched next to him. They stopped talking and turned to me. The inspector looked directly into my eyes and I felt a pang deep inside. Dammit, I couldn't be distracted now.

'Welsh Elsie has taken her young daughter onto a container ship on Quay Five to introduce her to the job, and I think we need to go and get her,' I blurted.

Alan stood up and Inspector Tyrrell jumped from his perch.

'What? How long ago was this?' Inspector Tyrrell asked.

'I've only just received the call. I can't be certain how long it is since she went on board,' I replied. 'Do I pass it on to the Ports Police?'

Without answering, Inspector Tyrrell rushed through to the control room and I ran after him with Alan.

'Ray, get Steve's location and tell him I'll pick him up. Get Phil to pick up Ken and tell them to RV with me at Quay Five. I'll take Sam.' The boss turned to Derek. 'Start a job sheet: Welsh Elsie has taken her daughter onto a ship at Quay Five. Then ring the Ports Police to meet us.'

Ray gasped and even Derek looked disturbed, but then he spoilt it by saying, 'What do you expect? It was inevitable that any child of Welsh Elsie's was going to end up on the docks.'

In my admittedly limited experience, although their lives were a million miles away from mine, the working girls had a clear code of conduct. Not all were as open and friendly to police as Karen, but they knew right from wrong, and Welsh Elsie had crossed that boundary.

'I'll contact social services,' Alan said, breaking into my thoughts.

'Ring the Children's Hospital too,' Gary said. 'We might need to take her there.'

'I'll let Sergeant Lewington know.' Ray turned to the radio.

'Belay that. Normal life goes on and we need some supervision on the street,' the boss said.

Ray hesitated, then nodded and started to direct the patrols as instructed. Interesting that the boss didn't want Brian involved. As patrol sergeant, he should have a part in this, but perhaps I was reading too much into it. As the boss said, we needed supervision on the street to assist with other incidents.

'Alan, if Brian comes in, kick his arse back out. I don't want him getting in the way.' The boss definitely wanted Brian sidelined. Very interesting.

Alan nodded once and returned to his office.

'Come on, Sam.' Inspector Tyrrell and I ran to his car and we shot off to collect Steve, who was waiting a few streets away.

'What's going on, sir?' Steve asked as he climbed into the back.

'Welsh Elsie has taken her daughter onto a ship,' Inspector Tyrrell replied.

'Why would she do that?' Steve asked.

I twisted around and lifted an eyebrow. Steve stared back for a few seconds, then the penny dropped and so did his jaw.

The inspector stamped on the accelerator and we raced to Quay Five where Phil and Ken were already waiting.

The sun was setting, which cast a golden glow across the scene.

An artist would have been in raptures about the light and colours, but we had more urgent things to consider.

Phil and Ken came over almost before Inspector Tyrrell came to a stop.

'We're going on that ship to get Welsh Elsie's underaged daughter.' The boss pointed to a huge, orangey red painted ship.

'I thought we needed special permission to board the ships, sir?' Ken said.

'Sam has received good information that there is a child in immediate danger on there. We don't need permission for that.' Inspector Tyrrell moved towards the gangplank and we went after him. The metal rail was hot to touch from the relentless sun, so I put my hands in my pocket as I ascended and hoped I wouldn't fall.

At the head of the gangplank a crewman, African in origin with a round face and a flat, wide nose, stepped in front of the boss.

'You have permission?' the crewman rumbled.

'There is a child on this ship, and we have come for her,' Inspector Tyrrell stated.

'No child, no child.' The man tried to jostle us from the ship.

Gesturing for us to follow, Inspector Tyrrell brushed past the man and headed off into the living area of the ship. The man ran after us shouting in a clicking language none of us understood.

Following the inspector's lead, we walked up and down white-painted corridors that all looked the same, opening closed doors.

'Bernadette,' I called in the hope she would reply before the growing group of crewmen became aggressive. 'Bernadette, I need to know you're all right.'

I pulled open one door and found myself in a recreation area furnished with metal tables and several soft chairs with violent-orange cushions. A television bolted high onto a wall blared out inane adverts. A girl sat at one table with two men. A small pile of banknotes lay on the table between them. I gave thanks that we had arrived in time.

'Here!' I called to the others.

The girl looked up and I saw a flicker of recognition in her eyes, but I couldn't place her.

Steve and Ken dashed over, and each stood over a man.

Inspector Tyrrell picked up the notes. 'Let's see how much an underaged girl is worth these days.' He counted out the money. 'Twenty pounds.'

'Come on, Bernadette. Let's get you out of here and safe.' I deliberately kept my voice low. I didn't want to alarm the child, but she shrank away from me.

'Mam!' she called.

A large woman with matted, yellow-blonde hair stormed into the room.

'What the fuck's going on?' she shouted in a heavy Welsh accent. This had to be Welsh Elsie and I could see how she got her rough reputation. 'Don't you lay a fucking finger on her or I'll break your fucking arm!' she bellowed.

'But you don't mind them screwing her for twenty quid?' Phil gestured towards the men and the money.

'Twenty?' Welsh Elsie turned to the crewman who had tried to block our entry. 'Molly promised me fifty!'

Molly again!

'Twenty is still twice what we pay you.'

Welsh Elsie swung a meaty fist into his face and his lips exploded in a spray of blood.

'Phil, help Sam get Bernadette out of here,' Inspector Tyrrell said.

Phil and I took an arm each and pulled the screaming child off the ship. As we disembarked, the Port Police arrived.

'They're in the recreation room, mate,' Phil called to the newcomers.

They waved and ran up the gangplank, evidently more accustomed to being on ships than we were.

Phil and I took Bernadette to the Panda and sat her down. I climbed in beside her. She had stopped screaming and now just sniffed as tears ran down her cheeks.

'You're safe now,' I said.

'I haven't done anything.' Bernadette sniffed again.

Phil got into the driver's seat and set off for the station.

'You're not under arrest; we rescued you,' I said as calmly as possible.

'Rescued me?' Bernadette dried her eyes on the back of her hand.

'Do you know what was going to happen?' I asked.

'Mam said they would give me money if I showed them my foo.'

'Those men wanted sex, Bernadette.'

Bernadette's eyes widened. She didn't say another word as we drove back to the station.

Inspector Tyrrell passed responsibility for Bernadette, and the paperwork, to me. It was quite a major job for someone with as little service as I had. Whilst I was waiting for social services to arrive, I sat with Bernadette in the report writing room to begin the file. Apart from my own statement, I would need statements from everyone involved. I would have to get a copy of the social worker's report, speak to Karen to see if she was willing to go to court: although I knew the answer to that one. I had to do a crime booklet, a full report on the circumstances and the reasons for removing Bernadette, and CID would marry up my file with the files on Welsh Elsie and the men. There was a lot to do and it would take days. Meantime, more jobs would come in and more paperwork would be generated. I already had a dozen files in various stages of completion in my box. I would have to come in early tomorrow to keep on top of it or I could easily be overwhelmed.

Bernadette sat across the table, watching me write. 'I know you.'

'Do you?' My workload distracted me.

'I saw you once at our school. You were talking to Miss Ashton.'

I looked up and a memory triggered. 'I remember. You were going on a camping trip.' That meant Bernadette had not long had her fourteenth birthday. 'I hope you enjoyed it.'

Bernadette looked pleased. 'It was ace. We had to be careful with the campfire because of the drought. I remember you smiled at me.' She paused and traced circles on the table with her finger. 'Can I ask you something?'

I put my pen down and smiled in what I hoped was an encouraging manner.

'Does the first time hurt a lot?' she asked.

I chewed my lip. I wasn't the best person to answer this. I would have to resort to theory.

'It can be uncomfortable the first time.'

'Why would anyone want to do something that hurts?' Bernadette picked at the edge of the table with bitten fingernails.

Why indeed? I took a deep breath. 'I think this is where feelings come into it. When you're with someone you care for, your body gets you ready to have sex with them. It might be tricky to start with, but you're happy and you want to make them happy too. If they care for you, they will be gentle. If you're with someone you don't care for, your body won't prepare you the same, and they won't be as gentle, so it might hurt more.'

Bernadette nodded as I spoke. 'Sex is better if you love him.'

'For me, there has to be love and trust before there can be sex.' As I spoke Bernadette's eyes moved to the door behind me.

'The social worker is here,' Inspector Tyrrell said.

That man was quieter than a cat; I would have to think of a way to attach a bell to him to save me from embarrassing moments like this.

In my peripheral vision, I saw him hold a hand out to Bernadette. 'They want to meet you.'

Bernadette looked more childlike than ever, walking hand in hand with the boss. I really hoped that the social services would find her a decent foster home, but I suspected that, if Welsh Elsie managed to dodge a custodial sentence, Bernadette would return home to a mother who thought prostitution was a valid career move for a fourteen-year-old.

Welsh Elsie was the talk of the station. The consensus was that Bernadette would inevitably finish up like her mother. I hoped not. I would have a chat with Karen when I next saw her; maybe she would be able to keep an eye on Bernadette if she returned home, and I knew I could rely on Karen to tell me if there was anything amiss happening. From our chats, I had gleaned that she was something of an agony aunt for young girls in the area, and some not so young.

Thinking of Karen made me think of our conversation about Brian. Events had overtaken me before I could pass that on, but I had to bring it to someone's attention, someone of a higher rank.

I went to the inspector's office and, as usual, the door was ajar. The boss sat writing at the desk. He looked up.

'I'll have my statement for you if you hang on a minute,' he said.

I went inside and shut the door, which caused the inspector to raise his eyebrows. 'Sir, can I tell you something that might or might not be true?'

'Go on.' He put his pen down and sat back.

'It might be nothing, but I heard that Brian is in with a criminal gang. They specialise in porn and prostitution. Apparently, he protects them and deflects police interest in exchange for sexual favours. I was told he prefers young girls. I can't prove this but I thought I should say something.' I felt foolish for bringing it up. 'It's probably nothing. Forget I said anything.' I turned to leave

'Did Karen tell you this?' Inspector Tyrrell asked.

I felt my cheeks flush.

The inspector drew a long breath. 'Right. Okay, thanks. If there's nothing else, you can go.' He handed me his statement and I opened the door.

'Sam.' Eamon Kildea was hurrying towards me. 'Are you busy? I could do with you to sit in while I interview Welsh Elsie.' He peered into the inspector's office. 'Will that be okay, boss?'

Inspector Tyrrell looked up and nodded. 'Yeah, fine.'

Eamon led me to the interview room in the bridewell where Elsie was sitting, arms folded and glaring at Ken, who was standing in the doorway.

'How long are you going to keep me here?' she demanded.

'A little while longer yet.' Eamon sat at the table and I took a seat tucked away in a corner. 'We need to ask you a few questions.'

'Fuck you.'

'Not right now thanks, Elsie,' Eamon shot back deadpan. 'Now, why don't you tell us why you decided to take Bernadette onto the ship? She's a lovely girl by the way.'

Elsie's laugh sounded like a cinder being ground underfoot. 'Fancy a bit, do you, *cariad*? It'll cost you.'

'So this was all about money?' Eamon leant on the table.

'Isn't everything?'

'Who offered you £20 for Bernadette?'

'It was £50, robbing buggers. I want to make a complaint about that, and I hope you're going to do something about it.'

'Civil action, Elsie,' Eamon said. 'Go to the small claims court.'

I knew they'd laugh and kick her out.

'So, what's this got to do with you taking your fourteen-year-old daughter onto a ship?' Eamon asked.

Elsie thought for a moment. 'Our Ruthie was talking to Connie Jones and she said she stopped going on the ships because she earned more doing films.'

'Naughty films?' Eamon asked.

'No, Hollywood cast her in their next blockbuster. Knob.'

Eamon chuckled.

'Is Ruthie your daughter?' I asked, earning myself a look from Eamon. I was supposed to be chaperoning, not interrogating.

'Course she is,' Elsie replied.

I recalled meeting Ruthie as she fled something. I wanted to ask more questions, but they weren't relevant to the current situation so I remained quiet, probably to Eamon's relief.

'Carry on, Elsie,' Eamon said.

'Well, to cut a long story short, I went to see Glynis, Connie's mum, about getting Ruthie into films but Glynis said Ruthie looked too well used. Fucker. Like her Connie is Miss World.'

'What happened then?' Eamon asked.

'I got thinking maybe they'd prefer someone younger, so I went back to speak to Glynis and asked her about Bernadette, but she said she's too young for her to take on. Lying cow, I know she takes on youngsters. Glynis gets her Connie to find girls, and if they're taken on, Glynis gets a cut.'

I tasted acid in my throat.

'How did this go from films to taking Bernadette to the ship?' Eamon cocked his head, awaiting the answer.

'I waited around Glynis's place until I saw Molly. I asked him about my girls and he said he wasn't interested in Ruthie because she's an addict and he expects his girls to be clean. She isn't an addict; she likes a bit of whizz sometimes that's all. Then he said he didn't want Bernadette because she didn't have proper tits yet but to speak to him next year. Then, a couple of days later, he called around to my house and said he had been told about someone on a ship that was due in who would be interested in Bernadette. He said I'd get fifty quid for her.'

Molly was a man! What would generate a nickname like Molly? Brian Lewington got called Lew, so Molly could come from… I knew at once who Molly was and kicked myself for not realising sooner.

'That's a lot of money. Tell me about what happened on the ship,' Eamon coaxed.

'We got to the ship. Molly wasn't there but he'd given our names to someone who showed us where to go. While we were there, I was offered a quick job, so I left Bernadette in the recreation room. Then you lot came. I didn't get the fifty quid Molly promised me and I didn't get my tenner either. I don't work for fucking free.'

Eamon smiled. 'Do you know this Molly well?'

'Not really,' Elsie replied. 'Glynis is the one to speak to there. He's knobbing her and Connie. And probably Lana too.'

'Right then, Elsie, that'll do for now. Samantha here will take you back to the cell and get a nice cup of tea for you.'

'Eamon, can I speak to you before you disappear?' I asked.

'Sure, Sam. I'll be in the charge office.'

I stood up and escorted Elsie to the female wing of the bridewell.

She paused before she went into the cell. 'You know, if you get fed up here, you're just the type of girl Molly would want.' She looked me up and down. 'Yeah, you'd do well in films you would, and you'd probably earn more than you do now.'

I ushered her into the cell and locked the door. I would never ever be enticed to have anything to do with films like that.

I made Elsie the promised tea and went to the charge office to see Eamon. He was alone as the sergeant was doing the rounds in the male wing. Good, the fewer people who heard us, the better.

'Right, Sam m'darlin'. What's on your mind.'

'Molly. I thought Molly was a woman, a madam, but Molly is a man. I also know Molly is connected to Ted Bulwer who runs a pornography operation in the city.'

Eamon nodded. 'That fits with some information we have.'

'Do you have any idea who Molly is?' I asked.

'We have suspicions but nothing concrete,' Eamon replied.

'I believe he's Robert Molyneux. The owner of that Lotus Elite I keep seeing. I saw him give money to Janice outside the Jones's house.'

'That also fits,' Eamon said.

I glanced around to make sure nobody was in earshot. 'I'm not sure I should be saying this, but don't trust Brian. I've been told he has a business arrangement with a gang involved with prostitution and pornography. I saw him searching around the DS's drawer.'

'Did he see you?'

'No.' I was relieved that Eamon seemed to be taking me seriously, so I ploughed on. 'And I might be jumping to conclusions, but he saw me put information in the basket, the information that went missing, and I wonder, if he is protecting Molyneux and Bulwer, did he remove it?'

'You'll never prove that, but I will mention it to Irene.'

I felt I had done all I could do for now, so I left Eamon to write up his interview notes and went to work on my enormous and complicated file.

Chapter Nineteen

Life at Wyre Hall settled a little as July melted into August. Standpipes appeared in parts of the country as the drought dragged on. Ladybirds infested everywhere and crunched underfoot and obscured road signs. I didn't know the little buggers could bite, but they can and there was no avoiding them. Even I, a fan of warm weather, was getting fed up. The heat drained energy but I did have a lovely, flattering tan.

Finally the weather broke, and rain bucketed down. It was still warm, and I could imagine there were parties in gardens and allotments all over the country.

I worked lates that week. On the first day, I was in the 3pm parade, jotting down my duties, when my pen ran out. My own fault: I knew it was getting low and I should have thrown it away. I put my hand in my open bag to get a new pen but, instead of the usual paraphernalia I felt something smooth and a little moist. I peered in and gasped as a frog clambered over a packet of tissues and looked up at me. I couldn't be sure who had put the poor creature there, but I guessed Steve was back to his old tricks! He was jotting in his notebook paying no attention to me.

I took the frog from my bag and placed it on his knee. 'I believe this is yours.'

Steve screamed, literally, and in one smooth movement pushed the frog to the floor and leapt backwards, knocking his chair over.

I scooped the frog up before he stood on it.

'What the hell, Steve?' Alan shouted.

'She put a frog on me.' Steve pointed a shaking finger at me. 'A real frog.'

Damn, the boy was genuinely scared.

Inspector Tyrrell looked from Steve and me as the others began to laugh. 'Sam?'

'I found a frog in my handbag, sir. I thought Steve had put it there.' I looked at the panicked man. 'Although after that display, I might have been mistaken.'

'Get rid of the damned frog,' Inspector Tyrrell barked.

I sidled out to the front of the room, cradling the frog in my hands. When I was clear of the table and chairs, I turned to face everyone.

'Just for the record, I'm not scared of frogs, toads, mice, rats, spiders, moths, worms, or any small creature.'

'What does scare you?' Brian asked.

'Bent coppers.' I retorted.

The inspector caught my eye. I took the hint and left the room, hurrying over to the fence that surrounded the car park. I placed the frog over the fence on the grass verge and shooed him in the direction of a small pond a short distance away. I saw a few other frogs moving in the grass. The rain was encouraging frogs to start roaming. Poor Steve.

I hurried back to the parade room, stopping only to wash my hands. No doubt Steve had been on the receiving end of ferocious teasing whilst I was away.

'Is it gone?' Alan asked.

'Yes, Sarge.' I took my seat and parade resumed.

'I have a nice little surprise for you, Sam,' Inspector Tyrrell said. 'My recommendation that you receive a chief constable's commendation for rescuing that baby has been approved.' He passed an envelope to me.

Everyone clapped and I stood up and did a little curtsey.

'Now let's get on.' The boss flicked though his files

Ken nudged me. 'Let's see your letter.'

I opened the envelope and pulled out the official notification. I felt Steve lean in from the other side, curiosity overriding his annoyance. It wasn't anything fancy, simply a white card informing me that because of outstanding bravery, the chief constable wished to personally thank—*Insert name here*—Constable Samantha Barrie at a ceremony to be held at HQ on—*Insert date*—Monday January 31st 1977.

'You might end up with a national award,' Ken said.

I spotted Alan looking our way, so I put the notification down and tried to focus on parade.

'Just for your information, Janice Alderman was reported missing again after we went off duty. She returned home this morning. She refuses to say where she's been,' Inspector Tyrrell said.

'Her father will be bringing in an exorcist,' Phil muttered.

*

On my way out to patrol, I called into Irene's office to have a ten-minute chat.

'I have some gossip for you,' she said.

'Good gossip?' I pulled a chair up.

'Depends on your perspective. Derek got off with leaving the radio. Brian said he'd been asked to stand in.'

I sagged in my seat. 'But he wasn't there.'

Irene grinned. 'That's the second part. Ken saw him in the locker room and let it slip, not realising what had happened, so Gary's put Brian on a charge for leaving the radio. And he's gone after Derek for unprofessional conduct for sending you to the men's showers.'

I laughed. 'Don't cross the boss.'

'Exactly.'

Eamon Kildea came in, wrapped his arms around Irene, kissed her neck, and winked at me. 'How are my favourite ladies?'

'Well, thanks Eamon.' I was glad Eamon and Irene had started dating. Things seemed to be going well for them and I hoped I would receive another engagement invitation at some point.

'Has there ever been any follow-up on that information Elsie gave us about Molyneux?' I asked.

'I passed that information on to the vice squad but they don't want to bring him in yet. They're hoping he'll lead them to the big boss, but he's been a bit slippery. I can't say any more yet.'

I hated being the last to know things.

*

The afternoon after the frog incident, I opened my locker and a large rubber spider fell out at my feet. Someone must have spent quite a long time pushing it though the vent holes after I had gone home. I picked it up and put it on the top shelf. My six-year-old cousin would like it. I grabbed my hat and hurried off to start my shift.

In the parade room, someone had taped pictures of frogs across every notice board and on the walls. A stuffed toy frog sat on Steve's chair. Phil and Ken were the only ones there.

'Did you do this?' I asked.

'Not us,' said Phil, gesturing to Ken. 'Word gets around, you know.'

Several more people came in and laughed aloud when they saw the frogs. Then Steve came in and was greeted by a chorus of croaks and ribbits. He stopped dead in his tracks and looked around the room.

'Sam, was this you?'

'Not me, nor them.' I picked up the stuffed frog and waved a furry little hand at him. 'Sit down, Steve. It's only a little frog, it won't hurt you.'

'Wazzer.'

I held out the stuffed frog, but he batted it away.

'Bog off,' he growled.

'Can I have it then?' I asked.

'You can stuff it up your arse for all I care.'

I studied the frog for a minute. 'I think I'll call him Steve. He'll make a good addition to the rubber spider I found in my locker. Would you know anything about that, Steve?'

Before Steve could answer, Alan, Brian and Inspector Tyrrell came in and burst out laughing.

'Sam, is this your handiwork?' Alan asked.

'No, Sarge, but I wish I had thought of it.' Well, I was being honest.

'Steve, before you go out, clear up this lot,' Alan said.

'But I didn't do it,' Steve argued.

'I didn't say you had. Hop to it and you'll soon be finished.'

I wasn't sure if Alan had deliberately made a joke but the sniggers around the room told me that I wasn't the only one who picked up on it.

'He doesn't like frogs, Sarge, he's gone green,' someone said.

'Perhaps you can wade in and give him a hand then,' Alan replied deadpan.

Phil laughed then began to cough.

'Are you all right, Phil? You're not going to croak, are you?' Inspector Tyrrell said, causing much hilarity.

'I'm fine thank you, sir. It's just a frog in my throat.'

Steve sat stony-faced, with his arms folded across his chest as parade descended into hysterics.

'Wazzers,' he muttered.

It took a couple of minutes for everyone to regain control of themselves and for parade to begin.

'Don't worry, Steve. They'll get bored with it soon,' I said between giggles, but I don't think he appreciated it. He glowered for the rest of parade.

On the way out, Steve grabbed my arm. 'I thought we were friends.'

'I told you it wasn't me.' I yanked my arm away. 'Given your past form, it was reasonable to think you had put the frog in my bag. I didn't know frogs scared you until you screamed.'

'I was just surprised. And I didn't scream,' Steve protested.

'Yes, you did: high and loud,' Alan called from his office. 'If she hadn't been in sight, I'd have thought it was Sam.

Steve stamped off to the locker room and I swear I could hear his teeth grinding. I didn't want to fall out, we were supposed to be going to Ken's engagement together in a couple of days, so I trotted after him.

'I'm sorry. I really thought it was you who put the frog into my bag.'

'I wouldn't touch a frog, or a toad. I can't stand them. I'm not keen on eels or snakes either.' Steve said.

'Is this a phobia or a general distaste?' I asked.

Steve sighed. 'Phobia, I think. My beloved big brother, Richard, used to amuse himself by tormenting me. Once he put a frog in my bed; it crawled over my foot just as I was going to sleep. I was only eight and I thought it was going to eat me. I've hated them ever since.'

Poor Steve. I patted his shoulder. 'I won't tease you about it anymore.'

'The others will,' Steve grumbled.

'Think of it as being like when you first arrived here. They'll get fed up and move on to something else eventually.' I gave him a little hug. 'Come on, let's go out and get started. I've got loads of paperwork to do later so I want to stretch my legs.'

He slammed his locker door closed and together we left the building. As we crossed Nelson Square, Steve turned off to go to his beat and I walked on past the maisonettes.

I spotted a familiar yellow car coming towards me. I waited for it to pass but it turned off before it reached me. However, I spotted Lana in the passenger seat. That sighting was definitely going to Irene.

*

On the day of Ken and Gaynor's engagement party, I put on my new outfit, bought specially.

'Let's take a look,' Mum said as I came down the stairs.

I gave a little twirl and stood before her with my arms outstretched. 'Do you think a boob tube is a bit risqué?'

Mum adjusted the top to show a little cleavage. I pulled it back up, high under my arms. 'I can't wear a bra with this and it's only held up by elastic. I don't want my boobs to fall out.'

'You're young and firm enough not to need a bra every day. Don't pull the top up so high, it looks wrong.'

I allowed Mum to adjust the top again. I saw she wanted to feel needed. When Dad had come home on leave she had relaxed a little, but now he was back on the rig, Mum had reverted to hyper-protective mode. I couldn't complain as this too was a legacy from Hogarth Acre.

'Try not to worry, Mum. I'll be with Steve and it's the police club, not The Capstan. If I do have a drink, I'll call a taxi.'

'He's a nice lad, Steve.'

'Yes. Annoying sometimes, but basically nice.'

'It keeps things interesting.' Mum wiggled her eyebrows at me.

'We're just mates so don't get excited. He said he doesn't want a girlfriend.'

'Doesn't he like girls?'

'Yes, of course.' I thought for a second. 'Actually, I don't know. Do you mean...?'

Mum shrugged. 'You're a pretty girl, why else wouldn't he want to go out with you?'

'I'm not looking either. It doesn't mean I'm a lesbian.'

'I know,' Mum agreed. 'But you have a good reason. Maybe he's been hurt.'

'I don't know. For now, though, we're just two mates who are going to enjoy a night out together.' I went upstairs to finish my make-up and put on my shoes. Platforms were a little out-of-date, but they went well with the wide-leg, velvet trousers I was wearing. When I was ready, I kissed Mum goodbye, picked up the gift-wrapped crystal vase I had bought on her advice, and drove to

Steve's house.

*

Steve's brother, Richard, answered the door. He leaned against the door frame and allowed his eyes to roam over me. Even without Steve's warning, I could see this was a man used to attracting female attention.

'Well, hello.'

'Hello yourself. I'm Samantha. Is Steve ready?'

Richard bellowed up the stairs, 'Oi, maggot, your girlfriend's here. She's out of your league you know.'

I didn't correct Richard. A girl needs a compliment occasionally.

Mrs Patton came into the hall. 'Richard, don't keep the girl on the doorstep.' She hip-bumped Richard aside. 'Come in, dear.'

'Thanks Mrs Patton.' I stepped inside.

'It's so nice to meet you. Steve speaks about you quite often.'

'Does he?' I was surprised.

'I always thought he was queer,' Richard said.

That was the second time tonight I had heard someone suggest that Steve was gay. He didn't look gay, but then what did "gay" look like?

Mrs Patton slapped Richard's shoulder. 'Stop being so horrible about your brother. He's just fussy, unlike you.'

'Can you two please stop discussing me in front of Samantha,' Steve said as he came downstairs. He took my arm and pulled me out of the house.

'I have a few days before I'm due back at camp,' Richard said as we passed. 'And I've got a car. Call me.'

'Get lost, Dick,' Steve snarled.

'You know your brother hates that name,' Mrs Patton said.

'I wasn't calling him by a name.' Steve flumped into the car and I set off for the police club.

'Ignore Richard, he's a berk.'

'He seemed quite nice.'

189

'No, he's just a berk.'

Sometimes I was glad I was an only child.

*

Music boomed from the club. I put the present under one arm, pushed open the door, and went to the bar with Steve.

'What do you want, Steve?'

'You drove so let me get this.'

'Fair enough. Coke please.' As I waited for my drink, I surveyed the room. Phil was already sitting with Jo, his wife, and Alan and his wife, Edna.

'Phil and Alan are over by the stage,' I said when Steve passed me my drink. Stage was the grand name for a small dais hung with silver lametta, where a DJ was playing his records and bellowing into a microphone from time to time.

We wended our way through the tables and joined the others. I saw Phil and Alan wink at each other. No doubt commenting on Steve and I being there together.

'I'm going to give Ken and Gaynor my present; back in a tick.' I went over and hugged Ken. 'Congratulations.' I handed the vase to him.

'Thanks.' Ken placed it on a table already groaning with gifts. 'This is Gaynor, my fiancée.' Ken tightened his grip on Gaynor, who met his eyes and smiled.

I held out my hand. 'I'm pleased to meet you, Gaynor. I'm Sam.'

Ignoring my outstretched hand, Gaynor gave me a short hug. 'I've heard about you. You've had a hard time of it, haven't you?'

Not being a natural hugger, I gave a quick half-hug in response. 'It's not so bad, just teasing and practical jokes,' I said. 'Are you looking forward to going to the training school?'

'Yes, I am. But I'll miss Ken while I'm away, Gaynor replied.

'I enjoyed it there. It's challenging, but there's a lot of fun and you'll be home at the weekends,' I said.

'Ken said that too, but I want to spend every minute with him.' Gaynor turned to Ken, who gazed back at her. There was a joy there as if they were facing the rising sun. I wanted to face the sunrise too, but that wasn't likely anytime soon. I hadn't allowed anyone to get close enough.

'I'll let you get on.' I went back to the table and sat next to Steve.

Ray arrived shortly afterwards, accompanied by Irene and Eamon.

'You two make a nice couple.' Irene nodded towards Steve.

'We're not a couple, we just came together because neither of us have a partner.' I was getting tired of explaining this to people.

'Maybe tonight will be the start of something big.' Irene leant towards me and whispered, 'You have to start somewhere, Sam, so why not Steve?'

'He doesn't want a girlfriend. He panicked when I kissed him.'

'You kissed him?' Irene's eyes lit up.

'It was just a thank you peck on the cheek. That's when he told me he wasn't on the market. I didn't mind because I'm not either.' I gestured for her to come closer. 'Do you think he's homosexual?' I whispered.

Irene looked past me to Steve then back at me. 'Why do you think that?'

'Something Mum said, and his brother openly said he thought he was queer.'

Irene laughed. 'That's just brothers for you.'

'Come on, Sam, let's dance.' Steve grabbed my hand and hauled me onto the dance floor.

Steve bounced around unselfconsciously, and I couldn't help but join in with his enthusiasm. Did he prefer men? I couldn't tell, but it didn't matter, I was out with my friends and I felt completely safe.

*

Steve and I shared several dances during the evening. I even had a dance with Ray, Phil, and Alan, cheered on by their partners.

'The boss is here!' Steve said as he returned from another trip to the bar.

We all turned and saw Inspector Tyrrell handing a gift to Ken and Gaynor. I couldn't hear what was said, but Ken shook his hand and Gaynor hugged him. Inspector Tyrrell then came over to the table and we all shuffled along to make room for him to sit down. There would have been room next to me, but instead he slid in beside Phil's wife.

'I've put some money behind the bar, so please all have a drink on me.'

'Nice one,' Phil said.

'Thanks, sir,' Steve and I said in unison.

Ray, Phil, and Steve went off to collect the drinks for our table.

'We thought you weren't coming,' Edna said.

'I tend to hang back at social occasions. I'm aware that our junior members might feel inhibited by my presence, so I give them time to have some fun before I arrive,' the inspector replied.

Edna and Jo laughed aloud.

'Oh, hark at Methuselah,' Edna said. 'How old are you, Gary? Thirty?'

The boss laughed as well. 'Not quite, Edna. I was referring to rank rather than age.'

Alan returned with some drinks and placed them in front of Edna and me.

'May I borrow your wife?' Inspector Tyrrell asked.

'Please, take her,' Alan replied.

Inspector Tyrrell took Edna to the dance floor, where they did a passable hustle. Then he danced with Jo and Irene, and then with Edna again.

'You haven't danced with Sam yet, sir,' Steve commented when Inspector Tyrrell brought Edna back for the second time.

I'd noticed too, but I hadn't intended to say anything. I felt Inspector Tyrrell's eyes slide to me and I wondered if he was gauging my reaction. Nope: when I turned to him, his eyes were following the line of my boob tube. I self-consciously tugged the garment higher and Inspector Tyrrell dragged his attention back to the crowd.

'I'm sure the boss just wants to sit and enjoy his drink,' I said.

'Dance! Dance! Dance!' Irene chanted. Everyone joined in and banged the table with each chant until Inspector Tyrrell held his hands up, laughing in surrender.

'Okay, okay, I give up.' He held a hand out to me. 'Sam, would you care to dance?'

Everyone cheered as I took his hand and allowed him to lead me onto the dance floor.

We faced each other as the music changed to a slower tempo. Normally, at this point, I would flee back to the table, but I made myself stay. If I wanted to live a normal life, I had to stop panicking if a man held me. I put my outstretched hands on his shoulders and hoped he wouldn't notice them shaking.

'I can't waltz or anything, sir.'

'Neither can I, but I can manage a shuffle around the dance floor.' He pulled me a little closer and I stiffened at the first pangs of panic, but I pushed them down. This was the boss for goodness sake. We began to move in time to the music.

'I think given the circumstances you can call me Gary.'

'Yes, sir.'

This was one of my all-time favourite records and I hummed along as we moved. Inspector Tyrrell's hands slipped further around my waist and glided up my back. It felt nice and, for the first time ever, I relaxed in a man's arms. Gradually, my hands slid around his shoulders and we moved closer until there was no space between us. I didn't worry about him hearing my pounding heart. I laid my cheek against his shoulder, courtesy of my platform shoes, and I felt his chin rest against my head. I shivered as his fingers stroked the bare skin of my back. I could have stayed like that forever, but the music ended. However, he didn't release me. He lowered his head and for a second, I thought—hoped—he was going to kiss me, but he put his mouth by my ear and whispered, 'I think we'd better sit down quickly.'

I looked around and saw that every eye on our table was locked on us. I stepped away from the inspector—Gary—and scurried back with my cheeks burning.

Irene leant towards me. 'Keep Steve away from Gary. After that dance, he'll be obliged to punch him on the nose.'

'Steve and I are not together, so he's not obliged to thump anyone. And even if we were together, it was just a dance,' I protested. 'You all wanted me to dance with him, remember?'

Irene chuckled. 'There's dancing and then there's what you two just did. I don't know what he said to you, but you visibly melted into him.'

'I did not.'

Ray began to talk cricket with Phil a little too loudly. Jo and Edna whispered together and Steve just gaped. Dammit, I supposed it was too much to hope that everyone would have forgotten it by the next shift, because one thing all bobbies love is a juicy bit of gossip.

Chapter Twenty

We were on earlies when I next arrived at Wyre Hall, and it seemed everyone who had not been at the party had heard about me dancing with Inspector Tyrrell. Only it had been ground up by the rumour mill and a spicier version churned out.

'What's this about you and the boss snogging at Ken's do?' Brian asked as I walked past the sergeants' office. 'I heard that you snogged on the dance floor, right in front of everyone.'

'We didn't!' I cried.

The boss had left the party soon after we'd danced. I'd remained to the end, making sure I paid a lot of attention to Steve, which I think had alarmed him. He had almost run up his path when I dropped him off at home. I'd fooled nobody. Something had happened between Gary Tyrrell and me even though we hadn't kissed, and everyone there had seen it.

Gary didn't look my way once during parade. I didn't expect him to be blowing kisses, but I didn't want him to ignore me either. Even when parade ended, he just picked up his folder and walked out. If he could carry on as normal after I had caught him in the shower room, why was he aloof now? *'Because it meant something,'* my brain whispered. I shuffled out of the parade room to get my radio, ignoring the comments from the lads. It was going to take a while to live this one down.

Before I could begin patrol, I received a call from Karen asking if I could call around to her house. Curiosity piqued, I told Ray that I was going to do some follow-up enquiries and asked him only to call me if something was urgent. I had deliberately been vague and withheld the address, as I didn't want a certain sergeant to see where I had gone. Ray jotted a mark against my number on the shift sheet, and I went around to Karen's house.

Karen wasn't her normal outgoing self when I arrived.

'Is everything okay, Karen?' I asked.

'I've got something to show you, but first I'll put the kettle on.'

I sat at the small Formica table in her tiny kitchen and waited for the kettle to boil.

'This is pretty, where did you get it?' I pinched at the embroidered table cover.

'Thanks, I made it,' Karen said, smiling for the first time since I got there.

I examined the sewing. It was neat enough to rival any professional job. 'It's really good, Karen.'

Karen smiled as she put a mug of tea in front of me. 'Thank you. I make most of my clothes too, especially trousers because I can't get anything long enough for these.' She shook out a long, long leg.

'I had no idea you were so talented.'

I could tell she wasn't used to receiving genuine compliments. She shrugged.

'Sewing is just something I like to do. I enjoyed it in school and I did once think I could get a job and do it properly, but you know… we needed money… life gets in the way.'

'You still could do it properly, Karen.'

She shook her head. 'I've got responsibilities, and I'd never earn what I get now.'

She put a plate of bourbons on the table indicating the discussion was over.

'Tuck in, I'll get the magazines I want to show you.' Karen pulled out a cardboard box from the under stairs cupboard and dumped it on the table. Inside were several magazines and a couple of cine films.

'Have a flick through those.'

I hesitantly picked up one of the magazines. I had heard of the *Fiesta* and *Playboy* magazines, but this was in a different league. I hadn't realised there were so many positions, or that a penis could be that long. In a couple of pictures, I wasn't sure what part of the body I was looking at, so close was the camera

'This isn't run-of-the-mill stuff,' I said.

'Some customers like it, so I keep a supply. It comes from abroad. I get them from the ships.' She took a bourbon and dipped it in her tea.

I took a sip of my tea and picked up another magazine. Bondage this time, lots of black leather and chains. I couldn't imagine anything worse. Bad memories.

'People actually like this type of thing?' I said to myself.

Karen thought I had been speaking to her and nodded. 'Wait until you get to the SM book.'

I pushed the bondage magazine aside, picked up another and leafed through it. Sadomasochism. Some things looked painful. Definitely not my thing.

'Try this one.' Karen handed me another magazine. This one was in the form of a photo story. A flimsy tale of a turbaned sultan with baggy trousers and a lot of wives. One wife fell in love with the bodyguard. In it, people performed acts that I wasn't certain were even legal on a long couch surrounded by brightly coloured swathes of hanging material. How did people behave normally with each other after doing that? Incredibly, as I looked at the photos, something clicked. Suddenly, I wasn't in Karen's kitchen, squirming in embarrassment; I was on duty, looking with a detached, professional eye, and my professional eye thought it recognised someone.

'I think that's Janice Alderman... with the sultan.'

Karen leant in and tapped the photo below it. A girl on a bed with a huge bamboo headboard, entertaining another man. 'And I think that's Lana Jones.'

'It could be Lana. It's hard to tell with that mess on her face, but I'm certain that's Janice,' I said.

The sultan looked familiar too, but I couldn't place him. I put my hand over his turban so only his face was visible. Gerald Mount!

'Can I keep hold of this, Karen? Those girls are only fifteen and I think we need to act. This is evidence.'

Karen looked uncomfortable. 'I don't know, Sam. I'll get into trouble if anyone finds out you got them from me, and I don't mean from the cops. It doesn't do to get a name as a grass around here.'

I could see her concern, but I needed proof.

'I won't say where I got them,' I promised.

'I suppose that's all right.' She pushed the cine films towards me. 'You might find them useful too. I'll get you a carrier bag.'

I had learnt more about sex in half an hour with Karen and some mucky books than I had in a whole half term of sex education at school. Now I had to get them back to the station. I needed a car but, if I sent out a radio call, anyone might come, and I thought it best if Brian didn't know I was here.

In the end, I went to the phone box on the corner of the street and rang Inspector Tyrrell via the switchboard. When I explained the situation, he agreed to come and meet me. I went back to Karen's and waited for the boss to arrive.

I heard a car draw up and looked out of the front window. It was the boss. Karen opened the door and let him in.

'Thanks for coming, Gary. Sam, show him that magazine.'

I handed the magazine over and tried to control the spreading heat across my face. Failed.

'Right,' Inspector Tyrrell said after he had looked at the pictures. 'We need to speak to Lana and Janice.'

'They'll just deny it.' I said.

'I don't see how they can now that you have those pictures,' Karen commented.

'Let's get back and get this lot booked in. Thanks Karen,' Inspector Tyrrell said. 'What will you say if anyone asks why we're here?'

'I'll tell them I give cheap rates to coppers.' Karen winked.

'You need a cover story, one we can corroborate if necessary,' Inspector Tyrrell insisted.

'Yeah, I know. I'll tell them a customer got a bit rough last night and I reported it.'

Gary nodded. 'Okay, that should do.'

We got back to the Panda and I tucked the bag down by my feet as the boss headed back towards Wyre Hall.

After a few minutes, he said, 'About that dance.'

At last he was going to acknowledge what happened. I didn't know if I was pleased or scared.

'I was out of order,' he said. 'I'm sorry.'

I was disappointed. 'You don't need to apologise; it was just a dance.'

'We both know it was more than that.' Gary glanced my way. 'For a few minutes, as I held you, I could imagine…' He exhaled loudly. 'I won't get in the way of your relationship with Steve.'

'Steve and I are just mates. What you and I had was more than a dance and I'm glad it was.' There. I'd said it.

Inspector Tyrrell shook his head. 'It's a bad idea, Sam.'

Okay then. That was that.

'Karen is a useful contact to have. I've found her very helpful over the years.'

And now he was changing the subject. All right, I'd go with that. I hadn't thought of Karen as a contact; I enjoyed her company and felt if circumstances were different, we could have been good friends.

'She's given me some good information,' I said.

As we pulled up the ramp to the station, I sneaked a sideways look at the boss and wondered where his preferences lay. Karen had said it had been a while, and he had arrived at Ken and Gaynor's engagement alone. Then a wave of remorse hit me. Two children I knew of were being exploited and I was wondering about the boss's sex life. That guilt pile of mine was getting bigger and bigger.

*

'Wow,' Irene said as she leafed through the magazine I had put in front of her.

'Wow indeed,' Eamon echoed. 'Now I understand why you called me, Irene. Where did you get these, Sam?'

'An informant.' I wasn't going to break my promise to Karen. I turned the pages until I came to the pertinent pictures. 'The one in the yashmak is Janice and I think the other one is Lana. Also, the sultan is Gerald Mount.'

'It is too.' Irene tapped the page. 'Over to you then, Eamon.'

Eamon loaded the magazines and films into an evidence bag. 'I'll take these upstairs. Good work, Sam.'

I glowed with pleasure, even though the evidence had dropped into my lap.

'Inspector Tyrrell said we needed to speak to Lana and Janice.' Okay, I admit I was angling for an invitation.

'We will. I might need you to come with us,' Eamon said. 'I'll clear it with Gary.'

Pleased, I left Irene and Eamon to discuss the magazines and went back out.

*

Hari was cleaning tables as I passed and called out to me, 'Hello, Constable Sam. You haven't been to see us for a long time.'

'Hello, Hari. I've been very busy.'

Hari said. 'Sergeant Brian is here collecting the insurance.'

'What insurance. Hari?'

'Police insurance,' he replied.

'Police don't collect insurance, Hari.' A nasty niggle started in my gut.

We faced each other for a few seconds before Hari said, 'I must be mistaken. He must be here for something else.'

'Hari...' I began.

Hari waved a hand. 'Don't you worry, Constable Sam. It's nothing.'

I had to say it. 'Hari, there is no reason I can think of why Brian would need to collect money from you.'

Hari's shoulders sagged. 'I must go now. I will see you again.' He disappeared into the restaurant.

I had to report this. I didn't want to make waves, but some things could not be ignored. I jumped out of my skin when a car horn pipped beside me. I hadn't noticed Phil draw up beside me.

'Hey, Sam. You're in a world of your own.'

Phil! Just the person. I hopped into the passenger side. 'Can I ride with you for a few minutes? I need to talk,' I said.

'What's happened?'

I took a deep breath. 'Remember the rumours about Brian and bribes?' Phil nodded. 'I've just been speaking to Hari Kapoor and he said Brian is in the restaurant collecting police insurance.' I spotted Brian emerging from the alleyway beside the Golden Temple. He had exited via the back door. 'There he is.'

Phil accelerated away and parked up around the corner near Belvedere House.

'Hari actually used those words?'

'He did, Phil. I'm not wrong, am I? This is proof that Brian's bent.'

'Bent as a nine-bob note. I'll take you in to speak to the boss. Don't say anything to anyone until Inspector Tyrrell gives you some guidance.' Phil swung the car around and drove me to the station.

As soon as we got back, I went to see the boss. He listened to everything I said then sat back and chewed his thumbnail for quite a long time. I didn't interrupt him.

'You're quite sure Hari said, "Police insurance"?' Inspector Tyrrell said.

'Positive, sir.'

The boss chewed his thumbnail some more. Finally, he said,

'You did the right thing coming to me. Okay, off you go but say nothing for now.'

'Yes, sir.'

It was almost knocking-off time so, although I'd spent a fair bit of time in the station, there wasn't much point in going back out. I had a couple of files to finish so I would get them done, but first, I would visit the ladies' toilet.

I was retouching my lip gloss when I heard the outer door of the toilets open. The inner door opened, and Brian came in. My stomach clenched.

'Wrong door, Sarge,' I waved the wand of my lip gloss. 'Gents' is on the other side.'

I had hoped he would just apologise and leave but he stood, staring, between me and the only door out. I put my lip gloss away and zipped up my bag with a shaking hand.

'Can I help you?' I asked.

Brian took a step towards me. I pressed the transmit button on my radio just once. A warning.

'I saw you chatting to Hari.'

I held my nerve and remained silent.

Brian smiled. 'He's a nice boy but his English isn't quite up to scratch. Sometimes he misunderstands things.'

'I have no trouble understanding him.'

'The Kapoors have made a decent life for themselves in England.' Brian took a step forward and I stepped to the side. 'It would be a shame if they had to abandon it all and go back to India.'

I understood the threat; I had to remain quiet or he would cause trouble for the Kapoors. He didn't seem to know that I had already been in with the boss, on two counts. I wasn't going to enlighten him.

'You need a friend, Sammy.'

'I have friends,' I replied.

'You need a friend with a bit of authority who can look after you.' He took another step forwards and I backed to the wall. 'I can make life easy for you. We all play for the same team, Sammy.

I just want to be included with any information you get. I can be helpful to friends that help me. Just think, you wouldn't have to worry about passing your probation.'

Brian grabbed my arm. My calm exterior shattered. I shoved Brian away from the door and wrenched it open.

'I don't need friends like you.'

Brian shook his head. 'Sammy, Sammy… What you don't need is to piss off someone in authority.'

'I'm going to report this,' I said.

'Report what? I've come to you offering my assistance and you reject it. In fact, you strike me. It's not me that's committed an offence, Sammy.'

'I didn't strike you.'

Brian suddenly slammed his arm hard against the edge of the sink. He cried out and pulled his sleeve up. A livid mark that was sure to bruise, ran across his skin.

'Oh look, Sammy, I fell against the sink and hurt my arm when you shoved me. Maybe I should get it x-rayed?'

I gawked at the Sergeant. 'You're unhinged. Stay away from me.'

I ran back to the control room, wanting people around me.

'All right, Sam? You look a bit flustered,' Ray asked.

I could report this, but Brian would deny everything and then would start proceedings against me because I had supposedly assaulted him. He had faked proof of his own story and had shown me he would go to extraordinary lengths to get what he wanted. He was a dangerous man. I had to trust that the boss was dealing with things in the background and that Brian would soon be removed from Wyre Hall.

'I'm fine, thanks. I just came downstairs so I'm a bit breathless.'

Ray cocked an eyebrow and opened his mouth to speak, but then one of the patrols called up. He spun his chair back to the radio and I went to the report writing room. A couple of other lads were there, so I felt safe…ish.

Chapter Twenty-One

A couple of days later, DS Mike Finlay—Eamon's immediate boss—and I went to St Agnes' school to interview Lana Jones. She was in the fifth form now. It would probably be her last year of education; I couldn't see Glynis letting her go to college when she could be earning money. The DI had decided that we couldn't speak to her in front of Glynis or Connie, so it was pointless going to her house or asking Glynis to bring her in. We would have to have a teacher sit in on the interview.

The school secretary greeted us. 'Miss Hughes, head of pastoral care, is going to sit in with you. I'll take you to her office.'

We walked a short way down a wood-floored corridor and she showed us into a study, similar to Miss Ashton's. A surprisingly young blonde woman sat at a desk, her elegant nails tapping on a typewriter. I furtively checked out my own, plain, short nails.

'The police officers are here to speak to Svetlana Jones, Miss Hughes. I'll go and get her.'

'I'm DS Finlay and this is Constable Barrie,' Mike said. He smoothed back his auburn hair and noticeably straightened his powerful shoulders, used to good effect on the divisional rugby team.

Miss Hughes came around the desk and shook our hands. 'I'm Jill Hughes. DI Webb phoned and gave me brief details of the reason for your visit. Would you like to sit at the desk or would you be more comfortable on the sofas?'

We glanced between the upright chairs at the desk and the two saggy sofas facing each other over a shabby coffee table.

'We want Lana to be comfortable, so we'll take the sofas please, Jill. May I call you Jill?' DS Finlay's smile rivalled Eamon's for twinkliness.

Jill's own smile widened. 'Of course.'

'Thank you, Jill. Call me Mike.'

'Mike,' Jill said.

'Jill,' Mike said.

And my name's Gooseberry, I thought. 'I'm Sam,' I said, not that either of them noticed.

The secretary arrived with Lana in tow. Lana did an about-turn and tried to leave when she saw us, but Jill stopped her.

'Relax, Lana. The officers just want a quick word. I'll be here the whole time.'

'Let's sit down,' Mike said. He and I took one sofa, and Lana grudgingly sat opposite with Jill. Mike placed his briefcase on the floor beside him. If necessary, we would bring the magazine out.

'We're worried about you, Lana,' Mike said. 'My friend, Sam, here has seen photographs of you in a magazine.'

Lana's eyes bulged. 'I… I don't know what you mean.'

'Lana, let's cut the tosh. There are pictures of you in that magazine that would shock Miss Hughes.' Mike leant back and waited for Lana's response.

'Lana, do you want to tell us about the pictures?' Jill asked.

'I can't. He'll find out and it'll be bad.'

'Who will find out?' I asked. I wanted to suggest a couple of names, but Mike had warned me not to put words into her mouth.

Mike opened his briefcase and pulled out the magazine and placed it on the table in front of Lana. Jill gasped at the front picture, which was pretty mild in my opinion, but my perception had altered somewhat over the past few weeks.

'You're not in trouble, Lana, but someone is exploiting you and we need to find out who before they can exploit others.' I said.

Lana picked up the magazine and flipped over a few pages. Jill's eyebrows disappeared into her fringe.

'I remember this. It wasn't that long ago.' Lana put the magazine down. 'It was a film. Ted must have taken stills from it to make a photo story.'

'Ted Bulwer?' Mike asked.

Lana nodded.

'How did you get involved with Ted Bulwer?' I asked.

'Molly took us over.'

'Us?'

'Me and Janice. The money wasn't bad.'

'Did your mother know?' Mike asked.

Lana laughed softly. 'She let Molly sleep with me for the first time about a year ago, and she recruited Janice.'

Jill gave a little cry and slapped a hand over her mouth.

Mike reached over and touched her shoulder. 'Are you all right, Jill?'

She nodded. 'I'm just shocked at what I'm hearing. Lana, why didn't you come to me with this? I would have tried to help you.'

'How?' Lana snarled. 'Tell the Welfare so I'd be dumped in some kids' home? No thank you.'

'You're in danger,' I said.

'You've put me and Janice in danger by coming here. It'll get back, you know. Grasses are not tolerated where I come from.'

She had a point. I glanced at Mike, who didn't meet my eyes.

'You're not grassing, Lana. We came to you with some questions, that's all.' I wanted to reassure her, but I suspected that Mike had deliberately ignored the danger to Lana.

'That won't make a difference. Molly won't put up anyone drawing attention to his operation. Me mum's been warned about reporting me missing so often, but the school board would get on to her if she didn't.'

'All right, Lana, we'll finish this,' said Mike. 'Just to clarify, Molly has been sleeping with you, with your mother's knowledge, since you were fourteen. Your mother recruited Janice, who's fifteen. Molly handed you both over to Ted Bulwer, who has used you in blue movies and pornographic books.'

Lana gave an almost imperceptible nod.

'Will we need to speak to Janice?' I asked Mike.

'Eventually, but I think we have enough for today,' Mike replied.

'I'm not going to court. I'll deny everything,' Lana warned.

'We'll let you go now, Lana. Normally I would tell you to let your mother know we've spoken to you in the presence of Miss Hughes, but given the circumstances I'll leave that to you.'

Mike and I stood up and together we walked with Lana to the corridor.

'Hang on, Sam. I just want to have a quick word with Jill.' Mike slipped back into the office.

Lana turned to me. 'Will you please explain to everyone at the station that, when Mum reports me missing, I'm not really missing. I'm usually working.' She toed a sweet wrapper on the floor.

Poor Lana. I wanted to hug her.

'If you're reported missing, we're obliged to act. We don't have a choice,' I explained. 'And we don't have a choice here either.' And neither did Jill Hughes. I didn't voice that; I didn't want to panic Lana, but I knew Miss Hughes would have to inform Miss Ashton, who would probably have to bring in social services. I hoped she would see the bigger picture and hold back on that.

A bell sounded, doors flew open, and dozens of green-uniformed girls walked to their next class. Janice Alderman clocked us, and her head turned almost a hundred and eighty degrees as she went past.

'Oh shit,' Lana said.

Janice came over. 'What's going on?'

'We're in a magazine and they've seen it. They asked me some questions about it.'

'Shit. We're buddies. If you've grassed, Molly will find out and it'll be me that gets it,' Janice whispered, but I heard her.

That was twice I had heard Janice refer to buddies. I expected to hear that word in American films and shows, not in a British school. Buddies; best buddies; buddy system. I suddenly had a lightbulb moment. A shared experience, each responsible for the other. Janice would get it if Lana grassed. Molly kept order by using the buddy system. One girl stepped out of line and her buddy was punished. That was far more effective than straightforward threats.

'Girls,' I said, 'if anyone threatens you, ring and speak to me and I will do my very best to help you. Janice, maybe you should tell your parents what's really going on. We're going to have to visit you soon and it would be better for them to hear it from you first.'

Janice and Lana stared at each other for a long moment.

'Yeah, we might just do that,' Lana said.

Janice went to her classroom but Lana stayed close to me. 'You know there's no way out of this for us,' she said.

'There's always a way out,' I said.

She shook her head sadly and walked away.

I looked back into the office. Mike was laughing with Jill. He looked up and nodded to me. 'I'll see you then,' he said to Jill.

She twirled a lock of hair as she watched him leave.

'Did you get a date?' I asked as we walked back to the car.

Mike grinned. 'I might have.'

'Janice Alderman clocked Lana and me talking outside Jill's office,' I said. 'Lana wasn't happy. I think Molly—Molyneux—runs a buddy system to keep the girls in line. One plays up and the other is punished. Mike, do you think we might have made things worse?' I could feel an addition to my guilt pile coming on.

'There was no safe way to do this,' Mike said. 'Wherever we spoke to her, it was going to cause problems.'

'You knew that and didn't tell me?'

Mike shrugged. 'What was the point? We do our best.'

But sometimes our best wasn't good enough. Dammit.

*

Later on, DS Mike Finlay and I knocked on the Aldermans' door but there was no answer. While Mike peered through windows, I looked at Maud's house next door. She must still be in Australia. A shame really. I was pleased she was spending time with her remaining family, but she had been useful in getting information about her neighbours.

'Definitely out,' Mike said. 'We'll have to call back.'

I was a bit disappointed. Mike would continue the enquiries while I was on rest days. I would miss the next instalment, so to speak.

I followed him back to the car. As we drove off I looked back, half expecting to see Maud peering from her window. She must be lonely without Henry. I hoped her nephew was giving her a great holiday in Oz.

Chapter Twenty-Two

A few days later, I arrived in the parade room ready for the night shift. I took my seat, tucked my bag under the chair, and listened to the usual banter as more people arrived. The room was almost full when Steve sauntered in wearing a pair of mirrored sunglasses. Everyone stopped talking and stared at him as he tried to look cool when he stumbled over my handbag, almost landing in my lap. I shoved him onto his own seat.

'Sunglasses?' Ken asked. 'It's eleven o'clock at night.'

'Not just sunglasses; these are aviators and they look good.' Steve leant back on his chair.

'You need to really be an aviator for them to look good,' I suggested.

'I was going for *The Choirboys* look,' Steve said. 'The book by Wambaugh. You should read it.'

'You look like a wazzer. No choirboy I've seen wears sunglasses like that, especially at night. You're mad.' Phil rotated a finger by his temple. 'Who wears sunglasses on nights?'

'I wouldn't expect you to understand,' Steve said.

'I don't have to walk around half-blind to look cool,' Phil said over his shoulder.

Everyone stood as Alan, Brian, and Inspector Tyrrell came in to start parade. I was disappointed to see Brian. I had hoped after speaking to the boss he would have been fired or something by now, but I had to trust there were things happening in the background. Sometimes I felt frustrated at my lowly status. One day, things would be different.

'As you were,' said the inspector.

Everyone sat except Alan, who stared over at Steve.

'Are those shatterproof lenses?'

Steve touched the glasses. 'I don't know, Sarge.'

'One smack and you could be blinded. Get them off!' Alan thumped the parade book onto the table and sat down, shaking his head. Steve removed the glasses and put them in his top pocket.

'Leave them in the sergeants' office before you go out, Steve,' the inspector said.

'But sir...' Steve began.

'No buts. You heard Sergeant Bowman. I don't trust you not to put them back on when you get outside. That goes for you all. I don't mind glasses with "eyeguard" glass but I won't have anyone risk their sight, no matter how cool they think they are.' The inspector turned to Alan. 'Over to you, Sergeant Bowman.'

Alan gave out the duties and I tried to ignore Brian's never-ending smirk. I had to hide my own smirk. He thought he had me, but the boss was on to him.

'Sam, I want you to cover the control room with Ray tonight. He's by himself at the moment, so go there now.'

'Yes, Sarge.' I would have a flick through the parade book and briefing sheets later. I liked working with Ray, he always had the most entertaining stories from his time in the Merchant Navy. I gathered my things and hurried to the control room.

I settled myself into my seat by the phones and gathered the incidents ready to be allotted when the lads came to collect their radios. Inspector Tyrrell came in first.

'Sam, when you get a minute, can you come to my office?'

'What have you done?' Ray asked when the boss went out.

I supposed it was all about Brian, or maybe the mucky books, but I shrugged. 'Nothing, I think.'

'Running off to the boss's office again, Sammy?'

I spun my chair to face Brian, who was standing at the door to the enquiry office.

'The inspector has told me to go to his office. I don't know why,' I said.

'Haven't you given him his oats today?' Brian said.

'I beg your pardon!' I exclaimed.

'Everyone knows you snogged him at Ken's do,' Brian said.

'I was at that party and Sam did not snog anyone.' Ray spun his chair to face Brian and held his gaze. He didn't exactly curl his lip, but the sentiment was there to see.

'Right, right.' Brian sauntered off.

'I hate that man.' I screwed up a bit of paper and launched it at the wall. It bounced off and rolled back to my feet. I didn't feel any better.

Ray watched me as he lit another cigarette. 'He has been quite complimentary about your physical attributes.'

'Nothing that man says would be a compliment. I bet he just commented about my boobs.'

Ray snorted, making smoke puff from his nose. 'And your behind. He said he would love to get you on film.' He blew smoke across the radio. 'Hey, this might be your big chance, he said he knew someone who did films.'

Ted Bulwer probably. Karen's information had been good up to now. I laughed for effect. 'Yeah. Hollywood, here I come.'

'I'd ten minutes alone with him, though,' Ray said. 'I'd knock his block off.'

I chuckled. 'You'd only get yourself arrested.'

'Wouldn't be the first time,' Ray said.

'What? You have to tell me everything.' I turned my seat towards him and waited agog.

'I used to box in the navy. I was quite good. One night I went out with a couple of shipmates and someone in the pub said something he shouldn't so I punched his lights out. One punch. He was a big bloke, as tall as me but twice as wide. I expected his mates to wade in, but they hauled him away. I spent the night in the cells but, because he hadn't complained, they let me go next morning without charge, and I got back before I was logged as AWOL, which would have been bad. It did my reputation on the ship no end of good.'

I stared at Ray's sinewy forearms and big hands, so at odds with his slim body. It must have been like being hit by a hammer. 'Didn't that count against you when you applied to the police?'

'I declared it like you're supposed to and told them how, when I got back to the ship, I had been disciplined and fined a day's leave. I had no criminal record and I left the navy on good terms, so they considered the matter dealt with and my application went ahead.'

'I'm working with a violent criminal!' I joked. *Apart from Brian*, I thought.

Everyone bustled in and, for a few minutes, we were busy with test calls and demands for batteries. I allocated my list of non-urgent incidents and gradually everyone cleared away to begin the night's patrolling.

'Is it okay if I go to see the boss now?' I asked Ray.

'Should be. Let me know if you'll be more than ten minutes.'

I trotted upstairs and knocked on the boss's door.

'Come in, Sam. Close the door and sit down.'

Uh-oh, this felt like the lead up to a rollicking. I sat down and folded my hands in my lap.

Inspector Tyrrell rested his elbows on the desk. 'Sergeant Lewington came to me earlier because he has concerns about you. He thinks you're becoming too friendly with prostitutes and they might be using you for their own ends. Feeding you false information or maybe trying to get information from you that they can use.'

So Brian was trying to get in first to throw doubt on any information I had. Why would he do that if he didn't have something to hide?

'He's trying to discredit any information I get by disguising it as concern for me,' I said.

'I know that you are friends with Karen,' Inspector Tyrrell said.

'So are you!' I lowered my eyes, shocked at myself for my disrespectful outburst. 'Sorry, sir.'

Instead of rebuking me he chewed his thumbnail, as was his habit when he was thinking something through.

'I am friends with her, which is why I trust information she gives.' The inspector stood up and paced the few feet beside the desk. 'Maybe it would be better for you not to see Karen for a while.'

He believed Brian! No, that couldn't be it, I knew Inspector Tyrrell didn't trust Brian. Then, I saw it.

'Oh hell. Karen's placed herself in danger by talking to me.' I groaned.

Working independently didn't make a difference. If she came to the notice of the wrong people, they would be out to get her. I had made life risky for Lana, Janice, and now Karen. More for my guilt pile.

'Let Brian think I've warned you off,' Inspector Tyrrell said.

I enjoyed my chats with Karen and I would miss seeing her but, if Brian had contacts with gangsters, he would report back if he saw me going to her house. I didn't want to be responsible for her getting another beating. Again, the boss's instincts were spot on. He was also telling me he was on my side and he believed me. That compensated nicely.

'Does Brian know about the magazines and what Hari said?' I asked.

'I can't discuss that right now, Sam. Rest assured that it's all in hand.'

'Has anyone spoken to Janice about the pictures, sir? Only, DS Finlay said we would, and I haven't been approached to accompany him.'

'Mike Finlay took one of the women DCs with him while we were on rest day, but they were out. I can tell you that social services have been informed about Lana and Janice,' the boss continued. 'Lana has been taken to Merrymoor, the secure children's unit in the city, and Janice will be closely monitored in the home environment.'

'The way they are monitoring Bernadette, who has remained with a mother who has tried to sell her, twice?'

'Now you sound cynical.'

'Sorry, sir. I suppose there is a big difference between Elsie and the Aldermans.'

The inspector dismissed me and I went back downstairs where Brian was hanging around again.

'What did the boss want?'

'To discuss a concern you had.'

There was no mistaking Brian's look of triumph. He would think I had been well and truly rollicked and his path was clear, which was probably the best thing for now.

'Right then, Ray,' he said. 'I'm off out.'

'At last,' Ray muttered when Brian was out of earshot. He relaxed back. 'Put the kettle on and tell me what's going on.'

I clicked on the kettle and put tea bags into four mugs; I had learnt always to include Alan and the boss.

'I can't tell you everything, Ray; but Brian has gone to the boss to tell him I am making myself vulnerable to disinformation by befriending prostitutes.'

'Are you befriending them?' Ray asked.

'I have a professional acquaintance with one, that's all.' That seemed to answer any questions. Although really, I felt affection when I thought of Karen. I'd taken to calling in on her from time to time when I was working lates. We chatted comfortably and not just about policing and prostitution concerns.

Ray nodded. 'We all need an informant or two.'

'Well I've been told to stay away.'

Such was Ray's disdain for Brian, I knew he wouldn't tell him anything. But it wouldn't be a bad thing if that filtered back to Brian from another source; he would think his plan was working. Maybe Ray would mention it to Derek, then Brian would be sure to hear I'd been warned off.

I saw the inspector go past on his way to the bridewell for the mandatory review of prisoners. He would be done in about fifteen minutes, so I placed a saucer over his drink to keep it warm. I put a mug in front of Ray and then carried another mug through to Alan in the sergeants' office.

On my way back to the control room through the enquiry office, I saw Mr Kapoor come in with Hari. The restaurant must be shut, because there was no way they would have left while there was the possibility of business.

'Hello, Mr Kapoor, Hari. Can I help you?'

'Hello, Constable Sam, we want to see the man in charge,' Hari replied.

'That's Inspector Tyrrell, but I'm afraid he's with the prisoners. If you want to take a seat, he'll be finished in about ten minutes.'

Mr Kapoor peered at me and said something to Hari who replied, speaking quickly and quietly. Mr Kapoor glanced at me a couple of times as Hari spoke, then both men smiled and nodded at me. Hari and his father sat on the hard, plastic chairs and I returned to the control room.

Ray had been watching through the glass partition. 'What was that about?'

'I'm not sure. But they want to speak to the boss.'

Brian crashed into the station from the yard.

'Someone's in a hurry,' Ray murmured.

'He's only just gone out,' I whispered back.

Brian rushed through the control room to the front desk. Ray and I left the door open and, remaining in our seats, feigned indifference while we watched through the glass wall. This could be interesting. I hoped that the phone wouldn't ring.

'Mr Kapoor and Hari, how nice to see you,' Brian said.

Hari stood up. 'Sergeant Brian, we don't want to speak to you,' he said.

'Is it some problem about your continued residence in this country?' Brian asked in a friendly tone.

Another threat? I turned to Ray, who shrugged in answer to my unasked question.

Mr Kapoor said something to Hari who hushed him.

'You foreigners are subject to so many regulations to live here; I wouldn't like you to fall foul of them.' Brian smiled with a nasty, wide, smug grin.

'Sam, go and get the boss,' Ray whispered to me.

I slipped away and ran to the bridewell where I found Inspector Tyrrell in the charge office talking to the bridewell sergeant.

'Sir, you need to come to the front office right away. There's something going on between Brian and Mr Kapoor from the Golden Temple restaurant.'

Inspector Tyrrell came at once and marched into the front office. I took my seat at the phones, and Ray and I continued to watch proceedings through the glass partition.

Hari stood up and came to the desk. 'You are in charge, sir?'

'Yes. I am Inspector Tyrrell.'

'It's all right, boss. I think Mr Kapoor and his son are leaving.' Brian looked pointedly at the two men.

'My father and I wish to discuss a matter of great concern, but we do not want to speak to this man.' Hari gestured towards Brian.

'Very well. Come to my office and we can talk.' Inspector Tyrrell cut through the control room and brought the Kapoors through to the corridor.

Brian came up behind me. 'You have been a busy girl, haven't you Sammy?'

I turned to face him. 'What am I being blamed for this time?'

'Always the innocent.' Brian went into the sergeants' office.

Ray lit another cigarette and drew deeply on it. 'I think it's about to hit the fan.'

Chapter Twenty-Three

A couple of hours later, Inspector Tyrrell rang down and asked us to get Phil to come in to see him. Ray called him up and, in a few minutes, Phil arrived.

'What's happening?' he asked.

'The Kapoors are with the boss.'

Phil held my gaze for a moment. He understood. 'Hellfire.'

'You'd better go straight up,' Ray said.

Brian had been hanging around, jumpy as the proverbial cat on a hot tin roof, but he had eventually gone out. I didn't doubt he would remain close to the station to monitor when the Kapoors left. If my guess was correct, the boss thought Brian would intimidate them into withdrawing their complaint. Phil was to get them home, and I hoped he would stay around there until the morning.

After a few minutes, I saw Hari and his father leave the station with Phil.

Alan came in from the sergeants' office. 'Sam, the boss wants to see us both. Ray, he said to put a "Gold Response" on the Kapoor's restaurant and home address.'

'Roger that, Alan.' Ray replied.

Gold Response. That meant Gary thought they would have need to ring us and he wanted to make sure they would be given top priority. Surely Brian wouldn't be so stupid as to turn up there, but he had already demonstrated how far he would go to perpetuate his dodgy dealings. Now things were crumbling around him, he was getting careless, even reckless, so he might try to intimidate them. Both Ray and I had heard him threaten the Kapoors. Once his protection scam had been uncovered, which in itself would be enough to have him sacked, other illegal activities might be revealed. Interesting times ahead.

*

I followed Alan upstairs and waited for the inspector to invite us in.

'Shut the door after you,' Inspector Tyrrell said.

Alan adopted his position leaning against the wall and I sat on the chair opposite the boss.

'Mr Kapoor and Hari have come in to make serious allegations against Brian. It's as you told me, Sam: he's taking money. He was holding the threat of deportation over them to ensure they kept quiet.'

'We have to take direct action now, Gary,' Alan said.

The inspector nodded. 'I had hoped we could give him enough rope to hang himself and let the surveillance team do the rest.'

'Surveillance team?' It wasn't my place to comment but I was shocked to hear that.

'Brian has been subject of quite a high-level operation, some of it concerning information you passed on, Sam. However, now I have to be seen to take action.'

'Suspension?' Alan said.

'That would be normal practice, pending full investigation. It'll have to be effective immediately.'

Part of me was glad Brian would be out of the way, but a larger part was filled with trepidation. Brian would be angry; that would make him more dangerous, to me and the Kapoors, and maybe Karen.

'Right, I'll draw up the report and inform the brass. Sam,

I'll ring down shortly for Ray to call Brian in.' He paused. 'I'm parched. Would you bring me a brew while I'm doing this, please?'

'Of course, sir.'

Alan and I went downstairs. Ray said nothing as I went into the telex room and boiled the kettle, but I could feel the questioning waves coming from him.

'Brian's being suspended,' I whispered as I placed a mug in front of him.

Ray didn't reply, but I saw the slightest movement of his head to indicate that he had heard.

I took Alan his mug, then ran upstairs with the inspector's drink. He reached out just as I put the mug down and our hands brushed. For a second our eyes met and, instead of fleeing, I smiled.

'Thanks,' the boss said.

'You're welcome.'

I walked towards the stairs, hoping that the boss had picked up my not-so-subtle cues that I liked him: really liked him. As a result, I didn't see Brian until he was on me. He seized me and pushed me into an empty office. I slammed through the door and turned to face him.

'What are you doing?' I shouted.

Brian pressed himself hard against me, trapping me between him and the wall. I tried to scream but he put his hand over my mouth, smothering any noise.

'Did you know that more police lose their jobs over property than anything else? We do random locker searches from time to time and I would be shocked if something from the property cupboard or the safe were to be found in your locker. Even the boss couldn't protect you then,' he whispered into my ear. He took a step backwards, releasing the pressure on me. 'But I could. You scratch my back... et cetera.'

I tried to get away from him, but his arm shot out and blocked my way.

'Make your mind up, Sammy, I have limited patience and time is running out.'

Didn't Brian realise he was about to be suspended? Hadn't it occurred to him that he was facing the sack? Was he so deluded?

'You won't get away with this,' I hissed. 'Everything you do now is just one more nail in your coffin.'

'Wrong answer. Don't forget, I'm still bruised from when you assaulted me. Make any waves and I'll be the one putting a report in. An ex-cop with a conviction for assault and theft would be virtually unemployable. You'll end up alongside your little friend on the docks.' He stepped towards me again and I pressed myself back against the wall. 'You won't be able to be so fussy there, you might even welcome my assistance.' He put his cheek next to mine and I strained away. 'But it comes with a price.'

I turned my head and looked directly into his eyes. 'You're the one going down, you bent bastard.' It was the wrong thing to say, but I was so angry and scared it just came out.

'Then I'm taking you with me.' Brian sneered.

All pretence was over. I pushed him with all my strength and he moved enough for me to get to the door. I crashed open the door and ran to the control room.

'Brian's just threatened me! He grabbed me and put his hand over my mouth and threatened me!'

Ray grabbed his phone and quickly dialled the inspector. 'You need to get down here fast, boss.'

Brian arrived a second later but Ray, bless him, abandoned the handset, leapt up, and stood between Brian and me, his big fists clenched, ready to thump Brian. A moment later Inspector Tyrrell arrived, closely followed by Sergeant Bowman.

Brian rolled up his sleeve and thrust his bruised arm in front of Inspector Tyrrell. 'I wish to make a formal complaint against Constable Barrie. She assaulted me a few days ago: ask Derek when he comes back, he'll be able to corroborate it. I showed him my injury at the time but didn't report it as I didn't want to endanger her probation.'

I stepped from behind Ray. 'It's a lie. He did it himself to try to blackmail me. He's protecting gangsters. He's been threatening me to make me share any information I get so he can pass it on to his masters.' I was shaking so badly, my voice wavered.

Brian lashed out and the back of his hand cracked against my cheek, causing me to cry out.

Instantly, Ray's fist shot out and connected with the side of Brian's face. He dropped to the floor.

'He assaulted me, I want him arrested,' Brian shouted.

'I didn't see anything,' Alan said.

'Me neither,' I said.

Inspector Tyrrell grabbed Brian's arm and dragged him up. 'Brian Lewington, I am arresting you for assault on Samantha Barrie. You do not have to say anything unless you wish to do so, but anything you do say will be taken down in writing and may be given in evidence.'

'She assaulted me! I have bruises to prove it.' Brian waved his arm around. 'So did that big fairy.'

Ray raised a fist. 'You want another one?'

'Go ahead. I'd like to see them deny you hitting my twice, you pouf,' Brian cried.

Eyes blazing, Inspector Tyrrell said, 'Enquiries will be made about the alleged assault on you by Constable Barrie. Meantime, we need to have a chat about a little insurance scam you have going.'

Brian blanched. 'You can't believe those people; they barely speak English, they probably misunderstood me.'

'Hari is fluent,' I said.

Brian turned a look of such malevolence on me, I shrank back.

'This is your fault, you put them up to this. I've seen you whispering with Hari, putting ideas into his head,' he shouted. 'I bet you're fucking him.' He turned to Ray. 'And as for you, I know you're queer and I'm going to make sure everyone else knows too. About both of you: the queer and the slut.'

'Alan, get him to the bridewell; I'll join you shortly,' Inspector Tyrrell barked.

Alan escorted Brian, still shouting insults to us all, out of the office. My knees felt weak and I sagged against the wall. The tears I had held back bubbled up and I covered my face. Inspector Tyrrell put his arms around me and I burrowed my head under his chin and wept while he stroked the back of my head and made shushing noises.

When I calmed down, the boss sat me down and chewed his thumbnail for a moment.

'Sam, given that an allegation of assault has been made against you, C&D will have to talk to you.'

C&D: Complaints and Discipline. It was to be expected, but my heart sank.

'Will you have to arrest me? What about Ray?' I looked at Ray sitting quietly in front of the radio, puffing on another cigarette and flexing his fingers.

Inspector Tyrrell shook his head. 'Nobody is going to arrest you, and I don't know what you're talking about with reference to Ray.' He grinned. 'C&D will have to look at this, but word against word works both ways. I arrested Brian because we all witnessed an assault on you. The fact that he assaulted you in front of us supports that he would assault you when nobody was around. Anyway, let's leave C&D to worry about that. I should suspend you pending investigation, but I think if you take a few day's leave instead, that will suffice.'

Suspension was supposed to be a neutral act but, for a probationer like me, it could mean the difference between passing and failing. By offering me leave instead, the boss had thrown me a lifeline that could save my job. I nodded, grateful for the chance. Nothing to do now but wait to be interviewed and for the result of the investigation.

'Should I go home now, sir?'

'Brian's safely in the bridewell. See out your shift if you feel up to it, then begin your leave tomorrow.'

Inspector Tyrrell went to deal with Brian in the bridewell, leaving me alone with Ray.

'Thanks, Ray,' I said.

'I've been wanting to do that for a while,' Ray said, shaking his hand out. He sat back in his chair. 'Well, aren't you going to ask me?'

'Ask what?'

'If what Brian said is true?' Ray said.

'I don't care if it is,' I said.

Ray nodded and sat silently for a moment. 'It is true.'

'That's why you came alone to Ken and Gaynor's party,' I said.

'I'm not alone, Sam. I have someone I love very much.'

'Then why not bring him to the do with you?' I asked.

'He's wary of us being seen together. Being homosexual wasn't always legal. Even now, many people disapprove.'

I stood up and hugged him. 'You're the toughest man I've ever met and I'm glad I'm working with you.'

Ray smiled. 'Thank you, Sam.'

*

Brian's allegation against me was quickly found to be unsubstantiated, so I returned to work with no stain on my record, unlike Brian. He remained on suspension.

A surreal atmosphere had descended on B Block with his departure. No police officer likes to know that they have been working with a corrupt colleague and, if Brian thought he was going to garner support, he was mistaken. Even Derek remained quiet on the subject and he'd been Brian's biggest fan. Inspector Tyrrell did speak to Derek in more depth about the alleged assault by me on Brian, but he had not supported his supposed friend's account.

Everyone knew the charges against Brian were so serious it was unlikely that he would ever enter a police station as an operational officer again. I was a little concerned that Brian was being so quiet. The Kapoors hadn't been visited—or at least, they hadn't phoned in—and I hadn't seen Brian around. I didn't trust him; he had to be plotting something.

Chapter Twenty-Four

I pushed open the door and Inspector Tyrrell and I entered the CID Office.

'Sam m'darlin', Boss, glad you're here. Take a seat,' Eamon said.

I perched on the edge of a chair.

'Where's Norman Webb?' Inspector Tyrrell asked.

'Just taking a call, boss. He'll be here in a minute.' Eamon went over to the kettle. 'Do youse want a cup of tea?'

'Yes please,' we said in unison.

Eamon plonked mugs of tea in front of us and handed around a tin of biscuits. I took one, but even I could see he was trying to get the boss and me in a good mood.

DI Norman Webb—Webby to everyone—appeared with DS Finlay and Irene, who came and sat beside me.

'What's going on?' I whispered.

'Wait and see,' Irene answered.

'Thanks for coming,' DI Webb said, his double chin wobbling as he spoke. 'I'll cut straight to the chase. Gary, you know we've got an operation going on at that warehouse in the city: Operation Hollywood?' Gary nodded so DI Webb continued. 'It's run by Ted Bulwer. Robert Molyneux is connected and we suspect he uses his security firm to launder money. There is a suspicion that our erstwhile colleague, Brian, is somehow connected.'

'He protects them,' I said.

DI Webb clicked his sausage fingers. 'Exactly. So we need someone to get in, so we can close the operation and put the whole bunch away.'

'You have Benno,' Inspector Tyrrell said.

'Yeah, but he's only at the periphery. His contact is a runner for the organisers, not on the inside. We need somebody who can get close to the girls and the main man, and who can bring me enough bloody evidence for me to charge the bastards.'

'Our female detectives are too well-known,' Eamon explained, 'and, well, I don't mean to sound unkind, but they're too old to be able to get in. These criminals like kids. We need someone young-looking, who can pass for maybe sixteen, and who is not well-known to the gang.'

Everyone fell silent and looked at me. I gazed back, waiting to hear the plan.

'No,' Inspector Tyrrell said. 'Sprogs can't go into situations like this.'

Realisation dawned. 'You want me to go into the warehouse and get evidence against Ted Bulwer?'

'That's right, Sam,' DS Finlay said. 'And anyone else who has a stake in the operation.'

'Why have you asked me? Why not someone who knows what they're doing? There must be young-looking female DCs in other areas. They wouldn't be known by our local criminals.'

'You fit the preferred profile: dark hair, fresh complexion, generous... chest and, most importantly, an air of innocence,' the DS replied.

I blushed as the others scrutinised me against Mike's description.

'Even Welsh Elsie said you'd do well in the movies,' Eamon grinned.

'I didn't take her seriously,' I replied. 'Besides, I'm too old for them.'

'But you look young,' DS Finlay said.

'Can I have a word with you, Norman?' Inspector Tyrrell went into the DI's office and the detective inspector followed him.

I watched them through the interior window that faced onto the CID office. The barely controlled anger in Inspector Tyrrell's gestures told me this was more than a professional disagreement.

'You might have asked me first. You know her history, you know about Hogarth Acre. I don't think she should be put into this position. I'm going to have to think extremely hard about releasing her for this,' I heard Inspector Tyrrell say.

The DI pointed his finger towards Inspector Tyrrell, and I heard him say, 'This is a CID operation. I'm the DI and you do as you're told.'

Inspector Tyrrell erupted. He banged his fist on the desk, pointed right back and shouted, 'I'm sick of you strutting around like cock of the walk, Norman. Detective is a job description, not a rank. We're equals, so don't you dare talk to me as if I'm a sprog. That girl is under my command, she is inexperienced and vulnerable because of her past. Find someone else.'

I grimaced. This was so awkward, but I couldn't look away; none of us left in the office could.

DI Webb smirked. 'I've already had clearance from the chief. If Sam agrees, she's mine for a few days. I only asked you out of professional courtesy.'

Inspector Tyrrell looked up and caught my eye. I wondered if he would say something to me, but he reached over and dropped the blind on the office and the door slammed shut.

'Someone is not happy at all,' Eamon murmured.

A couple of minutes later, the door to the DI's office opened and the bosses came out, speaking in a relatively normal manner but Inspector Tyrrell's brows were low, his normally upward-curving mouth turned downwards.

'We're not talking about a pub staying open too late or a club serving underage kids here. This is an organised gang who are procuring teenagers to take part in hard-core pornographic films and prostitution. If they discover Sam's undercover, she could be in real, deadly danger.'

The DI snorted. 'Jeez, Gary. Danger comes with the job. You're so protective of her; I'm beginning to wonder if your interest is purely professional.'

There was a moment when everyone, including me, drew a breath. My jaw dropped as Inspector Tyrrell briefly met my gaze then looked away. A distinct pink tinge crept along his high cheekbone.

'All right,' Inspector Tyrrell said after a few seconds.

He hadn't corrected the DI. Irene caught my eye, raised one eyebrow, and half smiled at me.

'Sam will be as safe as we can make her, boss. We'll be nearby, waiting to move in.' Eamon winked at me.

'Molyneux will know her,' Inspector Tyrrell argued.

'I did only see him face-to-face the once,' I said.

'We're agreed then. Sam is going to go into the warehouse and help us round up these pervs. This side of the operation will be called Operation Elstree.'

'Do you agree, Sam?' Inspector Tyrrell asked.

'If I hadn't been asked, I'd have volunteered. Sorry, sir, I know how you feel, but people like this must be stopped.'

DI Webb rubbed his hands together, and DS Finlay and Eamon pulled out the whiteboard and several coloured markers.

'Right then. Let's get cracking.'

*

When I got home that night, I had to think about what I was going to tell Mum. I couldn't tell her about the operation, scheduled for a few days away, but she would notice if I didn't come home. She was still angry with the police force in general over the whole Brian thing, and I almost had to physically restrain her when she'd heard how Brian had threatened me. She would not react well to this operation.

'Have you had a good day?' she trilled when I opened the door.

'Not bad, just routine stuff,' I called back from the hall.

'There's some stew in the pressure cooker if you're hungry.'

Mum popped her head out from the kitchen.

'Thanks.' I was always hungry after a shift.

I sat at the kitchen table while Mum heated up the stew and ladled some into a bowl.

'I might not be home for a few days next week,' I said.

'Oh?' Mumspeak for *"Go ahead and give me all the details"*.

'It's a work thing. I have to stay over.'

Mum put the bowl in front of me. 'You're a terrible liar, you know. What's his name?'

'What?! No, it's not that,' I cried.

'Really?' Mum looked disappointed. 'I'm sure I picked up fib vibes.'

'It really is a work thing, Mum.'

Mum sat opposite me and watched me eat stew.

'And stop trying to read my mind, Mum.'

'There's something you're not telling me.'

I sighed. 'Mum, please don't be upset but you are going to have to accept that there are some things I can't tell you.'

Mum bristled. 'I have the right as your mother—'

I put my hand up to stop her. 'No, Mum. I'm sorry but you have no right. I'm an adult. You must accept that I will sometimes have things in my life that I cannot, or might not want to, share with you.'

Mum seemed to shrink, which made me feel terrible.

'I love you, Mum, but you must trust me to do what I do and not demand answers.'

'It's dangerous isn't it?' Mum sounded flat.

'I'll be one of many with lots of back up.' True…ish.

Mum threw my empty bowl into the sink. 'I'm tired. I think I'll go up.'

'You have to let it go, Mum. You did nothing wrong that night, I was just unlucky.'

Mum faced me. 'I can't let it go. Every time you go out of that door, I make a mental note of what you're wearing in case I need to report you missing again. I'll never let it go.'

I hugged her. 'I do know how you feel, but seeing you like this makes me feel guilty. I carry enough guilt from that night, so please don't add to it. I spent a long time too scared to go out, simply existing between home and school. I cannot live like that again. You must let this go, you must let me go and let me try to live a normal life.'

A fat teardrop ran down Mum's face. 'Dad would know what to say now, but I don't. I don't want to make you feel guilty, but I can't help how I feel. I don't relax unless I can see you, or I know exactly where you are and that you're safe.'

'I think this is something we both must learn to live with,' I said.

Mum nodded. 'I think it might be. Tell you what, let's make a pact. I won't nag you about what you're doing, and you don't tell me to stop worrying. We just accept that's the way it is.'

'Sounds like a plan,' I said.

Mum kissed my head and went to bed.

*

A few days later, I walked along a long road looking for the address I had been given. I found number 453, a typical council end-of-terrace house. Like its neighbours, the garden was a brown scrub with the skeletons of bushes in each corner. The rain had not revived them after the hot summer; rather it had swept the dry soil away, exposing the roots.

I checked the note that DI Webb had given me for my contact's details then knocked on the door. A scruffy man with the omnipresent Mexican moustache opened the door. This wasn't what I had expected. His hair was too long to be a police officer.

He looked me up and down, removed the cigarette from his mouth and said, 'What?'

'I'm sorry. I think I must have the wrong address.' I backed away

'Who are you looking for?' he asked. Less gruff this time.

'Benno. I was given this address.' Dammit, I didn't want to draw attention to myself or Benno. 'Elstree.' I said.

'Come in.' The man stepped back. I hesitated but he waved his hand to hurry me in.

The living room was furnished in typical fashion. Slightly out-of-date suite, teak coffee table and bookcase, and an orange plastic, coin-operated television atop a matching pedestal.

'Is Benno here?' I asked.

'I am,' he said with a laugh. 'You must be my mole. I don't want to know your real name in case I slip up. What's your alias?'

I hadn't thought of an alias. 'Sa...lly. Sally.'

'Sally.' Benno held out a hand. 'I'm Benno, just Benno.'

'Hello Benno.' I shook his hand.

'You have the back bedroom. The front one's mine because I live here.'

'All the time?' I asked. Then worried I was being thoughtless or rude.

'Pretty well. The house belongs to the force, but those of us working difficult cases get to live here. It stops the neighbours getting suspicious if there's a tenant here, and it means we don't have to worry about undesirables getting near our families.'

'Right.' I hefted my backpack onto my shoulder. 'I'll take this up.'

'I'll put the kettle on and make us some tea. *The Bionic Woman* is coming on soon. Have you seen it?'

I had. It was a spin-off from *The Six Million Dollar Man*. I wasn't a great fan, but I said. 'Great, back down shortly.'

My bedroom was about eight foot square with a bedside table, a single wardrobe, chest of drawers, and a single bed, neatly made. I wondered if Benno had done it that day when he was told about me. I threw my bag on the bed and went back downstairs.

Benno had put digestives on a plate and opened a tin of Quality Street. He seemed like a decent bloke.

'Help yourself,' he said as he put two mugs of tea on the table. So I did.

*

I slept well despite the chocolate overdose. I waited for Benno to shower and go downstairs before I got up. Benno had warned me not to look too groomed, so I put on a plain white t-shirt, jeans, and scuffed sneakers. I combed my hair out and left it hanging loose.

Benno was sitting at the dining table, which was set for two. He looked up from his cornflakes as I came in. 'Not bad. You've still got a tan from the summer and the white t-shirt sets it off. They'll like that.'

'Do I look like a runaway? Do I look seventeen?'

'I thought you were supposed to be sixteen?'

'I was, but I don't think I can get away with it.'

'Overdo some purple eye shadow and make sure your mascara clumps, and you're sixteen.'

'You seem to know a lot about teenaged girls.' I sat at the table and poured myself a cup of tea from the pot.

'Yeah,' was all he said. I thought there was a story in there, but I didn't pry.

He pushed the box of cornflakes towards me. 'There's bread in the kitchen if you want toast.'

I wasn't a big breakfast cereal fan, but I wasn't sure when I'd get to eat again so I poured cornflakes into the bowl Benno had thoughtfully put in my place and sploshed on some milk.

'There's no point in rushing; nobody will be awake yet so take your time. I'm off to the shops to get a paper and some fags. Want anything?'

I couldn't think of anything. Benno picked up his dishes and took them into the kitchen. He left the house and I heard him greet his neighbour. He wasn't wrong when he said having a tenant stopped neighbours becoming suspicious.

I finished my breakfast and took the dishes into the kitchen, which was pleasingly clean and tidy. Benno's bowl was already washed and draining on a dishrack, and a washing machine was midway through a cycle. I rinsed my bowl and the teapot and left them to drain too. Then I went upstairs to experiment with make-up.

I put bronzer across my cheeks but didn't blend it in, I put a thick ring of black liner around my eyes and flicked up the outer edges and covered my lids in lilac crème shadow. Plenty of clear lip gloss, and my face was done. My hair naturally fell into a side parting, so I created a centre parting to alter my appearance a little. I gave my hair a good brushing until it fluffed out and I resembled Crystal Tipps, a popular children's character. I made two thin braids at the front and tied them at the back to contain the mass of hair. Sometimes I wished my hair wasn't so thick but then again, at times like this, it was a good disguise.

I heard Benno return, so I ran downstairs.

'What do you think?'

'Bloody hell, Cleopatra meets a Brillo pad.'

'Do I look over-made-up, trying-too-hard, sixteen?'

'Yes, that's fine. Someone called Neil's coming over in a little while, so get into character and follow my lead.'

Game on. I felt my pulse increase.

The washing machine clicked off and, to kill time, I helped Benno peg the wet washing out in the small back garden.

'You're quite domesticated,' I commented.

'And they talk about men pigeonholing women,' Benno muttered. 'Welcome to the new world, where men cook, clean, and operate washing machines.'

I hadn't meant to offend him so, to make amends, I made us a cup of tea.

I had just poured hot water into the cups when the doorbell rang.

'This will be Neil. Be nice,' Benno said as he went to the door.

He admitted a suited man who scrutinised me as I brought in the drinks.

'Would you like a cup of tea or coffee?' I asked, nicely.

'Coffee please. Milk, one sugar,' Neil said.

I went back into the kitchen and, as I assembled the coffee, I listened to Benno and Neil discussing me.

'She's pretty enough,' Neil said. 'Have you broached the subject yet?'

'Sort of. I said I knew someone who could get her a job as a model.'

Neil laughed. 'She's a bit dumpy for catalogue work, but our clients like big tits.'

Dumpy! I carried in Neil's coffee and fought the urge to pour it in his lap.

'I am not overweight. If you want a skeleton, go find a heroin addict. There are plenty at the bus station.'

Neil took the coffee from me and smiled at Benno. 'Oh dear. I think I've hurt her feelings.'

'I'm right here,' I snapped, ignoring Benno's warning look.

Neil studied my face for a long time. 'Yes, you are. I like a woman that isn't afraid to speak out, but not everyone does. If I take you to meet my client, you must keep that tongue still.'

'Then don't insult me.'

'Sally!' Benno had had enough.

'Where did you find her?' Neil asked Benno.

'The railway station,' Benno replied.

'They often turn up there.' Neil sipped his drink. 'Where were you headed, Sally?'

'I thought I might go to London, but I didn't have enough for the fare.'

'London, where the streets are paved with gold.' Neil gave a short laugh.

'She asked me for spare change, and I ended up inviting her back here,' Benno said.

'Don't you have a job?' Neil asked me.

'I was a waitress, but I got fired.'

'She wouldn't fuck the boss,' Benno added. I shot him a look.

Neil looked at me with interest. 'You live at home, with parents?'

I rolled my eyes. 'Okay, you want my life story. Mum left, Dad drinks. I was saving for my own place but now I'm jobless. Dad hit me for getting sacked so I left. I met Benno. I had nowhere else to go so I came back with him. He said you could get me a job. Can you?'

'I can introduce you to someone who is looking for models, not necessarily the skinny type. You're not shy, are you?' I shook my head. 'Good, because he might want you for glamour work.'

Glamour, as in stripping? I turned, wide-eyed, to Benno.

'I'll talk to her about that,' Benno said.

'Good. Because if she is going to work for my client, she will be expected to perform to order.' Neil finished his drink and handed a card over to Benno. 'Go to the shop this afternoon and give them that card.' He turned to me. 'Take off some of that make-up and do something with that hair before you go.'

'It makes me look older,' I protested.

'My client will not want you to look older.'

Benno showed Neil out.

'I'm not stripping!' I cried when Benno returned.

Benno sat down and indicated that I should also sit. 'You can walk away whenever you choose.'

'I don't want to walk away, I want to help stop these people. I also don't want to get dragged into "performing", as that Neil put it.'

'Then you have to make a choice.' Benno said. 'You're like an actress, playing the part of a snotty runaway: and playing it very well, by the way. You're quite obnoxious. Are you going to immerse yourself into the role and do what's necessary, within reason, to get the evidence we need, or are you going to go against the role and play Miss Prim?'

I stood up and paced up and down the hearth rug. 'Nobody said stripping was part of the deal. I don't want to strip. What's the next step? Drugs?'

Benno smiled. 'Puts a whole different light on "taking a hit for the team".'

'It's not funny!' I threw myself down onto the sofa and chewed my nail for a minute. 'I suppose I could go along with it to a point, just to fool them. But if they ask me to strip, I'm off.'

Benno laughed.

'It's all right for you,' I complained. 'You aren't expected to expose yourself.'

'Like I said, Sam, we're playing roles. I'm a detective sergeant, but I've lived like this for four months. I've had to help these pervs so I can get close, but even that hasn't been enough to get the right evidence.'

'Have you been able to help any of the girls?' I asked.

'A couple of times I knew I was going to transport a youngster, so I alerted the local police and we were stopped during a "routine document check".'

'But other times you've had to watch girls being exploited so your cover is not blown?'

'You have to think of the bigger picture, and sometimes the girls actually want to be there.' Benno stood up. 'It's in your hands Sally. Stay, go, just don't blow it.'

I could see what he was saying. I could pretend to go along with things and, if I felt uncomfortable, I could find a non-suspicious way to back out. I could throw a strop and storm out, classic teenage behaviour, but would I be allowed to leave once I had infiltrated them? I thought about those magazines and the pictures of Lana and Janice. Dammit, did I really have a choice?

'Okay, let's do it.' What was I letting myself in for?

'Okay then. Chippy's open. I'll nip over and get a couple of fishcake dinners then we'll take a ride to the city.'

Chapter Twenty-Five

We drove through the city to a derelict-looking warehouse close to the river. Benno pulled up beside a barn-sized sliding door and pipped his horn twice. A small door in the big door opened and a woman looked out. She waved and went back inside. Next thing, the great doors slowly opened and Benno drove in and pulled up next to a pile of old machinery.

'Come on, Sally.'

As we got out of the car, a screech rang out from across the vast space, and a young girl sprinted towards us and launched herself at Benno. He staggered back under her weight.

'Benno! They let you go, I'm so glad.'

'They couldn't prove anything,' he laughed. 'You have to let go, Lisa, you're choking me.'

Lisa released her grip on Benno. 'Next time you see a police car, make sure you go the other way. I couldn't believe it when they arrested you.'

'You were arrested?' I asked.

Lisa turned to me. 'It was awful. The police stopped us and took me to the station and called the social services. Another cop threw Benno into the back of a police car and took him away. Who are you?'

'This is Sally,' Benno said. 'I wasn't expecting to see you back here again. Lisa.'

Lisa snorted. 'Where else will I earn enough money to go to America?' She turned to me. 'I'm going to go to Hollywood. Ted says I've got talent so they're bound to cast me in something and meantime I'm getting experience here.'

I caught the look of deep sadness in Benno's eyes before he hid it. Lisa must be one of the ones who wanted to be here. She believed the lies Ted Bulwer fed her.

'So this is an apprenticeship,' I said.

'Yeah, that's it,' Lisa said. 'I'm a 'prentice.' She eyed me for a moment. 'You could be a 'prentice too.'

'That's why we're here,' Benno said. 'We'd better not keep Ted waiting.' He took my arm and guided me to the metal stairs, which led up to a mezzanine floor. Our footsteps rang out across the dusty warehouse.

'How old is she?' I asked.

'Fifteen,' Benno replied.

I noticed a camera pointing down onto the cars. 'Security camera.' I said. I looked across the wide space. 'I can't see any others.'

'Ted just has it covering the door and the cars. Not much point anywhere else, there's sod all there,' Benno said.

At the top of the steps, Benno opened a peeling door and I gasped at the change of surroundings. I stepped into a reception area that any company would be proud of. Plush seats lined a lilac painted wall. Glossy magazines covered a glass coffee table and a coffee machine bubbled away in a corner. A wide, white desk almost filled another corner, and a receptionist with immaculate make-up smiled a greeting.

'Hello, Benno. Who's this?'

'Hi, Sonia. This is Sally.' Benno handed over the card Neil had given him.

'Ted's in the office,' Sonia said. 'Go right in.'

Benno pointed to the seats. 'Wait here, Sally. I'll be back soon.'

I obediently sat down, and Benno disappeared into a doorway.

'Help yourself to coffee.' Sonia pointed at the coffee machine.

'I'm all right thanks.'

'So, Sally, where did Benno find you?' Sonia asked.

It seemed Sonia was the first line of defence here and would try to glean enough information to decide if I could be trusted to go on through the next doorway.

'I met him at the railway station. I asked him for change.'

'Did you stay at Benno's last night?' she asked.

'I had nowhere else to go. Benno let me use his bathroom.'

Sonia smiled knowingly. 'Right. I thought you looked a bit less dishevelled than some we see here. How old are you?'

'Twenty-one,' I responded automatically. Dammit! I had blown it already. Benno would kill me. DI Webb would kill me.

Sonia half smiled. She didn't believe me! Maybe I was better at this undercover lark than I thought.

'Seventeen.' I lowered my eyes. 'Okay. Sixteen.'

Sonia's smile spread. 'Don't be in too much of a rush to grow up. You're an adult, with all the responsibilities that go with it, for a long time. Enjoy being a kid.'

I wanted to say that any kid coming into this office would have to grow up very quickly, but I bit my tongue.

Benno reappeared. 'Come on, Sally. Ted wants to meet you.' He showed me through the lounge to a large space that stretched the length of the warehouse and smelt of cabbage, mildew, and dust.

It looked like most of the filming took place here. In one corner, a cheap nylon carpet had been thrown down and a few beanbags scattered around. Opposite, a double divan with candy-striped bedding awaited its next occupants. A few dirty magazines were piled next to it. I guessed that was to get everyone in the mood. Nearby was a pile of sand. Beach scenes? Beyond that was a cream vinyl bar unit with four tall stools along it. At the farthest end of the room, a white shag pile carpet covered the floor. On it was a long sofa covered with brightly coloured cushions: deep purple, royal blue, scarlet, burnt orange, yellow. More cushions lay on the floor, and voile sheets floated down from wires suspended from the metal beams overhead. The overall effect was quite exotic. This was the set from the photographs in which I had seen Janice and Gerald Mount. I could do with photographing that as evidence for DI Webb. The rest of the space was taken up with lights and camera stands.

Benno pushed me forward towards a shortish man. Short, but taller than me. 'Ted, this is Sally.'

Ted didn't look like a criminal mastermind. He was about fifty. His belly hung over too-tight, too-young jeans and caused the buttons on his shirt to pull. He circled me, inspecting every inch. His thick gold bracelet clunked as he grabbed my breast. I swatted his hand away and stepped closer to Benno.

'Are they real?' Ted asked.

'You should know after grabbing them like that,' I snarled.

'Take your top off,' Ted demanded.

'I'm off.' I spun on my heel, but Benno grabbed my arm and pulled me back.

I was about to give him a mouthful when I caught the warning in his eyes. I could leave, but I had to think of the bigger picture. Ted might guess I was undercover, which would risk exposing Benno and losing all the evidence he had built up. Neither of us would be safe, so, I slowly removed my top and stood in my bra. Benno wandered off and stood with his back to us, flicking through a magazine over by the divan. I had complied so far, but if Ted wanted me to take anything more off, he would have to wrestle me to the ground and forcibly strip me.

'Not bad,' Ted pronounced.

I put my top back on and Benno rejoined us.

'Bring her to the studio in half an hour so we can do a screen test.'

Benno took me back to the lounge and we sat on a huge corner sofa.

'So what does the screen test involve?' I asked.

'He wants to see what you look like on screen.' Benno eyed me. 'I think you'll be quite photogenic.'

'Thanks Benno. Tell me again why you need me? Only it seems to me that you are quite close to Ted.'

'Normally I don't get past Sonia. The card Neil gave me confirmed that I had a potential recruit, you, and that allowed me in to meet with Ted. I haven't seen the sets before. Even now, I can't get as close as you can.'

'Is he the big boss?' I asked.

'There's always a bigger boss,' Benno replied.

'And that's who you're going for?'

'I wish. These people are very slippery. It's unlikely we'll get much above Ted. It depends how talkative he is when we bring him in.'

I felt that we would always be playing catch-up. We could close Operation Hollywood, Elstree, and others like them, but there were the shadowy characters in the background that would simply start another. Would girls like Lana, Janice and Lisa ever be safe?

*

Half an hour later, I stood in front of a table with a home-made console glued to it. It wasn't high tech, some of the buttons were bottle tops. Lisa came in and stood beside me. Benno leant against the wall at the back and Ted sat on a swivel chair next to a photographer, who set up a cine camera.

'What are we expected to do?' I whispered to Lisa.

'Follow instructions,' she whispered back.

Ted clapped his hands. 'Right, girls. You are the crew of a cargo ship on the way to a distant planet. Space pirates are after your cargo and invade the ship.'

I held my hand up. 'What are our lines?'

'I want you to react to what's happening. I want to see how you improvise.'

'It's hard to feel spacey without a costume,' Lisa complained.

'If I choose you for a film, you'll get a costume. I just want to see how you look on camera. Make it real. Action.'

I glanced at Lisa and jabbed at a couple of buttons while she strutted around, chest thrust forward, staring at an imaginary screen. The photographer snapped polaroids of us while the cine camera whirred on. I felt ridiculous, until a group of men stormed onto the set and grabbed us. Lisa squealed and pretend-struggled, taking care to pout and flutter her eyelashes at the camera. I didn't pout or flutter anything: my survival instincts kicked in and I went crazy.

I threw my head back and butted the man who had pinned my arms to my side. Simultaneously, I drew up both legs and smashed them into the stomach of the man attempting to hold my legs. They dropped me and fell to their knees. I immediately rolled over and brought the heel of my palm into the face of the man holding his stomach. I shakily stood up and realised that Ted, the cameraman, and Benno were staring at me, open-mouthed. What's more, the camera was still rolling. I had to remain in character.

'Get off my fucking ship!' I shouted.

The men groaned. 'Ted, we don't get paid enough for this. I think my bastard nose is bust,' cried the man behind me.

Ted stood up. 'What just happened?'

'You said to improvise,' I answered. 'That's how I deal with people who grab me.'

'It looked incredible,' Ted said. 'You honestly looked like you were fighting for your life. You're in. You two, go and get cleaned up.'

The actors staggered off. 'You can count me out of anything she's involved in,' one called back.

'What about me?' Lisa asked.

'You can be an extra,' Ted said in rather a distracted manner.

'An extra? But you said I was talented,' Lisa complained.

Ted curled his lip. 'Sally's got talent. You're an extra. Take it or leave it.'

'I'll take it only because I need the money for America.' Lisa flounced off the set.

'Yeah, yeah.' Ted couldn't have cared less. 'Come into my office,

Sally. We need to talk money.'

'I want Benno with me.'

Ted was already several yards away. He waved his hand, which I took as assent, so Benno and I followed.

Ted's office was ordinary: a desk with a row of drawers on one side, a locked cabinet against a wall, two hard-backed visitor chairs, and a wilted plant in a corner. We sat down and, while Ted and Benno discussed how much I would be paid, I looked around the office, trying to see if there were any cameras and where he was likely to keep the keys. If Ted commented, I would play the bored teenager.

'Does she do anal?'

And Sam's back in the room. 'No!'

'Could she be persuaded? It's very much in demand and she would be suitably compensated.'

The figure he quoted didn't seem anywhere near what I thought would be suitable compensation. And why was he asking Benno?

I rapped on the desk. 'I'm here so talk to me.'

Ted sighed. 'Let me explain this to you, Sally. My audience wants excitement: something different, daring. The more adventurous you are, the more you get paid and the more sales I make, which will make me very happy, so I'll use you again.'

I gave Benno a pleading look, but he didn't step in to help me. Then I remembered that I didn't really have to appear in a film. Okay then, I could have some fun.

'Oh, what the hell. All right.'

Ted sat back. 'Anal?'

'Yeah, whatever. The money will be useful.' I signed the sheet Ted pushed in front of me.

Benno gave me a sideways look. 'You're a fast learner.'

I knew he wasn't referring to the negotiations.

'If you're stuck for somewhere to stay, I have a couple of houses in the city that some of the girls share. Sonia will give you details.' Ted pushed himself away from the desk. 'I have a meeting in Manchester. Sonia will see you out.'

'Is it okay if I stay a bit longer and look around, maybe meet the other girls? I've never been on a film set before today.' I fluttered my eyelashes, badly, but Ted grinned.

'Sure, take your time.' He locked his desk and placed the key in a cabinet. I watched as he spun the numbers to lock it. His fingers didn't cover all the rows, just the last couple. Useful.

Ted ushered us out and we went to see Sonia.

'I'm going to my meeting now. Sally wants to look around,' Ted said.

'Oh, Ted, the lock on the door is playing up. Sometimes it doesn't catch.' Sonia pointed to the door off the stairs.

'So ring a locksmith,' Ted answered.

'I did but he can't come for a couple of days.'

Ted rolled his eyes. 'Do your best then. I have to go.'

'Can I go back and look at the sets?' I asked once Ted left.

'Sure, enjoy yourself,' Sonia oozed.

'I can't be bothered trailing around. You go, I'll stay and chat to the lovely Sonia,' Benno said.

Great. With Benno occupying Sonia, I had more time to check out the office. I hadn't been able to see any cameras, so I might be all right. I went through the film sets, then on towards the office.

'Where are you going?'

I turned to face Lisa. 'Ted said I can look around.'

'I'll show you around,' Lisa said. She linked my arm and guided me back to the sets. Dammit.

'I'm sorry you didn't get the part you wanted,' I said to Lisa. 'You were very good.'

'Thanks.' Lisa sighed. 'You were better.' She pointed to the bar unit. 'That's where they film parties. The sand is for desert and castaway stories and the bed is for straightforward fucking.'

The word sounded wrong, even jarring, coming from Lisa. She looked like the child she was. I pointed to the voile-festooned set. 'I bet that set is used for harem films.'

Lisa nodded. 'And Roman orgies and stuff like that.'

'Does this place have security cameras?' I asked.

'Why bother? There's not much to steal here.' Lisa picked up a champagne glass from the bar unit and pretended to drink from it. 'Dead sophisticated, eh?'

I laughed but I needed to keep her focused on the security. 'I bet Ted's got cameras everywhere.'

'The garage and the photo room because that's where the expensive stuff is.' She leaned towards me and whispered. 'There's a secret camera in the big, grey cabinet in Ted's office. There's a little hole in the door for the lens. It isn't on all the time. He thinks there's no point when he's there unless he has a meeting. I'm the only one who knows that because I heard him talking about it. Don't tell anyone.'

I shook my head vigorously. 'Cross my heart.'

'Is there a camera in reception or on the sets?' I asked.

'No point,' Lisa said. 'There's nothing to steal there and anyone coming in will be filmed in the garage.'

'I suppose so,' I said. 'You know loads about this place, Lisa.'

Lisa preened.

'There you are,' Benno called out. 'Have you had a good look?'

'Got to go, Lisa. Nice talking to you.'

'And you. You'll be dead good at this, you know.'

'Thanks.' I left her pretending to drink champagne and let Benno show me back into the office.

'While you were looking around, Sonia gave me the details of the house you'll be going to. So let's get your stuff and take you there,' Benno said. I was sure it was for Sonia's benefit.

'Thank you,' I called to Sonia as we left. She waved goodbye back.

'We've got to try to get Lisa out of here,' I whispered as we went down the stairs.

'She doesn't want to be helped,' he whispered back. 'Anyway, did you find anything?'

'Not much. Lisa says there's cameras in the garage and the photo room. Ted has a secret camera in the grey cabinet, but he only switches it on when he's in a meeting, or out of the building.'

Benno lit a cigarette and blew out a cloud of smoke. 'That means we have to disable it somehow.'

'Or risk searching the office when Ted is around.'

'Too risky.'

'It might be a risk worth taking,' I said.

'We'll think about it.' Benno tossed his half-smoked cigarette away. 'Let's get your stuff and I'll take you to the house. Don't let your bag out of your sight because some of them aren't above "borrowing" other people's stuff.'

Chapter Twenty-Six

The house was nothing like Benno's neat accommodation. I was allocated a bed in the large front bedroom that I would share with two others. Two more girls had beds in the back room. The tiny bathroom was grey with limescale, and black mould crept along the seal and grouting. Downstairs, the living room was shabby and crowded. The kitchen was a wreck of Rose and Arthur proportions. A plastic bin was rammed full of empty chip wrappers, and the cooker looked as if it hadn't been used in several months. The girls were friendly enough though.

'How long are you going to be here?' one asked.

'Dunno. I suppose I'll save enough to get myself a bedsit or something then move on.'

'That's what normally happens,' said another.

'What's your name?' said a third.

'Sally.'

'I'm Lesley but I use the name Lacey in the films. Luscious Lacey.' She swayed her hips, and everyone laughed.

'So what do you want me to call you?'

'Lesley's fine. What name are you going to use?'

I smiled. An alias for an alias. 'I can't think of anything. I'll just stick to Sally.'

'You can't do that, you need a stage name,' said the first girl. 'I'm Donna; Bella Donna.'

'Isn't that a poison?' I said.

'It means "beautiful lady".'

'I'm Busty Barb,' said the girl with large breasts whose name, I presumed, was Barbara. 'And that, over there, is Wendy.'

'Wondrous Wendy,' said Wendy.

'*Underage Wendy*,' I thought. She looked the youngest of us all.

'Okay then, how about Saucy Sally?' I said.

Wendy shook her head. 'Makes you sound like a boat. The "Saucy Sal".' We all laughed.

'Got it!' Lesley said. 'Something classy. Fiery Flora or Fizzy Flora, depending on whether you want to be fierce or peppy.'

I thought for a moment. 'I like fierce. How about Boudicca?'

'Bloody strange name if you ask me,' Lesley said.

I thought for a moment. 'Got it. Valkyrie.'

'That's a great name,' Wendy said.

'Valkyrie it is.'

Donna put the television on and scooted in beside me on the sofa.

'Did Benno bring all of you here?' I asked.

'Molly brought me,' Lesley said.

'And me,' Donna added.

Interesting. 'Molly? He lives in a posh flat, doesn't he? How did you meet him?'

'Janice, a girl from our school, told me about him. She said he could get me into films like he did for her. She says she's earning a packet,' Lesley replied.

Janice Alderman? It had to be. 'What school were you at?' I asked Lesley.

'Aggie's. I left this summer. Do you go there?'

'No. I went to the 'sec,' I replied.

'I don't remember you,' Wendy said in a challenging tone.

I held my breath a moment waiting for her to unmask me, but then attack was often the best form of defence.

'I don't remember you either. You weren't in my year, were you?'

Wendy flushed. 'I left last year.'

'Who was the head teacher when you left?' I recalled reading in the local paper that the headmaster had recently moved on and a woman had taken over.

'Miss…Mr Thomas,' Wendy said.

'You haven't left school, have you? You're a runaway. How old are you, fourteen?'

Wendy refused to meet my eyes. 'It's none of your business.'

Benno was definitely hearing about this. I held up my hands. 'Okay, calm down. I really don't care how old you are. I just wondered if we were going to get police knocking on the door.'

'I don't want police here either. We're buddies don't forget, Wendy,' Lesley said. 'Ted would go ballistic, and you know what would happen.'

Wendy stormed off to the bedroom.

'Buddies, like in a buddy system?' I asked Lesley.

'Yeah. You'll be given a buddy. Probably Lisa because she hasn't had a buddy since Julie died.'

'Julie?' I felt hairs lift on my neck.

'Yeah, she drowned. You must have heard it on the telly a few weeks ago.'

I nodded. 'Yes, Julie Wynne.'

'That's right. We think she ran away and topped herself. Normally, Lisa would have copped it if her buddy ran away but, with Julie dead, there wasn't much point.'

'Lucky,' I murmured.

'I suppose,' Lesley agreed, not seeing the irony.

'What if someone doesn't run away but is picked up by the police or something?' I asked.

'That's nobody's fault. It happens sometimes,' Lesley said.

'Remember that girl who got sent away by social services?' Barb said. 'Nothing happened to her buddy.'

'Yeah, that's right,' Lesley agreed.

I'd really wanted to question Lesley about Janice, but now it would seem odd. I would have to bring it up again sometime. Meantime, I had to make friends. 'Seeing as it's my first night, I'll go to the chippy and get us some scoff.' Oops, I had to be careful not to use police jargon in case I was uncovered. I got away with it this time because the girls responded enthusiastically and called their orders to me.

I went to the foot of the stairs. 'I'll bring back some sausage and chips,' I called up.

'And gravy,' Wendy called back down. I smiled. She was okay.

*

While I was out, I stopped at a phone box and told Benno about the buddy system and what I had been told about Julie.

'We know now that she had been working for Ted Bulwer.'

'Yes, but that doesn't mean that she was murdered. The coroner ruled accidental death,' Benno said. 'I'm not sure there's anything to be gained by investigating that. Let her family grieve in peace.'

He had a point, but I felt it had to be relevant somehow. Then I told him about Wendy.

'I don't think you should ask the local lads to come and get her; she'll know it was me and I don't want to blow my cover.'

'Maybe I can alert them tomorrow and get her picked up on the way to the warehouse,' he said.

'Also, Lesley was talking about a girl called Janice from St Agnes', who's been boasting about how much she earns doing blue movies. I suspect it's one of our persistent mispers, Janice Alderman. Can you pass that on, please?'

'Leave it with me.'

I trusted Benno totally. Happy in the knowledge I was trying to help Wendy, I purchased five sausage dinners with gravy and five cans of cola, and returned to a rapturous welcome at the house.

*

Next day at the warehouse, I was indeed buddied up with Lisa.

'You understand what that means?' Ted asked.

'She misbehaves, I get punished and vice versa,' I intoned.

'You are a bright one. Most girls like to assume a stage name. Have you chosen one?'

'Valkyrie. Nobody messes with me.'

'Valkyrie?' Ted rubbed his chin. 'Yeah, that's okay.'

I smiled in satisfaction. I was enjoying the playacting.

'We need to get some promo shots done. Go to the dressing room and choose yourself a couple of outfits.'

'What type of shots?' I asked suspiciously.

'Various. You'll have to speak to the camera guy. He controls that type of thing.'

'How much will I get paid?' I asked, to make my character seem more believable.

Ted laughed. 'We're doing you the favour by not charging you for the pictures. And you have to pay something for your lodgings.'

'So I do these pictures for free, then afterwards I suppose you take a cut of my earnings. How much do you take?'

'Sixty percent.'

'How much is rent?'

'You pay twenty-five percent of what you earn. Christ, you're a nosy one.'

That left fifteen percent which, to me, seemed an exceedingly small reward for what we had to do. I didn't condone what was happening here but, as Benno said, some didn't want to be helped so I might as well try to improve their conditions.

'I do all the work and come away with fifteen percent? That's rubbish.'

'I invest my money in you. I want a return.'

'I want more,' I said.

'I could use someone else,' Ted threatened.

'Then do so. Lisa will probably accept those terms.' I turned to leave and Ted started to laugh.

'Valkyrie certainly suits you. Twenty percent.'

I turned back. 'Fifty.'

'Forget that. Twenty-five percent.'

251

'Forty-five.'

'Okay, thirty. But that's my last offer.'

I paused for a moment. 'Okay, but I want Lisa and the others to get the same.'

'That's too much,' Ted said.

I jutted my chin and held his gaze. Knowing that this film would not happen was liberating; I could agree to anything, challenge anything, say anything because in a few days everyone involved in this would be under arrest and the girls would be returned to their families, or taken to a place of safety.

'All right then.' Ted was annoyed and dismissed me.

'Where's the dressing room?' I asked Lisa when I got to the sets.

She pointed to a door I hadn't noticed behind a screen at the far end. 'Have you seen Wendy?' she asked.

'Isn't she here? She left the house to go to the sweetshop this morning and I haven't seen her since,' I replied, happy that Benno must have managed to get her picked up and, for now, she was safe and Lesley couldn't be held responsible if Wendy had been picked up by the police.

'Ted's going to fire her if she doesn't show up,' Lisa fretted.

'More chance of you being used then,' I nudged her.

Lisa's eyes glowed with wicked pleasure. 'Oh yes.'

I left Lisa to her glee and went into the dressing room, which was cold and dusty. I hadn't taken part in drama at school, so I had no idea what to wear. I rifled through some of the racks and immediately rejected most of the outfits. Then I gave myself a stiff talking-to. I was not an actress, it didn't matter what I wore, I was not appearing in a film. Dressing up was fun though.

One rail held the men's clothing. I selected what appeared to be a Roman soldier outfit. A skirt with fake leather thongs encircling it and fake leather, studded straps intended to cross the chest. I pulled out a cavewoman outfit, which consisted of a chamois loincloth and bra. I decided it was okay to show some midriff and put on the bra, topped it with the crossed leather straps, then put on the skirt. It was a little large but settled on my hips and the outfit seemed to work together so I rooted around a bit more and found a set of vambraces, which I put on. Then I found a plastic mace, a long sword, and a long, double-sided axe. I did a few swipes with the axe and giggled, then immediately felt guilty. Girls were being exploited; I was here to gain information and evidence, not to play dressing-up. But then, was I being too hard on myself? Part of this operation was to pass myself off as a sixteen-year-old, and didn't teenagers find fun in things? I was supposed to immerse myself into this environment, so the others wouldn't become suspicious of me.

'Oh. My. God!' Lisa squealed. 'What are you?'

I banged the handle of the axe on the ground and planted my fist on my hip. 'I am Valkyrie!' I cried.

Lisa clapped her hands. 'Great, but sneakers don't go. Put on the gladiator boots.'

I complied and had to admit, Lisa was right.

'You need something on your head.' Lisa delved into a box and pulled out a selection of headwear from a plastic Viking helmet to a tiara.

I looked daft in the helmet, and the tiara, and pretty well everything else we tried.

'Do you know, I think I'll just leave the hat.' I gave my hair a good fluffing and shook my head.

'Wild hair is good, but you still need something.' She grabbed a fake leather belt and held it against my head. 'That's it.' She threw the belt aside and rummaged in the box again. 'Here.' She passed me a suede thong and I tied it around my head. Maybe she wasn't much of an actress, but she was good at costume design.

'I think that works,' I said.

Ted came into the fitting room.

'Knock, knock,' I muttered. There was no privacy around here, but why would I expect there to be when they filmed people in what should be their most intimate moments?

'We're ready,' Ted said.

I followed him into a small photographic studio off the sets and stood like a spare part until I was directed to stand in front of a white backdrop. Lights beamed from each side and a small camera sat atop a tripod. A short distance away was what appeared to be a video camera. They didn't stint on technology.

A photographer peered at me through gold-rimmed glasses. 'Brunhilde?'

'Valkyrie,' I replied.

He picked up a polaroid camera and fired off a couple of shots. The photographs ejected from the machine and the photographer peeled them and waited for them to develop.

'We'll just see how these go before we use the film.'

In other words, he was going to see if it was worth wasting celluloid on me.

After a couple of minutes he appeared satisfied with the result and had me leaping around, looking fierce, and waving my axe while he moved between the cine camera and the still camera. It was all quite good fun, until he told me to remove my clothing.

I had no intention of undressing, but I couldn't just refuse without losing my chance to gather evidence. I resorted to my snotty teenage persona.

'I don't work for free.'

The cameraman stared. 'You're here to get your tits out and any other part I tell you to get out.'

'If I was a shopkeeper, you wouldn't expect to take the goods before you paid for them, would you? Pay me and I'll put tassels on them if you want, but…' my voice trailed off when Ted arrived with Molyneux. Oh crap!

I pulled my hair across my face and tried to look inconspicuous and, for good measure, I adopted an expression of disinterest.

Robert Molyneux looked at me, right at me, but not a flicker of recognition passed his face.

'How are you getting on?' Ted asked.

'She's rather uncooperative,' the cameraman replied. 'I was just trying to get her to undress but she said she doesn't work for free.'

Ted half laughed and shook his head. 'I've got a feisty one here,' he said to Molyneux. 'Benno found her but she's got an attitude problem. Questions everything.'

Robert Molyneux laughed. 'She needs to learn her place. Come and meet the one I've brought. She's in the car.' He lowered his voice. 'She'll appeal to your... more privileged audience.'

Ted snapped his fingers at the photographer. 'Let's see the polaroids.'

The cameraman handed them over and Ted scanned them. 'That's fine. She's what we want. Filming starts on Monday.' He looked over at me. 'Monday. And you'd better be a damned sight more cooperative than you've been up to now or you're back on the street.'

I nodded vigorously.

The cameraman switched off his equipment. 'Go on. Piss off, Brunhilde.'

Chapter Twenty-Seven

I scooted off the set and back towards the dressing room but then realised that Ted was outside with Molyneux, checking out some other poor girl, and he probably hadn't activated his secret camera. Now was my chance to get into his office without worrying about that camera being on.

I slipped into the office and checked the camera cupboard. To my amazement, it was open. I opened the door to see there was indeed a camera. I furtled around behind the equipment and yanked at a couple of leads until they came loose. Maybe, with a bit of luck, Ted wouldn't notice and when he was away I could return for a good mooch around.

I then checked the key cabinet. That, too, was open. I noted the code. The drawers to Ted's desk were locked, however. I was about to go through the keys when I heard movement along the corridor. I scurried to the door, but Ted was already close; I would have to brazen it out. A quick scan of the office and I was satisfied all was as he had left it. Now I knew the code, I could come back.

Ted jumped when he saw me. 'What are you doing here?'

'I came to see you,' I replied. 'I wanted to apologise for being so awkward.'

Ted looked at me through narrowed eyes. 'Go on.'

I fidgeted as I struggled to think up a response. 'I do appreciate you taking me on, I really need the money, but…'

Ted pulled open the camera cupboard then checked the key cabinet as I was talking. He appeared satisfied by what he saw and sat at his desk. He surreptitiously tugged at the locked drawers. I gave him my best wide-eyed innocent look.

'You were saying?' Ted prompted.

'I haven't undressed in front of strangers before.'

Ted leant back, making his chair creak. 'Get used to it. By Monday I want you to be able to walk around naked. You will do as directed, you will fuck who we tell you to fuck, and you will fuck as many times as we tell you. Lisa is waiting in the wings to take your place.'

'I know.'

'Go on, get out of here.'

It looked like I had got away with it, which was a relief. I went to the dressing room to change into my own clothing.

*

That evening I slipped out and phoned Benno, as per our arrangement. He was interested to hear about Molyneux and promised to pass the information on, but he was less happy about my behaviour.

'You're causing some problems,' he said. 'Ted sent Neil around and he said you were being truculent and insolent.'

'I wouldn't undress for the camera,' I explained.

Benno sighed. 'I understand, Sally, but you're raising suspicions. I talked Neil around. I told him you told me you'd had a traumatic experience when you were younger.'

I gasped. 'You know about Hogarth Acre?'

'Yes, but I didn't elaborate.'

'You know I wouldn't undress for them anyway?'

'I guessed as much. Sally, I'll tell you straight, they're giving you until Monday. If you don't pass muster, they're binning you.'

'Then we have to do what we need to do before then. You need to get me out before filming starts.'

'I was going to suggest we extract you tonight,' Benno said. 'Gary Tyrrell has expressed his displeasure and I do wonder if he's right.'

'No,' I protested. 'I have the key code for Ted's office. I was going to go and search the place.'

'This wouldn't be a reflection on you, Sally. You don't have the experience. It was a daft idea to send in a probationer. We placed too much on you.'

'Leave me here. I'll get some evidence for you somehow, and I'll even go topless on Monday if I have to.'

Benno laughed. 'They'll expect more than topless, believe me.' I heard him draw on his cigarette. 'All right, we'll leave you for now, but get what you can by Sunday night because we're going to move in early Monday.'

I replaced the receiver and walked slowly back to the house. I had little time to gather evidence. Tonight would be a good time to check things out.

I hurried back to the house and pinned my hair up. There were bound to be cameras around an industrial area, so I wanted to disguise myself a little. I put on a black hooded top over my jeans, and slung my backpack over my shoulder. I had to assume that Ted would have some means of checking for fingerprints and might have a contact in the SOCO. I grabbed a torch and a pair of gloves and headed off. My housemates were engrossed in a film, so probably wouldn't miss me for a while.

*

The warehouse was in darkness, but there was nothing unusual about that. I didn't use the torch in case the light revealed my presence. I didn't want to use the door because of the camera, so I kept to the shadows and checked around the windows. Some were boarded up, which I decided was my best bet for access. I pulled at the boards one by one until I felt a little give in one frame. I worried away at it until I could get my fingertips underneath and then prised it free. I found an abandoned milkcrate, put it under the window, stood on it, and put my hand through the broken pane to release the catch and pull the window open. I had to assume there were cameras hidden around the place despite Lisa thinking there were not, so I pulled my hood tight around my head before heaving myself up and slithering inside head-first, landing in a heap beneath the window.

I stayed still for a few moments and listened for any sounds, but all was quiet. I remained in the shadows and, using only the moonlight, crept to the staircase. I paused for a minute then, as lightly as I could, I ran up the steps and crouched down outside Sonia's reception office. Everything was so still, even the birds that normally nested in the girders remained quiet.

I pushed at the door, but it felt secure. Then I remembered what Sonia had said about it not catching all the time. That had happened to our door at home once: a screw had come loose on the lock, which caused it to slip. Dad had taken five minutes to fix it. I gambled on Ted not having the knowhow or inclination to do a repair before the locksmith came out, so I rattled the door and it clicked and opened. I slid into reception and ran through to the lounge. I began to relax a little. I walked quickly through the lounge and peered in to the sets to make sure the coast was clear before racing to the far end.

I gave silent thanks when I found Ted's office door unlocked. I slipped into the office and the first thing I did was to check the camera cupboard. Locked. I hoped the camera was still unplugged but I couldn't rely on that. Next, I went to the key cabinet and entered the code. The door opened, and I had free access to the contents.

I found the camera cabinet key and unlocked the door. A quick furtle behind the camera confirmed that the wires were still unconnected from when I had pulled them free. A blinking red light warned me that the camera was active. I examined the equipment further and found that, by chance, I had disconnected the link between the camera and the recorder. I couldn't have done better if I had planned it. Ted would have seen the camera activate, but wouldn't realise until later that nothing had been recorded.

I carefully replaced the cabinet key and then located the drawer key. This was going to be interesting. I sat at the desk, unlocked the drawers, and began a search.

The first thing I saw was the large handgun. I had no idea what make, size and so on it was; I had only passed the firearms act exam at training school by memorising it by rote then spilling it out onto the exam paper. I had forgotten most of it by the time I left initial training, as I didn't think I'd ever need it unless I went into the firearms department, which was unlikely. I considered taking the weapon, but then I didn't want Ted to realise that I had been here, so I left it in place. It was useful information to pass on to Benno, although he probably already suspected that Ted had weapons. In fact, I wondered why it hadn't occurred to me that Ted or Molyneux might be armed. That was something to think about later; for now I needed to concentrate on the search.

The rest was mundane stuff: receipts and so on that would be found in any office. I pulled open the bottom drawer. This was deep, with document folders running along it. I pulled out a file and opened it. It was a script. Pretty feeble but plot wasn't really what Ted's films were about. I replaced the script and pulled another file from the drawer. This once contained a brief profile and photographs: apparently a screen test, and this girl was not so fussy about removing her clothing. Neither were the girls in the next two files I pulled out. No wonder the cameraman was confused when I didn't want to undress.

As I put the files back, I felt the rear of the drawer wobble a little. I pulled the files forward and jiggled the back, which came free. Behind were more files. I took them out and flicked through the contents. These photos were more explicit—much more explicit—and I had a feeling that they had not been posed. I picked one up and looked closely. In the background was a living room, decorated in ostentatious style with a white shag pile carpet and a white leather couch. A girl—no, a child, with little pinches of skin where her breasts budded—grimaced as a man thrust into her. This wasn't staged.

I picked up another photo and almost dropped it when I recognised Brian Lewington. I checked back to the first photo. The man's face was blurred, however the second photo featured the same girl in the same living room and it was undoubtedly Brian with her. Karen had once told me that Brian preferred young girls, but I hadn't realised she meant *this* young. The quality of the photograph wasn't great, which made me think there had been a hidden camera and neither Brian nor the girl had been aware. These photos were clearly intended to keep Brian complaisant if he were ever to cause Ted problems. They were also excellent evidence against Brian that I would enjoy handing over to Benno.

I heard a rumble from the lower floor. The large doors were being slid open and, in a minute, somebody would come up the stairs. I had been so engrossed I hadn't heard the motor. I stuffed the photos into my backpack, replaced the false panel, and locked the drawer. I put the key back into the cabinet and dodged into the little photographic studio. I had been lucky up to now, I just hoped my luck would hold out a little longer. I could hear footsteps ringing out on the metal stairs. Whoever they were, they were not trying to be quiet.

'How many do you need?' Ted's voice echoed around the empty building.

'There'll be a dozen guests, so at least twelve. More if you can.'

I peeped out of the door and saw Robert Molyneux follow Ted into his office.

'You're getting careless, Ted. Why didn't you lock your door? Anyone could have come in. I provided a decent security system here, but you have to do your bit and at least lock things.'

'I didn't expect you to keep me out so long, so don't start. I pay you well enough,' Ted replied.

The lights flickered on and I heard the creak of Ted sitting in his chair. Someone shut the door and I couldn't hear what they said any more. I should try to get evidence that Molyneux was in a meeting with Ted. DI Webb probably already had some evidence, but another photograph would always be useful. I looked around the studio and saw the polaroid camera. I could take a snap but the camera was quite noisy; they would be bound to hear it and, in the dark, the flash would certainly give me away. I picked up the camera anyway; there had to be a way to disable the flash. It would be too dangerous to hang around the office—escape routes were limited—but maybe I could hide amongst the sets and get them as they left. I pushed my worries about the camera to the back of my mind.

My heart hammered as I tiptoed past the office. As soon as I was clear of the door, I ran to the sets and looked around to choose the best place. I could hide under the divan, but then, if I was discovered, I would be trapped. The harem set might be better: the sofa, cushions, and voiles would break up my silhouette, and I could photograph them almost face on as they left. Also, if I was discovered, I had a better chance of putting up a fight and escaping. I pushed away thoughts of Lisa being punished as I dived behind the sofa and fiddled with the camera until I found how to disable the flash. That was one worry out of the way.

The voices grew louder, the lights came on, and Molyneux and Ted came onto the sets.

'I'll ask at the house, they always want more money,' Ted said. 'Will it be filmed?'

'Aren't they all?' Molyneux laughed. 'It keeps our fractious guests onside.'

So they did take secret pictures to blackmail people into silence if necessary, and Brian was probably amongst them. Was he even aware or would they be the big guns to be brought out as a last resort?

I clicked the polaroid and a film whirred out of the bottom of the camera. Ted paused and looked around and I almost fainted with fright, but he resumed his conversation.

'I have a couple of high-profile guests coming and Lew is bringing a little special something. A couple of new faces for my regulars would be good,' Molyneux said.

'We do have a couple of new ones.'

I risked another photograph. Ted paused again.

'Did you hear that?'

'Probably a bird or a bat at the window,' Molyneux said.

'Who's there?' Ted shouted. A couple of pigeons squawked and took off from the window ledge.

'See, it was a pigeon.' Molyneux laughed and slapped Ted's shoulder.

They opened the door to the lounge and left the sets. After a moment, the lights went off and released the breath I'd been holding.

My eyes took a little time to adjust to the darkness. I peeled the photographs and an image slowly appeared on them. They were not the best photographs, but sufficient. I had my evidence.

I heard the rumble of the big doors and a motor starting up and going away. I climbed out from behind the sofa and paused for a moment, listening out in case one of them had stayed behind. I heard the door to the sets open again and dived behind the sofa. Ted strode to his office and shut the door. I hoped he wouldn't be there for long.

After fifteen minutes or so, Ted left the office, carefully locked the door, and hurried out of the building. I didn't move this time, waiting instead to hear the rumble of the big doors and the sound of a vehicle driving away. Then I slowly straightened up and listened for a full minute. Satisfied it was all clear, I took a photograph of the sets for comparison with the magazine, then hurried through the lounge and into reception. Everything was quiet. I tried to pull the door open an inch. It was locked. Not to worry; I could see that one side of the lock was loose. I rattled the door again until it clicked open. I went out and took care to close the door behind me. It wasn't as safe as when Ted had done it, but it would do.

I wriggled out of the window, ran to a nearby phone box, and dialled Benno.

'You have to meet me ASAP,' I gasped. 'I have photographic

evidence that Robert Molyneux and Ted Bulwer have met up here. And I have indecent photographs of Brian Lewington.'

'Slow down,' Benno said.

'I've been back to the warehouse. I photographed Molyneux and Ted together and I found a secret compartment in Ted's desk and there were photos of Sergeant Brian Lewington with an underage girl.'

'You broke into the warehouse without telling anyone? Bloody hell, Sally!'

'That's why I'm here, isn't it?'

'Not to go breaking into places without back up. Where are you?'

I gave Benno my location and hung up. I had about fifteen or twenty minutes to kill before he'd get to me.

I paced around the phone box, glancing along the road from time to time. A police car approached and drew up. I wasn't alarmed, until I remembered I wasn't in uniform and not many in the city knew me.

'It's late to be hanging around by yourself,' the bobby said through the open window. 'Is business slack?'

'I'm not a prostitute!' I was offended he would think such a thing.

'Then why are you loitering around here?'

Who used the word "loitering" in normal conversation? A policeman considering a charge of CPL, that's who.

'I told you: I'm not a cow, I'm just waiting for my friend,' I replied.

He climbed out of the Panda and a young bobby, probably their sprog from the latest intake, climbed out of the passenger side. Not a good sign, it meant he was planning a stop check. All very useful to the sprog but I didn't need that, not with those pornographic photos in my bag.

'What's your name?' the senior man asked.

I thought quickly. Alias or real? He didn't know me, and probably wouldn't know about Operation Elstree. 'Samantha

Barrie,' I replied.

'And what is in your bag, Samantha?'

'Just my stuff: purse, comb, and so on.'

'Mind if we look?' The sprog looked on as the older constable held out his hand.

Yes, I absolutely did mind. I leant forward and whispered. 'I'm actually a police officer, undercover. I'm waiting for the DS to meet me.'

I could tell by his expression that he didn't believe me. He jerked his head towards my bag and the sprog stepped forward to take it. I moved the bag behind me.

'I really am a police officer. I have photographs in there that I need to pass on.'

'Nice gloves.' The young bobby nodded towards my hands. 'I didn't think it was that cold.'

'Well spotted, lad,' said the older man.

Dammit, now he was thinking I was going equipped to steal. Phil once did a similar stop with me. The torch in my bag would just confirm his suspicions.

'Look, I understand why you tugged me, but I'm not going equipped and I'm not CPL. I just coughed what's going on.' I said, trying to use as much jargon as possible so they knew I was one of them. 'I had to screw an office to get the photographs but it's okay, the DS will explain everything when he gets here shortly.'

'You use jargon quite fluently,' the older bobby commented. 'You must have had a lot of dealings with police.'

'I'm a policewoman.'

'Why would a policewoman need to break into an office?'

'I can't tell you that. It's an ongoing operation.' I understood now why patrols were warned away when an operation was ongoing.

'Let me see your warrant card.' The older constable held out his hand again.

My warrant card was in the safe in Egilsby police station along with all other ID relating to Samantha Barrie, placed there in case

I was searched by Ted.

'I don't have it with me. You'll have to ring Egilsby.'

'Police officers always have their warrant card.' He turned to the younger bobby. 'Going equipped. Off you go, lad. Not a bad collar for your first one.'

Dammit, I was going to be the sprog's first arrest. The sprog laid his hand on my arm and said, 'I am arresting you on suspicion of…'

I ran. They immediately gave chase and caught me before I had gone very far. The older bobby snatched my bag and the sprog snapped on handcuffs. Strangely, I didn't freak out; but then I had other things to worry about, like how was I going to explain to Benno.

A car rounded the corner then accelerated towards us, it's headlights flashing.

'What the hell?' the senior policeman said.

Benno's Cortina screeched to a halt and he leapt out brandishing his warrant card. 'Release her. She's an undercover police officer and you are in danger of disrupting an operation.'

The bobby took Benno's warrant card and scrutinised it while the sprog stood uncertainly to one side.

'It doesn't look like you,' he said.

Benno sighed. 'I wasn't undercover there, my hair's longer now. Get your control to ring the force control room. Tell them Elstree and give password Magenta.'

'The photos are in the backpack,' I said to Benno. He reached out, but the older bobby moved it away from him.

'I think we'll check on you first.' He radioed their control room. 'Could you contact force control room and check if they are aware of a WPC Samantha Barrie?'

'Give the operation and the password,' Benno insisted.

'Tell them Elstree and password Magenta, over.' the bobby relayed.

We all waited in an awkward silence until the control room contacted them.

'From the control room inspector. All in order.'

As he transmitted, in the background I heard someone say, 'Svetlana…'

'What was that about a Svetlana?' I asked.

'Svetlana Jones has been reported again,' Benno said. 'It's been a couple of days now.'

That would explain why she was being spoken about in another control room. Perhaps they had had a sighting in the city.

'She's normally back within a day,' I said.

The older bobby looked from Benno to me and back again. 'Right, I suppose that's okay then.'

The sprog looked quite crestfallen. I turned my back to him and he released my hands.

'Sorry, mate. Better luck next time,' I said.

Benno took my arm and pulled me, none too gently, to his car. I got in and he sped away.

'This is going to be all over the bloody city now,' he muttered.

'It wasn't my fault. I was waiting for you and they stop checked me.'

'You shouldn't have been there alone!' He took a deep breath. 'Okay. Leave the damage limitation to me.' He pulled over. 'Let's see the photographs.'

I pulled the photos from my backpack and handed them over. 'The one with the girl is Brian Lewington. The others aren't so good, but you can see Molyneux and Ted by the sets.'

Benno looked at the photos of Brian and whistled through his teeth. 'Bloody hell.'

'I thought something similar. He's going to go to prison, isn't he?' I said.

Benno nodded. 'Let's get you back, then I'll hand these over.'

Benno drove me to the house. 'Just so you know, I'm going to mention in my report that I've had to warn you about going in half-cocked. You do not put yourself in such situations without backup. I know it isn't the first time you've gone off like this. Gary Tyrrell is paying close attention to this operation and he will not be happy.'

No, I could imagine he wouldn't. I had promised him I wouldn't rush off, but surely he would appreciate the circumstances. Surely Benno should appreciate the circumstances.

'Tonight you were completely alone. The surveillance teams concentrate on the main players; they don't sit by the house to watch you girls all night. You should have mentioned your plans to me and then I could have come over and alerted the force control room in case we needed backup. This shows a lack of judgement that you must address if you want to complete your probation.'

'You wanted to pull me out. I went on impulse and I'm glad I did because I got photographs. Surely that shows initiative.' I argued.

'It worked out this time, but what if you'd been caught? You could have been dead before we'd even known you were gone. These operations are planned meticulously to keep the people involved as safe as possible and to ensure evidence gathered is admissible.'

'I got a lot of evidence tonight.'

'Yes, you did,' Benno agreed. 'But you also got yourself arrested and almost lost it. And who knows what the fall-out will be now the local lads know about you. Don't think you can be the maverick cop that cuts through bureaucracy, that only happens on telly. Rushing off just makes you a liability and risks the whole operation.'

I sighed.

'I don't want to moan at you, Sally. You were brave and you did get some useful stuff, just stop trying to be a one-man-band. When you finish your probation, consider getting your CID aide's course in. You'll be able to work alongside CID every day until you are experienced enough to transfer to the department permanently.'

'I'll think about it.' I went into the house and Benno drove off.

'Where've you been?' Lesley demanded when I got into bed. 'I saw Benno drop you off.'

'I got arrested.'

'Really? What for?'

'Going equipped to steal,' I said truthfully. 'Benno came and got them to release me.'

'Without charge?' Lesley asked.

'Yep.'

'I bet he gave you an alibi.'

'Yeah, he did.' I hadn't had to lie once.

'Benno's great.' Lesley turned over and, in a few minutes, was snoring.

If only she knew just how great he was. I got into bed and thought about what Benno said about getting my CID aide's course. I hadn't really enjoyed my attachment there when I had come out of training school; but as an aide, and eventually a DC, I could go out on enquiries and I wouldn't be expected to do the filing or make tea, probably. It was something to consider.

Chapter Twenty-Eight

Apersistent knocking on the front door woke me up the next morning. I groaned and struggled upright.

Barb was already up; I heard her open the door.

'Where is everyone,' Ted asked.

'Still in bed,' Barb answered.

'It's ten o'clock. Tell the lazy cows to get up, I want to speak to you all.'

Barb yelled up the stairs, 'Get up, Ted's here.'

'What's Ted doing here?' Lesley said to me. 'He hardly ever comes to the house.'

We all trudged down.

Ted curled his lip. 'I was going to ask if anyone wanted to earn a little extra at a party tonight, but I think I've come to the wrong place. Look at you all.'

This party must be the thing Ted and Robert Molyneux had been discussing last night. It must be special because Lesley said he seldom came to the house.

'I'll go, Ted,' Lesley said.

'Use me. I've been before, the guests like me,' Barb cut in.

'Me!' Donna hopped on her toes like a schoolgirl desperate to attract teacher's attention.

The girls clamoured like seagulls fighting over the last chip.

'All right, I'll send you all. How about you, Sally?' Ted asked.

I shrugged. 'I suppose so.'

'You suppose so!' Barb cried. 'The parties are amazing.'

'How do you know?' Lesley said. 'You've never been to one.'

'Lisa told me about them. She said the pay's great and, if you're very good, the guests sometimes give you decent tips.'

'Money is always useful,' I agreed. Lisa lived in Ted's other house and she had not mentioned these parties to me. I would have to speak to her when I next saw her.

'All right then. I'll send someone to collect you all at seven.' Ted eyed us all. 'Make an effort; you look like vagrants at the moment.' Muttering, he left.

Lesley went into the kitchen to put on the kettle. I needed to go out and warn Benno, so I ran upstairs and got dressed.

'I'm going to the sweetshop,' I called. 'Anyone want anything?'

'Get me a Galaxy, please,' Lesley called. 'Or a Mars Bar.'

I went to the shop and bought the Galaxy bar, and a packet of mints for me, then on the way back I stopped at the phone box and dialled Benno.

'Do you know where the party is?' he asked. I didn't know. 'If Molyneux is involved, it will probably be at the flat in Belvedere House. We'll have to put a surveillance car on the house,' Benno exhaled loudly. He smoked almost as much as Ray did.

'Oh, by the way, Gerald Mount has been charged with USI along with a lot of other stuff, and denied bail,' Benno said. 'Those photos you got were the main evidence.'

'Denied bail?' Blooming heck, the courts normally took the attitude that everyone was entitled to bail. It took a lot for them to refuse it.

'Unlawful Sexual Intercourse is a serious matter. He's being very cooperative. I think he thinks if he sings loud enough, he'll be released. We have several names, some quite high in the social pecking order. They'll be brought in over the next couple of days.'

'Are Hollywood and Elstree ending?' I asked.

'Soon. We still want Ted and co.'

I was glad. I didn't like this sordid, dangerous world I was living in. I wanted to get back to my comfortable life, but I wouldn't walk away until I was sure I had done all I could.

Benno ended the call and I replaced the receiver. I paused for a moment, then rang home. I had expected to be back by now and I knew Mum would worry about me.

'Hi Mum,' I said brightly when she answered.

'Sam! How are you, where are you?'

'I'm fine, I told you I would be. I just wanted to say hello.'

'It's lovely to hear from you. When are you able to come home?'

'I don't know, Mum.'

'I miss you.'

'I miss you too. Love you, Mum.'

'Love you.'

I put the phone down and gulped back the lump in my throat. I pushed the door open and Barb stepped out from behind the hedge she had been lurking in.

'Who were you talking to?'

'Did you follow me?' I demanded.

'I wondered why you were taking so long,' she said.

'I stopped off to ring my mum,' I answered.

'Why?'

I folded my arms. 'I miss her.'

'So are you going back to her?' Barb asked.

'No. She left home a few years back. There isn't room for me, but we speak from time to time.'

Barb's expression relaxed. 'Families, eh?'

I held out my mints. 'Want one?'

Barb took a mint and we walked back to the house. That had been too close; I had to be more alert in future.

*

That evening, I borrowed an outfit from my housemates for the party. The dress was a short, tawdry creation in a shocking pink, perfect for a sixteen-year-old. I overdid my make-up and put on the slightly too big high heels.

'What do you think?' I asked the others.

'Perfect,' Donna said. Lesley looked on in approval.

I wasn't so sure, but it matched their gaudy, pink outfits.

I looked out of the window, hoping to see a covert surveillance vehicle, but there was nothing out of the ordinary to be seen. Which was the whole point of covert, I supposed.

'They'll be here soon,' Lesley said.

I dropped the curtain and sat on the sofa, worrying whether Benno had been able to set up the surveillance as I wouldn't be able to let anyone know where we were going.

Someone knocked at the door and Donna opened it.

'Our ride's here,' she called.

Oh well, too late to worry about Benno now. I had to start thinking about how I was going to extricate myself if things got a bit hairy.

I had assumed a driver was collecting just us, but no: a minibus sat outside. A group of equally gaudy girls were already on board. Pink was definitely the preferred colour. Barb and Lesley squealed a greeting as we boarded and hugged a couple of them. Evidently, they had worked together before.

I spotted Lisa, who gave me a wry smile. I sat next to her.

'I wasn't expecting to see you here.' I said.

'Nor me you, but money's money isn't it. I can't afford to be choosy where it comes from.'

'Where are we going?' I asked her.

'They never tell us the address, even when we get there. You just have to keep your eyes open for street names.'

Smart girl. I looked around to see if I could spot the surveillance but, if I could, they'd be doing a rotten job of it.

*

Twenty minutes later, we turned into the car park of Belvedere House. Oh crap, this was too close to home and there was a chance that I would run into Janice and Lana. My cover would be well and truly blown.

'It's the posh flat!' One girl trilled.

'Have you been here before?' I asked Lisa.

She nodded. Her subdued demeanour unsettled me.

'Why so glum?'

She forced a smile. 'This is where the extra special parties are held.'

'Extra special?' I was becoming increasingly nervous.

'At normal parties, the rules are quite strict: no kinky stuff. The clients pay more to go to special parties because the rules are more relaxed, they can play out a particular fantasy. Extra special is, well, all that and extra.'

'Like what?' I was seriously alarmed.

'Anal, toys, DP, underage...' She slapped my knee and in an over-bright voice, said, 'Don't worry about it. The money's good.' Her smile slipped almost immediately. 'Julie's last party was here. Julie was my buddy. She died.'

'I heard about that. Had she been upset?' I asked.

Lisa looked sideways at me. 'You think she killed herself?'

I felt my cheeks burn. 'The other girls said...'

She snorted. 'They know nothing. Julie wasn't sad or depressed, but she was fed up with having to do what Ted and the others said. She told me that if anyone wanted anything kinky, they could sod off.'

'What do you think happened?' I asked.

'She told the wrong person to sod off.'

Murder? The coroner had ruled an accident. I opened my mouth to clarify, but then the driver slid open the door and wafted his arms to hurry us along. I remained silent and huddled with the other girls waiting for instruction. There was no chance I could make a run for it without being seen, or dropping Lisa in the muck. The yellow Lotus elite was not in the car park, so I was surprised when I saw Molyneux coming toward us. I tried to blend into the centre of the knot of girls.

'What are you waiting there for? Get going, there are clients waiting,' he barked.

Like a flamboyance of flamingos, we followed him into building, up to apartment 11 and into a large living room, which was a tacky homage to Ancient Greece. All around was decorated in gold and white with enormous mirrors on two walls. A large, white, shag pile rug and an ornate, glass coffee table completed the look. Several men lounged around the long, white leather sofas watching a pornographic movie or inhaling white powder from the coffee table. Drugs as well! I should have anticipated that.

'The entertainment is here.' The man, fifty if he was a day, openly rubbed his crotch.

I was relieved that Lana and Janice were not here, although I would keep alert in case they arrived later.

Lisa leaned in and whispered, 'Leave your dignity at the door. You can pick it up on the way out.'

It seemed Lisa was more switched on than I had given her credit for. I wondered if her apparent enthusiasm really was a keenness to get to America, or if it was to keep her from Julie's fate. That might explain why she went back after Benno had rescued her. I wanted to cry for her and for the other girls, for all girls forced to endure such humiliation. I had to let Benno know about Lisa's theory about Julie's death.

'Come here, little girl.'

The girl leading our pack giggled, pranced over to the client, and knelt at his knees.

Donna looked uncertain as a client unbuttoned her blouse. Others, perhaps more experienced, had no inhibitions; they enthusiastically screamed as men pulled clothing from their bodies. I got it, they were acting: this was just another role to them.

'Keep something back, remember, we have a special treat later. I want your bids in a sealed envelope,' Molyneux announced to the room.

I looked at the couple writhing on screen: the girl was young, no surprise there. The man had a tattoo of some sort of writing on his upper arm. I couldn't make it out. The background looked vaguely familiar, but I supposed white shag pile was ubiquitous in the porn industry, as was white leather furniture. The girl looked around and smiled, an attractive smile despite the crossed front teeth. Something clicked; I had seen that smile before.

'Come on, don't be shy.' A lanky man with a patchy Mexican moustache wrapped his arms around me. 'I have something new I want to try.'

'Try self-restraint.' I shoved him back and he slapped me across the face. I immediately responded with a knee in the groin.

'Hey, Ron, don't damage the merchandise. If you want to try some S & M, take her to the bedroom. There's gear in there,' Molyneux shouted.

'I want my money back,' Ron shouted back. 'The bitch just knackered me.'

Molyneux laughed. 'No refunds. Ron.'

Ron glared at me. 'No tip.'

I could live with that. I gave him the finger and turned back to the film, then it came to me in a horrible punch to the gut. The girl with the crossed teeth was Julie Wynne. Julie's onscreen partner turned around and I sagged against the wall as I recognised Brian Lewington. Julie had been a few days short of her sixteenth birthday when she died, yet here she was onscreen, having sex with my disgraced sergeant.

I looked around. Men, old enough to be my father and older, were with teenagers, most underage. Some girls had no qualms about public sex; others, like poor Lisa, looked vacant, as if they had taken themselves somewhere else in their mind. I was nauseated. This was wrong, so wrong. I had to speak out, stop this. I was a police officer dammit, it was my duty. I would stop them… But what about the operation? What about the bigger picture?

Lisa tried to stand up, but her client pulled her back down. She tried to smile but I could see the tremor at the corner of her mouth and the tears welling up. I moved towards her but then stopped. I was useless by myself, and I would jeopardise everything and everyone if I revealed my true identity. I had to get out, get a message to Benno, to anyone.

'Where are you going?' Molyneux said as I sidled towards the door.

'Toilet, unless you think your clients would like to see me pee on the shag pile.' Oh, that was too much. I didn't want him to pay much attention to me and there was a distinct possibility that some of the men might actually like that sort of thing.

Molyneux pointed back to the hall. 'Off there. Don't be too long. I paid Ted a lot of money for you lot, and don't think I haven't noticed you're not joining in. When you get back, you'd better get involved.'

I nodded and scurried off.

When Molyneux returned to his guests, I quietly opened the front door and slipped out. I couldn't risk waiting for the lift, so I pelted down the stairs and out to the nearby phone box. I quickly dialled Benno's number, constantly scanning the area as I waited for it to be connected. Someone would soon notice I hadn't gone back and Molyneux might come after me.

'Benno, you need to get to Belvedere House,' I shouted as soon as he answered. 'There's an orgy going on, drugs, porn, underage girls, the lot. Robert Molyneux is hosting it...'

'Sally, Sally! Calm down. We know where you are.'

I took a breath. 'You do? There really was someone following us?'

'Yes. We have everything covered. The troops are gathering as we speak.'

'I can't see anyone.'

'They'll be nearby.'

Right, of course. They would use a rendezvous point away from the target.

'Sally, someone will be with you very soon.'

'Benno, they're playing a film and it's got Julie Wynne in it, the one who drowned. Brian Lewington is also in it.'

'In a blue movie, with Julie Wynne?' He exhaled.

'Yes. He's taking a very active part.' I glanced around, half expecting someone to have come after me. 'I have to get back; they'll miss me and might get suspicious.'

'No. Stay where you are, someone will be with you shortly.' Benno rang off.

I didn't want to stay by the light of the phone box, so I crept into the scrubby bushes nearby and ducked down. Dammit, I forgot to tell him about Lisa's theory. I would have to wait until someone met me here and tell them.

Chapter Twenty-Nine

'There she is.'

I spun around at the sound of Eamon's delectable voice.

'Over here, Sam.'

I moved towards his voice and found him crouched behind a wall listening intently to his radio.

'The RV point is over there.' He pointed to a car park some distance away. 'Keep down and follow me.'

We scuttled to the car park and I was delighted to see most of B block waiting for me.

Steve hugged me. 'Where've you been?'

'It's a long story and I'm not sure I can tell you,' I replied.

He looked me up and down. 'If you want to be a scarlet lady, you should go for a dark red with your colouring.'

'Hellfire, who are you, Norman Hartnell?' Phil said.

'Who?' Steve asked.

'Never mind.' Phil patted my shoulder. 'Good to see you back where you belong, even if you do look like a tart.'

I giggled; I felt a bit drunk with relief to be with people I knew. Speaking of which…

'Where's Benno?' I looked around but couldn't see him.

'Who?' Steve asked.

'He isn't here. He can't be seen to be a part of this,' Eamon explained. 'You probably won't see him again until the court case, and not even then if they plead guilty.'

That saddened me. I wanted to tell him that I admired him for what he was doing and to thank him for looking out for me.

Inspector Tyrrell appeared out of the darkness. 'Let's just run through what's happening,' he said.

We all turned towards him. Our eyes locked for a moment and I wanted to throw my arms around him but we simply smiled, then got down to business.

'CID and the Vice Squad are arranging themselves around the flats. We are to stay here until they are in place then we move forward. The caretaker will open the communal door for us, then the plan is to basically storm the building, up the stairs and into apartment 11. Who has the universal key?'

Ken held up the heavy enforcer. 'I do, sir.'

'Good.' Inspector Tyrrell looked around us all. 'When we get there, nobody leaves. CID and Vice will deal with the prisoners, we will seize any equipment and take the girls back to Wyre Hall. From there we will contact their parents. Ray is alerting the social services.'

'Make sure you get the porn film that's showing now. It's got Julie Wynne and Brian in it,' I said.

'Brian as in our ex-sergeant, with that girl who drowned? Shit!' Steve exclaimed.

I nodded. 'And Lisa, one of the girls, reckons her death wasn't an accident.'

'Bloody hell.'

Inspector Tyrrell held up a hand to silence us and listened to a transmission on his radio that didn't come through to everyone. It was normal practice to use a different channel during an operation, that way they didn't interfere with normal patrols' transmissions.

'Right, they're in place. We're to move towards the house and remain out of sight until called.'

We all scurried forward and crouched in a line behind the wall.

Inspector Tyrrell spoke into his radio. 'We're in position.'

'Roger. Stand by.'

I recognised DI Webb's voice. It felt as though we were waiting for a battle to begin. The air was electric, as if I could hear what everyone was thinking if I tried hard enough. Every eye was trained on Belvedere House, everyone waiting for the order to advance.

The yellow Lotus turned into the car park, and we all froze as Brian got out. He went to the passenger side and pulled Bernadette out. He gripped her upper arm and walked her towards the building.

'Robert Molyneux told the clients at the party he had something special lined up. I bet she's it,' I told the others.

Bernadette broke away and started to run towards us. I went to run to her, but the boss grabbed my arm and held me back. Dammit. I didn't want to wait, I wanted—no, needed—to go and help Bernadette, but I trusted the boss's instincts. I had no choice but to back into the shadows with everyone else.

I watched with a racing heart as Brian grabbed Bernadette and swung her around. 'You get in there. I paid Elsie a lot of money for you,' He shouted.

'I don't want to,' Bernadette cried, wriggling frantically to escape.

'I have to go to her, she knows me,' I whispered to Inspector Tyrrell.

'No, wait,' he said. 'Webby hasn't given the go yet.'

What was DI Webb waiting for? Bernadette looked petrified, and I knew too well how it felt to be powerless. But I was no longer a victim, I was a policewoman now, there to save girls like her. I clenched my fists. If I let my anger rule me, I could screw things up for everyone. I forced my rage down and huddled out of sight.

Brian tried to drag Bernadette back to the building, but she yanked her arm away.

'I won't!' she shouted. 'I know what you did to Julie. I'll tell if you don't let me go.'

Julie? Julie Wynne? Lisa thought Julie had told the wrong person to sod off. Brian could be the wrong person. He was a dangerous man. I had no time to process the information further.

Brian backhanded Bernadette across the face and she fell to the ground.

The boss tried to grab me as I instinctively rushed forward but I was too fast.

Behind me I heard him shout, 'Sam, wait… Shit!' He yelled into his radio. 'Go! Go! Go!'

Everyone surged after me. DI Webb and half the CID department came from the direction of the river, while the Vice and Drugs Squads closed in from the Nelson Square side. Maybe Norman Webb was glaring daggers at me, but I didn't notice as I stormed towards my target, my nemesis: Brian. I wanted to kill him.

Brian looked up, paused for a nanosecond, then abandoned Bernadette, turned, and ran towards the building.

'Sam, take the kid to the carrier and wait there for the other girls to come out,' Inspector Tyrrell shouted.

What?! I wanted to chase Brian into the apartment and drag him down to the bridewell, kicking his arse every step of the way. I clenched my jaw in frustration, but I had already overstepped the mark so I peeled off from the crowd while Inspector Tyrrell and DI Webb led the troops past the caretaker and into the building.

I helped Bernadette stand up. Her lip was bleeding and her cheek was already swelling.

'Do you remember me, Bernadette? I'm Sam.'

Bernadette nodded. 'You're the nice policewoman.'

'Let's go and wait for the others to be brought out. We're going back to the station, a safe place, and social services will be there.'

'Can I go back to me mam's?'

I sighed. 'You might be better off somewhere else.'

'She's me mam.'

Despite the horrendous situation, Bernadette wanted her mum. I wanted her mum too: I wanted to smack her repeatedly across the face. I wanted to smack her face more than I wanted to kill Brian. When did I develop these violent impulses? I put my hand on the girl's shoulder and guided her to the carrier van. We climbed inside and sat down. I needed to find a way to bring up what she'd said about Julie, but I couldn't just go charging in; besides, I had a more immediate concern.

'Bernadette, you might hear some people call me by a different name. Sally. It would be really helpful if you don't tell them my real name.'

'Are you undercover?'

'Yes I am. It would be good if they think I'm just one of the girls and I'm being taken back to the station with you all.'

Bernadette nodded eagerly. 'I won't blow your cover. It's just like a film, isn't it?'

I could use that. 'A bit, but this is real life, and you're in on the secret.'

Bernadette's eyes shone.

'What would you like to do when you leave school?' I asked. Perhaps I could get her to relax into a conversation, then bring Julie up

Bernadette shrugged.

'What do you enjoy doing?' I persisted.

Bernadette shrugged again.

I gave up and we sat in silence, listening to the shouting coming from the building. In a few minutes, the first arrests would be brought down.

'Do you know what I'd really like to do?'

I turned towards Bernadette. 'What would you like to do?'

'I'd like to be a hairdresser. At school, we do each other's hair at dinner time and I enjoy that. Everyone says I'm good at it. I want to be a hairdresser and have my own shop one day.'

Such an achievable ambition, but Bernadette spoke as if she were wishing for the moon. Elsie and Ruthie probably could not see beyond their narrow, wretched world and would not offer much support to Bernadette's wishes.

'Then why don't you speak to your teachers and tell them what you want to do? Maybe they can help you get an apprenticeship or something like that. Perhaps you'll have to do day release at college.'

'College?' Bernadette laughed but I could see the light in her eye. She wanted this very much.

'Only one day a week, that's why it's called day release. The rest of the time you work in a hairdressing salon. You'll sweep the floor and wash hair at first, but you'll soon qualify and then your future is in your own hands. If you like, I could speak to your headmistress for you.'

Bernadette looked almost beatific. 'I'd like that.' Then her expression turned serious. 'Can I tell you something important?'

'Go on.'

'Have you heard of Julie Wynne?'

'She drowned in the river a while ago,' I said.

'No. Lew killed her,' Bernadette announced.

I knew for certain that she'd drowned, so I waited for Bernadette to speak again to see where this was leading. I also knew that Julie had been in that film with Brian Lewington. Lewington, Lew, Lou. Suddenly, I knew in my bones that Brian was Lou, *my* Lou! He had been the one waiting for me at Hogarth's Acre that night. I was sure of it. But how would I be able to prove it?

'You don't look well. Do you know him?' Bernadette asked.

'I do know him. I don't like him.' I wanted her to know that in case she felt she couldn't tell me any more about Brian, and I really wanted to hear what she had to say.

'Why do you think Julie was killed?' I asked.

'I heard Mam, our Ruthie, Glynis, and Connie arguing in our house because Molly said Lew was going to pay extra to be my first.'

I knew that what Bernadette was saying was true, and hadn't tonight been described as an extra special party? Also, Karen Fitzroy had told me that Lew liked young ones. I wished I had been able to take more direct action earlier.

'Why were they arguing? Was it about the money?'

'Partly. Mam said it would be all right, but our Ruthie knew I was scared and said she didn't think my first should be Lew because she thinks he's a psycho. Glynis and Connie said that I could be used for pictures, but Molly said I should be broken in first and promised Mam more money for me, so Mam agreed.'

I really, really wanted to punch that woman.

'What do you mean: Lew's a psycho?' I asked.

'Everyone by us says so. After everyone had gone that night, our Ruthie told Mam she'd been there when Lew killed Julie Wynne because she wouldn't do what he wanted. She'd screamed when he tried to force her, so he put a cushion over her face to shut her up. She suffocated. I think Ruthie was worried he'd do the same to me if I screamed, but Mam told her to shut up.'

My mind went into overdrive. The coroner had said Julie had died by drowning, which meant water had to be in her lungs, so Brian couldn't have suffocated her. However, I could tell Bernadette really believed what she was telling me.

She continued. 'Ruthie said that Molly had helped Lew to get rid of Julie's body. They wrapped her in a rug and threw her in the river. Molly told the girls there that if they said anything, they'd go into the river too.'

A cold feeling ran down my back. Julie had been alive when she went into the water and she mustn't have been able to free herself from the rug and had drowned. The rug must have fallen away before she was washed up at Lyseby.

'Lew came for me tonight,' Bernadette said. 'I thought we were going to go somewhere quiet, but he brought me here. He told me it was a special party and that he could get his money back and more by letting someone else pop my cherry then going second. He said I wouldn't have had time to catch anything.' She shuddered, so did I. Bernadette nibbled at her nails. 'You'll protect me, won't you? I don't want to go to Molly's parties, I want to be a hairdresser.'

'Don't worry, Bernadette. We'll do our very best for you.' I stared out of the window and hoped our best would be good enough. I would tell the CID about Julie. Bernadette would have to be interviewed and removed from her dreadful mother ASAP.

'Here they come,' Bernadette said. 'Don't worry, I won't give you away.'

A gaggle of girls came towards us, flanked by Steve and Ken.

Lisa was first on board. 'Sally! I wondered where you were. Molly was furious. He rang Ted, but the fuzz had you all along. I knew you wouldn't run away on me.' She turned to Bernadette. 'Who's this?'

'This was tonight's something special,' I said. 'Her name's Bernadette.'

'Bernie,' Bernadette said.

'Hi Bernie.' Lisa sat next to Bernadette and it didn't take them long to chatter like old friends.

The other girls climbed on, some clucking their indignation. Ken and Steve didn't acknowledge me, for which I was grateful. They had probably been warned not to. Ken sat in the back with us and Steve rode shotgun while Phil drove us in the van to Wyre Hall. Normally a single male officer wouldn't travel with a van full of females but, for the purposes of the reports, I would be counted as an escort.

Chapter Thirty

At the station, with me still in role, we were taken off to the parade room—the only room large enough to accommodate us all—to await the arrival of a parent or some other appropriate adult prior to interview. Almost as soon as we got there, an unfamiliar policewoman called for Bernadette and me and we were taken straight to the interview room, where I could finally shed my Sally identity.

Ray goggled as we passed the control room en route and I winked at him; he'd get the full story later.

We were left alone in the interview room. We didn't chat; my head was too full of "what ifs" and I felt a little high on adrenaline. Bernadette—Bernie—seemed content to just read the notices on the wall.

A few minutes later, Irene put her head around the door. 'All right, Sam?'

'What are you doing here at this hour?' I asked.

'I've been drafted in to help with the operation. There's a couple of Egilsby peewees in too, to help with the girls.' She cast an eye over me. 'Bad dress.'

'It's borrowed,' I said.

'Thought it wasn't your usual style. Who's your friend?'

'Bernadette: a budding hairdresser,' I replied.

'I prefer to be called Bernie. When I'm a hairdresser I'm going to call my shop *"Bernie's Beauty Salon"*, because a salon is posher than just a shop.'

Bernadette must have decided we were all right.

'Great name for a hairdressers',' Irene said. 'I'd go there, especially if you did manicures too.'

Bernadette—Bernie—preened. 'I just thought of it. I can learn to do nails when I'm learning to be a hairdresser.'

Irene sat on the edge of the table. 'Bernie, the social services are coming. They'll want to talk to you about going to stay with a foster family.'

'Can't I go home?' Bernie asked.

'Your mum is probably going to go to prison for a while and maybe your Ruthie too. But even if she doesn't, she won't be able to look after you properly.'

Bernie wiped the tear that trickled down her cheek. 'I understand. Will it be a nice place?'

'I'm sure they'll do their best. You might have to stay somewhere for a day or two until they get you a longer placement.'

'Bernie, you can write to me when you get settled, let me know how you get along,' I said.

'If you're serious about being a hairdresser, you could find a Saturday job in a salon when you're settled into your new place,' Irene said.

'Could I?' Bernie looked from Irene to me.

'You'd get paid a little and the experience would be useful when you go to college,' I said.

Bernie beamed. 'Me, at college.'

Irene grinned. 'You hold that thought. I need to get on.'

Bernie didn't seem to notice Irene leave; she was lost in thought about a bright future.

Eamon came in with Mike Finlay.

'Bernie, why don't you tell the detectives what you told me about Lew?' I said.

'Are we talking about Brian Lewington?' DS Finlay asked.

Bernie squirmed in the seat and glanced uncertainly between

the two men.

'Would you rather I told them?' I asked.

Eamon sat down and gave Bernie his best, twinkliest smile. 'Sergeant Ward told me about your plan for a shop. Great idea. Maybe you'll end up with a chain of salons, like Vidal Sassoon. *"Bernie's Beauty Salon".*'

It sounded exotic when Eamon said it. Bernie grinned so wide I could see her back teeth.

'Bernie, m'darlin', why don't you tell me what you told our friend, Sam.'

'Lew killed Julie Wynne. He suffocated her and Molly helped him get rid of her.' She turned to me.

'Cause of death was drowning' I said. 'Maybe they thought she was dead, but it looks like she was still alive when they threw her in the river.' I felt sick and shaky; the adrenaline was leaving my body.

'Whichever way it was, the bastard killed her,' DS Finlay muttered.

'Thanks, Bernie.' Eamon lingered over her name. Sneaky devil was playing her with his beautiful voice.

'A word, Sam?' Eamon cocked his head towards the door. 'Elsie knows about this?' he asked when we went into the corridor.

I looked through the doorway to make sure Bernie couldn't hear us, but she was deep in conversation with Mike Finlay, who was making a good effort to show interest in her shop plans. 'She must do. She was being paid for Bernie, although I'm not sure if she knows Bernie is here now. Don't forget what she told us after that ship incident.'

Eamon sighed. 'This is going to get really huge. We've got to bring in Elsie, Ruthie, Glynis, and Connie as well as those we got tonight, and there are some important people there. Ted Bulwer and the filming crew are being rounded up by the city lads. We also need to speak to Lana and Janice.'

'Last I heard Lana was AWOL again. Has she returned?' I asked.

Eamon shook his head.

'Neither she nor Janice were at the party. I think they normally would have been. Lucky for me, but I wonder where they are?'

'Social services are here and the first of the parents have arrived,' Steve called down the corridor.

Eamon waved an acknowledgement. 'Stay with Bernie until social services take her, Irene and I will deal with the parents.'

'By the way, how are things going between you two?' I asked. I wouldn't normally be so nosy, but it had been ages since I had had a good natter with Irene.

Eamon grinned. 'Pretty good actually. Very good.'

I was happy for them. Eamon went to the enquiry office. I still felt shaky, so I went back into the office to sit with Bernie and Mike Finlay, who was sketching a logo design for Bernie's future shop on a scrap of paper.

'I think the background should be pink, bright pink, and the writing white.' Bernie tapped the paper. 'Maybe I could get it in lights.'

'Black might be easier to see,' Mike said. Bernie shook her head. 'White.'

'Then how about an outline around the words? Silver glitter or something like that.' Bless him, he was really getting into this.

'Oh yes, that would look dead classy.' Bernie shivered with joy.

I had been just a year older than she was when I was taken. I hadn't realised how young I had been, not in age, but in maturity. I escaped, and Bernie had been rescued, but there were girls for whom it was too late. And then there were girls who didn't want to be helped: they chose the life. I wished they would see sense but perhaps for the first time I realised that I couldn't force things. Bernadette was safe, and that would do for now.

*

When the social worker took Bernie, I slipped off to the deserted refs room and phoned home.

'I'm so happy, Sam.' Mum said. 'I'll stay up until you get in.'

'It's going to be really late,' I warned her.

'I've missed you and I've worried about you. I want to stay up and see you.'

'Okay, I'll be back when I can. There's still lots to do here.'

'I love you, Sam.'

'Love you too, Mum.' I hung up and sat heavily on one of the armless chairs. I felt drained and close to tears.

'How is Liz? I bet she's relieved.' Inspector Tyrrell came in from the kitchen carrying two mugs of tea.

'She is,' I said.

He sat next to me, put the drinks on the table and pushed one towards me. 'And how are you?'

'I'm fine thank you, sir. A bit tired.' I picked up the tea and took a sip. It was just as I liked it and it felt good as it hit my stomach.

'You have a habit of rushing off on your own. Benno told me about the warehouse, and there was that time at Belvedere House. You must wind in that impetuous streak if you want to complete your probation. You're part of a team.'

I didn't want to hear it. I had almost ruined everything, I knew that, but I also knew that I would do the same again. I was tired, queasy, and grumpy. 'Please don't be cross with me, sir. We all know what would have happened to Bernie if Brian had taken her to the apartment, and we all saw him hit her. I had to do something.'

'This was not the Sam Barrie Show. We should have waited for DI Webb to give the signal; he should not have had to follow us.'

'Then they should have got their fingers out and moved sooner.' I spat. 'Everyone was in place. What was DI Webb waiting for? Did he want to make a grand entrance like some prima donna?'

Inspector Tyrrell lifted an eyebrow.

'Sorry.' I clenched my hands in my lap. I was letting emotion get the better of me, that would not do. 'I get frustrated that the jacks treat us like the country cousins because we're in uniform. Even worse, I'm a probationer and a female, which makes me bottom of the heap. Every time I get anything interesting, it's taken from me and handed to them as if I can't see what needs to be done.'

'Because we all have our areas of responsibility, but we're all on the same side.'

'Phil once told me something similar. When I finish my probation, I might try for CID and, if I get in, I'll make sure the bobbies know I appreciate what they do.'

Inspector Tyrrell smiled. 'You'll have a different perspective then, and don't forget: every police officer has started out on foot patrol, even the Chief Constable. They know exactly what you do, you just don't know everything they do.' He reached out and lifted a strand of my hair and placed it behind my ear, then traced his finger along my cheek. It was the most erotic moment of my life and I turned my head towards his touch. He smiled and flicked my nose.

'Phil's right; you do look like a tart in that outfit.'

I laughed aloud. 'I can't wait to get undressed.' I blushed. 'To change into my uniform,' I added.

'Shame.' Inspector Tyrrell had a playful light in his eyes but there was something else behind it, something that would normally send me racing in the opposite direction. But in the boss's eyes it wasn't threatening; I wanted to explore it.

Reluctantly, I stood up. 'I'd better get back and lend a hand with the girls,'

'No,' Inspector Tyrrell said. 'You shouldn't be seen to be part of this either. Let the girls continue to believe you've been brought in like them.'

'Bernadette knows I'm undercover,' I said.

'She was kept away from the others and is unlikely to meet them for a while. You may as well go home now.'

'There's so much work to do,' I protested.

'You can do it tomorrow. You did better than anyone had the right to expect. Get some rest and come back tomorrow afternoon with a clear head.'

I finished my tea then stood up, paused, then demonstrated my impetuosity as I leant forward and placed a soft kiss on his mouth.

I stepped back as Inspector Tyrrell stood up. Knowing we were attracted to each other was one thing, for me to kiss him like that was something else completely. I gave a wry smile and waited for the rollicking, but Inspector Tyrrell pulled me to him and kissed me properly. It was wonderful. I didn't even think of Hogarth Acre. I kissed him back and wanted more.

We broke apart when we heard the door opening.

'Sir, the Bridewell Sergeant would like you to come down.' Ken grinned at me. 'All right, Sam?'

'All right, Ken.' I hoped he hadn't seen anything.

Inspector Tyrrell said, 'Tell him I'll be there in a moment.' He turned back to me. 'I'll tell Webby I've spoken to you.'

'Yes, sir.'

He went downstairs after Ken. So that was that: the last barrier between us had broken down. Now what?

Chapter Thirty-One

Next afternoon, I felt a whole lot more comfortable in my uniform than in the tawdry dress I had worn the previous night. I bagged the offending article and the nasty shoes and handed them in to be returned to the owner, then I went upstairs to the CID office.

'Sam, m'darlin', good to see you,' Eamon called as I entered.

'Inspector Tyrrell said you wanted to see me.' And that was all he had said. No mention of our kiss. I'd laid my feelings before him and, as I didn't want to appear as a crazy stalker, the next move was his.

'We do. We're going to search the apartment over the next couple of days and, as you've been there before, your input would be much appreciated.'

'What happened with the girls last night?' I asked.

'Most returned to their parents, some happier than others about that. A couple went with social services, like Bernie.'

'Did you see a girl named Lisa?' I asked.

Eamon nodded. 'Social services.'

'Good. You got that film they were showing?'

'Aye. It made interesting viewing. Brian…' Eamon stopped speaking as DI Webb and DS Finlay came over.

'Has Eamon told you what's happening?' DI Webb asked. I nodded. 'Good,' he said. 'You can point out where everything is and help with the search.'

'Eamon told me you saw the film they were showing. What did Brian have to say about it?'

'We don't have him,' DS Finlay said.

'I don't understand. I saw him run towards the building with dozens of police on his tail.'

'One of the Vice Squad lads got him; but he attacked him, broke his nose, and made off. He didn't see where Brian went,' DI Webb said.

'Surely there were enough of us around to see where he went?'

DI Webb's face darkened. I could see that one more word from me could lead to a severe and public rollicking.

'The rest of us were focused on that flat. We had to get there fast to stop the destruction of evidence, seeing as we had lost the element of surprise.'

Ouch. That was a barb that hit home.

Mike Finlay interrupted the face-off. 'We suspect the caretaker helped him, maybe by coercion. However, with your information and what the girls told us last night, we have enough to charge them all. Excellent job, Sam.'

I could see he was doing the same thing to me that Eamon had dome with Bernie, but I wasn't having it. That bastard was on the loose and I refused to take the blame. I felt my anger rise. Not good.

'Stop trying to distract me with flattery. Brian is a dangerous man and he's wandering free.'

'We know, Constable Barrie, and I can assure you that we are doing our damnedest to find him.' DI Webb sounded quite terse. Right: this was his circus, not the Sam Barrie Show. There was stuff happening I didn't know about. I needed to rein in my feelings.

'I want to take Sam to visit Janice Alderman, boss,' DS Finlay said. 'There's been no reply the last few times we've been, and we need to speak to her about Gerald Mount and tie up a couple of loose ends there.'

'Her parents are likely to be upset,' I said. 'They're very religious.'

'Maybe they'll feel better when I tell them that Mount has been charged.'

I wasn't convinced, but I remained quiet. I didn't want to antagonise DI Webb any more than I already had.

*

An hour later, DS Mike Finlay and I pulled up outside the Aldermans' house. The sagging *"For Sale"* sign in the front garden matched the sign in Maud Albiston's garden. Mike knocked at the door to no avail.

I peered in the windows. 'It's empty.'

'They've done a flit!' Mike kicked a stone across the path.

I remembered advising Janice to speak to her parents when we last met in the school. Had they fled the same day? Was this their way of dealing with it and protecting Janice? Had I done the wrong thing again? I turned away from the house and spotted Maud peeping out of her window. She waved and dropped the curtain.

'Who was that?' DS Finlay asked.

'Maud Albiston. I met her a while back when her brother died.'

Maud came to her door and I went to the fence. 'Hello, Maud. How was Australia?'

'It was wonderful, just wonderful.' She scuttled to the fence. 'I have some news. My nephew has asked me to move to Australia, and this time I have agreed.'

'Maud, how exciting!'

'I know. I've no ties here anymore, so I'm going to spend my remaining days by my family. My nephew, his wife, and their children are so easy to get along with, and the little ones are a delight. They made me feel so welcome. I have my pension and some savings, so I won't be a burden on anyone, and I've already put a deposit on a flat near their house. It won't be long now before I leave.'

'I see the Aldermans have already gone,' I said.

Maud looked across at the house. 'Yes, it's all very strange. I came back from Australia and found a note pushed through my door with a forwarding address in the Lake District.'

'We need to speak to Janice, so may we have it, Maud?' I asked.

'Of course, I'll go and get it now.' Maud hurried into the house.

'Sounds like they moved away quickly,' I told DS Finlay. I decided not to mention that it might be a result of my advice to Janice.

Maud returned with the address. 'I won't pry.'

I smiled. 'I couldn't tell you if you did. Thank you, Maud.'

'You're the second person who wants to speak to the Aldermans.'

I cocked my head, encouraging her to tell me.

'It was a few days ago when I was just getting back from Australia. I got out of the taxi and saw a man hammering on their door. He saw me and came over wanting to know where they could be. I told him I had no idea as I had been away. I hadn't found the letter at that point.'

'Did he give you a name?' I asked.

'No, but another man in a car called out, "Come on Lou.".'

Brian had been looking for Janice! Her family were right to flee. 'What colour was the car, Maud?'

'Blue. Is it important?'

'Probably not. Thanks, Maud. I hope your move goes well.'

'Thank you, my dear. You make a fine police officer.'

I knew I probably wouldn't see Maud again and it made me feel a bit sad: she was a nice woman. I reached out and squeezed her hand. 'Take care.'

'Come on, Sam,' Mike Finlay said.

I followed Mike to the car and handed him the address.

'Kendal. We'll have to get Cumbria to pay them a visit. We need a statement from her about her involvement with Gerald Mount, Molyneux, and the film making. It's going to take forever. This has been going on for a few years; the roots go deep. Some of the original girls will be adults, possibly with families by now, and they won't appreciate us raking over old coals. Also, some men involved won't have been there last night so, as we get names, we'll have to question them. And there are a few "pillars of the community" in the frame already.' Mike Finlay's tone told me how little he thought of these "pillars".

'So this is going to turn into a journalist's dream?' I asked.

'And then some.' He started the car. 'Let's get going. We need to send a request for enquiries to Cumbria.'

'Maud told me that Brian Lewington was here a few days ago. Well, she didn't name him, but she said he was with someone in a blue car, no make or model, and she heard them call him Lou.'

'Interesting. I'll get Eamon to check who in that circle drives a blue car.' Mike glanced my way. 'Did she say why?'

'No. I think he might have been looking for Janice specifically. He must have been annoyed because Maud said he was hammering on the door.'

Mike sucked his teeth.

'What?' I asked.

'He's being reckless. He's showing himself at the addresses of potential witnesses. That isn't a good sign; he must be getting desperate.'

'It was before the orgy; he probably wanted her to be there.'

'I hope that's all it was.'

So did I.

*

Back at the station, Eamon came over as Mike Finlay and I entered the CID office.

He handed me a large padded envelope addressed to Constable Barrie. 'A kid brought it to the front office and said a man had given him a pound to deliver it. No description of the man.'

I took the opened envelope and looked inside. It contained a film reel and a note. I tipped the contents onto a desk and picked up the note that had just one word: *"Sammy"*. My pulse ratcheted up.

'Brian Lewington sent this! He's the only one who calls me Sammy.'

Eamon turned to the DI's office and shouted, 'Boss! You need to see this.'

Mike Finlay and DI Webb came over.

'What have you got?' DI Webb asked.

'A film sent to Sam. Apparently by Brian Lewington,' Eamon answered.

DI Webb snatched up the reel and held a short length of film up to the light. 'Mike, set up the projector in my office. Eamon, tell Irene to come up.' As he strode to his office he shouted to the few detectives in the room. 'The rest of you, bugger off, come back in an hour.'

A few minutes later, Irene arrived in the newly-emptied room and we all crowded into the DI's office. Eamon threaded the film through the projector and pressed play. A naked girl flickered into view on the screen.

'That's Lana,' I said.

'Just stand here?' she asked the person behind the camera. 'Why aren't we on set? Where's the props?'

It was hard to see the dark background beyond the lit area she stood in, but her voice had an echoing quality, which made me think it was a large space. I thought of the ground floor of the warehouse in the city.

Four men, all wearing ski masks, stepped into view and surrounded her.

She glanced around and bit her lip. 'What's going on? What sort of film is this? I don't want to do this anymore.'

'Where's Janice?' A male voice off camera asked.

'I haven't seen her; she hasn't been in school.' Lana backed away but was pushed back to front and centre by one of the men.

'You spoke to the police.'

'I didn't…'

'We know they went into your school and spoke to you. What did you tell them?'

I felt as if a brick dropped into my stomach. I glanced over to Mike, but he just stared at the screen.

'I told them nothing!' Lana shouted.

The man that had pushed her, punched her hard in the stomach. Lana gasped and sank to her knees, clutching her abdomen. The camera followed the action. She was still retching when another man punched down on the top of her head, knocking her to the ground. She lay whimpering. A third man kicked her in her back. Lana screamed, and I slapped my hands over my mouth to stop myself screaming out too.

DI Webb paused the film. 'Sam, love, I want you to wait outside.'

I didn't want to see poor Lana being beaten, but the film was addressed to me and I felt I should watch. However, it would not do to go against a direct instruction from a boss I had already vexed several times.

I stood up and left the DI's office.

'Just make sure you don't mention what you've seen to anyone,' DI Webb called after me. 'That goes for everyone.'

'Irene, why don't you go with Sam,' Eamon said.

'No, I think I should wait here,' she replied.

Then the door was shut, mercifully blocking the sound and the screen from me, but they hadn't shut the blinds. I stood in the empty CID room watching them watch the film.

I watched as Irene flinched then turned her head away. Her eyes met mine and she visibly gulped, and I understood why Eamon had tried to get her to leave. At one point I saw Mike draw a finger across one eye as if wiping a tear. DI Webb kept his arms folded, his hands tucked into his armpits and stared resolutely ahead.

After about ten minutes that had lasted a century, the film must have ended. They glanced around at each other, except DI Webb, who remained staring ahead. Irene handed Eamon a handkerchief; I could see the embroidered initial *"I"* in the corner. He blew his nose into it. She got another handkerchief from somewhere and held it against her own eyes. I could see her shoulders shaking. I knew the outcome of that film: Lana had not survived, was never meant to survive, her ordeal. I became aware of tears running down my face too. My determination to remain strong crumbled, and I ran from the room and into the ladies' toilet.

*

A short time later, a red-eyed Irene came into the toilet.

'How are you feeling?' she asked.

I dabbed my swollen eyes with toilet paper. 'She's dead, isn't she?'

Irene nodded. 'It was all on film. There's no doubt.'

'The last time I spoke to Lana, Mike Finlay and I had gone to the school to speak to her about those pictures. Janice was there. Molyneux and Ted run a buddy system and Janice was worried because she thought she'd be hurt if Lana spoke to us. I told Janice to tell her parents about what was happening. They must have moved to the Lake District to get her away.' I took a deep breath. 'I've done it again, Irene; I've made things worse, I've caused another death.' Fresh tears ran down my face.

Irene grabbed my chin and made me look at her. 'This isn't your fault, Sam. Hogarth Acre wasn't your fault, and this isn't your fault. Sick, perverted criminals are the only ones to blame for this.'

'Brian's taunting me,' I said. 'He wants me to feel guilty.'

'Or it's a threat,' Irene said.

Yes, a threat: that was more Brian's style. I gulped.

'Mike told us that Brian's been to Janice's address. He's losing control and that makes him careless and dangerous. He's arrogant too: sending that film and letting you know it was from him was pure hubris. I think we need to get a Gold Response on your address, just in case he turns up there,' Irene said.

'Mum will have a fit.' I put my head in my hands and slid down the wall to the floor.

*

301

'Feeling better?' Mike Finlay asked when we returned to the office a short time later.

'I just don't know how I'll get those images out of my mind, and I didn't even see all the film,' I said.

'You probably won't,' DS Finlay said. 'When you meet the offenders, they will probably seem like nice, normal blokes. Use what you feel now to strengthen your resolve then.'

'Thanks, Sarge,' I said, but I still didn't want those pictures in my mind.

I sat on Eamon's desk. 'I wonder where her body is hidden?'

'In the river probably,' Eamon answered.

I hadn't heard of any bodies turning up in our division. 'Have you heard if any bodies have washed up in the other divisions?'

'Not recently,' Irene said. 'But then, she might not wash up; she might have been washed right out of the river and into the open sea.'

There were outstanding mispers, some from decades ago, and I didn't doubt that some of them had finished up feeding the fishes.

'We need to tell Glynis,' Eamon said. 'But we need to get clearance first.'

'I'd like to come,' I said.

'I think you've been through enough,' Mike said.

'Sarge, I've been deeply involved with this and I'd like to follow it though.' I wanted to be there when Glynis was confronted with the consequences of her actions. I wanted to see if she actually cared.

'I don't see why Sam shouldn't be involved if she wants,' DI Webb called over. 'But we do the talking, Sam. Got that?'

'Yes, sir,' I responded. I must remember my place. I must remember my place. I must remember my place.

*

A few hours later, all formalities completed, DI Webb, Eamon, and I went to Schooner Street. It had been decided back at the station not to tell Glynis about the film yet. Glynis let us in and invited us to sit down. She took the chair by the kitchen door. Connie was curled up on the armchair, her hair uncombed and her face pale. Eamon and DI Webb took the sofa, and I perched on the arm of the chair closest to Glynis. She lit a cigarette and waited for someone to speak.

DI Webb looked at Glynis. 'I'm afraid I have some bad news—'

Connie wailed.

'Shut up, Con. Let them speak,' Glynis snapped.

'Lana is dead,' DI Webb continued. 'I'm sorry to say, we don't know yet where her body is hidden, or when exactly she died.'

Glynis's face looked like stone.

'How can you be sure if you can't find a body?' Connie sobbed.

'We received information that we have been able to verify. I'm sorry but there is no doubt.' DI Webb shifted position on the sofa, making it creak.

Truthful but nicely vague. I had to get to grips with this skill.

'How?' Glynis puffed furiously on her cigarette.

'She was beaten,' DI Webb answered.

Glynis nodded; a single tear trickled from her eye. So she did care.

'Janice?' she asked.

'She moved away,' the DI said.

'It should have been her. Nothing but trouble that girl,' Glynis almost whispered.

'It was Jan they wanted,' said Connie. 'Always bringing the police around…'

'Connie, I said shut up and let the police speak,' Glynis retorted.

'It should have been neither of them,' I said.

Glynis looked at me. 'You wouldn't understand, stuck in your cosy little world. I bet you've never had to worry about money or someone knocking on your door…'

I did worry about someone knocking at my door. And I bet she'd never been abducted, leapt for her life from a moving vehicle, or watched someone being beaten to death. 'I have…' I saw the warning in DI Webb's eyes. Oh yeah, I wasn't supposed to speak, I was there to make tea. 'I have experience of predatory adults targeting children. I understand more than you believe.' There: she could read into that what she wanted. I tried to feel sorry for her, but I kept thinking that we were going to have to arrest them for their part in Operation Elstree. Irene was right; I shouldn't feel guilty. Glynis had brought her girls into this seedy environment: her girls, and several others. Lana had paid the price.

'Do you know who would have done this?' DI Webb asked, regaining control of the situation.

Connie and Glynis exchanged a look, and Connie's head dropped. Connie knew, and she wanted to tell us—I could see it in her eyes—but she shook her head. Fear? Of whom?

'No,' Glynis said.

'Let me give you some names,' Eamon said. 'Molly. Ted. Lew.'

Glynis winced and Connie buried her face in a cushion to hide her sobs.

'Which one of them wanted Janice?'

Connie lifted her head from the cushion. 'Tell them, Mum.'

'Shut up!' Glynis snarled. 'Do you want to end up dead too?'

'They need to be stopped, Mum.' Connie turned to us. 'You know what a buddy system is?' We nodded. 'Molyneux and Ted use it to keep the girls in line. One plays up, the buddy suffers. Lana…' Connie's voice trailed away. She sniffed, then took a deep breath. 'Lana was trying to bring Jan into line because she knew she'd be for it if Jan's parents didn't stop bringing in the police every time she stayed out.'

'You think Lana was killed because Janice's parents kept reporting her missing?' DI Webb asked.

'No. Lana would have been slapped around a bit for that, nothing more. Molly came around a few days ago and we thought he'd run out of patience with Jan and was going to beat Lana, but he said he'd heard Lana had been speaking to the police in school.'

I felt my cheeks go red.

'We didn't know anything about it, but we knew Lana wouldn't speak to the police willingly and told him so. He said he'd had it on good authority, so Lew was going to advise Janice.'

'Lew,' Eamon said softly and shook his head.

'By "advise", he meant give her a thumping,' DI Webb said. It wasn't a question, more a statement of facts.

So that's why Brian had been hammering on the Aldermans' door. What if Janice's parents had answered? Would they have been "advised" too?

'Janice has moved away,' I said.

Eamon picked up on my train of thought. 'They couldn't get Janice, but they still had to set an example to the other girls so they came back for Lana.'

'Exactly.' Connie threw the cushion to the floor. 'Five days ago, she was told to go to the warehouse for a film and she never came home. We weren't too worried when she didn't come back the first night…'

'But why kill her?' I asked.

DI Webb scowled at me, but Connie said, 'This was more than misbehaving, they think she's a grass. They won't tolerate that.'

'It's all that bloody Elsie's fault.' Glynis stubbed out her cigarette and lit up another.

'How do you know that?' DI Webb asked.

Glynis blew out a rush of smoke. 'It's got to be her. Elsie's been trying to get me to take Bernadette for months, but I keep refusing because Bernadette's built like a boy and I need girls with tits. Elsie came around again last month and kicked off when I turned her down again.'

Glynis was admitting to procuring girls!

'To shut her up, I told her my book was full, so she said, *"We'll have to have a vacancy then".*' Glynis imitated Elsie's Welsh accent. 'I didn't think much of it, but then Molly came round like Connie said, so it stands to reason it's her. How the fuck did she know police had spoken to Lana?'

I thought about the meeting in St Agnes'. Mike and I would

have left at once, but Mike went back to get a date with Miss Hughes and, like an idiot, I hung around in the corridor in full view. I felt the weight of another bundle of guilt land on me. I was going to have to say something.

'All right, we'll finish here for now. I'm truly sorry for your loss,' DI Webb said, and actually sounded like he meant it.

'A family liaison officer will contact you. Meantime, is there anyone we can call for you? A neighbour?' Eamon asked.

'Auntie Rose,' Glynis said quietly. 'She lives in Gilmour Street.'

'And maybe the priest,' Connie added.

'Our Lady's?' Eamon asked. Connie nodded. 'All right, I'll radio control and ask them to ring them. We'll speak to you again soon,'

Glynis showed us out.

'I think this might be my fault,' I almost whispered when we were back in the car.

'What?' DI Webb stared at me.

'From when DS Finlay and I went to St Agnes' school.'

DI Webb sighed. 'Listen, Sam, police go into schools all the time, so try not to blame yourself.'

'And if Glynis hadn't got her into the industry in the first place, this wouldn't have happened at all,' Eamon added.

And if I had died at Hogarth Acre, Tina Smiley and Lana would still be alive. If, if, if.

Chapter Thirty-Two

As we arrived back at Wyre Hall, we almost collided with Phil's Panda as he bailed out of the yard with the blues and twos going.

'What's happening?' DI Webb yelled out of the window as Phil passed us.

'Kick-off at Schooner Street.' He raced away.

'We've just been there! Hang on, you two.' DI Webb spun the car around and razzed back to Schooner Street.

We took the corner into the street on two wheels and screeched to a halt. I saw Karen with her arms around Connie, who was sat on the pavement rubbing her stomach, while Phil and Ken tried to separate Glynis and Welsh Elsie, who were trying to pull each other's hair out. Surprisingly, given the considerable difference in size, Glynis seemed to be holding her own against the powerful Welsh woman. Most of the street were out, enjoying the free show. Elsie broke away, leaving a clump of hair in Glynis's fist, and punched Glynis full in the face. Glynis crumpled. Connie screeched, wrenched herself away from Karen and threw herself on Elsie's back, raking her nails across her neck.

We rushed over, and I pulled Connie from Elsie while Eamon and Phil kept Elsie from Connie. Glynis took advantage, picked herself up, and kicked at Elsie's head. Elsie roared and almost managed to escape. Glynis was dead if Elsie got at her now. DI

Webb grabbed Glynis and pulled her to the side. I was relieved to see Steve arrive with another Panda car. Steve helped DI Webb with Glynis.

'Our Lana's dead because of you, you fat bitch. You and your big flapping gob, you're a fucking grass. I'm going to kill you!' Glynis screamed.

A collective gasp went through the crowd. Elsie was going to find it hard to remain around here now. Nothing was worse than being thought a grass in this area. Connie wasn't putting up a fight anymore; she sagged against me and sobbed. Karen came to her other side, rubbed her back, and made soothing, cooing noises.

'What happened, Karen?' I asked. She was probably the only one who would give me a truthful answer.

'I saw Connie race out of her house and attack Elsie. Elsie gut-punched Connie, then Glynis ran out and went for Elsie. Is it true? Lana's dead?'

Before I could consider how I should answer, Connie shouted, 'It's true, Karen! That big-mouthed bitch has been shit-stirring. She wanted Mum to take Bernadette, but Mum said no, so that Welsh twat talked to Molly and now our Lana's dead.'

Karen turned, wide-eyed, to me.

I gave a one-shouldered shrug. 'We still need to establish facts.'

'Jesus.'

Inspector Tyrrell arrived.

'It's okay, Gary. No rush, we've got it under control,' DI Webb shouted.

Casting a baleful look at the DI, Inspector Tyrrell went over to help Eamon and Phil force Welsh Elsie into the car.

'Get her back to Wyre Hall ASAP,' Inspector Tyrrell said.

Glynis went in the other Panda.

'Can Sam and her prisoner go back with you, Gary?' DI Webb shouted.

My prisoner? I had simply taken her out of the fray and was holding her to stop her going after Elsie.

'Sure.' Inspector Tyrrell gestured towards his car. 'Hop in.'

*

I sat next to Connie in the rear of the car. I felt bad for doing it while she was still in shock about Lana, but I recited the caution and told Connie she was under arrest on suspicion of assault. The same thing would be happening in the other Pandas. We could sort the exact charges, if any, back at the bridewell.

I looked back at Karen as we pulled off, and she held her thumb and pinkie to her head like a telephone handset. As she didn't have a phone at home for me to ring her, I guessed she intended to ring me. The neighbours would think she was signalling Connie. Clever move.

'I wish I'd killed the bitch,' Connie snarled. 'You'd better make sure we're kept apart at the station because I'll have her, and so will Mum.'

'Noted.' I hoped Welsh Elsie would be safely in her cell by the time we got back.

*

DI Webb called Welsh Elsie for interview. Again, I was drafted in to chaperone.

While we were waiting for her, he said, 'Try to contain yourself. If you think of a question, either slip me a note and I'll ask it, or wait to the end and I'll ask if you have anything to add.'

'Yes, sir.' I said. I had to remember I was at the bottom of the pile.

'They attacked me, remember?' Elsie proclaimed as soon as she came in. She turned her head to display the scratches across her neck and bruising to her face. Her voice grated on me.

'Don't you worry about that now, Elsie. Sit down. We want to ask you some questions.' DI Webb pointed to the chair opposite us.

'You don't need to. It's simple: I was walking home, minding my own business, when Glynis and Connie came out, screaming like bloody *Gwrach-y-Rhibyn* and attacked me. I wasn't having that, so I fought back. It was self-defence.'

From what Karen had told us, that sounded about right. But what about the rest of it?

'To be honest, Elsie, it wasn't just the fight I wanted to speak to you about. I wanted to ask you about you trying to sell Bernadette again,' DI Webb sounded almost bored. I trusted that it was a ploy.

Elsie looked from him to me. 'You. You're everywhere, aren't you? I've seen you in Schooner Street loads of times; you're here whenever I come in. Wasn't it you who got Lew sacked?'

I snatched up a sheet of paper from the desk and scribbled, *"How did she know about Brian?"* and handed it to DI Webb. He glanced at it then screwed it up and dropped it into the bin.

'If you're referring to Sergeant Lewington, he has not been sacked,' DI Webb said.

'You mean he's still a pig?!'

'For now.' DI Webb slapped his hand on the table. 'Stop trying to divert attention and let's get on. You went to Glynis again and tried to get her to take Bernadette. She told you her book was full, and you said you would get a vacancy. What did you mean by that?'

'What does it sound like?' Elsie snapped.

'It sounds like you threatened to create a vacancy.'

Elsie paused; she had realised what DI Webb was getting at. 'No, I meant we'd have to wait for a vacancy.'

'To create this vacancy, you went to see Molly: Robert Molyneux. How did you know the police had been into the school?'

'Bernadette told me she'd seen the nice policewoman come out of Miss Hughes's office with Lana.' Elsie sniffed. 'Dunno why she likes you so much. Where have you sent her?'

'Did she tell you why the police had been there?' DI Webb asked, ignoring Elsie's question.

'How would she know that?' Elsie countered.

'Exactly. So why did you rush off to Molly, if not to cause

trouble for Lana?'

Elsie inhaled deeply. 'I need a fag.'

'Sorry, Elsie, we need to get this done first.'

I guessed that DI Webb was using this as a lever, because I had seen other prisoners smoke during interview.

Elsie sighed. 'Okay then. I thought if I told him that Lana had been speaking to the police, he'd stop using her and that would open the way for our Bernadette. I didn't say that she'd been speaking about him, so it wasn't a lie.'

This woman was unbelievable. I had to bite my lip to stop myself from speaking out.

'So you went to Robert Molyneux and told him that Lana had spoken to the police.'

'I just said that. Are you fucking deaf or thick?'

'And, although you know Molyneux, you didn't think of the ramifications?'

'Ramif… What sort of fucking word is that?'

'It means consequences, Elsie. You didn't think about what would happen to Lana or her buddy, Janice?'

Elsie bit a piece from the corner of a fingernail. 'I did think of it. I thought he would stop using her.'

'It didn't occur to you that either of the girls would be hurt?' DI Webb folded his arms and sat back in his chair.

Elsie's gaze wandered around the room.

'Lana is dead, Elsie. Beaten to death because she spoke to the police. You have admitted that you went to Molyneux with that information.'

'You're not pinning that on me!'

'We know you didn't take part in the killing, but your actions contributed to her death,' DI Webb said.

'A lot of things could have contributed to her death. That posh girl, Janice, was always getting reported missing. Molly wouldn't have liked that. And what about you eh?' Elsie nodded in my direction. 'I saw you going to the address loads of times. Don't you think Molly would have known that?'

Didn't she realise I was already thinking that?

'You think Molly was responsible for killing her?' DI Webb said.

Elsie brought her attention back to DI Webb. 'He has people he can call on.'

'Who?'

'I don't know.'

'I think you have a good idea,' DI Webb said.

'If I say I don't know, I don't fucking know!' Elsie pushed her chair back from the table and stood up. 'Why are you giving me a hard time? I told you what I know. I bet you weren't like this with Glynis, oh no. Her Lana's dead. Well she's not the only one to have lost a daughter; you bastards took our Bernadette.'

'There is no comparison!' I blurted out.

Elsie leaned on the table and pointed a finger at me. 'Isn't there? Think about it. You judge me because I tried to get Bernadette a decent amount of money. That Glynis only cared about herself. She took on loads of girls and got a fucking fortune for them. I'm sorry Lana's dead, but some would say this is karma.'

'Get the BP, Sam,' DI Webb said. 'I think we're done here for now.'

I went to the door and called the bridewell officer.

'Aren't I getting bailed?' Elsie asked.

'Not yet; I might want to question you some more later. Besides, it's probably safer for you here just now. You might want to think about staying somewhere for a while when you do get out.'

Elsie opened her mouth but hesitated before saying. 'Yeah, that cow called me a grass in front of everyone.'

She went off with the bridewell officer without complaint.

'Bloody hell,' I muttered.

DI Webb laughed. 'You should have heard Glynis. Those two are as bad as each other. Glynis is facing the more serious charges, though.'

'Was she bailed?' I asked. I had been dealing with Connie while Glynis had been interviewed.

'No. Glynis will probably go to the remand centre once she's been before the magistrates tomorrow.'

'Will Elsie be charged as an accessory to murder?'

'We probably won't be able to make that stick, although we'll interview her again later and see what we can get. I think trying to sell her daughter again is serious enough, and she's already got one of those in the pipeline so she'll certainly go down.'

Good. And if Elsie admitted to her part in procuring girls during interview, even if she didn't go to prison, she wouldn't be seen as a fit person to look after Bernadette, so Bernie should be able to stay safely with her foster family.

DI Webb looked at his watch. 'You should have knocked off a couple of hours ago. Get off home now. I'll see you again tomorrow.'

*

As I turned into our road, a movement in a van parked a little way down from our house caught my eye. I slowed down and peered in as I passed but couldn't see anyone because the street lights shone across the glass. I was a bit jumpy at the best of times but, since Brian had escaped, I was seeing shadows everywhere. I would feel a whole lot better when he had been caught. I pulled onto the path and hurried indoors.

'You're late.' Mum stood at the top of the stairs. I noticed the dark circles under her eyes and felt guilty again.

'Sorry. I had to sit in on an interview. I couldn't get to a phone until it was over, and then it was really late. I thought you'd be asleep.' Stupid thought: I knew Mum wouldn't go to sleep until she knew I was safe. I should have thought to ring her before the interview. I helped myself to a couple of slices of bread and put them in the toaster.

'Someone dropped something off for you earlier.'

I spun around. 'Who?' My heart felt as if it was jumping in my chest, I went light-headed so I sat down and tried to hide my rapid breathing from Mum.

'I don't know. He said it was from Benny. Some things you'd left behind when you were working away. It's in the living room, I'll get it for you.' Mum disappeared.

If Brian had been to my house... If he had been here, what could be in the parcel? Something unpleasant or dangerous, and Mum had touched it! I had to get us out of the house and ring for help.

Before I could do anything, Mum came back carrying a plastic carrier bag.

'It's just some clothes you left behind.' She lifted a pair of jeans out of the bag so I could see them.

I relaxed.

'There's a note with it.' She read it quickly. 'It's from Benno, not Benny.'

I smiled. 'He's a good 'un.'

I considered telling Mum about the Gold Response that Irene had insisted on putting on our address, but I didn't want to worry her. That made me think of the van outside. I peered out of the window. The van was still there but there were no signs of life around it. I could ring in and be assured of a swift response, but I didn't want to overreact. 'I'm not expecting any more callers or parcels, so if anyone else comes around don't let them in, don't accept anything from them, and ring the station, would you Mum?'

'Why, what's wrong? Who's likely to call?'

'Oh, I don't know. Reporters, maybe.'

'Reporters? Have you been part of a really big job?'

'It'll be in the papers soon enough. You mustn't tell anyone.' I told myself that I wasn't really lying to my mother because a reporter might somehow trace me and want an interview when this all came out. I just wasn't mentioning the escaped, possibly homicidal, psychopath with a personal grudge against me.

'All right. Don't stay up too late, you look a bit washed out.' Mum pecked my cheek and went upstairs.

I buttered my cold toast and sat at the table. I saw the sense in placing undercover police in alternative accommodation. Perhaps it was time for me to start looking for my own place: then I wouldn't have to worry about Brian, or anyone else, getting to Mum.

How did I get into this predicament? Because I wanted that terrible night at Hogarth Acre to count for something: for Tina's death, my curtailed adolescence and trauma, to mean something. I came home from Canada because I wanted to use my experience to help others, to make my mark. And, yes, to honour Tina by living a full and meaningful life for us both. Part of me wanted to jack it all in and run back to Canada, but I had to see this through, see Brian brought to justice. I understood that there would always be predators feeding on the young, the stupid, and the misguided but, one operation at a time, I would do my best. If the only thing that came from this one was Brian going down for a long time, and Bernie living safely and training as a hairdresser, I would be satisfied. I just had to keep my wits about me until Brian was found.

I finished my toast and took one last look out onto the street before going to bed. The van was gone.

Chapter Thirty-Three

The following afternoon I was again sent to assist the CID. I couldn't wait to get back onto my own block, but DI Webb wanted to start the search of the flat. He borrowed Steve and Phil for the heavy moving. SOCO had been in the previous day and had taken prints from everywhere. The prints were with the records office, being compared to the hundreds of fingerprints on file. Now it was our turn.

Before we left the station, DI Webb allocated areas for searching. I wasn't allocated an area, he wanted me to be able to move around, assisting wherever I was told. We piled into a personnel carrier and Eamon drove us to Belvedere House. Phil followed with the van to transport any property we seized.

'I heard Molyneux was remanded in custody,' DS Finlay called above the engine noise.

'That's right. So was Bulwer; and Glynis.' DI Webb called back.

'What about Connie?' I asked.

'Bailed.'

'And the guests from the party?' I hadn't heard much about them since the party had been broken up.

'Dunno yet. I'd be surprised if they weren't bailed too. The city lads are dealing with the warehouse studio. I heard most of the blokes are playing daft and claiming they had no idea the girls were underage,' Mike Finlay said.

'Welsh Elsie's place has been trashed,' Eamon said. 'Someone put in the windows and painted *"Grass"* all over the front. I heard Ruthie's gone to stay with a friend.'

'What about Glynis's house. Has that been trashed too?' I asked.

'Not that I've heard,' DS Finlay replied.

'Why is that? She procured loads of girls while Elsie was just touting Bernadette around,' I said.

'Elsie's been branded a grass, and they don't like grasses around there. Glynis might have been doing wrong, but she's still one of them.' Mike shook his head.

'Glynis was quite forthcoming with information in interview,' DI Webb called back.

'They don't know that yet' DS Finlay said.

Eamon pulled into the car park and we all piled out and squeezed into the lift to the third floor.

'All right, Sam,' said Ken as we spilled onto the landing.

'All right, Ken. You got guard duty?'

'Yeah.' He leant forward and whispered. 'It's not so bad, the woman across the landing keeps bringing me coffee and biscuits. I think she just wants to have a good gander at what's happening.' He held out a clipboard. 'I need to sign you all in.'

We took it in turns to sign the sheet and enter the apartment. Large portable lights were lined up in the hall ready for use if we lost lighting in the apartment. The living room looked just as large as I remembered. Someone had opened the heavy drapes, and the scratches and scuffs on the white leather sofas were evident in the light. The shag pile looked cheap and stained, rather like the shag pile square in the warehouse set. Policemen moved around the apartment, pulling out cushions, lifting the carpet, even trying to dismantle the electric fire.

'They were sniffing powder from that table.' I pointed at the glass coffee table, that looked vulgar in the daylight. The glass top was smeared with dried booze, powder and Lord knows what else.

The screen was still there but the projector had been taken back to the station. I stood where I had been the previous night and looked around. In my mind's eye, I could see the men sprawled around the furniture and the queasiness came back. I went into the bedroom Molyneux had said was for sadomasochism. This wasn't a bedroom in the conventional sense: there was a mattress on the floor but nothing else apart from manacles on the wall and a collection of whips, riding crops, and paddles beside the mattress. I shivered.

Back in the living room, Steve and DI Webb were moving the sofa so DI Webb could inspect what may be hidden beneath it. I heard Eamon's voice coming from the kitchen, so I went to join him.

'What's happening here?' I asked.

'Nothing much,' Eamon replied. 'We're just sorting through the cupboards. Lend a hand, would you?'

I opened a drawer that contained only a couple of bottle openers. I checked the back and base for false panels then closed it again.

'What are we looking for?' I asked as I pulled open another drawer.

'Anything,' Eamon replied without looking up from the large double oven he was checking. 'Anything that would indicate who is involved: any money, receipts, drugs, photos. Anything.' He sat back on his heels. 'That's the cleanest oven I've ever seen. I don't think anything has ever been cooked in there.'

I opened the pantry, which was empty apart from some wine boxes. 'There's no food.' I pulled open a couple of other cupboards. Apart from a couple of plates and wine glasses, there was nothing to indicate that anyone ever stayed here.

A little scratch began at the back of my mind. I went from the kitchen to the master bedroom. It was an extravagant palace of clashing themes and bad taste, from the huge, bamboo headboard surrounded by purple velvet, to the glitter ball set in a mirror-tiled ceiling, and the mock mediaeval wall torches.

Eamon had followed me from the kitchen. 'Bloody hell, pretentious or what?'

The itch in the back of my mind got worse. I needed to think this through. 'It's like a doll's house. A couple of rooms seem luxurious but aren't really, and other rooms are barely functional. In fact, this doesn't seem like a home.' The scratch crystallised into a coherent thought. 'Because it isn't.'

'It's a set!' Eamon said.

'You're right. I recognise the bamboo headboard from those photographs in those magazines with pictures of Lana. They had to have been taken here. This is visual evidence to tie Molyneux to Ted Bulwer's operation and that would back up the statements.'

'Where there's film sets, there's cameras,' Eamon said.

I gasped. I suddenly remembered Ted and Molyneux talking in the warehouse about a party being filmed. 'You're right. Molyneux has a security company, but he specialises in door staff and so on,' I said.

'Who's to say he wouldn't have a sideline in covert surveillance?' Eamon said.

We looked around the room, but no cameras were evident. Photographs for a magazine could be done with a conventional camera. Where would I hide a camera for those unguarded, candid shots?

One of the mirror tiles had a slightly different light effect than the others, sort of translucent.

'Eamon look.' I pointed to the ceiling.

'I see it.' Eamon stood on the bed and pushed at the tile. It didn't move. He pushed at the one next to it, which did move. 'Pass me that stool.'

I handed him a silly, gilt, fluffy stool. It wobbled on the bed as he stood on it.

'There's a camera here. That's a two-way mirror for the lens.' He jumped down and strode back into the living room.

'Boss, this is one big film set. There's a hidden camera in the bedroom and I'll bet there are more around.'

DI Webb scanned the room. 'Look for hidden cameras,' he shouted and directed a detective to dismantle the light fitting. We had been in the flat for a while and the sun had set, so DI Webb called for the portable lights to be brought in.

A camera would have to be front-on and quite high to capture all the action. They hadn't found a camera, or anything else, when they had dismantled the fire so maybe they would find one in the light fitting. There could be others as well.

I went over to the far wall and looked across the room. My jaw dropped. From this angle, I recognised the shag pile carpet and the white sofa: it was where Brian and Julie had been in that film. More visual evidence that linked Molyneux with Brian, and Brian with underaged sex. This, on top of what he was already facing, would be enough to earn him the death penalty in some countries. Shame he didn't live there.

'DI Webb, the film that was seized last night was shot in here.' I pointed to the sofa. 'On there. And those photos I found in Ted's office were recorded there too.'

Steve and Phil involuntarily wiped their hands against their jackets.

I turned back to the wall and saw an air vent painted the same colour as the wall. It blended in well so it could easily remain unnoticed, especially after a few drinks or a noseful of coke. This was an outside wall, at least double thickness; it wouldn't be a big job to get a camera in there.

'There's something here.' The detective working on the light pulled out a hidden camera.

'Good work,' DI Webb said. 'Keep looking, there might be more.'

I turned back to the vent in the wall.

'What are you thinking?'

I jumped. I hadn't heard DS Finlay come up behind me. 'We need to get the front off that air vent.'

'Do we have a stepladder?' he called to the room in general.

'There's some high stools at the breakfast bar in the kitchen,' Eamon replied.

A DC brought a stool, and DS Finlay climbed up, removed the

front of the vent, and furtled around inside. 'There's a camera here, the wire drops down the wall cavity. I can't see where it goes.'

I didn't doubt it would connect to a receiver somewhere, and everything that happened in this disgusting flat would be recorded.

DS Finlay pulled himself higher up and tried—and failed—to put his head inside the cavity. He shone a torch into the hole, reached in, and pulled out a plastic box, like the boxes SOCO carried with them. In fact, exactly like the SOCO boxes. Waterproof and strong, they were perfect for protecting something important, such as recordings. Could Brian have got hold of some and provided one to Molyneux?

DS Finlay passed the box down to me, took one final look into the space, and jumped down.

'Open it,' he said.

I knelt on the floor and opened the plastic lid. Inside were envelopes: brown, unremarkable apart from the dates written on each one. DS Finlay nodded permission for me to open them.

I picked up one dated two years previously and ran my finger under the flap. Inside were photographs. I looked at the first photo—a naked woman, mouth open, hand held up towards the camera—then handed it to DS Finlay.

'What's this?' he murmured as he looked at it.

The second photograph was more graphic. It was a little fuzzy, the lighting wasn't good, but I could clearly make out the distressed female. It didn't look staged. Two men were attacking her. No, there had to be three men in total as one would have been holding the camera. Two men had abducted me, but another waited at Hogarth Acre. I was looking at the fate I had narrowly escaped. I felt bile rise and swallowed hard. I wiped the tear that formed in the corner of my eye and passed the photo to the DS.

'Bastard,' DS Finlay hissed. 'Boss, over here.'

DI Webb came over and everyone else pretended they weren't trying to see what was happening. DS Finlay handed him the photographs.

'Not the sort of thing you can hand into *Boots* for developing.

He must do it himself.'

'Or have access to someone who can do it,' I murmured.

'Like someone with a film studio. Someone like Bulwer.' DI Webb said.

'Or Bulwer's photographer has gone freelance,' Mike Finlay added. 'What's the date on the envelope, Sam?'

'May 1974.' I held the envelope up. I had been in Canada then, learning how to function again in the outside world.

DI Webb turned away and spoke into his radio. He wanted to know what rapes had been reported then, but what if this hadn't been reported? A lot weren't. Then I heard him ask the operator to check on outstanding missing persons and murders. I wrapped my arms around myself and closed my eyes. This was not Tina. Gradually, I brought my breathing under control.

He turned back to us. 'This might take some time; we have no idea where this photograph was taken.'

'It's reasonable to assume it's local isn't it, sir?' I asked.

'We can't assume anything,' he replied.

As we were speaking, DS Finlay took out another envelope and opened it. He recoiled when he looked at the picture and handed it without comment to the DI. I didn't want to see it.

'What's the date, Mike?' DI Webb asked.

'September 1969.'

'Margery Barnes,' DI Webb said quietly. 'I worked that case. It's still unsolved.'

DS Finlay rubbed his top lip. 'Boss, this is a trophy box. Someone is saving souvenirs of their crimes.'

I picked up the next envelope. June 1970. The date was engraved in my mind. It was when I had been kidnapped and Tina Smiley had been murdered. I gave a little cry and threw it to the floor.

DS Finlay picked it up and took the photos out. 'Tina Smiley.' He passed the picture to DI Webb and I noticed his hands shook.

I leant heavily against the wall. 'Are there any other clues in there, something in the background?'

DS Finlay shook his head. 'I know it's Hogarth Acre, but the photo won't prove that. It's just a lot of trees.'

'Look at the other photos, maybe you'll recognise the men,' I suggested.

As DS Finlay shuffled through them, I caught sight of one photo; a naked man looming over a weeping girl. The blow that killed Tina might have been swift, but who knows how long she had been in anguish before that. I felt my heart thump and my thoughts whirled until I thought I would pass out. Then something struck me about the photo.

'Is that a tattoo? Like writing?' I pointed a trembling finger to the mark on the man's arm. It looked a bit like the tattoo I had seen on Brian in that film, but it was hard to make out.

'It's too indistinct. Crap quality.' DS Finlay gathered the envelopes together and put them back into the box. 'We'll examine these at the station.'

I felt nauseous and it wasn't just adrenaline. I stood up and made my way to the front door.

'All right, Sam?' Steve called as I fled the flat. I didn't answer. He followed me into the stairwell, sat beside me on the top step, and put his arm around me. 'Come on, tell me what's happened.'

'There's a trophy box behind the wall, next to the hidden camera,' I replied.

I felt Steve stiffen. 'What's in it?'

'Photographs, of rapes. Tina at Hogarth Acre. Brian was there.'

'Sergeant Lewington is a…' Steve seemed to have trouble saying the words, so I filled them in.

'A rapist, murderer, racketeer, pervert…'

'Bastard!'

'Steve!' DI Webb shouted from the apartment.

'You go in and speak to the DI, Steve. I need some air or I'm going to throw up.'

Steve stood up, pulled me to my feet, and watched me for a moment. 'Okay, but you stay close.'

'Yes, Dad,' I replied with a feeble grin.

Steve returned to the apartment and I went downstairs.

Night had fallen since I had entered that apartment. Lights dappled the surface of the river. I sucked in a large, healing breath and walked across the car park to sit on the wall and enjoy the peace. The black water lapped against the bank and I remembered Brian's comment about the river hiding things. Brian thought he had hidden Julie Wynne. I imagined Julie trying to escape her rug shroud until she drew water into her lungs. And Lana's body was probably out there somewhere. Suddenly the water didn't seem so beautiful. It was time to get back, not to dwell on events that I couldn't change.

I hadn't taken more than a step when someone jammed a sack over my head. I reached up but the man—I was sure it was a man—wrenched my hands behind me and fastened them with… handcuffs? Yes, handcuffs. I could hear the short chain. He squeezed them tight and the metal bit into my wrist. This wasn't like when we practised with them in training school: this hurt.

My colleagues were close by, just three floors up, but I couldn't get to my radio. I yelled for help, but he put a hand across my mouth and cut my voice short. I could taste the hessian grinding against my teeth. I kicked back, but I couldn't see where to land my blows and most were just a wasted effort. He dragged me a short distance then roughly threw me onto a hard surface and I heard a door slam. This was just like that night on Hogarth Acre. I began to cry. I couldn't help it, but it wasn't going to help me. I had to calm down, think things through, look for my chance to escape. Just like last time.

Chapter Thirty-Four

The vehicle rocked as my attacker climbed in. He yanked my radio from its harness and I heard the *clunk* as it hit the metal floor. He moved away from me, the engine started, and the vehicle lurched forward. I tried to remain calm, to take note of smells and sounds, to judge how far we had travelled before we slowed, turned and accelerated forward again. Then I heard a familiar voice cursing another driver.

'Brian Lewington,' I called. He didn't answer me. 'I know it's you.'

The vehicle veered to the right and I heard the bad-tempered blare of a car horn.

'Wanker cabbies,' Brian muttered.

A couple of minutes later, the road surface changed and I felt the vehicle rumble, as if we were on cobbles or going over tracks. I knew where we were: Brian had left the road and was taking me onto the docks. If I could get hold of that radio, I could alert the patrols that he had me.

We pulled up and Brian climbed into the back.

I struggled to a sitting position. 'What are you doing, Brian?'

'Ah yes, this is the part where I'm supposed to spill my plans about world domination isn't it? Well, that's not going to happen.' He pulled the bag from my head. 'Welcome to the real world, Sammy.'

The meagre light from a distant streetlamp seemed dazzling after the darkness of the sack. I looked around at my surroundings: a van, so like that dreadful night.

'Don't worry, we're well hidden,' Brian said.

He moved behind me and I felt the cuffs on my wrists release. At once, I leapt up and tried to open the door. Brian simply sat back and watched as I clawed at the handle. 'You won't open it; it's properly locked this time. You can scream, shout, and fight if you like. In fact, I would quite enjoy it if you did.'

I sank to the floor, defeated. His words confirmed what I already knew.

'You were at Hogarth Acre. You knew those thugs were going to abduct someone, and you were waiting there for them to bring a girl to you.'

Brian slow handclapped. 'Give the girl a gold star.'

'Did you plan it?'

'Do you think those two could have concocted anything alone?'

'You let them have their fun after you'd finished and that kept them quiet. Did you know they killed Tina Smiley?'

Brian just smiled. 'She made a break for it after I left, but they brought her down with a heavy branch.'

Which would have been when her skull had been fractured. I fought to keep calm, but my heart pounded and my breath came in gasps. 'I won't keep quiet about this.'

Brian laughed. 'Sammy, you won't get away this time.'

I had to keep him talking. 'What does your tattoo say?'

Brian raised an eyebrow. *Solus Deus me judicare potest.*'

'Only God can judge me.' Latin at school had been useful after all.

'I'm impressed. How did you know about the tattoo? You been peeking in the men's shower room again?

'I saw the film of you and Julie Wynne. Did you know there are secret cameras all over the apartment in Belvedere House? I've also seen photographs in Ted Bulwer's office of you and a child. An actual child! CID have them now.'

'You're lying. There are no photos.' I heard uncertainty in Brian's tone.

'Secret camera again. Ted kept files. Insurance.' I was starting to enjoy this. 'We found your trophy box, the one hidden in the wall at the apartment. DI Webb has taken that.'

Brian blanched. 'Molly said that would never be found.'

'Molyneux knew about your box?' I screeched. Of course he did. They all did. 'You've protected criminals, joined in as they preyed on children; you've conned and threatened your way through the police; terrorised and blackmailed businesses. You and Molyneux threw Julie Wynne into the river. She wasn't dead, you know. You killed her. You killed Tina Smiley in Hogarth Acre, and who knows how many more.' What about Lana? I hadn't recognised him in the short bit I had seen of that horrible film, but I had to know. 'Were you involved with Lana's murder? Were you there when she was beaten to death? Was it at Bulwer's warehouse?'

'Good. You got my present. You had to understand what your meddling led to. You had to see what happens to grasses. We have a thousand eyes and long arms. We are untouchable and you cannot compete.'

'I'm taking you down, Brian. We'll take you all down,' I shouted.

Brian ran a finger down my cheek. 'You put up a much better fight than she did. I like that.'

Pyroclastic anger burned through me. Sod waiting for rescue: Brian had to die, it was the only way. To hell with the consequences.

'Only God can judge you?' I shouted. 'Bollocks! I judge you, Brian. I judge you and find you guilty. May you rot in hell.' I launched myself at him and tried to gouge my nails into his eyes, but he punched me in the stomach. It felt like my stomach had exploded, and I fell to the floor retching and writhing in pain. It wasn't like this in films; this really hurt but I had to get up, had to keep going, had to stop Brian for good.

Before I could get up, he punched me again, in the face, and I almost lost consciousness. It would have been so easy to close my eyes and let the beckoning darkness take me away from the pain, but rage kept me going. I staggered to my feet and Brian punched me again, but now I was beyond pain, beyond reason, beyond words. Despite the limited space, I charged at him and he fell backwards against the side. I took advantage of his momentary lapse of concentration and tore his hair and gouged his eyes. He flailed his arms and legs but I kept close to him so he wouldn't have the space to put any weight behind his blows.

Suddenly, he stopped trying to hit me and reached around my waist to pull me even closer to him. I could tell by the way he bared his teeth that he was going to bite whichever part of me he could get at. Well, two could play that game. I pulled his head close and bit hard on his ear. I gagged as the blood slid down my throat but I kept biting, wishing it was his throat. Shrieking, Brian scrambled away. I spat his flesh out and wiped away the blood, snot, and spit with the back of my hand. Then, I spotted my radio on the floor. My chance of back up.

I lunged at it. '4912, scramble, the docks…'

Brian ripped it from my hands and threw it aside. I'd thrown away my advantage. Stupid, stupid, stupid.

Brian threw me down, dragged up my skirt, and tore at my underwear. No! I would not be raped, not then and not now. He'd have to kill me first.

He howled and squirmed when I twisted his ruined ear and gnashed at his face and throat. I reached down and tried to wrench his balls off. Roaring in pain, he squeezed my neck and banged my head against the floor.

Bang. Bang

'Fucking bitch!'

Bang.

I lashed out, but I was choking, exhausted, stunned. He couldn't win, I was the good cop. As my consciousness faded, I thought I heard sirens.

'Here!' A voice outside cried, then I heard lots of running feet. Brian's grip loosened and I took a gulp of beautiful air.

'Help me!' I wheezed. I felt the oxygen spread around my body, clearing my mind.

Brian covered my mouth with his hand. Big mistake. I bit hard on his fingers. He snatched his hand away leaving a good bit of skin in my mouth and punched me hard in the face and my cheek exploded with pain. The analgesic properties of adrenaline had worn off sooner than I would have liked.

The whole area illuminated as the floodlights came on: the ones that were normally used when a ship needed to be loaded overnight. The van reverberated as something heavy slammed against the door: once, twice, then the lock mechanism collapsed. Two Ports policemen rushed in, dragged Brian out of the van, and restrained him by one arm each as he writhed and kicked to escape. Spit and blood flew as he screamed and cursed at me.

'Watch your back, girlie, because I'll be coming for you and everyone you care about.'

'Hard to do that from prison,' A Ports policeman said.

'I'm not going to prison. I'll die first!' Brian screamed. 'And I'll take that bitch with me.' He pounced forward, almost dragging the Ports police with him.

I crab-scuttled away and cowered in the corner, but they managed to hold onto him.

More police arrived, both Ports and Wyre Hall. Brian would not be able to get at me now.

It was now I was safe that I felt worst. Everything hurt, I felt dizzy, my stomach churned, and I trembled. But at least this time nobody else would die. I tucked my knees under my chin and wrapped my arms around my head.

Phil peered into the van. 'Hellfire.' He turned to Brian, who was still struggling, and planted a fist deep into his stomach. Brian doubled over and dropped out of my sight. Phil had not finished, he kicked hard and Brian groaned. Phil pulled his foot back again but one of the Ports policemen pulled Phil aside.

'You'll only get yourself in the shit, mate.'

Phil grunted and moved away.

Steve, Ken, and Eamon peered in at me.

'Bloody hell,' Steve said. 'Look at the state of her.' He climbed in and put an arm around my shoulders. 'It's okay, you're safe. We're here now.'

I leant against him and dried my tears. 'You should see the other guy,' I croaked.

Steve chuckled. 'I just did. I want you at my back the next pub fight we go to.'

'Oh, Sam m'darlin'.' Eamon turned to Brian with a look of utter disgust. 'Gobshite. I hope you spend the rest of your life in prison and get fucked up the arse every day of it, and I'm going to personally make sure they know you're a cop.'

Eamon had such a rich variety of insults. I tried to laugh but it hurt my throat and ribs and mouth, in fact, it would be easier for me to list what didn't hurt: nothing

'We have her, sir,' Ken transmitted.

'Roger. Is she injured?' I recognised Inspector Tyrrell's voice. He sounded tense.

'We need an ambulance. She's bleeding quite badly and seems semiconscious.'

I wasn't semiconscious, was I? I closed my eyes, too tired to bother arguing.

Eamon hopped into the van and Phil kicked Brian again.

Eamon wiped my face with his handkerchief. 'There's a nasty looking gash here. You need stitches. What did he hit you with?'

'Fist. Floor.' The effort of talking exhausted me.

'It might be a fractured skull,' Ken said from the doorway. 'She's slurring quite badly.'

Steve groaned as I vomited across his boots.

I wiped my mouth with my sleeve. 'Sorry.'

'Don't worry, they'll wash,' he said through gritted teeth.

'Definitely a fractured skull,' Ken said.

'How did you find me?' I rasped.

Steve answered. 'Webby sent me back out to check on you because you'd been so upset, but you were gone so I went out to the car park and saw your hat on the ground. I guessed something bad had happened and told DI Webb. He shouted you on the radio a couple of times but you didn't answer, so he sent me and Phil to search by the apartments and spoke to Inspector Tyrrell. Inspector Tyrrell told us that Ray had put out an observation on their channel a short time previously for a possibly drunk driver in a Bedford van driving erratically near to the docks. A taxi driver had rung in complaining about him almost wiping him out on a roundabout. The boss said he'd send a couple of Pandas to the docks and alert Ports Police.

'A short time later, someone said you'd shouted a scramble to the docks so we all piled down here. Meantime, Ray said the Ports Police had told him their security camera had picked up a Bedford van entering the container section, so we searched around the containers until we found you.'

A commotion outside drew our attention and Eamon climbed out to investigate.

'Those eejits have let the gobshite go.'

Steve followed Eamon out of the van. I crawled after them and lay at the entrance. I saw Brian bolting for the riverside. Phil, Eamon, and several Ports policemen chased after him.

'What are you, *Keystone Cops*?' I grumbled.

A Ports policeman eyed me. 'An ambulance is on the way, sweetheart. You just relax.'

'A man who has killed and who wants to kill me has escaped—again—and you want me to relax?' I began to laugh but it hurt, then I cried again. Steve gently rubbed my back as I brought myself back under control.

'He's going up the crane!' Eamon shouted in the distance.

I sat up despite the dizziness and watched in shocked fascination as Brian climbed higher and higher. He reached the top and looked over at his pursuers, who were calling for him to come down.

'There's nowhere for you to go, gobshite,' Eamon yelled.

'I'm not going to prison!' Brian yelled back.

Steve and I both screamed as Brian deliberately stepped into empty space. I heard the thud of the impact from where we were standing.

Steve ran towards the crane and I began to climb out of the van, but the Ports policeman gently pushed me back.

'Jumpers are always messy. Let the lads deal with it.'

I did feel unwell so sat back in the van and let Steve go on his own. I could hear the Ports policemen radioing in to their control, asking their boss to attend and to inform ambulance, although we all knew Brian could never have survived.

I didn't try to hide my wide, wide smile. Brian was dead and, even better, I wouldn't be in trouble for it. He couldn't hurt anyone else ever again. Ted and his crew were going to prison, as were Molyneux, Glynis, Connie, and Elsie. We had helped as many girls as we could.

Chapter Thirty-Five

I was admitted to hospital for a few days. I felt a bit of a fraud because, despite Ken's diagnosis, my skull wasn't fractured. However, I did have a concussion and a couple of broken ribs, and my cheekbone was cracked. My swollen throat was a bit of a problem. Nobody had said anything, but I knew I looked a mess.

I was put into a side room, for which I was grateful as it meant I could sleep relatively undisturbed, but I think the nurses anticipated rowdy visits from my block and wanted to keep the main ward peaceful.

Meantime, my mother paced the small room as she ranted. 'You've had hardly any service in and you're injured again! What are they playing at? Weren't they looking out for you?'

'This is unusual, Mum,' I croaked.

Finally, she sat down. 'I don't suppose you would consider becoming a teacher?'

'It's not normally like this,' I argued.

'Well, it seems to me like it is.' Mum began pacing again. 'Anything dangerous, anything messy, send Samantha Barrie. Gangsters, murderers, pimps, terrorists: it doesn't matter, she's your girl. It's not good enough!'

'Stop it!' I snapped. I felt guilty, again, that Mum was upset but this had to stop. I was proud of my career choice, and, in general, happy at Wyre Hall. 'Policing isn't like *Dixon of Dock Green*. In fact, Dirk Bogarde shot him, so policing has never been entirely safe. I'm sorry you worry, but we discussed this and I thought we'd come to an agreement. I'm a police officer. It's what I am, it's what I do.'

Mum opened her mouth as if to say something but then closed it again and stared at me. I had to win this one, so I held her gaze until she looked away.

'I've phoned Dad; he'll be home tomorrow.'

'He doesn't need to do that, Mum.' It was no easy matter for Dad to leave the rig. He couldn't just hop on a bus.

'He wants to. He wouldn't rest out there. Sleep. I'll go and find us a cup of tea.'

I lay back down and, although I hadn't felt tired, I was asleep before Mum returned.

*

When I opened my eyes again, Mum was sitting reading a magazine. I wriggled to a sitting position and noted the cold, congealed tea on my bedside.

'I could murder a nice hot cup of tea,' I said.

'I'll go and get you one.' Mum put down the magazine just as Inspector Tyrrell arrived. 'Oh good. Gary, I want a word with you.'

'Mum, don't,' I cautioned, but she was too annoyed to be restrained.

'I'm going to get Sam a cup of tea but then I want to speak to you.' She blew me a kiss and left.

'I'm for it,' the inspector said when she was out of earshot.

'I think so. Mum might be short, but she has a mighty tongue and she's very protective of me.'

'How are you feeling?' Inspector Tyrrell took Mum's vacated seat.

'Better. Do Molyneux or Bulwer know Brian is dead?' I asked.

'They didn't seem that bothered,' he chuckled.

I snorted. 'Do you know if Brian paid into the funeral fund?'

'I suppose so. Most of us do,' Gary replied. 'I can't see the fund wanting to get involved with him, though. I expect they'll just pay out to his next of kin, if he has one, and let them sort something out.'

'He doesn't deserve a funeral. I'd throw him on the tip and let the rats and seagulls take care of him.'

He grimaced. 'Remind me never to get on your wrong side.' He sighed and stood up. 'I suppose I had better go and face your mother's wrath.'

'Sorry,' I said. 'She cares about me.'

'Quite right too.' He paused by the door, then came over to me and gently kissed me.

'Get well soon. Most of the block are planning to drop in.' He kissed me again then left. So now the ball was back in my court…

*

I had missed Karen Fitzroy so, when I went back to work, I called in to see her. I wanted to thank her for her information. I had argued that she had been the catalyst that had brought an end to the exploitation of children by Molyneux and Bulwer, and Brian. I wanted her to have some formal recognition. After all, I had been nominated for another commendation on the back of this, but Inspector Tyrrell had pointed out that the local rag loved things like that and it might make life difficult for her. I was safely back in my own world, but Karen's world was still the docks. I could take her a box of chocolates though, so I stopped at the shop on the way and bought a decent sized box of Milk Tray.

Karen squealed when she opened the door and saw the chocolates. It seemed poor thanks for what she had done, but she was delighted.

'My favourite! I can't remember the last time anyone bought me chocolates.' She invited me in and put the kettle on.

'I wanted to say thank you, Karen. That information you gave me, and those magazines, paved the way for this case to be successful.'

Karen placed a mug of tea beside me and opened the chocolates. She popped one in her mouth and held the box out to me. I selected a strawberry cream.

'I'm glad it worked out. But you do know that there will always be another Molly, another Lew, don't you?'

I nodded. 'I've learnt that I can't solve everything, but I can make things better for some.'

'Get them young, before they get stuck in this sorry life.'

I chewed my chocolate and eyed Karen. She looked pensive as she sat cross-legged on the armchair, a bundle of sewing beside her. I felt sad for her. Perhaps if someone had intervened when she had been a teenager she would be living a different life now, maybe earning a living by sewing.

'What are you making?' I cocked my head towards the material.

'A dress.' She shook out the material to show me. 'One of the girls is getting married to a bus driver and has invited me. You might remember her; she was with me the first night we met.'

I did remember her. 'Doesn't her fiancé mind...?' how did I finish that sentence without insulting Karen.

Karen smiled. 'He knows about her and doesn't care about her past, as long as she doesn't do it any longer. They're getting hitched at the registry office, then moving down south.'

'A new start,' I said.

'Yeah,' Karen agreed. 'I'm happy for her. Something like this doesn't happen often for people like us.'

I finished my tea. 'You're a good woman, Karen. Don't ever forget that. I'd better get back out now before I'm missed.'

'Don't be a stranger,' Karen called as I resumed patrol.

As long as Karen remained discreet, there was no reason I shouldn't be able to visit my friend occasionally. Maybe I could call in on a rest day from time to time.

*

A few weeks later, Sergeant Bowman tossed an envelope across to me during parade. 'A letter for you.'

It was from Bernie. As soon as parade was over, I scurried off somewhere quiet to read it.

'Dear Sam Barrie,' she wrote.

'I have moved to Manchester. It's good here, my foster parents, Tom and Maureen are really nice. I have my own room. The social worker said I can stay here until I'm old enough to live by myself, but Maureen says I can stay longer if I want to...'

I was pleased that she was away from her dreadful mother. Not that Elsie would be able to look after her now that she had been remanded in custody pending her trial, along with Connie and Glynis. How those women had the nerve to plead not guilty... But they were alleging that Molyneux had coerced them. Molyneux, in turn, was saying that he was a poor foot soldier caught between criminal masterminds: Brian Lewington and Ted Bulwer. Brian's suicide was a gift to him. It was up to the courts to sort it all out. I would attend, give my evidence, and trust our legal system to do the right thing.

'...My new school is good too. I've made friends with a girl called Beverley and we might start a salon together because she likes doing hair too. Maureen said we should call it Bibi's, because both our initials are B. I did what you said and got a Saturday job at the hairdressers Maureen goes to. Mostly, I brush the floor, wash the towels and make tea for the customers. Sometimes they let me wash hair with an apprentice watching to make sure I do it right. It's hard work but I really like it and sometimes I get tips just like the proper hairdressers...'

I was elated for her and that reminded me, I had a promise to keep. I would phone St Agnes' school to speak to Miss Ashton about Bernadette's ambitions. She could pass it on to her new head teacher and Bernie could start to build her CV right away.

'*…I don't know if I will ever forgive Mam for what she did, so I think I will stay in Manchester even when I'm grown up. I miss our Ruthie, but I don't want to be like her. I'm better off here…*'

Amen to that.

'*…Maybe, if you're ever in Manchester, you'll visit me. Tom and Maureen say it's okay for you to visit.*'

Maybe I would.

'*…Anyway, I hope you are well and you manage to put the crinimals in prison.*
Love Bernie.'

Crinimals! I smiled. It was things like this that made this job worthwhile. I couldn't help everyone but I could change things for some, and that would do for now.

*

At scoff time, I dropped into Irene's office to show her Bernie's letter. She quickly read it and handed it back to me with a smile.

'I'm glad things are working out for her.'

'Me too,' I put the letter into my bag. 'I hope the other girls have a break too…' My voice trailed off as I caught sight of the solitaire on Irene's ring finger. 'Oh my God!'

Irene laughed and wriggled her finger, making the stone sparkle. 'He's making an honest woman of me.'

'When's the party?'

'We don't need all that fuss. Eamon took me for a romantic meal a few days ago and proposed in the restaurant. I accepted and the staff served us with real champagne. Then we went back to my flat and celebrated in the customary fashion.' Irene winked.

'Where and when's the wedding?' I asked.

'The registry office, soon. I'm still working on the details. You'll get an invitation when it's all arranged.'

I hugged her. 'Congratulations, soon-to-be Mrs Kildea.'

Irene laughed. 'Irene Kildea. I'll have to get used to that.' She leant back in her chair. 'I've been hearing rumours about our newest sprog and a certain inspector. Are they true?'

'You know what this place is like for rumours.' I smiled, tapped my nose, and left to start patrol.

The End

Did You Enjoy This Book?

If so, you can make a HUGE difference

For any author, the single most important way we have of getting our books noticed is a really simple one—and one which you can help with.

Yes, you.

Us indie authors and publishers don't have the financial muscle of the big guys to take out full-page ads in the newspaper or put posters on the subway.

But we do have something much more powerful and effective than that, and it's something that those big publishers would kill to get their hands on.

A committed and loyal bunch of readers.

Honest reviews of our books help bring them to the attention of other readers.

If you've enjoyed this book I would be really grateful if you could spend just a couple of minutes leaving a review (it can be as short as you like) on this book's page on your favourite store and website.

Thank you so much—you're awesome, each and every one of you!

Warm regards

Trish

Acknowledgements

I have so many people I want to thank.

Thanks to my family who have listened to me banging on about Blue Bird for years and have got used to me staring into space as I unravel a plot knot or start to talk about my characters as if they are real people who probably live next door.

Thanks to the Ace of Scribes gang, John, Sam, Jason, Di, Jenny, and the late Anne Blair (who was the voice of Sam during our sessions at The Bridge Inn). I appreciate how you all listened to the various versions of Blue Bird and offered good advice.

Thanks to Graham Smith, for your invaluable advice, and for organising *Crime and Publishment*.

Thanks to my friend, Christine, who told me about Burning Chair, and thanks to Simon Finnie and Peter Oxley of Burning Chair, who took my manuscript and whipped it into shape.

Finally, thanks to the beta readers: Kirsti Wenn, Andreas Rausch, Alison Belding, Eve Clark, Alex Jones, Roger Owen, Joyce and David Oxley, and Richard Wood. Your enthusiasm thrilled me and I appreciate your feedback.

You all have helped me shape Blue Bird into the book it is today.

Trish Finnegan

About the Author

Trish Finnegan has spent her whole life living on the Wirral, a small peninsula that sticks out into the Irish Sea between North Wales and Liverpool. She has always had an overactive imagination and enjoyed writing and reading, sometimes to the detriment of her schoolwork.

She first met her husband, Paul, in the charge office of a police station: where they both were serving as police officers. She has three grown up children and currently spends her time wrangling grandchildren and writing.

About Burning Chair

Burning Chair is an independent publishing company based in the UK, but covering readers and authors around the globe. We are passionate about both writing and reading books and, at our core, we just want to get great books out to the world.

Our aim is to offer something exciting; something innovative; something that puts the author and their book first. From first class editing to cutting edge marketing and promotion, we provide the care and attention that makes sure every book fulfils its potential.

We are:
- Different
- Passionate
- Nimble and cutting edge
- Invested in our authors' success

If you're an **author** and would like to know more about our submissions requirements and receive our free guide to book publishing, visit:

www.burningchairpublishing.com

If you're a **reader** and are interested in hearing more about our books, being the first to hear about our new releases or great offers, or becoming a beta reader for us, again please visit:

www.burningchairpublishing.com

Other Books by Burning Chair Publishing

The Demon Inside
Beyond the Aether
The Old Lady of the Skies: 1: Plague

The Wedding Speech Manual: The Complete Guide to Preparing, Writing and Performing Your Wedding Speech, by Peter Oxley

www.burningchairpublishing.com

Blue Bird

Blue Bird

Blue Bird

Printed in Great Britain
by Amazon